THE RANFURLY MYSTERIES BOOK TWO

DANGLING
— AND —
DANGEROUS

K.M. KRENIK

Free e-book!

Download the e-book of the prequel novella, *Inevitable Danger*, for *free* when you subscribe to the author's monthly newsletter. Get notified about giveaways, new releases, and behind-the-scenes bonuses.

Visit **kmkrenikbooks.com** to subscribe.

Capture clues to solve the mysteries!

Before you begin, have you read *Danger Lies Within*, The Ranfurly Mysteries Book One?

Find it in paperback, hardcover, e-book, and audiobook wherever you purchase books or at **kmkrenikbooks.com**

Support local bookstores!

Request the hardcover or paperback copies at your favorite physical bookstore. Let them know The Ranfurly Mysteries can be ordered through **IngramSpark.com**

DANGLING AND DANGEROUS Book Two of The Ranfurly Mysteries

Written by K.M. Krenik

knoxworks.net

ISBN Hardcover: 979-8-9993420-0-3

ISBN Paperback: 979-8-9906296-9-1

Developmental and copy edits by Jessica Powers | Catalyst Press

Proofreading editor: Kim Beckham

Book Cover Design and Interior Formatting by 100Covers

Map design by Nathaniel R. Krenik and K.M. Krenik

Title page typesetting by Miblart

Dedicated to the Fantastic Four
Nathaniel, Lucas, Keira, & Bethany

CONTENTS

Author's Note

Trigger Warning: There are no explicit sex scenes in the story. Profanity is indicated by special characters. Due to sensitive situations, alcohol, and violence, parental guidance is advised.

Timeline: This story takes place in another world where dragons exist, and technology is more advanced. In my first two books, some readers have been confused by the timeline. To clear up any confusion, this is a different world, with its *own* timeline. It is *not* the future of our world.

Continuation: While *Dangling and Dangerous* (The Ranfurly Mysteries #2) can be read as a standalone, it will be far more easy to follow if you read the prequel first, followed by book one.

Fashion: Imagine Renaissance and Victorian era fashions (in our world) have a baby, then splash in the best of the 1900s. The Ranfurly world's fashion is a mashup, with the added benefit of having materials that we can't get here. *Dragon skin, for one.*

Offensive Language Matters: The use of special characters to indicate swear words is a nod to the old era of comic book writing.

Maps: The new addition of maps is all thanks to my son, Nathaniel. He insisted I have them and helped me design them.

The World - PAX Era

The Old Map with Languages

The Green Isles: Uplandish

Highland: Highlandish

Chantelle: Chantellian

La Belle Terre: Bellaise

Gutland: Gutish

Vinosa: Vinosian

Felizia: Felizian

Sollam and Qud: Sollamish

Tsur: Tsurish

The Northlands: Norrian

Loong Islands: Loongese

Ortus: Ortese

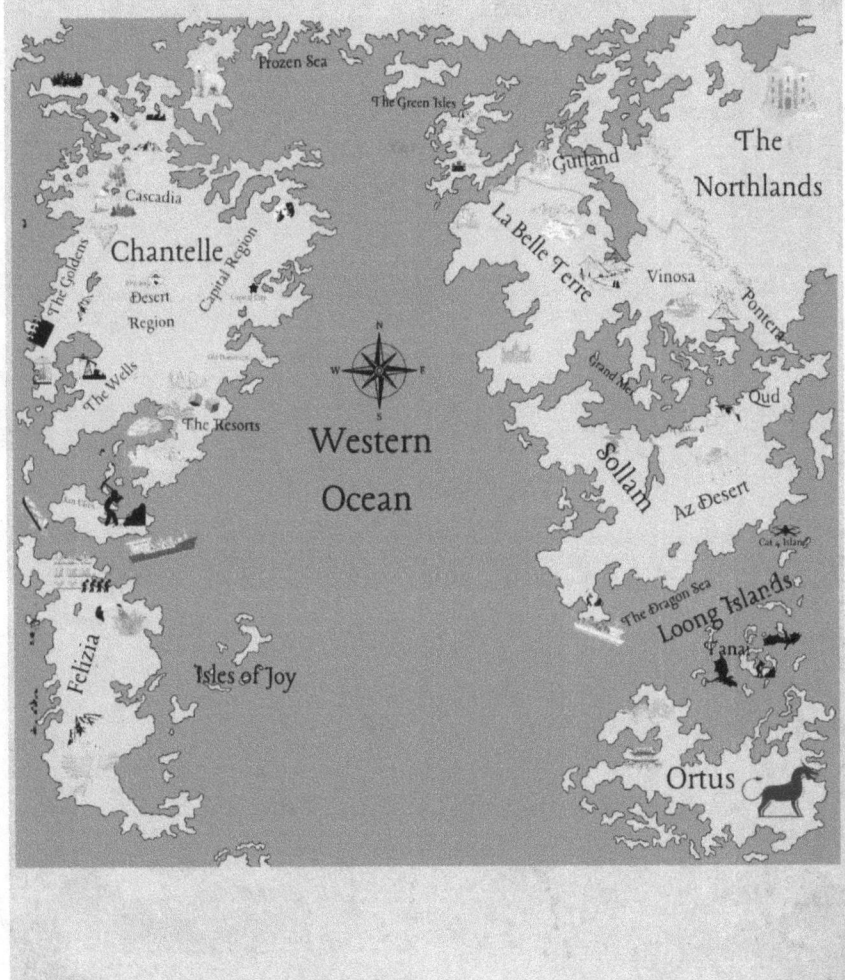

1

STUNNED BY BEAUTY

❧ Sean ❧

ONE YEAR AGO
Capital City

"Sean Knight?"

Sean glanced up from the cubicle that he'd been assigned. It was his first day working as a field agent for PAX Intelligence.

The vision that appeared in front of him was a splash of warm sunshine in the gray, windowless office. Bare and bronze shapely legs. Very nice. As he moved his gaze upward, he found everything else attached pleasing, all the way up to her lovely heart-shaped face, cascaded by rich, dark, flowing hair. But it was her warm eyes, deep brown dusted with a starlight twinkle, that caused him to lose his balance—he nearly fell out of his chair.

For a moment, he was stunned by her beauty, tongue-tied. It was unusual for Sean Knight to be at a loss for words.

The woman arched a brow, waiting for a reply.

Sean cleared his throat. "Um ... yes. Right. That would be me." He flashed a smile, the one that made women swoon.

Her eyes shimmered. She initiated a handshake. "I'm your new partner. Jasmine Lopez."

He allowed his fingers to linger and brush against her palm before letting go of her hand. Working as an intelligence agent just got more fun.

Jasmine exuded sophistication, a radiant confidence that Sean instantly admired. He could have sworn he caught a glimpse of an upward curve on the corner of her mouth, but it didn't last. She was all business. "There's a meeting in the conference room and the boss wanted me to show you where it is, since you're 'New Guy.' Follow me."

"'New Guy' huh? Is that how I'm known around here?"

"If you want to be known for anything else, you'll have to earn the title. But until then, you're 'New Guy.'"

They arrived in a large room, where the other staff members at the Intelligence Agency were taking their seats. Once everyone was situated, a short, bald man of Felizian descent addressed the room. The man was Alejandro Hernandez, Directorate of Zone B Intelligence (ZBI) who had hired Sean. Standing next to Alejandro was a man Sean had never seen before.

"Welcome, everyone," Alejandro began. "As you know, the merge between Zone A and Zone B Intelligence is now complete. We are officially PAX Intelligence West.

"This leads me to my announcement today. With the merger, a new Directorate will be taking my place. Some of you might have met him when he served as the Directorate of Zone A Intelligence: Lord August Wellington." Alejandro stepped away from the microphone and bowed to Lord Wellington.

Jasmine made a sound, a bit like a gasp. There was no mistaking the expression on her face. My new partner doesn't look too thrilled about the new Directorate.

Lord Wellington stepped up to the microphone. Sean guessed him to be in his forties. Tall and lean, with pointed features and thinning white hair, he had a vampire-like vibe. His voice was clipped, and he spoke with a posh Uplandish accent.

"Thank you, Alejandro. Your faithful service to the agency is appreciated."

Everybody clapped. Once the applause died, Lord Wellington continued. "I feel incredibly honored to accept the appointment to serve as Directorate of PAX Intelligence West." He flashed a tight-lipped grin. Bleached white teeth gleamed under the stage lights. "I'm sure you've heard the rumors that our agencies would likely be shut down now that The Peace Alliance Ten has brought world peace. After all, global turmoil has been job security for people in our ranks, hasn't it?" He chuckled.

The room rumbled with murmurs.

"Lovely," Jasmine scowled. "He's here to tell us we're being laid off."

As if he'd heard her, he announced, "Ah, yes. I can tell you're all squirming right about now. Well, I'm here to bring you good news. ... You get to keep your jobs today."

Sean could feel the tension in the room allay as everyone broke out in cheers and applause.

Lord Wellington nodded his head in acknowledgment before continuing. "PAX has repurposed us. We must now shift our gazes to a new global problem that is growing larger by the day: The Resistance.

"As you all know, many of the groups forming are disorganized, sloppy, and easy to dismantle. But unfortunately, there are a few groups who have powerful people on their side—some who even used to be our colleagues. They are the new threat to global peace, and they must be stopped at all costs."

The meeting ended soon after, the agents and office employees piled out. Before Sean and Jasmine left the room, Alejandro approached them holding a file in his hand.

"Hello Sean. I see you've met your new partner," Alejandro said, smiling warmly at Jasmine.

"Yes, I did. It seems I will be in excellent hands," Sean said.

The innuendo didn't fly over Alejandro's head. He narrowed his ebony eyes at Sean, shooting him a look that could kill, before continuing, "The new Directorate, Lord Wellington, would like a word with both of you."

Jasmine asked Alejandro, "How long have you known that Wellington was going to take your job?"

Through gritted teeth, he replied, "Now is the wrong time to speak, Jasmine."

They approached Lord Wellington and bowed to their new Directorate, as was the new PAX custom. The man's icy blue eyes shamelessly lowered and lingered on Jasmine's curves.

"Lord Wellington, this is our newest agent, Sean Knight. Here is his file." Alejandro handed it over to the new Directorate.

Up close, Wellington was waxed and plastic looking. A dragon was embroidered into the breast pocket of Lord Wellington's suit, a design that was the signature of the di Bianco brand. A whiff of one of the finest colognes for men filled Sean's senses. *Wellington is obviously getting a much fatter paycheck than I am,* he thought.

All through their introduction, Wellington remained glued on Jasmine. The vampire looks like he's ready to feast on my new partner for lunch, Sean thought. At last, Wellington flipped open the file. "Mr. ... er ... Knight, is it?" He read from the file. "Says here you fought with the reserves in the Tsur War, is that right?" He raised an eyebrow.

"Yes, Your Grace."

Wellington appraised Sean's physique. "You still look to be in excellent shape."

"I stick to a strict routine and diet, Your Grace."

"Hmm." Wellington blinked twice, then once again thumbed through Sean's file. "Says here you were born in Highland?"

"Yes, sir."

"I thought so by the accent. When did you relocate to Cascadia?"

"When I was ten, Your Grace."

"I'm surprised you didn't lose it—the accent."

"I can turn it on and off when needed," Sean said, with no hint of his Highland accent.

"Ah. Well, the reason I'm interested in speaking with you, Mr. Knight, is because when I browsed your file yesterday, it caught my attention that the house where you grew up was called Ranfurly Manor."

"Yes, Your Grace."

"Strange. A manor in the wilderness of Cascadia. Is it made of logs and twigs? I thought there was nothing but grizzlies and wolves in those parts. The Wild West, they call it." Wellington laughed. "The only known civilization is the coastal city of Emer Aude. But even it has a reputation for being the most feral city in the world."

"True. Cascadia is mostly wild," Sean said.

"Ranfurly Manor, hmm." Lord Wellington drummed his long, bony fingers on his waxed chin. "Funny coincidence, there's a Ranfurly Castle back where I come from in The Greens."

"Yes, I know. My father comes from a long line of chauffeurs who drove for the Ranfurly family in Knoxfordshire. Now, my father drives for the Mr. Ranfurly in Cascadia."

"Interesting. When was the last time you were back at the manor—the one in the wilds of Cascadia?"

"Oh, haven't been back in years."

Lord Wellington closed Sean's file. "Do you know who runs the manor now?"

"Mr. Theodore Ranfurly, Your Grace."

Alejandro shook his head. "That's impossible. Theodore Ranfurly died in a plane crash four years ago. I was part of the team that investigated the case. The plane was never found and it's still a mystery what happened."

Sean hesitated before he replied. "I had no idea." He swallowed down the knot that formed in his chest. He was always fond of Mr. Theodore Ranfurly.

Lord Wellington went on. "You weren't aware of this, Mr. Knight? Your father didn't tell you?"

"No. We don't speak, Your Grace."

"Ah. I see. … Well, someone must be running the place now. And, coincidentally enough, the Viscount of Knoxfordshire who owned Ranfurly Castle disappeared without a trace … also four years ago. Just after he was exonerated of killing his wife."

Sean raised his eyebrows. "Really?"

"Odd, that Lord Ranfurly would disappear concurrently with his cousin's death. Makes one wonder. Rumors spread that he must have died. His financial advisor shut down his company RanCorp, donated all the proceeds to charities."

Sean frowned. "That is odd."

"Yes," Wellington said. "But we've had recent reports from people claiming they've seen him. Mostly in The Capital region. But there was one sighting that was called in from Emer Aude." Lord Wellington squinted at Sean. "Mr.

Knight, I'd like you to go back to Ranfurly Manor. Come up with a story of why you need to be there. Shouldn't be difficult for you to do that, should it?"

Sean's eyes widened, but he didn't allow the rest of his face to convey his true feelings. Going back to Ranfurly Manor wasn't what Sean had signed up for when he decided to become an intelligence agent. "I don't suppose so."

"Good. It should be an easy enough job. I simply want you to find out who is running the place now. Your job will be to report his comings and goings, and anything that might seem ... suspicious."

"Yes, Your Grace."

Lord Wellington turned once more to Jasmine. He breathed in through his nose. "Mm. Ms. Lopez. It has been far too long since our last meeting." His eyes found her cleavage, and he addressed it, "We'll see to it that you get a job as a maid at Ranfurly Manor where you can assist your new partner. You will slip out of the manor once a month to report everything that goes on directly to me."

Wellington turned back to Sean. "A maid ... perfect cover, don't you think?" The vampire-like grin overshadowed the rest of his face.

Sean bowed in submission, resenting everything about the new boss and the new assignment. Going back to Ranfurly Manor meant seeing his father. And seeing his father was the last thing he cared to do.

THE INTRUDER

Courtney

PRESENT
Ranfurly Manor

Perhaps it was nature's way of protesting evil, sending long winters.

When I first came to interview for a job as a nanny at Ranfurly Manor, it was like the talons of winter were piercing into the earth, blocking out the sunlight.

It was strange, how it felt like I'd been there for months already. But the interview had only been a little over two weeks ago.

That was the day I met Ms. Stern, the frightful household manager, who seemed perturbed all the time. (You knew she was especially mad when her Gutish accent came out.)

It was also the day I met Elizabeth and Luke Ranfurly, the cute little five-year-old twins who I would be caring for.

Despite feeling a little overwhelmed by the immense manor and having misgivings about Ms. Stern, I couldn't deny I was magnetically drawn to the children.

That same day, I also met Sean Knight, the charming Highland-born chauffeur, who turned out to be more than just a chauffeur. (I still wasn't sure exactly what he was. *A PAX Intelligence agent? A member of The Resistance?*)

True, I was initially attracted to Sean. But I soon realized my feelings for him weren't romantic. No ... but I did consider him a friend.

After that, I started my job at the manor. Was it really only a week ago? It felt like much longer. That first day of work–the same day Jake the gardener was murdered. The same day I met *him–Lord Robert Ranfurly.*

The feelings that man awakened inside me ... *oh my.* Feelings I believed had died when I lost my husband.

Lord Robert was ... where to begin? His striking appearance left me tongue-tied. Raven hair that fell to his shoulders; penetrating green eyes; the physique of a superhero. I felt like a person feels when in the presence of a movie star ... or a prince.

But I quickly found there was far more to the man than just a dishy shell. He was thoughtful, reflective, intelligent. And when our eyes met, there was an uncanny soul connection between us.

Which is why, on this particular day in the barn, when he confessed to me his feelings, then *kissed* me, I was in a state of euphoric bliss.

For only but a moment.

All too soon, the moment was obliterated when Davey, the staff member who oversaw the equestrian program, rode into the horse stables. Lord Robert broke away from me to greet him.

"You seem to have a special bond with him." Lord Robert stroked the horse's mane. "Beaumont doesn't take to everyone."

Davey seemed alarmed.

"Something wrong?" Lord Robert asked him.

"There was someone out there. In your woods," Davey said.

"Someone?"

"A stranger," Davey said.

Robert shifted his attention to outside. "Where are my children?"

"Right behind me." Davey turned in his saddle to check on the kids.

On cue, adorable little five-year-old Luke rode in on his miniature horse, his curly strawberry mop of hair a matted mess as he removed his riding helmet. We waited, expecting Luke's twin sister Elizabeth to come in after him.

When she never came in, Robert asked Luke, "Where's your sister?"

"I don't know." He shrugged.

We ran out of the barn. Davey, still on his horse, followed us. "Elizabeth! Elizabeth!" We called her name several times, but there was no sign of her.

"Davey, take me back down the trail you just came from." Robert ran into the barn, mounted one of the other horses bareback, and followed Davey down the trail.

Luke started after them, but I grabbed the miniature horse by the bit and led him back into the barn.

"What's wrong with everyone?" he asked. "Elizabeth's probably just hiding. She likes to hide."

"Oh, I hope you're right, Luke." I sighed. "Why don't you put Sir Edgar back in his stall, and we'll play with Thor and Loki until they get back."

Over the course of the week, my dogs had taken a strong liking to Luke. Tails were wagging when he picked up their ropes and played a game of "fetch." It was thirty minutes later when Robert and Davey returned. Without Elizabeth.

"She has to be here!" Luke said. "She's probably watching us look for her right now! ... Elizabeth!"

We continued to call out for her, repeatedly. But when she never answered us, we became more frantic. Our worst fear had been realized. Elizabeth was missing.

After the horses had a chance to drink and rest, Robert and Davey rode back into the woods to continue searching.

Oh, you poor baby. Sweet, stubborn Elizabeth. The little five-year-old told me she didn't think she needed a nanny, that she could teach Luke everything he needed to know. I'd made it my goal to win her affection, and by the end of that first day on the job, I managed to conquer her heart! Just as she conquered mine. The thought that something terrible might have happened to her ... I couldn't let myself think about that.

Robert and Davey came back after searching a second time. "Still no sign of Elizabeth," Davey told me, his head hanging low.

Did the intruder kidnap her? None of us cared to say out loud the question that chewed away at us.

The sun disappeared behind grey patches, and a chill set in.

"I'm cold," Luke said, shivering.

"I've got to go into the manor and speak with Mr. Roth," Davey said. "I can take him in to get his coat."

Once again, Robert and I were left alone in the barn. "I have to keep looking for her." Robert said.

"What about checking the security cameras out in the forest?"

He ran a hand over his hair. "Unfortunately, the cameras on the property are out of order. Another reminder that I need to invest in a new surveillance system. I'm a fool for not taking care of that long ago."

"You couldn't have imagined something like this would happen out here, a hundred miles from the city. It isn't your fault."

He sighed. "The truth is, I didn't think I needed to waste money on upgrading the cameras. I put all my confidence in my other security system. I have triggers everywhere, even across the river."

"Don't animals set off the alarms all the time?" I asked.

"No. The system differentiates between animal type. A human breach should have sent out a high alert; alarms should have gone off."

"That's impressive."

"It would be impressive if it hadn't just failed!" He slammed his fist into the cabinet shelf.

I stepped back and gave him his space.

After he took a few deep breaths, he opened one of the cabinets and got out a backpack. We started to fill it with supplies.

"Hopefully you'll have everything you need out there," I said quietly. "Are you sure you don't want me to go with you?"

"No. I need you to stay here with Luke."

"Will you be alright out there ... alone?"

"I'll be fine. I've had more experience in those woods at night than you can imagine." He turned to me. "Forgive me. I'm not myself right now." He brushed a finger across my chin.

If only I could do something to help. I reached up to massage his powerful, broad shoulders ... his muscular torso was like a brick wall of strength and protection, yet deep inside him, I knew he was shattering into a million pieces. *This unbreakable man has a chink in his armor—his love for his children.*

"Someone might have opened the gate for the intruder," he whispered.

"Someone? You mean someone on staff?"

"I can't rule out the possibility." He had a faraway look. "...Well, let's just hope that's not the case. If it is, we have far more trouble on our hands."

I squeezed him. "You'll find her." I tried to sound strong and reassuring but my voice came out weak.

"God knows I won't stop looking for her." He gave me a peck on the forehead before he mounted the horse. Robert patted the beautiful Thoroughbred's mane.

"Good boy, Beaumont. You're getting your exercise tonight, aren't you? Let's go find Elizabeth."

The voices of Winnie and Luke could be heard outside the barn. "Watch after my little guy while I'm out there, will you?" Robert asked me.

"Of course."

Robert rode out of the back barn doors, just as Winnie and Luke came in through the front entrance.

"You look all bundled up now, Luke. Are you planning on being outside a while?" I asked him.

"I wanted to go with Daddy!" Tears welled up in his blue eyes as he caught sight of his father heading into the forest.

"Your daddy wanted us to stay here in case Elizabeth comes back." I clasped his hand. "Why don't we go to the staff quarters and see who else can go out to search for her. The more people looking for her, the better chances we have of finding her, right?"

"Right." Winnie agreed. Her soulful eyes were a deep brown, filled with depth, warmth, compassion. Even though she was a newcomer on staff, she seemed sincerely concerned.

But what Robert had just said disturbed me. *Someone on staff might have let the intruder on the property.* I shuddered. *Who on staff would have a reason to let the intruder in?* Picking Luke up, I nuzzled him close to me. I wouldn't let him out of my sight.

3

SEARCH PARTY

❧ Courtney ❧

Six Hours After Disappearance

The moon was hidden behind clouds, Thor and Loki curled up on the barn porch next to Luke. From where I sat, I could see nothing out in the woods, except pitch blackness.

Did the intruder kidnap her? And if not, then was she out there, lost somewhere in the forest? That would be terrifying for most people, let alone a five-year-old child. Robert's estate extended over thirty-thousand acres of thick, treed land. A river wound through part of the property, and this time of year, it was at its highest level, with a rapid current.

The thought of a raging river brought back a memory of the summer I turned fourteen, when I went white water rafting with my best friend, Meg.

We were headed toward a tree that had fallen across part of the river, which caused a dam effect that created a vortex. Meg hopped out of the raft in time, before it was vacuumed up in the whirlpool. I wasn't as quick as Meg at getting out. I grabbed onto the fallen trunk and clutched to it for dear life, kicking my legs as hard as I could.

Meg screamed, "Hang on, Courtney!"

I was losing strength in my arms. Just as I was about to let go, Meg yanked me up by my life vest and snatched me out of the raging water.

My dear Meg. She was stolen from me at the young age of seventeen … and the world lost a treasure that day. It still felt raw and painful to think about. *She's in a much better place now*, I reminded myself. It was the only comfort I had, knowing that with the kind of faith she had, she would be enjoying the afterlife. Especially considering how ugly the world had become with the war, and then the takeover of PAX.

I tried praying about Elizabeth, but it felt awkward. Deep down, I sensed there was a God. I just never took the time to explore the idea much. But with all the tragic circumstances I'd been going through, I knew I should probably at least try to pray.

Meg, I don't know if your God hears me … or even knows I exist. If He does, He might not be very happy with me since I've spent most of my life ignoring Him. But you were always close to Him. Maybe He'll listen to you. Can you ask Him to save Elizabeth?

A gust of wind swept through where we sat, and a chill came over me. Even Luke, bundled up as he was, shivered. "Come on, let's go brush the horses, Luke. That'll warm us up."

We headed inside the barn, Thor and Loki at our heels.

A few minutes after we started brushing the horses, the dogs barked. I soon saw the reason. Lord Robert had just appeared through the thick evergreens. We ran from the horse stalls to greet him.

"Daddy! Did you find her?"

"No, Luke. Not yet." His face muscles were tight, and I knew he was restraining himself from showing how much it was tearing him up. He stroked his horse's mane. "You've worked hard tonight, Beaumont. Let's get you some water."

A moment later, Mrs. Roth came from the manor, a thermos in each hand. Her cheeks were a rose shade that matched the color of her hair, a compliment to her fair, lightly freckled complexion. "I made Elizabeth's favorite soup … minestrone. One for you, and one for her, when you find her."

"Thank you, Mary," he said to Mrs. Roth.

"The soup was delicious," I told her. "Luke and I had some earlier."

She set the thermoses down on the table between the rockers. "If anyone gets cold, we keep clean blankets in the barn, inside the cabinets. Luke can show you where they are." She glanced at Robert and Luke, her brow creased with concern, before she excused herself.

Robert sat in one of the rockers, exhausted, and Luke climbed into his lap. I massaged his shoulders.

"Do you want me to pour you some soup?" I asked him.

He gently touched one of my hands. "I'm sorry, I can't eat right now. I have to go back out and keep searching."

After playing with his son's curly, strawberry mop for a few minutes, he stood and set his little boy on the rocker. "Don't stop praying, *mon petit guerrier*," Robert whispered in his boy's ear. He kissed him on the top of his head. Then he turned to me and said, "Keep him safe for me, Courtney."

"You know I will."

"Beaumont needs a rest. I'm heading back out on Llamrei. He's a pistol of a horse, not easily scared off. He'll do well in the woods at night."

"You could use a rest yourself."

"I won't rest until my daughter is safe and sound, back home with us."

He rode out of the barn, into the dark forest on the black horse Llamrei, looking like a warrior from the past. Dressed all in black leather, his hair flowing down. All he was missing was a sword.

"Daddy, wait!" Luke got up from the rocking chair and ran down the porch steps after his father. But Robert had already disappeared through the thick trees. The child began to cry.

"Oh! It's alright, Luke!" I scooped him up into my arms and held him close.

"It isn't fair. I want to go with my daddy!"

"I know. But the woods are dangerous at night."

Poor child. How could he understand? Truth was, I didn't like having to stay there any more than Luke did. Left behind to worry and wait, tormented by fears of what might be. It would be better if I had something to do.

15

Thor and Loki looked into the forest and whined. "What's the matter with you two? Do you wish you could go help Lord Robert look for Elizabeth too?" ... That was when an idea came to me. "Why didn't I think of it sooner?" I said out loud.

Luke blinked rapidly. "Think of what?"

"Thor and Loki. They were trained as search and rescue dogs when they were puppies! They haven't gone out on a search in a few years, but they used to rescue people in the mountains!" *With Keith.* "They just need to be put upon Elizabeth's scent. Can you find us something of Elizabeth's that they can smell?"

Luke shook his fists in excitement. "I know!" He ran over to a tray that held the children's boots and picked up a little yellow boot with pink flowers. "Here. This has her smell." He held the boot up to Thor's nose and let the dog sniff it. "Yuck! She left her stinky socks inside!"

"Stinky socks! They'll work perfectly, Luke! Now Thor and Loki just need to wear their special jackets, which reminds them it is their job to get busy searching. The jackets are in the cabinet where I keep their leashes."

I was thankful they happened to be in the same box that I brought with me from home. I got them out of the cabinets and fastened them around Thor and Loki. "Now stick those smelly socks up to their noses, then we'll tie them around their collars."

Luke obeyed. He commanded the dogs, "Go find Elizabeth!"

My dogs remembered their training. Noses to the ground, they were off.

"They won't stop searching until they find her," I told Luke.

The only thing I worried about was that they didn't have Keith with them. He used to act as their handler. *Hopefully those smelly socks will keep them focused.*

After the dogs disappeared, swallowed up in the blackness of the woods, Winnie walked into the barn with Davey. "Davey and I are heading out there to join the search," she told me. "We're experienced riders."

"And I know these woods better than anyone," Davey added.

"Oh, good. My dogs are on the search, but they're used to having a handler. It would be good if you can stay close to them."

"Okay. If we run into them out there, we will," Winnie said.

Davey started to open Beaumont's stall, but I stopped him. "Lord Robert told me that he wanted Beaumont to rest."

"Oh? Yeah, he looks tired," Davey agreed. "Well, we can't take Xavier. That's Sean's horse. We'll have to take the Arabians, Epona and Brid." Davey stood in front of Epona's stall. "Winnie, I hope you can handle a strong horse with an unpredictable temperament. Because Epona is a handful, and she won't let me mount her. I don't know what it is about the Ranfurly family and their thing for difficult horses."

Epona whinnied and snorted, blowing slime out of her nostrils. It landed on Davey's face. He wiped it off with the back of a hand.

Winnie put up a hand and let the majestic-looking white mare sniff her. Epona nuzzled Winnie on the neck. "She isn't difficult. She just has excellent taste in humans."

Watching Winnie and Davey saddle the horses, it was obvious Winnie had plenty of experience riding. They filled up canteens with water and loaded first aid supplies in their saddle pouches before they rode off into the dark forest.

"They are going to find her. I just know it," Luke said after they were gone.

I smiled and picked him up. "Let's sit for a while and wait, okay?"

"Okay." His little hands held onto my neck as I sat down with him on a rocking chair. After a few minutes, I felt him grow heavier as he began to drift to sleep. The peaceful sound of chirping crickets was a dissonant contrast to my racing mind.

Sean Knight's voice broke through my anxious thoughts.

"Good to see you're finally out and about after days of recouping in your room," he said.

"Sean! You startled me!"

"Sorry." His caramel-colored eyes regarded me with concern. "Something wrong? You look upset."

I let out a long sigh. "Elizabeth is missing. Her and Luke were out riding horses earlier today with Davey. There was an intruder on the property. Elizabeth didn't come back..." I decided not to say anything more in case Luke was still awake.

Sean squeezed my shoulders. "Do you know where she was last seen?"

"No. A few members of staff are out there searching right now. Along with Lord Robert."

"And Thor and Loki!" Luke sat up.

Sean lifted his thick eyebrows. "Thor and Loki are searching? Well, if I were to place my bet on anyone finding her, it would be on those two."

"I'm sure you're right," I agreed.

Just then one of the maids walked up – the exotic one who looked like she belonged on a movie set. Jasmine. I thought it a little odd that she gave me a not-so-very-nice glare. *Did I offend her somehow?*

She was all sugar and spice when she asked Sean, "Can I get some help? We need firewood brought into the house, and Davey was supposed to do it. Do you mind?" With a swaying of her hips, she turned and left. Sean watched her as she headed back to the manor.

"Always the knight in shining armor ready to rescue a damsel in distress, Mr. Knight?" I didn't mention to him that I'd seen them whispering like a pair of secret lovers from my balcony when I was recouping in my room.

Sean sighed and gave my shoulders a last, tension-relieving squeeze. "A knight's work is never done." He left me and caught up to Jasmine.

Of course, I couldn't blame him if he was attracted to her. She had every quality that men lusted after. A perfect body with curves in all the right places. Beautiful, bronze skin. A beautiful face. All those annoying perfections that other women envied.

4

INQUISITIVE MAID

❧ Winnie ❧

Six Hours After Disappearance

When Winnie's Uncle Peter invited her to join the group he himself began, she was honored. *Contending Alliance of Protectors against Evil*, or CAPE, was a sophisticated resistance group. Uncle Peter had once served as a Supreme Court justice, and was close friends with the last president of Zone B. PAX executed the president for not bowing down to their New Order.

At that time, many who were loyal to the president, including Peter and his wife, went underground. Due to his many connections, Peter formed a network of diverse and highly experienced professionals: ex-Intelligence agents, police, medical workers, technology geniuses. In addition, he recruited some wealthy contributors to the cause. Lord Robert was one of them.

Back when Winnie was a teenager, when she and her father lived with her Uncle Peter and Aunt Nina, was when she met Lord Robert. He was Uncle Peter's friend who used to visit occasionally. She came to think of him as a funny-talking uncle. As she grew a bit older, his visits stopped, for reasons unknown to her. But he never missed sending her birthday gifts and candles for Days of Light.

Days of Light were six days of celebration – a holiday observed by people who followed the Old Religion. It was also celebrated by those who didn't. The devout considered it sacred and spent time in reflection. Those who weren't so devout enjoyed the benefits of time off work and school. Many people would use the holiday as an excuse to throw parties.

Winnie's father, aunt, and uncle were devout, so she was raised to have respect for the Old Religion. Her father would retell the stories of The Dragon Rider—God Incarnate—who came to the planet over a thousand years ago to thwart the dark one and his army of red dragons from destroying mankind.

It was tradition to give out a candle to burn on the first five days, and on the sixth day to celebrate The Dragon Rider's victory with a feast. Some people would give special gifts to loved ones.

Lord Robert always sent Winnie a very nice gift on the Sixth Day of Light.

Last week, when Uncle Peter told Winnie she'd be working as Lord Robert's partner, she was elated. When McGregor and Kila went to Lord Robert's airport hangar on a recent mission, they were lucky enough to fly inside his protected dome that concealed the manor from satellites and anything that flew overhead. That gave them the opportunity to see his massive estate from the sky, but nobody in CAPE had ever been inside the manor. Winnie couldn't wait to explore it!

What she didn't know until she arrived was that Lord Robert had children. None of the CAPE team members had been told he was a father. Her Uncle Peter and Aunt Nina had kept that secret from her for five years!

Uncle Peter cautioned her to keep it a secret as well. "Lord Robert knows many people who have become loyalists to PAX since the regime takeover. He doesn't want any of them to learn about his children; he worries it might put them in danger."

Winnie would never want harm to come to Uncle Robert or his kids, so she promised to keep the secret.

"I am unofficially adopting you both, as cousins!" she told the children when she met them. She had no siblings or cousins of her own and fell in love with the adorable twins. She would stop at nothing to find Elizabeth. *She's family.*

So far, she hadn't seen much of Lord Robert since she'd arrived to work as his partner. *I don't think he's too crazy about having a partner.* She had to come up with her own ideas of how to help him. So, she did a lot of snooping around, eavesdropping, and observing the staff with a keen eye.

That's why, when Davey Reed lost track of Elizabeth, she considered it a red flag.

Not sure how this Davey guy managed to lose track of Elizabeth when they were horseback riding. He was supposed to be looking after the kids. I'd fire his butt if I were Uncle Robert, Winnie thought. She appraised him as he rode the stallion in front of her. *Not bad looking, though, if you're into the cowboy type.* She frowned as she observed the man with the cowboy hat that rode next to her. Thick, wavy black hair, a bronzed complexion, solid frame, broad shoulders. *And he's got those dark and sultry bedroom eyes. Bet he's a womanizer. Aunt Nina always warned me, "That old devil wears a beautiful mask, Winnie. Don't be fooled by it!"*

The other maids told her that when Sean Knight went AWOL and they were short a stable worker, Davey had to take over the stables and equestrian training. But before that, he'd worked in the kitchens. According to them, he was an excellent chef.

He might be handsome as sin, but he made a huge, unforgivable mistake. He returned home first, ahead of Elizabeth and Luke. He should have rode in last to keep the kids in his view. Nope. I don't trust him.

She caught up to him so that their horses were neck to neck on the trail. "So how long have you worked here at the manor?" she asked.

"Too long," he replied.

"What do you mean by that, exactly?" Winnie came off as defensive. She caught herself, remembering she was supposed to be a maid who didn't know Lord Robert. In a sweeter tone, she asked, "You don't like working here?"

"I don't know. Sometimes I'd like a complete career switch. You know, like on days like this. Or like on days when a fellow staff member is murdered. Hasn't really been the most positive work environment as of late."

Winnie tilted her head. "True enough. So, you still didn't answer my question. When did you start working here?"

"When I was sixteen. For the former employer, Mr. Ranfurly."

"Sixteen? You were young. How old are you now?" Winnie guessed him to be the same age as her.

"Twenty-six."

"Aha! I was right! I guessed you to be around my age. I'm twenty-four. So, you've been here ten years. Wow. You practically grew up at this place. What was he like, this Mr. Ranfurly guy?"

"Mr. Ranfurly. He was something else. A real cowboy, I guess you might say. Like you see in movies."

"Really? Did he have cows?"

"Yeah. Used to have cattle here. He left the herd to an indigenous tribe that borders the land."

"Huh. That's kind of cool. Was he friendly? Good to his employees?"

He glanced back at her over a shoulder. "You're sure full of questions."

Oops. I'm supposed to be a maid, she reminded herself. *But is there a law that says a maid can't be inquisitive?* "Well, that picture of him on the second floor made me curious about him. Was he anything like his cousin, Lord Ranfurly?"

Davey laughed. "Two men couldn't be more opposite. Lord Ranfurly doesn't fit into Cascadia. He's way too pretty for this rugged land. This is logger and miner territory. In fact, I'm from a long line of coal miners. But Lord Ranfurly, with his long, flowin' hair, the way he talks and dresses … he doesn't belong here."

"And your old employer—Mr. Ranfurly—how did he fit into Cascadia? I mean, he was filthy rich and built this house that looks like a castle."

"He didn't build it. His grandfather did. He left Ranfurly Castle in Knoxfordshire, he was the third son of the viscount, and according to their laws over there in The Greens, a third son doesn't inherit anything. So, his granddad made his fortune during the goldrush in Cascadia, and built this place to look like the castle back in Knoxfordshire. Only he made this place way bigger. Probably to show up his oldest brother over in The Greens," Davey laughed. "That's the story Mr. Ranfurly told us, anyway."

"Brotherly rivalry," Winnie said. "Why didn't Mr. Ranfurly call himself a Lord? Did he lose his nobility because he was born here?"

"I don't know about that. But he told me that his grandfather didn't want him to be raised with a title, didn't want him to be out of touch with reality. He made him work every summer as a logger. Then when the grandfather passed, Mr. Ranfurly inherited this place. But he always seemed like one of us."

"You really miss him."

"Yeah … you know, it was amazing the way he'd always remember everybody's name. He was funny too. Got a kick out of pulling pranks."

"Pranks?"

"Yeah. He'd do all sorts of stuff. One time he put plastic bugs inside the lampshades of everyone's rooms. We all thought there was an infestation." Davey laughed. "Then there was that time he hid inside the armor in the entrance hallway and jumped at me. I almost died of a heart attack!" They both laughed at that. "But the one he especially loved to mess with was Ms. Stern."

"Ms. Stern? Oh, I bet she hated his pranks!"

Davey shrugged. "I don't know. The only time I ever saw her smile was around him. She used to be prettier. She's aged a lot since he died."

"Really? She's so persnickety. I can't imagine what she would look like if she smiled."

He laughed. "Believe it or not, her daughter looks just like she did, when she was younger."

"I didn't know she had a daughter."

"Sure, she does. You work with her. The hot blonde, Gretchen."

"What? Gretchen is Ms. Stern's daughter?" Winnie had to let that sink in. "Who's the dad?"

"You know," Davey sucked in air, "nobody really knows. But rumor is that Mr. Ranfurly and Ms. Stern were once … you know." He moved his eyebrows up and down.

Winnie almost shouted. "No way! That's … wait! Then that could mean that Gretchen might be Mr. Ranfurly's daughter?"

"Well, nobody knows the truth. And you'd think if it were true, Ms. Stern would have shouted it from the rooftops, right? I mean, this place could belong to Gretchen if she is the true heir of Mr. Ranfurly." He whistled. "I'd sure say something if I knew I was related to him!"

"Yeah. You'd think…" Winnie said.

"Another thing I remember about Mr. Ranfurly … a person wouldn't want to get on his bad side. He wasn't kind to his enemies. Fortunately, he was always kind to me, though."

"You really admired him."

"Yeah. I liked to pretend he was my grandpa. He treated me like I was family, too. He used to hand me one-hundred pins, pat me on the back, and say, 'Go spend that on booze and women, son.'"

Winnie chuckled. "Did you?"

He laughed. "Well, I didn't have a car or any way to get to the big city of Emer Aude back then. Before I came to work here, I lived in the tiny town of North Ireland. There was never much action in that town. Just a bunch of people who worked at the coal mine. And loggers, of course."

"Miners and loggers, huh?"

"Yup. There used to be a logging mill out by the river, but now it's just an abandoned warehouse that nobody knows about."

"And you didn't want to be a miner? Or a logger?"

"No way! Not after I got a taste of what it would be like to live *here*. I was fortunate enough to be favored by Mr. Ranfurly. When I turned eighteen and got my license, he got me into a top-notch chef school in Vinosa. I learned all about the real world that year."

"But you still decided to come back here to be a chef?"

"Sure. I came back here for Mr. Ranfurly. I felt like I owed it to him since he paid for my education."

"But now you're a horse boy. Isn't this a demotion?"

"This is temporary until we find someone."

"So, you must have been sad to lose him and gain Lord Ranfurly as your new boss, huh?" Winnie asked, trying to sound casual and conversational, rather than too nosey.

"You have no idea," Davey said.

The trail narrowed, so Davey rode ahead in front of Winnie for a while.

Clouds had concealed the light of the moon. But as the clouds moved and revealed the bright bulb in the sky, the trail was lit up, and they could see it widening as they approached a large meadow. Davey tugged on Brid's reigns and halted so Winnie could catch up to him. He said, "Now it's my turn to ask you a question."

Their horses were side by side now, and Epona gave Brid a kiss. "Okay … ask away," Winnie said.

"Is there a reason you have a tattoo of a rose on your neck?"

Winnie was silent for a moment. Davey's dark gaze was on her, waiting for her response.

"Yes."

Davey shifted in his saddle. "Did I just ask the wrong question?"

Winnie paused, sensing she was making Davey feel uncomfortable. She still didn't trust him. *But what harm will it do to tell him about my tattoo?*

"I got it in remembrance of my dad."

"Oh. I'm sorry." He sighed. "I figured it had significant meaning."

"It's okay. I wear the rose proudly, in honor of him." She clicked and loosened up on the reigns. Davey kept up the same pace on his horse, so they were side by side.

"How did he die?" he asked her.

"Oh, he's still alive. Here." She put a hand on her chest. "Always with me."

"Yeah."

After that, they rode without speaking for quite some time. *Crunch. Crunch.* Horseshoes crushing leaves and twigs made a percussive kind of song.

Winnie's voice broke in, like a clarinet coming in at a measure. "He was killed on the Day of Cleansing."

A low groan came from Davey. "I'm sorry. How did you learn about his execution? Did PAX send a letter?"

"Yeah. But I wasn't shocked. PAX dragged my dad away for his bold stand on following the Old Religion. That was a few months before they showed their true nature to the rest of the world on The Day of Cleansing."

"Too many good people were executed that day. My grandfather was one of them."

"What law did they say he broke?"

"He protested the new government when they shut down all the coal mines. We weren't shocked either. Just mad as hell."

"I'm sorry," Winnie said.

Davey spat on the ground. "Did your dad really believe in the Old Religion? All that stuff about The Dragon Rider being God?"

"Yeah. My aunt and uncle believe it too."

"And you? Do you believe it?"

Winnie lifted her shoulders up. "I don't know. I did when I was a kid. But now, it sounds … outlandish. Yet the people who love me the most, who I trust and respect the most, believe the Scripture is God's message to us. They say He's going to come back and save us all. It's kind of confusing to me. I don't really know what I believe anymore."

"Yeah. But they're from a different generation. I think we know far more now than they did thirty and forty years ago. … I take a much more scientific view of things."

"Oh? What's your view?"

"I believe we are just matter."

"Just matter? You mean, you don't believe we have souls?"

"Nope. There's absolutely no scientific evidence that we have souls. But there is evidence that we're made of atoms."

Winnie raised an eyebrow. "Nah. I don't buy that theory. If we're just matter, then does anything really matter?" She became quite animated.

"What purpose is there in life for any of us? And what point is there to anything?"

Davey smiled.

Winnie went on. "I mean, think about it … where does our sense of purpose come from, if we're just soulless life forms? I mean, you know a great story needs a plot, right?"

"Of course."

"Well, if we weren't created by a being who instilled that concept into us, then how did we come up with it? If we're just *matter*, then you can't try to convince me there is a plot to anything in life."

"You are a person who asks a lot of questions, that's for sure!" Davey said.

"And as for our generation being smarter, look at how much worse the world is today. The Tsur War! Trafficking at an all-time high!" She sighed. "We sure aren't any better off considering how much more we know. I think your theory has way too many holes."

Davey laughed. "Well … it doesn't matter. Because we're just matter."

"Pff."

They rode through the vast meadow in silence for a moment. Epona was antsy, and Winnie ascertained that the horse longed to run through the large and open meadow. It was fine by her. The talk about her father caused her to feel more anxious about Elizabeth. It also stirred up the anger she had toward PAX. She wanted to be alone.

"Epona wants to run. I'm going to let her have her way." She clicked her tongue and her horse shot out into the meadow, leaving Davey and Brid to taste her wind. She grabbed onto the horse's neck, exhilaration rising from her belly to her throat. Her pulse raced to match Epona's rhythm.

She longed to be rid of the saddle, to feel no barrier between this noble and majestic creature and herself. Two united as one in their angst against those who used their power as a means to crush and control.

Through the tall meadow grass beneath the streams of moonlight, it appeared as if the horse and rider were flying. Winnie found her balance and sat up straight, lifting her arms up to her sides. She let out a sad, haunting cry, the refrain of a hymn that her father used to sing.

On the wings of the eagle

I will fly forever

Eternal joy, eternal joy

In the arms of my Maker

I will rest forever

Eternal peace, eternal peace

They crossed the open field and reached the edge of the meadow where dense forest began, just feet away. The horse stopped running of her own free will and munched on some grass. Epona would have been happy to stay in the meadow.

Winnie stroked the horse's mane. "Thanks, Epona. I needed that run as much as you did." She waited for Davey to catch up.

Davey whistled. "Wow. Epona hasn't been this happy since Mr. Ranfurly used to ride her."

"Lord Robert's cousin rode Epona?"

"Yeah. He was the one who broke her. And she hasn't let anyone ride her since. Until now."

The clouds covered the moon, and the dense forest was absent of moonlight. They turned their headlamps up a notch to a brighter setting. In silence, each of them scanned the surroundings for a sign of Elizabeth. At one point, Davey said, "What is that?" He pointed his light at a nearby bush.

"I don't know. Let's get a closer look." They stopped and Winnie knelt down by it. She held something up in her hand and inspected it by the light. "A blue ribbon."

"Elizabeth had blue ribbons tied around her braids," Davey said, as he roped off both the horses to a nearby tree.

They searched the area, Winnie checking up all the nearby trees. "If I were stuck out in the forest, a tree would be where I'd hide."

"Over here!" Davey called to her. Winnie found him near a large cedar stump that had a hollow. Inside the hollow, they found a ripped off piece of blue yarn.

"There's one out here too," Winnie said. "Smart kid, she seems to have left a trail."

"Perhaps this is one of the things Lord Robert did when he went into the woods with his kids and they acted crazy." Davey spun a finger next to his head.

"What do you mean, 'acted crazy'?"

"Oh, I guess you didn't work here yet. He once brought his kids out in the woods at night, and the three of them started howling. Ms. Stern sent me out to shoot what we thought were wolves. Thankfully, Lord Robert called out to me before I accidentally shot one of them."

Winnie chuckled. "No kidding. So, he could have been teaching his kids survival skills. Kudos to him if he was."

"Let's just hope Elizabeth is surviving," Davey said.

"At least we see a sign of her out here. I'm feeling more hopeful we might find her."

"Yeah. But I'm not sure I'd prescribe to Ranfurly's parenting methods."

"Hey, by the way, I haven't seen or heard from Courtney's dogs since we left the barn. Have you?"

"No. Not a sign of them. Wonder where they ran off to?"

5

HORSE SENSE

❧ Courtney ❧

Seven Hours After Disappearance

It grew too cold to stay in the barn, so I brought Luke back inside the manor and we waited in the Parlor. The poor little guy was exhausted, and fell into a deep sleep on my lap. But after a while, I got a cramp in my leg, which persisted until I could bear it no more. I tried not to wake him, but I needed to get up and stretch.

Sean came into the room as I was trying to lift Luke off of me. "Here, let me get him," he said.

"Oh, thanks."

Sean gently placed him on a nearby couch. Luke fidgeted to get comfortable but didn't wake. "Poor little tyke," Sean whispered.

I stood up to stretch my leg out. "Did you finish helping Jasmine?"

"Yes. I hurried so I could get back to you. Any word about whether they found Elizabeth yet?"

"No. It's like torture waiting here. I wish I could be out there looking for her."

"You're needed here to watch over the little guy." He surveyed Luke, whose mouth was slightly open as he slumbered peacefully away.

I smiled. "He fell asleep while praying that Thor and Loki would find his sister."

"I'm going to head out there and join the search."

"Oh, Sean. Thank you. But be careful."

"I'll be fine."

"And don't take out Beaumont. He's tired."

"I won't. I have my own horse. Had Xavier since I was a kid. We bonded then, and even though I was away all these years, it's like no time ever passed between us."

Luke startled me when he asked, "Have they found my Lizzie yet?" His eyes were barely slit open.

"Not yet," I whispered. "But Mr. Knight's going to help find her."

"Can I come?" Luke asked.

"No, sorry, little lad." Sean tapped him lightly on his head. "Mrs. Drake needs a brave man like you to watch after her. Promise me you'll keep her safe."

Luke contemplated that for a minute before he puffed out his chest and replied to Sean. "Okay. I'll protect her."

❧ Sean ❧

Sean left Courtney and Luke in the parlor and headed to his apartment in the staff quarters to gather some essentials before he joined the search. As he was leaving, he ran into Jasmine outside his door.

"Where are you off to?" she asked him.

"I'm going to help look for Elizabeth."

"Girls her age are worth a fortune in the trafficking arena. And people pay double for red hair. I hate to say it, but I have a terrible feeling."

"Let's hope you're feeling is wrong."

"I'll help you look," Jasmine said. "Smarter to team up out there."

"Alright," Sean said. "Grab a head lamp and jacket, and I'll meet ya out by the stables."

"Stables?"

"Yeah. I've got to saddle the horses."

"Um … I'm not exactly a fan of horseback riding. Horses and I don't get along." Jasmine made a sour face.

"What? Jasmine Lopez, not good at something? Here I thought there was nothing you couldn't do. Fine, you can ride on my horse with me."

Sean tightened up the straps of the saddle on his thoroughbred, Xavier. After he mounted, he held out a hand to Jasmine. "Okay. Hop up."

"Hop up?"

"That's right, Lass. Mount and straddle. We both know you're more than capable of doing that." He gave her a half grin.

Jasmine hoisted herself up and swung her leg over the horse, attempting to kick Sean as she did so. He leaned backward to avoid her foot.

"Be nice, Jasmine. I'm the one with the reigns tonight," Sean warned.

She snickered as she settled between his thighs and leaned back against him.

Sean kicked his heels into Xavier, and they headed out into the dark forest. "So, you don't care much for horses, huh?" he asked her.

"No. I do not."

"Have a bad episode with a horse once upon a time, or…?"

"No. I just don't like that they're infested with fleas, they stink, can't hold a conversation, and can't take care of themselves."

Sean chuckled. "Xavier and I take offense to that. Our stables have no fleas, and our horses are well-groomed and smell wonderful."

"Ha!" Jasmine mocked.

"And I happen to know firsthand that horses make fantastic conversationalists. Xavier and I spend heaps of time discussin' things."

"Oh, is that right?" Jasmine raised a finely plucked brow. "What do you discuss?"

"Women, mostly. How annoying they are."

"Mm."

"And horses know how to take care of themselves just fine. All you have to do is observe them in the wild and you'll find that out."

"But Xavier is not in the wild. You feed him, brush him, water him, shoe him, and shovel up his dung." Jasmine put a hand on Sean's leg and pinched his thigh muscle. "Don't try to tell me this beast is taking care of itself."

"He *allows* me to serve him. It's my privilege. If Xavier was in the wild, he could certainly survive without me."

"Yeah. Keep telling yourself that. ... Exactly where do you get this love for animals, Sean? Your mother? Because I don't see your dad as someone with a soft spot for pets."

"Definitely not my father. His stone-cold heart doesn't have room for anything except a love for cars. And I've never met my mother, so I can't tell you whether or not she was an animal lover." Sean choked on a piece of Jasmine's hair that flew into his mouth.

"Sean, stop the horse! I need to get off of this thing," Jasmine said.

Sean halted the horse and dismounted. He helped Jasmine off. "What's wrong?"

"I have a cramp! How do people sit on these things for hours? It's torment!" Jasmine stretched her legs and attempted to walk, bow-legged.

Sean snickered. "If you rode more often, you'd get used to it. You might even like it."

"Please, Sean. That's not going to happen."

Awooo! Awooo!

Jasmine gripped his arm, her head cocked. "Did you just hear that?"

"Yeah. Wolves howling in the distance."

"Poor kid. If she is out there alive, I don't know that she'll be able to survive a night in these woods."

"Are you sure you don't want to get back on the horse?" Sean asked her.

6

SURVIVAL SKILLS

❧ Elizabeth ❧

Seven Hours Earlier

Elizabeth liked to let Lady Rose stop and graze as often as she wished. She could still see her twin brother Luke ahead of her, even though she didn't see Mr. Davey. He was so far in front of them that he was out of sight. But that was nothing new. Ever since he'd taken Mr. Sean's job with the horses a couple of weeks back, he'd been in a hurry when they were riding. Elizabeth liked Mr. Sean much better. He didn't rush.

While Lady was munching grass, Elizabeth caught sight of *him*—the stranger. He had a face that reminded her of a snake. *Not a cute snake, either. Not like Luke's pet Elsie, who has a permanent smile and big round eyes that make her look like a cartoon.* No, the stranger was more like an ugly, mean snake.

When his black gaze met her curious stare, she gasped. *He sees me!* Fear rippling through her, she leaned forward and slightly raised herself off the saddle, communicating to Lady Rose that she wanted to run. *I have to catch up to Luke and tell him!*

But when Luke heard Elizabeth coming up behind him, he thought she was trying to race. "My horse might be small, but he can still run faster than your dumb pony!" Luke pressed his heels into his miniature horse, who started running.

34

Lady Rose tried to catch up, but something spooked her. She began to run off the main trail, into the forest. Elizabeth tried to stop her, but the pony reared and stood on two hind legs, throwing little Elizabeth off her saddle.

The snake-face stranger appeared out of nowhere, grabbed Lady by the reins, and mounted her. His beady black-eyed gaze rested on Elizabeth. She wanted to scream, but she couldn't find her voice.

"Well, aren't you a pretty little thing?" the man hissed. "With that red hair."

Elizabeth froze.

He dangled an earring that was designed to look like a snake, with sparkly green and red jewels. "Do you like it?"

She glanced around, looking for some place small that she could fit into, a place where he wouldn't be able to go.

"I'll let you have it if you come over here and talk to me," the stranger said.

She bolted into thick foliage, out of sight. Scrambling, she stayed low.

His scary voice called out. "Here, little Red. Come out, come out, wherever you are."

Elizabeth heard the crunch from her pony's hooves. The stranger called out again, sounding even closer.

She stayed on her stomach and continued to crawl away from the stranger's voice, until she came to an opening beneath a fallen tree. *I think I can squeeze through.* She crawled inside and tried not to make a sound.

She could see Lady Rose's hooves stepping through brush close to her hiding spot, then stopping inches from her face. Elizabeth held her breath.

It felt like forever and ever.

A familiar and eerie cry sounded nearby. *Cougar.*

The stranger was above her. "Suit yourself, kid. Stay out here and die in these woods. I'll be taking your pony with me."

She saw Lady's hooves back up and turn around. When she could no longer hear the crunch from her pony's hooves, and it grew silent around her, she let out a gasp. *He stole Lady Rose!* She burst into tears. *Lady!*

For a long time, all she could do was cry. At some point, face in her hands, her daddy's words came to mind:

When you're scared, your heart races too fast. Breathe with me. Her daddy would breathe very slowly. In and out.

Elizabeth did as she remembered. *In. Out. In. Out.*

She felt the sensation of creepy crawlies on her back and neck and rapidly squirmed out from the hole under the tree, swiping them off. As she stood up, she realized she was completely lost. *Uh oh. Where's the trail?*

After walking for a while, at last she found a trail. But it split and went three different directions.

Which way? She chose the widest.

Elizabeth came to several more forks, and was never sure which way to go.

Awooo!

Her head turned in the direction of wolves howling in the distance.

A screeching sound turned her in the opposite direction. *That sounded like a cougar!* She panicked and broke into a run.

The rushing sound of water grew louder, until it dawned on her that she'd come to the river. *Oh no.* Her father had warned her and her brother, "Stay away from the river; it's far too dangerous."

Which way is my house? Elizabeth was exceptionally bright for her five years, but her young mind couldn't grasp what her father meant when he told her they lived on miles and miles of land. What she understood was that it was a big, giant forest, and her house sat somewhere in the middle of it.

The sun had already fallen low. It would be dark soon. Shivering she cried out, "Daddy! Daddy!"

Elizabeth remembered the time her father showed her and Luke how to build a shelter out of branches. That had been fun when she felt safe with Daddy. But she couldn't build a shelter without him.

Daddy also taught them that if they were ever lost in the woods, they could follow the example of the little animals and look for places to hide at night. They even practiced by playing hide and seek. She was never afraid in the forest when her daddy was with her.

Elizabeth searched around the area, and spotted a hollow in a tree that she could fit into. She crawled inside before the sun completely went away. Hugging her legs, she peered out from her hiding spot.

She sat still, listening to the birds, mesmerized by the way the sun's fading light made the foliage turn from green to black in the hues of twilight. The distraction calmed her.

Eventually, the dim light of twilight disappeared, and the moon was hidden behind dark clouds. *Daddy, please find me.* Elizabeth cried.

She heard rustling in the bushes around her, and as she peered out, several red lights appeared. Daddy told her the eyes of different animals glowed in different colors at night. But she couldn't remember which colors belonged to which animals.

Two red lights were coming closer. She covered her face with her hands and bit her lip to keep from crying out. *Don't make noise.*

Sniff. Sniff.

What was sniffing her? Too terrified to peek through her fingers to see what it was, she thought, *What if it's a bear?* She shook uncontrollably and her breaths became audible.

She felt a cold, wet sensation on the knuckles of her hands, and shrank back further into the tree hollow. A scream desperately wanted to escape her, but she held it in.

Then … the sniffing stopped. The crunching noise in the dirt grew faint. Through her fingers, she stole a peek.

A white cotton tail of a rabbit bobbed as the animal hopped away. She let out a long breath that she'd been holding in.

It was just a cute little bunny! She laughed out loud, feeling silly about how afraid she'd been. Tears rolled down her cheeks.

Clouds parted and the forest floor was lit by the glow of the moon. What a difference even that small bit of light made. She could see everything around her. Bunnies hopping around, munching on plants. A white owl in a nearby tree looking down at her in curiosity.

She felt a new sense of gusto.

"I can see now! I can go home!" She crawled out of her hiding spot, and swiped off the feeling of dirt and creepy crawlies.

Another one of daddy's lessons came to mind.

She yanked hard on a piece of blue yarn from her sweater, and left it inside the tree hollow where she'd been hiding. As she walked, she continued to leave a piece of yarn every few steps, so she'd know not to return that way again.

She was on a very good trail now, with logs placed on each side to mark it well. *This looks right!* She suddenly felt very brave.

But after a little while, clouds once again blocked the moonlight.

What made the darkness even scarier was that she had the feeling she was being watched.

She searched for somewhere to hide, but it was too dark to make out her surroundings. "Mr. Moon. Please come out," she said out loud.

Something growled nearby. *Too close.*

She froze.

Another growl, this time directly behind her. Screaming, she ran, only to be tripped by a fallen log. She fell forward. Before she knew what was happening, something bit her leg.

The last thing she remembered before everything went black was being dragged along the forest ground.

7

ON THE TRAIL

Thor and Loki

Eight Hours After Disappearance

Thor and Loki showed up on the path where Lord Robert and Llamrei were searching, noses to the ground.

"Well, hello, you two!" Seeing their jackets, Robert said, "Looks like you're experienced at search and rescue! Very good, then. Let those sniffers of yours do their work."

Muzzles never leaving the ground, the dogs were relentless in their search. Robert confessed to his canine friends, "I can't think clearly. Not when it comes to my Elizabeth."

They stopped to look at him, heads tilted.

"I see why Courtney wanted the pair of you around. You must have been a comfort to her after she lost her husband."

Thor let out a whine, as if he understood. Then he was back to sniffing, continuing the search. Both dogs turned around on the trail to head back the way they'd come.

"Oh? You want me to go back that way again? Very well. Lead on!" Robert called after them, as he turned Llamrei around to follow.

The dogs led him back to where the last fork in the trail was, down the route that Robert had avoided earlier.

"This way? Alright! Onward!" Robert steered his horse to follow.

They started to pick up the pace, as if they had caught a whiff of a scent. Robert's heart raced. Dare he hope?

The dogs disappeared through thick brush, too thick for Llamrei to walk through. Robert had to dismount in order to keep up. A moment later, Robert heard a bark. He cut his way through the prickly bushes, then caught up to the dogs, who were wagging their tails.

When he saw what the excitement was about, Robert's heart caved. They'd discovered Epona and Brid. The horses were saddled and tied off to a nearby tree.

The dogs went back to sniffing. He followed them through a thicket of trees until he could see what appeared to be headlamp lights moving about. Robert reached for his gun, thinking it might be the intruder. A light shone in Robert's eyes and blinded him.

"Don't shoot, Lord Robert!" Davey called out. "It's Winnie and Davey! We're out here searching for Elizabeth."

"Ah." Robert put his gun back in its holster. "Any sign of her?"

"Yes! She left a trail by pulling off yarn from her sweater, but it stops here." Winnie handed Robert a piece of the blue yarn.

Robert's pulse throbbed in his temples, as blood rushed to his head. *My precious girl was here!* He scanned the area, looking for more strips of yarn.

"Davey said you brought your kids out into the woods at night. Were you teaching them survival skills?" asked Winnie.

Robert never stopped searching as he replied, "Yes. I taught them things they could do if they were ever lost in the woods. Showed them how they should leave a trail, so they would know where they've already been. Fortunately, Elizabeth was wearing that sweater today. It was made with yarn so her tiny fingers were able to pull it apart."

Thor and Loki abruptly stopped and froze in place, their noses in the air, each lifting a paw slightly off the ground. Robert flashed his light on them.

"They're pointing," Robert whispered. The dogs shot off. The three of them followed. After a few minutes, the dogs darted through a six-foot-high hedge of berry bushes.

40

"Ladies first," Davey said to Winnie.

She was about to suck it up and plow through the stabbing wall when Robert brought something out of his backpack.

"What's that?" she asked him.

He quickly swiped through the hedge, and a passage was cleared for them. "Laser cutter. One must be prepared when in the forests of Cascadia."

Loki and Thor were now barking and growling ferociously. Robert, Winnie, and Davey's headlamps found the source of the dog's aggression. They were in a faceoff with a wolf. Its eyes glowed white as it stared square into the beams of the headlamps and bared its teeth.

Robert drew his handgun and shot the wolf, sending it down with a yelp. But then they heard another vicious growl, and a pair of white eyes flashed, as a second wolf emerged from out of the darkness.

"Oh fantastic. It's a pack," Winnie said.

Thor and Loki snarled, their back hairs standing on end, fangs bared. Nobody could recall who lunged first, and confusion set in as growling, barking, and yelping echoed through the night. In the darkness, it was impossible to distinguish whether it was wolves or dogs crying out in pain.

The rest of the pack advanced toward the three humans. "It'd be nice if I could see what I'm shooting at!" Robert said, shooting at something he saw running toward him.

Winnie had out her gun and was shooting as well. "Davey, shine your light so we can see better!" She and Robert continued to shoot at more wolves in the pack. "I hope to God we're not shooting Courtney's dogs!"

At some point, whatever wolves remained had finally retreated into the forest. They heard whimpering, and ran over to where Thor and Loki were lying together.

Davey flashed the light on them. "I think Thor is hurt," he said. "It's okay, boy. Hang in there."

Winnie reached into a pack that was attached to Epona's saddle and brought out a first aid kit.

"Loki looks like he got out of the fight unscathed." Robert said.

"Thank God!" Winnie knelt down by Thor's side. "Oh, poor Thor. That wolf did a number on him. He doesn't look good." Blood was spilling out of Thor's side.

Lord Robert knelt down on the other side of Thor. "He's losing too much blood." He put pressure on the wound. "We need to get him home. You two head back on the horses and return with the forest trekker. You know where it is, Davey."

"Yeah, and there's a gurney in the shop. I'll bring it."

"Yes. Take Llamrei back with you. I tied him off close to where I found you. Hurry! I'll stay here with Thor."

As Davey and Winnie hurried to find Llamrei, Davey asked, "Do you always carry a concealed weapon on you?"

Winnie shrugged. "Only when walking around ... and sleeping ... and, well, pretty much all the time. Yeah."

8

DON'T LEAVE US

❧ Courtney ❧

Eight Hours After Disappearance

I'd been anxiously waiting in the parlor when Robert stormed in. "Courtney, help me move everything off this coffee table."

Winnie and Davey came in a moment later, carrying a gurney. My first thought was that they'd found Elizabeth and she'd been injured.

Then I saw my pup.

"Thor?" I hurried over and removed a vase and a couple of books to get the table ready for him.

Luke woke as he heard his father's voice. He stretched his little arms up and yawned. Then he saw my dog. "Thor!"

Loki quietly entered the room and laid down next to his littermate. He let out a soft whine.

"Do you have a vet who can help him?" I asked Lord Robert.

"Vet?" He didn't seem to comprehend the question.

"Yes. Surely you have a vet for the horses."

"The people I hire to look after the horses are qualified to care of them when they are sick or wounded."

"What about a family doctor? A doctor could probably help Thor, right?"

"Family doctor?" It was like it was the first time he'd ever heard the two words together in a sentence. "I don't really trust doctors, Courtney. They all work for PAX now."

"But ... when I accepted the job, Ms. Stern told me there would be medical and dental included."

Robert sucked air through his teeth. "I'm sorry, Courtney. I told Ms. Stern to make the job sound irresistible."

"Seriously?" I blinked quickly. "Speaking of Ms. Stern, where is she?"

Just after the words came out of my mouth, she snappily appeared. "Is there something you need?"

"Oh! No. I was just wondering where you were," I said.

She raised her chin and turned on her heels, then went back into the kitchen where she'd just come from.

"So, what do you do without a doctor when there's an emergency?" I asked Robert. "Like right now?"

"There's never been an emergency at the manor that I haven't been able to handle on my own," he said, as if it were common knowledge.

I blinked a few times. I understood not liking doctor visits, but Robert's reaction seemed a bit ... much. I thought back to the past week when I was recovering from the concussion and stab wound. Mr. Roth had done a great job tending to me. "Luke, sweetie, go into the kitchen and ask Ms. Stern to find Mr. Roth so he can help Thor."

"Good idea! Whenever we get sick and Daddy's gone, Mr. Roth takes care of us really good. He can help Thor!" Luke made a mad dash for the kitchen.

A few minutes later, Mr. Roth came into the room. "Oh my," Mr. Roth said. "What was it that did this to him?"

Robert glanced up, his face ashen. "Wolves. He and Loki tried to fight off a pack of wolves to save us. Courtney's dogs were very brave tonight."

I stroked Thor's fur. "Oh Thor, hang in there, boy. Please stay with us."

Mr. Roth spoke quietly. "It doesn't look good. ... I wouldn't hope."

"We owe that dog our lives," Robert said in a gravelly voice.

44

"Thor is not going to die! I won't let that happen!" Luke screamed. Loki whined and rested his head on his littermate's paw.

I draped myself over Thor. "Come on boy. Don't leave us."

"God, please, you can't take him! You can't!" Luke ran over to Thor, sobbing.

Mr. Roth asked, "Lord Ranfurly, do you know how to administer immunizations?"

"Yes."

"Come with me, I'll show you where the medical supplies are. We have globulin and rabies vaccines on hand."

"Really, Mr. Roth? You are full of surprises!" Robert said.

"I was a medic in the military before I came to work here." Mr. Roth said as he and Robert hurried out of the room.

Mrs. Roth came into the Parlor, and Luke and I moved out of the way as she put a warm blanket over Thor. "Poor pup," she said.

As his breathing slowed, I stroked his paw and watched him intently. I was vaguely aware of a warm hand on my back.

Sean Knight's slight Highlandish lilt broke into my silent sobs. "Ssh, there, there, boy." He knelt next to me and pet Thor's paw.

Luke sat on the other side of me. "Thor isn't really going to die, is he? He can't die."

I didn't want to give Luke false hope. "I don't know, sweetie. I'm not sure he can pull through this."

"It's my fault. I told him to go look for Lizzie."

"No, it isn't your fault. It isn't anyone's fault."

"Do you think God has a place for dogs?"

"Well, God made dogs, so why wouldn't he have a place for them to go when they die?"

"Yeah. I think he does. And I bet it's really, really, really big." Luke spread his arms out wide.

Winnie and Davey gathered around Thor. "Thank you, Thor, Winnie said.

"Yes, thank you," Davey said.

I wished he would open his eyes, move his paw, show some sign that he was alive. But it appeared as if he was no longer breathing.

Lord Robert and Mr. Roth came back into the parlor. Mr. Roth checked for Thor's heartbeat. He frowned and shook his head. "He's fading."

Robert stood behind me and put his hands on my shoulders. "I'm sorry, Courtney."

"Is this really happening?" I looked up at him. "But Robert, what about Elizabeth?" I whispered. "Did you see any sign of her?"

"Yes," he said. "She left pieces of yarn along the trail. I have to get back out there and search for her, but I feel terrible about your dog. He saved our lives."

It wasn't quite hitting me that Thor was already lost to me, even though word had spread quickly through the manor that my dog had died a hero. Gretchen came into the parlor and ran over to hug me. Mr. Knight, Sr. was there too, along with Jasmine, Dean, the Butters brothers—they were all there. Even Ms. Stern and the other grumpy ladies, old Eleanor and Mrs. Pemberley, came in with concerned expressions. Ms. Stern's usual scowl had softened a bit. It surprised me, the way the staff rallied together in dire circumstances.

How could I say goodbye? He'd been my greatest source of comfort since I'd lost Keith, since the kids left for college. That dog could read my thoughts, predict my actions, sense my emotions. And he would go to endless lengths to protect people. He was like a guardian angel.

Luke was drowning in sobs, and Lord Robert reached down and picked his little boy up to console him. Sean was still sitting on the floor next to me, stroking my dog's fur and whispering to him. I leaned forward to touch Thor's front paw.

Mr. Roth checked him once more for a heartbeat and had a disappointing reaction.

"Is he still breathing?" I asked.

"I'm sorry. His breathing stopped," Mr. Roth said quietly.

Loki whimpered and licked Thor's face. Robert sat down in a chair with Luke. The child held his hands together in prayer, head bowed, lips moving.

I spoke softly into Thor's ear. "Thor, you were so brave. I love you, boy. So much. If only you could have stayed with us longer. You're the best. The absolute best. … I don't know what I'm going to do without you."

A squeal from Luke startled me. He shook his head fiercely. "No! He isn't going to die! I prayed to The Dragon Rider!" he shouted.

It made it so much harder, knowing the disappointment he was going to have to face when he realized the truth.

"He is not going to die! He's not!" cried the child.

This is too hard. Unable to respond, I sat up, and pressed my fingers into my temples, lost in my own grief.

Then … a golden-brown eye opened, and was watching me.

No, I must have imagined that.

"See? I told you!" Luke jumped up on his feet and clapped. "He's alive!"

Both of Thor's eyes were open and he was trying to lift his head. He let out a soft whine. Loki stood and wagged his tail.

The whole room broke into cheers of joy and sobs of relief. Sean whispered, "There, there, boy. You're hurt. Too soon to try to get up."

Thor is alive? I'd stopped hoping too quickly, but Luke hadn't. I decided then that Luke must have more faith than anyone I'd ever met. Moving a finger over the bridge of Thor's nose, tears of relief spilled out of me. "Oh, Thor, thank you for coming back. I thought I'd lost you."

Luke ran to Thor and patted his head. "You sure did trick us good, Thor. You know how to play dead better than anyone!" Luke said.

Everyone laughed.

"He's quite the hero," Robert said, kneeling down behind me. "But let's not forget Loki. He fought hard against those wolves too." He reached out a hand for Loki, and he came over to get some petting from us.

"Oh, Thor. You do like to steal all the attention away from your brother, don't you?" I said, tears of joy dripping off of my face.

Mr. Roth brought a couple of bowls of water out and set them down by the dogs, one under Thor's nose. "Take a drink, Thor. It'll make you feel better," he said.

Thor didn't move.

"Give him some time," Sean said, standing up.

"Lord Robert, with your permission, I think it would be best if we can keep Thor inside for a few days while he recoups. I'll keep a close eye on him for the next couple of days," Mr. Roth said. "My wife and I can let him out to relieve himself when he needs to."

"Of course. Keep both the dogs inside," Robert said. He wrapped his arms around me, and I sank against him, relieved. Exhausted. Drained. Luke laid down and put his head on my lap, while petting Thor.

We sat in silence. Long enough for the rest of the room to clear out. By the time it did, Luke had fallen sound asleep.

Likewise, Thor and Loki were slumbering away, the rhythm of their snores music to my ears.

Robert whispered, "I'm going to head back out to look for Elizabeth now."

"Robert, I'm sorry. I would have understood if you weren't here during all this craziness with Thor. Your daughter is the most important one for you to think about right now." A good hour had passed.

"I felt I needed to be here," he said. "Now, get some rest. Sleep in here if you like."

There was no way I could fall asleep with Elizabeth missing. "I want to help you look for her, Robert. Please. Can't the Roths look after Luke tonight? They seem like good people."

Robert contemplated. "You're sure you want to leave Thor right now?"

"There's nothing I can do for him. He needs sleep, and I definitely won't be getting any while I'm worrying about Elizabeth."

"Alright, then. Let's get going."

MORE THAN COLLEAGUES—IT'S COMPLICATED!

❧ *Sean* ❧

Flashback—Nine Months Ago

Another nightmare.

Sean splashed his face with water. His nightmares had increased since the war ended. Almost always, it was the same haunting scene.

In the Sollam desert, he met the ebony stare of the "enemy." *He's so young*, Sean thought. Yet the fire of hatred was in the teenager's eyes. The boy's gun was aimed at him. But Sean fired his gun first. The flame in the eyes was extinguished. The lifeless shell of a body fell.

Sean would wake, dripping in sweat and uncontrollably shaking.

The dreams were disturbing, and he tried his best to forget. Forget, forget. *But the dreams kept him a prisoner to the memory.*

However, sometimes he would have a different reoccurring dream.

He was back in Cascadia at Ranfurly Manor. A woman, with long, flowing, hair of a brownish red would always show up somewhere on the grounds. Their gazes would meet, and he had a sense he knew her.

That dream was disturbing in a different way. Something about the appearance of the mysterious woman made Sean aware of how alone he felt. Flings with women, one-night stands, they seemed pointless lately. He longed for something deeper.

Now he was stuck back at Ranfurly Manor. He made a point to avoid his father, for the most part. Three months had passed since he and Jasmine arrived, and they still hadn't met the owner. Apparently, the other staff members had strict orders to keep tightlipped about his name. As the newcomers, Jasmine and Sean were not to be told.

Then, one day Jasmine waltzed into Sean's apartment in the staff quarters. "I'm a genius."

Sean raised a brow. "Getting in your daily dose of self-praise, Jasmine?"

"I found out his name," she sang happily.

"You did?" Sean perked up. "Well, what is it?"

"Lord Robert Ranfurly." Jasmine swooned.

"And is he Viscount of Knoxfordshire? The one Wellington suspects inherited this place?" Sean asked.

She shrugged. "More than likely."

Soon after that, Jasmine and Sean were invited to a staff meeting where the Viscount introduced himself, officially. Still, to catch a glimpse of him continued to be a rare occasion and to find out anything about him was next to impossible.

It was around that time when Jasmine began to show an interest in Sean. She became more flirtatious. This made his otherwise boring job at Ranfurly Manor much more bearable.

The flirting led to a more involved relationship. They kept their relationship a secret from everyone on staff by limiting their intimate moments to when they met in Sean's hidden bunker.

With Jasmine next to him, Sean slept through the night better than he'd slept since the war. The nightmares went away. Even the dreams about the mysterious woman went away.

Jasmine was different from all the other women Sean had been with. Others left him wanting nothing more than a one-night stand. With Jasmine, *he couldn't get enough. She was everything he could ask for, and nothing he deserved. Exotic, sexy, smart, funny.*

All of that was amazing, but what set her apart was how she seemed to know what he needed before he could speak it out loud. It was as if their souls were interconnected. He'd never experienced that before. He came to trust Jasmine more than he'd ever trusted anyone.

But one morning, everything changed. A morning Sean wouldn't forget, when the playful spark in Jasmine's eyes seemed to go out.

"What's wrong?" He traced a finger over the curve of her neck, concerned.

"Nothing." She pretended to laugh.

He wasn't fooled. "Jasmine ... I know you well enough by now to see that something is eating away at you."

She sighed. "I just ... I'm so sick of this, Sean. This assignment. It's a joke."

"What do you mean?" Sean brushed a wisp of her hair out of her eyes.

"You remember Director Alejandro, who hired you?" Jasmine whispered, even though they were in Sean's hidden bunker where they couldn't be overheard.

"Yes, of course, I remember him. They say he went rogue. He's on the blacklist now."

"Well, that's just it, Sean. I never felt right about it when they said he was blacklisted, it just seemed ... off."

"Off?"

"I knew Alejandro well. He was always a good man. Which is more than I can say about Wellington."

Sean narrowed his brow. "Yeah. I've never been crazy about Wellington. And the way that cringy vampire looks at you makes me want to knock every bleached tooth out of his plastic grin."

"You don't know the half of it," she said.

Sean wondered what she meant by that. He began to ask, but she cut him off.

"I haven't told Wellington that Lord Robert has kids, Sean. I don't know why, but I just had a hunch that I shouldn't. And lately, I've done some digging, and I've come across something that confirms the hunch I had about

him was right." Jasmine rose out of bed to pull a folder out of her purse. She tossed the file in front of Sean. *"Take a look at this."*

Sean sat up in bed and opened the folder. He flipped through some of the photos, his expression changing to a look of disgust. *"Sick."*

"I know. This is what has been on my mind ... why I'm having trouble working here. How can we trust PAX, after seeing this? Wellington is a demented pervert. Doing those things to kids! And these other men in the photos are in high-ranking positions with PAX, as well."

"It isn't like I don't care, but what is the point in showing me all this? What can we do about it?"

Jasmine stood, red-faced. *"Sean, we've been at Ranfurly Manor for over four months now. Have you ever wondered why we're still here?"*

"To report on Ranfurly."

"Report what? He's hardly ever home! And I personally don't get wife-killer vibes from him. And as for telling Wellington about those two sweet little five-year-olds, no way will I tell him after I saw those pictures."

"You're not falling for the dashing viscount bit are you? Pining away for him and wishing you could be his viscountess?"

Jasmine laughed. *"Sean, I don't pine away. Ever. Not my style. I just don't know ... my gut tells me something is off about this whole job."*

"Are you insinuating that Wellington put us here because he thinks we're too incompetent to do something more important?"

Jasmine was lost in her thoughts, not really listening to Sean's question. *"I don't know."*

"So, you think I'm incompetent."

"What?"

Sean glowered. *"Good to know how you really feel."*

Jasmine glared at him. *"Your ego is so huge, you can't see anything past it."*

"Oh, okay. I see we're getting out our true feelings now. Well, I can assure you, the feelings are mutual. In fact, I don't think I've ever met a woman as stuck on herself as you are."

Jasmine gasped. *"You're such a jerk!"*

"If that's how you really feel, why are you still here?"

A hurt expression crossed her face, but Sean never saw it. Jasmine was a master of masking her true feelings.

Fuming, she slipped on her maid uniform, snatched the folder off the bed, and put it back into her purse. She swung her purse over her shoulder and stormed out of the bunker, letting the door slam behind her on the way out.

That was their first fight.

PRESENT

The staff, chattery about Thor's miraculous resurrection, cleared the Parlor. As he watched Courtney lean back against Ranfurly, Sean quietly backed out of the room. *Aren't they just thick as thieves, now? Coorie-ing like a pair of doves.*

He decided to go back to his apartment before rejoining the search party. On his way, Jasmine came running up behind him and linked arms. "Seanster, can you walk with me? The sky's cleared and the stars are out."

"Not really in the mood for stargazing, Jazz," Sean answered in a gruff voice.

"Do you remember the last time we went stargazing? We found a place where we could be completely *alone*."

"No."

"Seriously?" She became annoyed. "You don't remember? You were in love with me back then."

"That's ancient history."

"That was two months ago. You were so in love with me, you even proposed. Don't expect me to believe you've already forgotten *that*."

This set Sean off. He snapped. "Why are you bringing *that* up? And why are you actin' so soppy about it? You declined my offer. I realized it was a stupid idea. We moved on. End. Of. Story."

"Oh, okay. Well, I hate to break it to you, but going on the rebound isn't really moving on, Sean. And boy did you pick the wrong one for a rebound." She put a hand on a curvaceous hip.

"Rebound? What are you yippin' on about?"

"The nanny. Yeah, it's obvious you have a *thing* for her. ... Although, I don't know why. She's so ... simple. But you men do seem to like that type. And how she managed to get her claws into a viscount is beyond me."

"Oh, please. I'm not interested in her."

"Mmm. Okay. Sure, you're not."

A silent moment passed. Sean was about to leave, but Jasmine grabbed his arm as he turned to go. "You know, she didn't even see what you did in there for her dog. But I saw. You saved that dog, Sean."

"No. I didn't save him, Jasmine. In fact, I swear he wasn't breathing for at least a good five minutes."

"Sean, I was in the room watching. He probably would have died had you not been there. But Courtney was too wrapped up in Lord Ranfurly's arms to even notice you. ... She doesn't deserve you."

"I was only thinking of Thor, Jazz. I could care less what Courtney was doin'."

Jasmine watched Sean for a moment, concern on her face. She gently touched his jaw. "You're sure you don't feel like stargazing with me?"

"That little girl is still missing. I need to go back out and help look for her."

Like a switch, Jasmine changed from sweet and gentle to demanding and forceful. She dragged Sean down an abandoned path that was lit by lantern lights.

"What in the devil's name is wrong with you, Jazz? You're rippin' my arm out of its socket!"

Through gritted teeth she said, "You are so clueless. How is that you got picked to be an agent? You didn't even catch one of the signs I gave you. I wanted to get you alone because I have some news. ... I found another secret passage."

He perked up. "Where? Inside the manor?"

"You'll never guess," she said. "But try to, anyway."

He scrunched his face and stood with a hand on his hip. She snickered.

"What?" he asked her.

"That's your thinking man pose," she teased. "You always do that when you're making your brain cells work too hard."

Sean frowned. "Do I really? Well, you should see the face *you* make when you're thinking."

"What? I don't make a face." Jasmine's plump bottom lip stuck out in a pout.

"Oh yes you do. You purse your lips like…" Sean puckered like a fish.

"Oh stop! I do not look anything like that! Please!" Jasmine smacked him on the shoulder.

"I know you better than you know yourself, Jazz."

"And I know you better than you know *yourself*." Jasmine pressed his chest with a finger and stroked downward.

Sean took a step backward.

Jasmine sighed. "Babe, when I said no to marrying you, I didn't mean I wanted to end things between us. But *marriage* … that's just … well, it isn't in the cards for someone like me."

"What's that supposed to mean?"

"Oh, come on. I'm a double agent. I'm the last person on earth who would make a good wife. Or God forbid, a mother."

"Oh. Okay. Maybe you're right – people like us shouldn't get attached. Which is why we need to move on. So can we quit talking about this?"

"If that's what you really want. … But no matter how *you* feel, my feelings for you haven't changed. And I'll always have your back, Sean. We've been through too much together." Jasmine traced his back with her fingers then made little circles up his neck, giving him the shivers. He fought an urge to touch her the way he used to.

"Thanks," he replied stiffly.

"Another reason I lured you out here is to tell you I have news from DART."

"What?"

"We have another assignment. Alejandro will be waiting for us at the usual spot, a mile away from the manor's security gate –four in the morning." She stopped talking when she heard the sound of the search party approaching. "I'll see you then," she said, walking in the opposite direction of the voices.

Sean headed down a different path. On his way back to his apartment, it dawned on him that Jasmine never finished telling him where the entrance to the secret passage was.

Courtney's Discovery

❧ Courtney ❧

Ten Hours After Disappearance

Robert met me at the bottom of the stairway, holding a jacket. "I brought you a jacket. It's chilly out there. ... You're sure you want to come with me?"

"Of course I'm sure."

"Alright, then. Winnie will be joining us. She's taking one of the horses and we will be driving the forest trekker. I've brought along a few shotguns in case we have a run in with any more wolves."

We set out to where they'd encountered the pack. The trekker's bright beams lit the forest around us, so we could see the carcasses of wolves scattered along the trail.

Did those wolves find Elizabeth? No doubt they would have torn her little frame to pieces.

We scanned the area. "It seems like the yarn trail ends here," Winnie said.

"Yes, I see that." Robert said, shining his light at a dead wolf.

"Are you thinking what I'm thinking?" Winnie asked him.

I somehow picked up on what they were thinking, and it made me ill. "Oh, dear God. You aren't seriously both going to do *that*, are you?" I asked them, disgusted.

It was a morbid idea, but it *would* be the best way to get confirmation if Elizabeth had been devoured by the wolves. I don't know how Robert managed keeping it together, considering this was his own child they were looking for. One by one, they cut open each of the carcasses to look in their abdomens for evidence that Elizabeth had been eaten.

While they did that, I continued my search. *Perhaps Elizabeth is hiding somewhere.*

Flashing my light around, I saw something shiny on the ground. I reached to pick it up and inspect it.

"This was one of the beads in Lady Rose's mane," I said out loud.

A thick silence answered me. I was alone. I'd gone further than intended. But I was on to something, so I continued to search for hoofprints. And then ... *there they are!*

I followed the tracks, too focused to think about how far away I was from the others. *These tracks could lead us to Elizabeth!*

Something lying in the middle of the dense forest caught my eye.

A backpack? Maybe the intruder dropped it.

It was heavy, like something was in it, but when I felt inside, it was empty. *Strange. But it* could *have fingerprints.* I held on to it and found my way back to the others.

Robert ran to me when he saw my light approaching. "Courtney! I've been worried sick. You can't just go off into the forest alone like that! You didn't even bring a shotgun. What were you thinking?"

"I'm sorry, but I saw these little beads that Lady Rose had in her mane, and then I found her hoofprints. So, I followed the tracks. That's when I came across this." I showed him the backpack.

"Is there anything inside it?" Winnie asked.

"I didn't feel anything, although it's kind of heavy, like it's weighted or something. Do you think the intruder dropped it?" I asked.

"Possibly. We'll certainly check it for fingerprints."

"How was the ... dissection?"

"Fortunately, we didn't find human remains," Robert said.

"Thank God."

"I just have this feeling she's still alive," Robert said.

"I know. Me too."

"Let's have a look at those tracks you were following," he said.

I led Robert and Winnie to the spot, and we shined our lights around the area. "The tracks end here," I said.

"… No, they continue out of the blue over here," Winnie said, a few feet away.

"It appears as he tried to cover up the tracks to throw us off," Robert said. "Let's keep following the hoofprints Winnie just found, see where they lead. I'll walk. Winnie, walk Epona alongside you so we can both keep the hoofprint trail in sight. Courtney, will you drive the forest trekker behind us? We could use the light it will give off."

"Yeah, good idea," I said.

The pony tracks eventually led back to the manor. They came out by the pool terrace.

"Perhaps she and Lady Rose have found their way home!" Robert said.

Our hearts quickened in anticipation. But when we arrived at the stables, our hopes were crushed. Lady Rose and Elizabeth weren't there.

"I thought for sure…" I said.

"Me too." An absent expression on his face, he seemed fixated on Lady's empty stall. We stood there, all of us, silent. Every time I tried to think of what to say, the words didn't come. Nothing could be said that would make it right.

Robert was the one who finally spoke first. "We all got too excited too soon and forgot to keep following the tracks. We need to go back to the pool terrace and see if they lead somewhere."

Back where we'd last seen the pony tracks, I found more hoofprints. "You're right," I said to Robert. "We stopped following them too soon. Here they are!" I pointed my flashlight at the trail.

We saw that the tracks continued on the terrace concrete and stopped in front of the entrance to a building. It looked like a cabana.

"I don't see any more tracks around here. It looks like the pony went into the cabana," Winnie said.

"This isn't a cabana, it's the pool pump house," Robert said. He opened the doors, and we flashed our lights inside. "Lady might have been inside here, but she isn't now. There's nowhere for an animal as large as her to hide in here."

He was right. It was a huge rectangular space, with nothing in it except pipes, filters, heaters, and pumps. A pony wouldn't have been able to fit behind the equipment, and the rest of the floor was visible from where we stood.

"What a waste of space," Winnie said. "You should enclose the equipment in a closet, and make the rest of it a pool cabana."

"Good idea," I agreed.

We closed up the pump house and searched some more. But it seemed, this time, we really had come to a dead end.

WELCOME TO THE NEW WORLD

❧ Sean ❧

FLASHBACK: SEVEN MONTHS AGO

Jasmine was still mad at Sean.

It had been three weeks since their first fight, that morning she showed him the file with incriminating photos of Wellington and the other PAX workers. She'd given him the cold shoulder ever since. And he was far too proud to let on she had him twisted up in knots.

One morning, when Sean was brushing Xavier, he saw Jasmine on her routine run around the property trails. It was the day before her monthly meeting with Wellington. He decided to be the first to extend a white flag. "Hello, Jasmine. How've you been?"

"Fine." She didn't look at him but kept jogging.

Sean dropped his brush, hoisted himself easily over the fence that kept the horses in, and caught up with her. "Any important info you'll be sharing with Wellington at your upcoming meeting?"

She grunted and sped up her pace.

Sean kept up with her. "I've been thinking about those photos you showed me of Wellington and the other PAX leaders."

"Mmhmm?"

"Maybe there is a way to expose them," he said.

"How?" Jasmine maintained her pace.

"Leak the pictures to the press."

"In the old system that might have worked, but not in the new one, Sean."

"What do you mean?"

"The Peace Alliance Ten owns the press. They shut down all the media outlets that spoke out against them, and executed the reporters on Cat 4 Island. Besides, with AI, they can tamper with the photos, so it looks like you're the one in those shots, instead of them." Jasmine broke into a full run.

Sean picked up the pace and caught up. "We could post the photos ourselves ... to social media. Use fake accounts. I'm no tech genius but I'm sure there's a way."

"Not sure how we would pull it off. They're always cracking down on fake social media accounts."

"There has to be something we can do, Jazz."

Jasmine stopped running. "You really want to do something to help?"

"Of course. Why? Do you have something in mind?"

Jasmine let out a long breath. She checked to make certain they were alone. Far from the barn and stables, there were only trees and birds in view. She closed the distance between them and brought her voice to a whisper. "Look, I've been wanting to talk to you about something, but I also had to gather more facts first."

She hesitated.

"I'm listening," Sean said.

When she spoke again, her words were slow and deliberate. "I decided to go looking for Director Alejandro. To see if I could ask him what happened ... why he went rogue."

"And? Did you find him?" Sean probed.

Twigs breaking nearby caused them both to stop and look around. When they saw it was just a deer, they both exhaled in relief. She led Sean back from the path into the bushes.

"Can I really trust you, Sean?"

"After everything we've been to each other, you still don't?" he asked.

She studied him intently. "I want to. I really want to."

62

Sean touched her arm. *"Jazz, if there's anyone who knows me, it's you. I let you in."*

"I know. ... Okay. But you can NOT. TELL. A. SOUL. Understood?"

"Scout's honor."

"Alejandro was in hiding. Along with many other blacklisted agents."

"How many agents are we talking about?" Sean asked.

"More than you can imagine."

"Really?"

"Every one of them worked for Zone B Intelligence before The Peace Alliance Ten took over. The ex-agents formed their own alliance. They call it DART."

"Hmm."

Jasmine squinted at him. *"What are you thinking right now?"*

"Just listening. This is my listening face. Go on."

"You look skeptical," she crossed her arms.

"No ... I'm not. I'm just trying to get the full picture."

"Alejandro showed me more of what PAX is doing. And the full picture is bad, Sean. Worse than I thought. After what I've seen, what I know ... I can't do this. I don't want to be one of their dirty little hands anymore."

Sean wrapped his arms around her waist. *"Is learning about PAX what you've been doing with all your free nights now that you aren't coming to see me?"*

Jasmine softened. *"Of course. Ever since I saw those photos. I can't sleep at night anymore knowing those poor kids are out there. I want to use my training to help them. To help the lives that PAX is destroying."*

"How? How can you or I do anything to help?" Sean asked her.

"I know how I'll help." She tilted her head and gazed at him. *"But what you decide is up to you."*

"I've already told you I want to help. So, what are you planning to do?"

Jasmine raised an eyebrow. *"I've already done it. I'm working with DART."*

Sean's jaw dropped. He let go of Jasmine and backed away. *"You're what?"*

"The only way I can see us making any difference is by joining DART, Sean."

Her announcement was like a splash of ice water in the face. Jasmine is with The Resistance? "The Resistance is our enemy. Stopping them was the mission we signed up for. And you're telling me you joined them?"

"Yes."

"Jasmine," Sean said it with a condescending smile. "You showed me a few sick and twisted men who work for PAX Intelligence. But that doesn't prove everyone in the agency is corrupt. I mean, what about The Ten? They stopped the war and brought peace!"

"They have peace by silencing people who don't share their views, Sean. Surely you can see that."

Sean didn't have a response.

Jasmine went on. "There are so many more layers to PAX." She spit out the name as if it was poison in her mouth. "They've been feeding us lies. They're not the good guys."

"They brought world peace when nobody else could, Jasmine. Stopping the war, eliminating people like our last president, who was a war monger. Before they stepped in, this world was a powder keg about to blow."

Jasmine jeered. "They're blowing rainbows out of their asses, Sean! They buried live footage of how the war really ended. You would hardly believe it if you saw. It was an act of God that stopped that war – not PAX. They just stole the credit for it."

"Buried live footage? Where are you hearing this stuff?" Sean asked.

"I've seen it. Do you realize that PAX is making a mountain of gold pins in profit on trafficking drugs and humans?"

Sean shook his head in disbelief. "Extremists will feed you with all sorts of stories to turn you, Jazz. No way is any of that true."

"These aren't stories I've been fed. I'm telling you … I've seen it. Drug dealers and traffickers get a little slap on the wrist by the new justices that were appointed by PAX. The slap on the wrist is all for show. Then those same traffickers are released in private. PAX workers slip them pins under the table to keep up the dirty work."

Sean's expression was dubious. "Alejandro is telling you all of this?"

"I've seen it," she said.

"So, you're telling me the ten leaders that are running the world are evil."

"Yes. And the fact that they hide themselves behind a curtain incriminates them all the more, in my opinion. It's like they want to give off the impression that they're wizards or gods – invisible and all-powerful."

"There are always two sides to every story, Jasmine. And the side you're hearing is a very bitter side. When people get laid off, they say all sorts of things about the boss who fired them."

"Were you even listening to what I've been saying? I'm not just hearing it from Alejandro. I've seen it firsthand! I've been to Emer Aude, seen traffickers commit crimes, seen justices let them go free, then, when they think nobody is watching, give them suitcases of gold pins to keep up the good work, courtesy of PAX. While you've been in this superficial bubble, the outside world has been getting darker by the day!"

Is she in her right mind? *Sean wondered.*

Jasmine's face clouded over. "Fine. If you don't believe me, come see for yourself. As soon as I get back from my meeting with Wellington, I'll be meeting with Alejandro. Come with me. Hear him out."

It was a risk. Meeting with the man who had once been Directorate of Operations for Zone B Intelligence, who was now blacklisted as a rogue agent.

On the other hand, Sean didn't want to lose Jasmine. She was the one woman in the world he could trust. Now she was inciting a curiosity in him, one that couldn't be squelched. He had to see for himself what compelled her to risk her life and join The Resistance.

"Okay, I'll go to your meeting with Alejandro, Jazz."

When he first saw Alejandro, Sean was surprised how much the man had changed in just a few months. He'd lost so much weight, his face was sunken in, and his salt and pepper beard had turned completely silver.

Alejandro played a reel of footage for Sean. The scenes depicted exactly what Jasmine had told him.

"How do I know this footage is real?" Sean asked them. "It could be tampered with."

"Perhaps you just need to spend a night in Emer Aude to see for yourself," Alejandro said.

"Crime and poverty have always been in our cities," Sean argued. "The Peace Alliance Ten has actually improved the economy by making sure everyone gets equal shares of pins."

"You believe they've been helping the economy, Sean?" Alejandro had a soft tone and always seemed to be calm, in contrast to the fiery Jasmine. It was easy to see why Jasmine liked him so much. Still, Sean wasn't sure whether he could trust him any more than he could trust Wellington.

"I can bet you're about to show me different," Sean replied.

The ex-Directorate of Intelligence pushed play on his computer screen, and they all watched as several scenes of horror unfolded. Drones patrolling cities, shooting innocent civilians. Rapists getting away with their crimes while police drones observed and passed over them. PAX workers grabbing food out of the hands of starving civilians on the streets of Emer Aude.

"Welcome to the new world under PAX's reign," Alexandro said.

"Again, I ask you, how do I know this footage hasn't been tampered with by AI?" Sean demanded.

"This footage was taken by my own agents," Alejandro answered.

Jasmine jumped in. "And those last few scenes, I was right there with the camera operator who filmed them!"

"What? When? You were somewhere nearby when that woman was being raped by the PAX agent?"

"Nearby? Of course not. I wasn't about to stand by and let that happen. I sent that rapist to face his Maker."

Alejandro played the reel of Jasmine defending the woman against the rapist.

"Unbelievable." Sean began pacing. He stopped to reprimand Jasmine.

"Those drones could have caught you!"

"You underestimate me." She blew on her nails.

"Sean, is our new government accomplishing everything they've promised us?" Alejandro asked him.

"I don't know. How can I know? As you've already pointed out, I don't get out much. It wasn't until Jasmine showed me those disgusting photos of Wellington that I started to question things."

As Sean turned things over in his mind, it didn't seem real. It was too extreme to be real. His head hurt from too much thinking.

"Tell him what you told me last week," Jasmine said to Alejandro.

Alejandro frowned. *"You know what they say ... always follow the money. Well, we followed the pins, Sean. Do you know what we found? PAX is taking ninety percent of the money made from trafficking. And there is nobody to hold them accountable. No congress, no senate. No House of Lords or Commons. The Ten have complete power."*

"You say they are distributing wealth, yet you saw the starving people on the streets. While PAX workers are living well." Jasmine pointed to a beautiful neighborhood on the computer screen. *"And do you know who lives there?"*

Sean shook his head.

"PAX's high ranking leaders. PAX just built brand new exclusive communities in the Isles of Joy and The Resorts. For PAX elites only. They're all rolling in the pins! The highest ranks get a harem of whatever they have an appetite for. Women, men, children. And you're telling me PAX is making the world better? That they are distributing wealth equally? Please!" Jasmine slammed her foot into a nearby wall.

Alejandro continued in his calming voice. *"Since the PAX takeover, the billionaires in the world are only gaining more wealth. Those who pass the test to become PAX workers get a comfortable life while the rest are forced to go without."*

After absorbing quite a bit more footage, Sean finally said, *"I can't believe things are this bad."*

Alejandro shrugged. *"You've been preoccupied."*

Jasmine gave him a pleading look. *"We could certainly use someone like you in The Resistance."*

It was difficult to refuse Jasmine anything. But this? *"This is a lot to take in. I need some time ... but don't worry. Your secret is safe with me. I won't rat you out."*

A few nights later, Sean decided to go with Jasmine to Emer Aude to see things for himself. When he experienced firsthand that everything Alejandro and Jasmine told him was true, he made his decision.

He would join DART.

TIGERS LIKE TO PLAY

❧ Sean ❧

Fourteen Hours After Disappearance

At five o'clock in the morning, Sean and Jasmine were boarding a private jet provided to them by DART. It was a fine interior, with six comfortable leather seats and a wet bar. The two of them had the plane to themselves, with the exception of their pilot, Jared. They sat in seats that faced each other.

"Did DART give us fake identities for this trip?" Sean asked Jasmine.

"Yes, of course," Jasmine said, painting her fingernails. "They're inside my purse. Can you find them? My nails need to dry."

"I was taught it was a no-no to look in a lady's purse." Sean raised an eyebrow.

"Unless the lady orders you to do so. In which case, ask no questions." Jasmine gave him a warning glare.

Sean slowly picked up her purse, as if it was a rabid animal that might bite him. He peered inside. "What am I supposed to be looking for in here, exactly? I see all sorts of strange things."

"A secret pouch." Jasmine blew on her fingernails.

"Apparently very secret. I'm not finding anything that looks like a pouch."

Jasmine huffed, impatiently. "Give me my purse. I'll do it myself." She reached to grab it.

"Shite, woman. Calm down. Can't have you messing up your finely painted nails. I'll find it!" Before she could snatch her purse away from him, Sean turned it upside down and rattled it. All the contents fell out on the floor.

"What is wrong with you, Sean? Really?!"

"Testy, aren't we?" Sean said, handing her the emptied purse.

She sighed loudly as she opened the secret pouch. She brought out two passports, smudging her fresh nail polish in the process. "You'll be needing this." She handed him a tiny chip. "We can't use our PAX-issued chips because that would alert PAX Intelligence we are in Felizia, so Alejandro managed to get these false ID chips that will clear us if scanned by any PAX drones."

"Huh. But PAX knows what we look like. Cameras will be everywhere. How are we going to avoid being spotted?" Sean asked.

"DART has that covered, too," Jasmine said. "We'll be wearing these incredibly real looking masks. And guess what? We get to be blonds."

"Oh goody."

Sean opened their passports. "Mr. Jack Kilmore and Ms. Justina Tigar. For once, DART didn't make us a married couple."

Jasmine looked at her passport. "DART saves pins when we share a room as a married couple. They don't need to book us a hotel room this trip, though. We won't be staying the night. Now, start picking up everything you just dropped out of my purse and put it back. ... You owe me big time for messing up my nails." Annoyed, she wiped off the smudged nail polish and reapplied a fresh coat while Sean put the items back in her purse.

Sean asked, "By the way, did you ever follow up about that serpent earring? The one that Courtney found in the Royal Rodney when she came to the interview?"

"Now, now, Seanster Monster. You know you have to pay me if you want information."

"Oh, #@*! Jasmine! Does everything always have to be a little game for you?"

She got out of her seat and whispered in his ear, "Tigers like to play." Then she sat back down and kicked off her heels. She put her bare feet on Sean's lap, and spoke as if she were the queen and he her slave. "You know my rules. You can start by massaging my feet."

Sean stayed focused on the airplane wing as he kneaded her heels and squeezed her toes. *I wonder what Courtney is doing right now.*

After hearing a lot of Jasmine's mews of satisfaction, Sean asked her, "Will this suffice, your majesty?"

"I suppose. What was the question?"

"Did you find any information on the earring?" Sean asked.

"Yesss…" a clever smile crossed her lips.

"And?"

"Mmm, my shoulders are so tight."

Sean grumbled. He lifted his hands up and held them in the air, waiting for her to get up out of her seat and turn around so her back was to him.

She smiled and situated herself between his legs on the floor of the plane. "Mmm. Mmm. Yes. Yes! Right there. … No, a little lower … ahh."

"Have I earned a response yet?" Sean asked her, focusing on the questions he needed her to answer.

"Mmhmm. Okay. Getting information on the earring was not my favorite gig. The guy I got it from … let's just say he was *creepy*."

"I hope you didn't break any Holy Commandments to get answers from him."

"I'd put a man out of commission before breaking that commandment. But the way I see it is that one of the powers God gave me is the ability to draw secrets out of men. I play a little, they talk a lot. And since when do you get off on acting holier than thou? Mr. I-romp-around-with-every-pretty-thing-on-two-legs."

"I'm deeply offended. … Now, you were about to tell me about the information you got out of Creepy Guy."

"Right. Creepy Guy works for someone named J.J."

"J.J.? Who's that?" Sean asked.

"I might know more, but it'll cost you." She pointed to her shoulders. "Squeeze."

Sean gripped her shoulders and gave them a firm squeeze. She mewed. A whiff of coconut and aloe made its way to his nose. Memories of their intimate past played out vividly in his mind.

What was my question? He tried to clear his head. "J.J.?" he asked her. Jasmine purred, as Sean continued to massage her neck and shoulders.

"J.J. is a jewelry designer. Creator of the earrings. Apparently, only certain girls are chosen to wear them for high-end clients."

"But why do the girls who wear them sometimes end up dead?" Sean asked.

"I asked that same question. He didn't know." Jasmine shrugged.

"Well. Nice work. You are never to be underestimated."

"Very true. Any other questions?"

"Yes, you told me you found a secret passage. But you never said where it was."

She twisted around so she was facing him. "I asked if you had any more questions."

Sean lowered his eyelids. "Where is the entrance to the secret passageway you found inside the manor?"

"That answer will cost you much more than the last questions did."

His resolve to resist her was waning. "What will it cost me, Jasmine?" Sean whispered.

A call from Alejandro rang in on his cell phone. *Saved by the smart phone.* "The island you are headed to is the island of San Ulios," Alejandro explained. "The language spoken there is Felizian. You'll be visiting a PAX controlled mine, and your mission is to fill containers with ore."

"Ore?" Sean asked. "Why ore?"

"We think there has to be something incredibly valuable in the ore because PAX increased the amount of miners tenfold in the past few weeks. DART has scientists in The Goldens on standby to run tests on it."

"Okay. So how do we get in?"

LUNCH BREAK

❧ *Sean* ❧

Sixteen Hours After Disappearance

By the time they arrived on San Ulios Island, it was nine o'clock in the morning and Sean and Jasmine had transformed themselves. Wearing their masks and blond wigs, they were unrecognizable when they sat down in the cafe and waited for their contact to arrive. Jasmine's foot was tapping in impatience when he didn't show up on time.

"Where is he?" she asked Sean through gritted teeth.

Fifteen minutes later, he finally drove up in front of the cafe in a food truck.

"*Hola.* I'm Jorge." The driver, who pronounced his name Horhay, was a large and wide man, with a bald head and a fat nose that covered most of his face. He had droopy eyes, a triple chin, and a thick waxed mustache, pointy at the tips. "Sorry I was a little late. Traffic jam."

"*Hola,* I'm Jasmine." She extended a hand.

"*Qué amable de tu parte unirte a la fiesta.*" [Nice of you to join the party.] Sean said in a not-so-good Felizian accent.

"That's my partner, Sean. *El cómico.*" Jasmine pointed at him with a thumb.

"Okay, no time for fooling around," Jorge replied. "Hop in."

They climbed into the truck and Jorge drove off. He pointed to two lanyards lying on the dashboard. "Those are your official IDs to get into the mine."

Jasmine and Sean put them on. "These lanyards are going to get us into a mine with PAX security?" Jasmine asked, doubtful.

"No, the food in this truck is going to get you in. Felipe's Fresh Felizian is the regular food service for the mine. It just so happens that I'm pretty popular in these parts. Known to the locals as Felipe. It's my middle name. I usually have other workers helping me, so if anyone asks, Jasmine's my cousin from Zone B, and *El Cómico*, you're her *gringo* husband."

"Well, surprise, surprise. We're back to being a married couple," Sean said.

Jasmine ignored him. "Alejandro told us you were with DART. Is the food truck one of your covers?"

"No, no! I owned my business way before I joined DART. I've only been helping the resistance for the last six months. I believe in the cause, you know? But working the food truck is what pays the bills. DART sure doesn't pay anything. What do you two do to make a living?"

"We get by on our good looks," Sean said.

Jorge guffawed. "Well, we aren't all so lucky. But I got brains to make up for it. And my world class tri-tip sandwiches get me through a lot of doors."

They drove forty minutes out of the city until they were in a plain, nothing but desert sand for several miles. Eventually the pavement ended, and they turned onto a rugged, abandoned gravel road that was concealed by giant boulders on each side of it. Jorge stopped the truck and climbed into the back. Jasmine and Sean followed.

"Okay. Here's the plan," Jorge said. "See those ten food containers there?" He pointed to a stack in a food cart sitting next to the refrigerator. "There're lunches inside for the miners. Beneath them is an empty compartment. That's where you'll need to store the ore."

Jorge pointed to a map on the refrigerator. "You'll enter the mine *here*." He circled the mine entrance. "The miners will love you. Trust me,

I know, because today is the favorite. My slow-cooked tri-tip. They'll grab their boxed meals and head outside for a thirty-minute break in this area *here*." He circled the eating area with a red pen. "Once the place clears out, look for the ore. It will be on the right side of the mine." He circled the area where they would find the ore. "Security workers usually eat lunch too, but they could pop in at any time, so you'll need to load the ore fast."

"Any cameras to worry about?" Sean asked.

"As far as I know, not yet. The mine is newly acquired by PAX, and they haven't put in the good equipment."

"That's good for us," Sean said.

"But they might frisk you. If you've got any weapons, leave them in the glove box."

Sean scrutinized Jorge. *Let's hope we can trust him.* He opened the glove compartment and placed his Glock inside, then held out a hand and waited for Jasmine to relinquish her gun. She hesitated.

"*Rapido!*" Jorge said. "Lunch break is starting soon."

Jasmine grimaced as she handed her gun over.

"Okay," Jorge clapped. "Let's roll, *amigos!*"

The rest of the ride was jerky, with a lot of potholes and large rocks along the dirt road. They passed some huge boulders before they at last came to a security gate. Two guards were on duty.

"*Hola.* What's for lunch today?" one of them asked in Felizian.

"The favorite. Tri-tip sandwiches. And tacos and burritos as always." Jorge replied.

"Oh yeah! I can't wait til my break, I'm starving," said one of the guards as he waved them through.

Jorge parked the truck near the entrance of the mine. Sean and Jasmine rolled the food cart past the workers, and Jasmine, as always, stood out. But instead of her sultry, dark hair, she had on a blonde wig and the convincing mask. Sean resembled a surfer in his wig style: long on top and short on the sides. They were dressed in beachy attire: cut-off shorts and tanks.

75

Jasmine's low-cut top showed off all her assets. Mine workers whistled as she walked by. She swung her hips, egging them on. "Tri-tip is waiting for you, boys," she sang out.

"Haven't seen you here before? Where've you been all my life, beautiful?" One of the men asked in Felizian.

"I'm Jorge's cousin, here for a visit. I live in Zone B." Jasmine was raised by parents who came from Felizia, and was fluent in the language. "And I'm married to *that* guy." She aimed a thumb at Sean.

"Oh. Lucky *gringo*. You better treat the lady right, or I might steal her from you," he smiled widely at Sean, showing a few missing teeth. He carried his sandwich, chips, and soda and made his way outside. The mine was quickly emptied out. Even the guards stayed outside for the break.

"Looks like we're in luck," Sean said.

"Except it looks like Jorge lied to us. Either that or he didn't know about the camera," Jasmine said, careful to be discreet in pointing it out.

"Jorge." Sean said through gritted teeth. "I hope he doesn't screw us over."

"Well, in case we're being watched, I'll provide a little entertainment. You fill the containers. Just be fast, Sean. *Rapido!*"

Jasmine grabbed a water bottle and casually walked over, close to the camera, so she was front and center in the lens, blocking the view of Sean behind her. She fanned herself, and slowly poured the water down the front of her top.

At first, Sean was distracted by her little performance, until she gave him a warning glare that reminded him of the mission they were on. He worked quickly to fill the compartments with ore as she worked the camera.

He was finishing up the ninth compartment when she asked him, "How's it going over there? Those miners are going to be coming off their break soon."

"Just one left. Trying not to be distracted by you, Jazz. You've been putting on quite a show."

"*Si. Todo un espectàculo, en verdad.*" [Yes. Quite a show, indeed.] The words were spoken by a female security guard who had just entered the mine.

Jasmine and Sean froze.

The guard eyeballed Sean, who held a few pieces of ore and was about to place them in the tenth container. "*¿Qué estás haciendo con ese mineral?*" [What are you doing with that ore?]

Sean noticed the guard had no weapon. "*Hola, bonita sodada.*" [Hello, beautiful soda.] Sean flashed his most charming smile. He meant to say, "beautiful soldier," but got the word wrong.

"Nice try, surfer boy," the guard replied in Sean's language. She lifted a radio out of a holster and was about to call more guards in.

Sean kicked the radio out of her hand before she had the chance, while Jasmine came around behind her and put her in a carotid choke. The guard passed out.

Jasmine searched her. "No weapons," she said. "But she'll wake up soon, and we don't know who else might be watching us on that camera."

"Help me fill this last one and let's get out of here," Sean said. They finished filling it and replaced the food shelves on top, then hustled out of the mine. The workers were still enjoying their lunches as Sean and Jasmine pushed the cart past them on their way to the food truck.

As they were loading the cart into the truck, a limousine parked next to them. Two men in white suits got out.

"Got any more of that tri-tip?" one of the men asked Jorge.

Sean was wondering who the limo belonged to, when two beautiful teenage girls popped their heads through the sunroof. "We're starving!"

"Sit back down!" One of the men in white suits barked at the girls. "We're getting you something."

"But I have to go to the restroom!" one of the girls said.

"Me too!" the other squealed.

Jasmine elbowed Sean. "Do you see what I see?"

Sean did see. The serpent earrings with rubies. Both girls were wearing them.

"Hey Jorge, I need to go to the restroom. Where is it?" Jasmine asked Jorge, who was handing the men in white suits their lunches.

Jorge said, "Sorry cousin. We have another job to get to. You'll have to hold it."

Sean whispered to Jasmine, "What? Are you *loco*? That female guard is going to wake up any second, and we don't want to be here when she does."

After Jorge gave the men their meals, he closed up the food service window and rushed to the driver's seat of the truck. "Take a seat, we gotta roll out of here," Jorge told Sean and Jasmine.

Two of the girls in the limo stepped out and ran to the portable restrooms. Jasmine stepped out of the truck's back double doors and hollered after them, "You girls look gorgeous! Where are you headed?"

"Jasmine! Get back inside!" Sean growled.

"We were chosen out of hundreds of teenagers from Felizia to perform for a big event," one of the girls shouted back, excited.

"Many important people will be there. It's going to be streamed live!" the other one said.

"Where is this event going to happen?" Jasmine asked.

"On an island in The Tropics!" they said.

Security guards came running out of the mine, headed in their direction. Leading the charge was the female guard they'd left unconscious.

Jorge revved the truck's engine.

"Do you know the name of the event? And when it will be streamed?" Jasmine asked. The girls shrugged.

"Jasmine, get in the truck! Now!" Sean roared.

Jasmine jumped in, and slammed the back doors closed. Jorge sped away, pedal to the floor. The blast of guns could be heard as guards fired after them.

The truck managed to reach the security gate without being hit. But the two guards at the gate were waiting for them. Now they had guns firing at their windshield.

"Get down!" Jorge warned.

Jasmine ducked just in time. A bullet came through the front window of the truck and whizzed over her head.

Sean got their guns out of the glove compartment and handed Jasmine hers. Rolling down his window, he sent a bullet through the forehead of one of the entrance gate guards. Jorge plowed over the other with the truck. Ramming through the gate, they made it out of the restricted area and careened down the abandoned road that led away from the mine.

Jasmine headed to the back doors of the truck and kept watch out the windows. A few minutes passed when she yelled, "Two motorcycles are gaining on us!"

"Open the refrigerator, and pull out the meat tray!" Jorge said.

Jasmine pulled out the tray, and a concealed door opened up behind the refrigerator, revealing a bathroom sized closet filled with an arsenal of weapons.

"Sean!" she yelled. "Check this out!"

Sean made his way to her and stocked up on weapons and a couple of grenades. As he stepped out of the arsenal, a bullet whizzed through the truck's back window and grazed his ear. Blood misted out, some of it splattering across Jasmine's face.

Dodging more bullets, Sean pitched a grenade out of the back of the truck at one of the motorcycles. The grenade exploded in front of it, sending the rider and motorcycle flying through the air in pieces.

Jasmine grabbed a loaded MP5, and shot at the other motorcyclist's tires. Pop. She hit her mark. The bike crashed, its rider was sent flying.

"Three more coming!" Sean yelled. "But only one more grenade. Keep shooting!"

One of the motorcycles gained speed and caught up to the truck. Sean threw the grenade, man and bike were lost in the explosion.

The other two motorcyclists caught up to the truck, one on the passenger side, one behind them.

Jasmine was shooting out of the back doors at the rider behind the truck. He sped up and jumped inside. Hand-to-hand, Jasmine fought for her life against the man, who was far larger and stronger.

Sean grabbed a sniper rifle out of the arsenal. He climbed into the passenger seat of the cab and aimed through the window. But the rider wasn't out there. "Where did he go?" Sean yelled.

Then he saw that in the truck's wake, a motorcycle was lying on the side of the road. *He must have jumped onto the truck.* Sean pulled himself up out of his window to check the roof. He caught sight of the rider as he was climbing down Jorge's side of the truck. Sean fired at him and missed.

Sean slid back into the vehicle, right when the rider came crashing through Jorge's window. The big driver was knocked unconscious. The food truck that had been moving at high speed swerved off the road.

The truck's front tire hit a large rock, and the vehicle flew up into the air. The rider who had kicked into Jorge still had his torso hanging out of the window. As the truck went flying, he toppled backwards and fell out, while Jasmine and the man she'd been fighting were thrown out of the back doors.

The truck landed on four wheels, but then it hit another large boulder which sent it rolling on its side.

As the truck rolled, Sean was slammed into Jorge. The man's large frame blocked both of them from flying out of his window. When the vehicle finally rolled to a stop, it was on its side, Jorge's window facing the ground.

Jolted around after rolling so many times, Sean took a minute to get his bearings. Once he had them, he realized Jorge was alive, but unconscious. The large man had padded him from the impact of the crash. He scrambled to the back of the truck in search of Jasmine. The back doors were open, and he could see her lying on the ground outside.

"Jasmine!" He ran out to check on her. The motorcyclist she'd been fighting was lying face down a few feet away. Neither of them were moving. Sean felt her for a pulse. "Baby, can you hear me?" Eyelids fluttered. "Baby?" After a few seconds, she gasped for air. He let out a breath. "Thank God. Jasmine?"

"Is the %#$! dead?" She turned her head to look at the motorcyclist. He hadn't moved.

"I don't know. Stay here."

"Oh. Okay. Like I could go anywhere in this state," she chuckled.

Sean checked the man for a pulse. "Dead," he said, pocketing his gun. "Don't ever scare me like that again, Jasmine. Understand?"

"Aww. Sweet. You still love me." She faintly smiled.

"Be right back. I'm goin' to check on Jorge."

"Okay. You do that," Jasmine said, then groaned. "You know, babe. Maybe we *should* get married. We make a great team."

Sean froze. *Was she serious?* A second later, he laughed. *Don't be a fool. She just got knocked in the head.* He climbed through the back of the food truck and saw that Jorge had come to.

"I can't feel my legs!" Jorge groaned.

"We've gotta get you outta here."

"You're going to need a crane," Jorge joked.

Sean tried to think. *Maybe Jasmine is feeling well enough now to stand, and she can help me get Jorge out of the truck.* Even so, it wouldn't be easy. He probably weighed four hundred pounds.

"Are they all dead? The bikers?" Jorge asked.

"Yeah. Looks like it."

As soon as the words came out of his mouth, he heard a gunshot, and realized the rider who had come through Jorge's window was unaccounted for. Out through the back doors, he could see that it was Jasmine shooting her gun from where she was lying. Sean jetted through the back of the truck and fired after the rider, but he darted around the truck for cover.

Seconds later, the biker dropped down through the sky-facing passenger window. Sean shot into the truck, but the biker dove behind the food cart. Sean crawled around the side of the truck for cover and intermittently shooting and retreating, reloading. More shooting and retreating.

Finally silence fell like a suffocating blanket.

Sean slowly peered inside the truck. The motorcyclist was face down, blood spilling out from under him.

"Jorge?"

No response. Sean climbed inside the food truck, over the top of the dead motorcyclist. He peered around into the driver's seat of the cab. Jorge had suffered a fatal bullet to the head. "I'm so sorry," Sean said.

Sean ran to check on Jasmine. She was too still. "Baby?" He fell on his knees next to her. "No. No! Jasmine!"

He placed his mouth over hers and breathed into her, quick short breaths, then pumped her chest. Two more times, he repeated the action. "Come on!" he yelled at her. He put his mouth on hers again in desperation. This time, her tongue playfully welcomed him. He collapsed into her, in relief. "Thank God, you little tiger. I thought I lost you."

"I couldn't very well leave you on your own. You're pathetic without me." She moaned. "But can you get off me. I can't breathe."

He pushed himself up. "I told you, no more dying."

Her face was a blood laced, swollen mess, but there was a smile in her eyes. Sean was about to kiss her, but was interrupted by a sudden vibration in the ground. "A vehicle is coming. We have to move. Now. Can you get up?"

Jasmine attempted to move. "No. My legs aren't cooperating. And I'm out of bullets, by the way."

Sean reloaded his gun and handed it to her. "Looks like you get a third take to play dead," he said. "Make it more believable this time. I'll cover you."

"Acting 101," Jasmine said.

Sean ran to the food truck's back doors. He opened the hidden arsenal and grabbed a gun, along with a couple of fun looking knives. The space in the arsenal was large enough for him to fit inside. He closed himself in, leaving the fridge door slightly ajar so he could hear what was happening.

Like a vampire in a coffin, he waited and listened.

The approaching vehicle came to a stop behind the food truck. Sean heard the car door open and was glad he understood Felizian well enough to comprehend what the voices were saying.

"She looks dead," a man said.

"Where's Filipe and the *gringo*?" a second man said.

"Check inside the truck." the first man said.

"If they're alive, they won't get too far on foot. It's twenty miles to the closest town," the second man said.

Sean heard the men come in through the back of the truck.

"Filipe's dead. Too bad. He made the best sandwiches," the first man said.

"Yeah. Looks like the *gringo* might have made a run for it. I don't see him," the second man.

"Can't worry about him. We gotta get the ore back to the mine now. Where do you think they put it?" the first man said.

Sean heard one of the men next to the refrigerator, trying to unlock the cart that had the stack of food crates containing the ore. He chose that moment to pop out of the refrigerator, the force knocked the man off of his feet.

Sean landed a hard blow on the man's chin, knocking him out cold.

A gun shot sounded outside the truck.

He leapt out of the back doors. "Jasmine!"

Jasmine was standing, holding the gun, the man she'd just shot face down in the dirt.

"Those beautiful legs are working again, I see," Sean smiled. She turned to face Sean and pointed the gun right at him. "What? You can't take a compliment?"

No, she's not aiming at *me, but* past *me.* The man he'd knocked out was back on his feet, about to ram into his backside. Sean ducked in time for Jasmine to fire her weapon, hitting a bull's eye in the center of the man's forehead.

"We're good now. There were only two of them," Jasmine said. "Looks like we're in luck. They left the keys in the ignition of their car."

Let's load the ore and get out of here," Sean said.

After they loaded it they sped off to meet the DART helicopter that was supposed to pick them up. Jared the pilot was waiting for them when they arrived. On their way back to Cascadia, they made a stop at the DART Laboratory in The Goldens to unload the ore. Alejandro was there to meet them. They briefed him on everything they'd found at the mine, including the girls they'd seen who were wearing the serpent earrings.

"One of those earrings was found in the backseat of Lord Ranfurly's car," Sean explained. "Ranfurly must have something to do with these girls."

"It's possible. See what you can find out," Alejandro told them.

THE WORLD KEEPS SPINNING

❧ Courtney ❧

Nineteen Hours After Disappearance

After a long night of searching for Elizabeth, I fell asleep as soon as my head hit the pillow. The next day, it was ten o'clock when I finally woke. At first, the bubble of sleep shielded my mind from the horror of reality. But then I remembered that Elizabeth was still missing. *God, I wish it was just a bad dream.*

My thoughts immediately went to my own kids. Maybe it was a mom thing, but I automatically started to worry that they were also in danger. My poor babies had no idea where I was! With no cell service at Ranfurly Manor, I hadn't called them since I'd started working there, and up until that moment, I'd forgotten that the manor had a landline.

In a few minutes, I was dressed and racing down the two flights of stairs to the little alcove in the grand entry of the house, where an ancient dial-up phone sat on an antique wooden table that had dragon claws carved into the feet of its legs. I rang Laurel's number first.

Laurel: "Hello?" Her voice sounded cautious.

Me: "Hi honey, it's me."

Laurel: "Mom! What number are you calling me from? I almost didn't answer. I thought it might be a solicitor."

Me: "Sorry, sweetie. I got a job as a live-in nanny and I'm calling from the house phone here."

Laurel: "You got a new job? You could have told us! Nick and I literally just hung up after talking about how neither of us have heard from you in over a week."

Me: "I know. I would have called from the landline sooner, but I forgot the house had one."

Laurel: "Why didn't you just use your cell phone? Don't tell me you lost it…"

Me: "No. Cell phones don't work out here. And there's no Wi-Fi service."

Laurel: "There are still places that don't have Wi-Fi? How is that even possible?"

Me: "I know. It's weird. But I'm out in the wildest part of Cascadia."

Laurel: "I didn't know there were houses in the wildest parts. Is it built into a cave or something?"

Me: "No. It's not *that* bad."

Laurel: "So, you're working as a nanny? How many kids? How old are they?"

Me: "Twins." A tear quietly snuck its way out and trickled over my nose. "They are five." Knots were tangling in my stomach. Worry for Elizabeth made it hard to think clearly.

Laurel: "Oh! Twins! How cute! What are they like?"

Me: "Amazing. A boy and a girl. Luke and Elizabeth. But… right now, things are not going very well. Elizabeth is missing."

Laurel: "What?!"

Me: "It wasn't because I lost her or anything … there was an intruder on the property." I couldn't finish.

Laurel gave me a moment before she said anything. When she did finally speak, her voice was a whisper.

Laurel: "Mom. That's the worst thing ever."

Me: "Yeah." I sucked in a sob that tried to audibly escape. "Is everything okay with you?"

"Yeah. I'm just buried under essays right now, trying to finish this semester strong. I can't wait to be done."

"I know. I look forward to when you're home. …. Listen, if you don't hear from me for the next few days, it's because I'm with Elizabeth's father. We're going to look for her."

Laurel: "Oh. Mom, that sounds kind of dangerous. Please be careful."

Me: "I will. I love you to the moon and back."

Laurel: "I love you too."

We hung up, and then I called Nick. He didn't bother with the usual greetings.

Me: "Hi Nick, it's your mom."

Nick: "Jeez, Mom, it's a good thing Laurel just texted and warned me you would be calling from a weird number, or I wouldn't have picked up. Where the heck have you been? I had the neighbors check in on you and they said you weren't there … that even the animals are missing!"

I explained to Nick about the new job, but didn't get to the part about Elizabeth missing.

Nick: "What happened to you working at the restaurant?"

Me: "It closed. So, I took a job as a nanny. But the house is off grid."

Nick: "A nanny? That's … kind of weird, isn't it?"

Me: "Not really. I mean I raised you and your sister, and you both turned out pretty good. Now I'm getting paid to raise someone else's kids. Really good pay, too. I don't think that's weird at all. And I didn't have to get chipped, so *you* should be happy."

Nick: "I am happy to hear that. But the pay as a nanny is good? That is surprising. Well, at least you could have let us know. Laurel and I had no idea where you were. And Nanny and Papa are freaking out."

Me: "I know, I know. I need to call them. … How have you been, anyway?"

Nick: "Super busy. ... I really want to hear all about your job and catch up, but I'm actually running late for a class right now."

Me: "Oh. Okay. We'll catch up later. Love you!"

Nick: "Love you, too, Mom. Call Nanny and Papa. They're probably ready to report that you've been missing to PAX police. Even though they know PAX police can't really be trusted. That's how worried they are."

Me: "Oh no," I moaned. "I will call as soon as we get off."

I realized I didn't get a chance to tell Nick I worked for Lord Robert. Nick knew Lord Robert, but he had no idea that I knew him. I'd have to fill him in on everything later.

I called my parents next. My dad answered.

Me: "Hi Pops."

Dad: "Well, if it isn't my long-lost daughter. Where have you been, Courtney Matilda?"

Me: "I got a job as a live-in nanny. Sorry I wasn't able to call. There isn't cell service or Wi-Fi at the house. You didn't report me missing to PAX police or anything crazy like that, I hope?"

Dad: "Well, actually, your mother and I were about to. Glad to know you are alive and well and weren't abducted by aliens or something."

Me: "No alien encounters, as far as I know."

Dad: "Well, I hear from Laurel and Nick more than I hear from you lately, so I know how *they* are. How are all my *fur* grandbabies?"

Me: "They've seen a lot of action lately. Thor and Loki saved three people from a pack of wolves. Thor almost died. Thank God he had a little miracle turn around and he's doing better today."

Dad: "Really? I'll have to send those dogs a special package of bones to let them know their Papa is proud of them."

Me: "They would love that. How are you and Mom?"

Dad: "We're fine. But I'm afraid I have to go. I'm expecting a phone call from an old client who wants me to help him out. Your mother is out shopping with Angela. But I'll tell her you called. She'll be happy to know you're alive."

Me: "Thanks, Dad! Don't work too hard! You're supposed to be retired, remember?"

Dad: "Yeah. Well, I've decided retirement is overrated. Good talking to you, kiddo. Miss you."

Me: "Miss you too, Dad."

I sighed. *My mom is* shopping? *She couldn't be* that *worried about me. Ah well. I guess it's good to know the world keeps spinning without me.*

CAPE OUT OF THE BAG

❧ Courtney ❧

Twenty-Seven Hours After Disappearance

Winnie, Davey, and other staff members continued to scout out the forest, while Robert and I searched all morning and afternoon on the trekker, only to come up with nothing.

Nearing the evening mealtime, we returned to the manor. Thor seemed to be doing much better. Mr. and Mrs. Roth were wonderful at taking care of him. They equally great about looking after Luke. When we returned, Mrs. Roth was letting him roll dough in the kitchen while she made dinner.

Robert gave Mrs. Roth a pat on the back. "Thank you for keeping Luke busy."

"Oh, he's a wonderful little helper. And he's got a special connection with Courtney's dogs. I had him read one of his little books to them. They enjoyed that!"

Robert went over to his son and scooped him up with one muscular arm. "What's this I hear? You've found a new audience to practice your reading on?"

"Yeah. I read them *Mr. Frog and the Dog*. They loved it."

"I bet they did. Come on, little man," he whispered. "Let's go get your pajamas on." He hoisted his little boy up on his shoulders and off they went.

"Thank you, Mrs. Roth, for looking after my dogs," I said. "Mmm." A whiff of the French loaf she was pulling out of the oven filled my nostrils. My stomach growled, and it dawned on me that I hadn't eaten anything that day. "The bread smells heavenly."

Mrs. Roth cut off a piece and smothered it with butter and honey. "Here. Have this. There's fresh coffee out on the dining table in case you decide to go back out again. No doubt Lord Ranfurly will. Dinner is buffet style tonight. I figure people will be coming in and out at different times, and I'm sure everyone is famished."

"Thank you!"

The bread was the best I'd ever tasted. I dished up a bowl of soup and sat in the quiet dining room, which I had all to myself. I reflected on everything that had happened since Elizabeth had disappeared, running through the order of things in my mind.

When I came to the part where I found the backpack, I paused and thought on it for a minute. It bothered me that the pack had been empty, yet felt so heavy. *Maybe I missed something.* I decided I need to search it again. I headed upstairs to my room to find it and brought it back down to the dining table where I finished my meal. Rummaging through the pack, I felt for any concealed pockets I might have missed.

"This is the strangest pack. It feels like it has two big cylinder-shaped weights in it," I said out loud to myself, thinking I was alone.

"What thing?" Sean walked into the dining room right then.

"Oh! Sean! I didn't hear you come in."

"What do you have there?"

"A backpack. We think the intruder dropped it in the forest."

"Interesting. What's inside it?"

"As far as I can tell, nothing."

"I used to own a pack just like that. It has some hidden compart-ments that are tricky to find. Let me check it." I handed it to Sean, and he felt around inside. In less than a minute, he found two aerosol cans.

"What the...? I searched that backpack thoroughly! How did I miss those huge cans?"

"I told you ... this kind of pack has well-concealed pockets. Oh, wait ... there's something else in here." Sean pulled out a clear plastic pouch.

"What's in the pouch?" I asked him.

"Looks like a couple of little ring boxes." Sean handed one to me.

When I lifted the lid, I let out a quick gasp.

"What is it?" Sean asked.

"Remember the earring I found in the back of the Royal Rodney, the day we met?"

"Yes."

"Look at these." I lifted out an earring that was inside the box and let it dangle down from my fingers. "Serpent earrings. With rubies. Just like that earring I found that day in the car."

"That *is* odd," Sean said, opening the other ring box. "This box also has a pair of those earrings. ... You say the intruder dropped that backpack?" he asked.

"I think so."

"You're certain it doesn't belong to anyone else here? Did you ask Ranfurly if it was his?"

I shook my head. "I'm sure it isn't. He was as surprised as I was to find it in the forest. Not to mention he had no luck finding the hidden pouch."

"Hmm." Sean scratched his five o'clock shadow. "I wonder what these aerosol cans are for?" He gave them a look over. "No markings on them. Strange. You know, I have a friend who is a chemist. I could ask her to do some lab tests."

"Oh, would you? But just take one. Lord Robert needs to see what we found."

"What *we* found? You mean what *I* found, don't you?" Sean winked as he snatched up one of the cans. I placed the other, along with the earrings, back inside the backpack.

A little while later, Lord Robert returned and joined me at the table. Robert's dark hair wasn't up in a man bun as he often kept it, but was loose, and fell to his shoulders. I couldn't stop myself from reaching out and coiling a strand of it around my finger.

"Is Luke in bed?" I asked him.

"Yeah." He put a hand around my waist, and kissed me, his stubble jabbing my tender cheek. He smelled like earth and evergreens. "Thank you for being here, Courtney. You know you don't have to ... I wouldn't blame you if you wanted to get as far away from this place as possible."

"You aren't getting rid of me that easily, Mister."

He smiled. "Is that the backpack you found last night?"

"Yes. I was looking through it when Sean walked in and said he used to have one like this. He found a concealed pocket immediately. There were two aerosol cans hidden inside. And these." I showed Robert the earrings.

Robert fixated on them.

"What? Have you seen earrings like these before?" I asked him.

"Yes. Unfortunately. Those earrings are connected to a string of murder cases."

"Murder cases? But ... Lord Robert..."

"Just Robert," he held my gaze.

"Robert," I whispered. "The day I came here for my interview, I found an earring just like those. In the backseat of your Royal Rodney."

"Really? Why didn't you tell me then?"

"Because I gave the earring to Sean, and he said he would look into it. After that I forgot about it, until just now."

"I see." Robert cocked his head. "Can I have a look at that backpack again?" I handed it to him, and he rummaged through it. "Didn't you say there were two cans of aerosol?"

"Oh, yes, there were. But Sean told me he has a friend who's a chemist, and that he'd ask her to test it."

"Courtney! You can't be serious!"

"What? I thought that would be helpful," I said defensively.

"First, you gave Sean the earring you found. Now, you're telling me you gave him one of the aerosol cans? Sean just happens to turn up at the right time, doesn't he? For all we know, he's working for PAX as one of their intelligence agents, Courtney."

"Robert, I really don't think so. I mean, maybe he used to. But Simon and Rayeena said that PAX hired them to sniff Sean out. They believed he went rogue."

"And you actually buy anything those two demented psychopaths have to say?"

"Why else would Rayeena have searched my house, then chased Sean off into the Wildwoods? And then later, Simon searched his room?"

Robert sighed. "I don't know. I just … I don't trust Sean Knight. And neither should you. Although, we *could* use a chemist right about now."

Robert searched the backpack again. This time he pulled out a piece of paper.

"What's that?" I asked him.

"Looks like an address … it's a location in Emer Aude."

"What? That could be a lead! What if that's where the intruder took Elizabeth?"

"That's precisely what I plan to find out."

"I'm going with you! Just let me run upstairs and grab a jacket." I got up from the table and started to run out of the dining hall.

"Courtney, wait…" Robert got up and followed me out into the hall-way. "I was hoping you would be here, in case Luke wakes up."

"Can't the Roths look after him? He'd be in good hands. But I don't want you to go alone to Emer Aude."

"Courtney…" Robert started to protest.

I gave him my best pouty face and batted my lashes.

"Oh, how am I supposed to say no to you when you give me that face? Fine. I'll have Mr. Knight Senior pull up a car for us."

I gave his scruffy cheek a peck.

While Robert and I waited on the front porch for Mr. Knight Senior to drive up, Winnie popped out of the manor's front doors. "Going somewhere?" she asked us, a mop in her hands.

"Lord Robert has a lead, in Emer Aude," I told her.

"Sounds like you could use my help." She let go of the mop. *Smack!* Its long handle dropped to the ground inside the foyer and Winnie stepped out the front doors, leaving it to lie there behind her.

I eyed Robert, wondering what he would do. It was definitely presumptuous of one of his maids to invite herself. To my surprise, he just said, "Fine. What's one more?"

Mr. Knight Senior rolled up in a black sports car. It had a sunroof and tinted windows, and when the doors opened, they raised up like wings.

In unison, Winnie and I said, "You have a Whipper?"

Robert smirked. "Another toy left to me by my cousin, Theodore Ranfurly. It's the fastest in the collection."

"I've never seen one of these in real life," I said. "Only in action films."

Mr. Knight Senior stepped out and waited for us to climb in, expecting to be our driver. Until Robert said, "Thank you Mr. Knight, but I'll be driving the car this time. Enjoy the rest of the evening off."

Winnie crawled into the small back seat, and I got in the front passenger seat. Then Robert sat in the driver's seat and the winged doors lowered and locked. We zoomed off down the driveway, Mr. Knight Senior staring after us.

"Oh yeah! Now this is a *serious* sports car." Winnie smiled as we flew down the road at one-hundred-thirty miles an hour.

I kept checking the side mirrors for drone police. "The last thing we need is to get pulled over right now, Robert. You might want to slow it down."

"Oh, come on. Live a little, Courtney!" Winnie said.

Robert heeded my warning. "Courtney's right, Winnie. As desperate as I am to get there quickly, I certainly don't want to be locked up in a PAX prison when my daughter needs me the most." He grabbed my hand. I gave a squeeze.

When we arrived in Emer Aude, Robert parked in front of a café. "This is the address," he said. "Winnie, will you go in with Elizabeth's photo and ask if they've seen her? I'm going to look around the building. Courtney, stay in the car and keep watch for anything suspicious, alright?"

"Stay in the car? Really?"

"Then we'll have eyes in *three* places. If you come with one of us, we'll only have eyes in two."

I sighed. "I guess you're right."

Scanning faces for Elizabeth, I saw a few kids, but none of them were small enough to be her. A few minutes later, Winnie got back in the car.

"Well? Did the café workers recognize her?"

"They said she was definitely here with a man that fit the intruder's description. The worker said that was right when she came on her shift, about three hours ago."

"That recent? They could still be close by!"

"Yeah. And the worker said she was kind of worried for the child, because the girl seemed scared of the man she was with."

"Oh! Poor Elizabeth! We have to find her, Winnie!"

Robert got back in the car and Winnie told him what she'd just told me. "The worker said she watched them get into a black SUV in front of the café."

"Really? If the worker could see them, they would have been in view of the café windows. And look up there." Robert pointed to a camera. "And there." He pointed to another camera. "There are cameras all around here," Robert said.

"But how can we view the footage on them? Wouldn't we need to ask the police?" I asked him.

"Not exactly," Winnie said.

"What do you mean? You know a different way of getting the footage?" I couldn't imagine how we would accomplish that, unless ... *unless we stole it*. But we had to find Elizabeth, and if that meant breaking the law, so be it. I'd do whatever it took. "Maybe we could..."

"Maybe we could what?" Winnie raised an eyebrow.

"I don't know ... there has to be a way to see the footage off of those cameras."

Winnie made eye contact with Lord Robert. It was a strange look she gave him, as if they had some sort of secret between them. But I didn't get the impression they were having a love affair.

Winnie wasn't your typical maid, that was for sure. *Why is Lord Robert shaking his head at her?*

"What's going on with you two?" I asked them.

"What do you mean?" Winnie asked me, a disgusted look on her face. "You aren't insinuating that Lord Robert and I..."

"No. I'm not insinuating *that*. But there is something that you two aren't telling me."

Winnie squeezed her lips together. She couldn't be more obvious that she was holding back a secret.

And Robert? *Oh yes*, I thought. *He is* definitely *keeping something from me.*

"You two are conspiring." I crossed my arms. "What is it you're not telling me? Lord Robert?"

The muscles in his jaw clenched and he stiffened his shoulders. By the strained look on his face, my suspicions were confirmed. Winnie, on the other hand, was about to burst.

"Winnie! Spill it!" I demanded.

She pleaded with Robert. "Come on! We have to tell her."

Robert's shoulders lowered. "Fine. ... But let *me* explain, Winnie," he said. "Courtney..." His eyes searched mine. "We're with The Resistance."

"And we know people who can get us the footage on those cameras," Winnie added.

"You're what?" I wasn't sure I'd heard him correctly.

"We're with The Resistance," he repeated. "And we have incredibly talented team members who can help us access the footage on those cameras."

"Oh." I said, dumbfounded. "That's not what I was expecting to hear."

"What *were* you expecting?" Robert asked me.

"Anything but that?" I said. Still shocked.

But as I turned it over in my head, things started to click. *So, this is the real reason behind why there's no Wi-Fi or cell service at Ranfurly Manor. This is why he has an ultra-insane vetting process, and why he knew everything about my life before he hired me. This is why he has rules about not being chipped! And why he doesn't allow outside vehicles onto the Ranfurly property!*

"Now I see."

"You do?" he asked. "The media has twisted the narrative, Courtney. Made it sound like The Resistance is made up of brainwashed terrorists. True, there are plenty of those to go around and sadly they also call themselves 'The Resistance.' But that isn't us. We're with a group of highly intelligent and capable individuals who work against crime. We fight trafficking. We help the people who are suffering under the new regime."

I dug my fingernails into my palms. "Let me see if I'm getting this right. Simon and Rayeena were sent here by PAX to investigate Sean because they suspected he went rogue and had joined The Resistance. But you said you thought he was with PAX. So then, you lied about that? Sean is actually working with both of you?"

"Sean?" Robert was the one who looked confused now. "He isn't with *us*. Like I told you, as far as I know, Sean is a PAX agent and can't be trusted." A flustered look came over him, and he changed the subject. "We have to find out where the SUV went that took Elizabeth."

Winnie nodded. "CAPE has the smartest geeks in the world on our side," she spoke quickly. "Which is why we have to call them ... now. They might be able to hack into those cameras."

"She's right. CAPE Tech is our best hope right now in tracking that SUV," Robert agreed.

I saw the desperation on his face, heard his voice breaking, and realized that in light of the situation, whether or not they were with The Resistance was not the issue. *We have to save Elizabeth. She is all that matters.*

"Okay. Call them."

They video called CAPE Tech and two people showed up on the screen.

Dillard, who was maybe in his mid-twenties, was a slight man, with giant glasses and a very serious disposition. He had a nasal voice and was everything I would imagine when I thought of a typecast tech geek.

Baca, on the other hand, was nothing I expected. She was a bubbly ball of girlish energy even though she was also probably in her early twenties. She wore a hot pink sweater and matching glasses. Her hair was in blonde pigtails that flopped around like bunny ears whenever she got excited. Which seemed to happen every other sentence.

A few short minutes into the conversation, the tech geeks had the plates of the SUV and knew exactly where it went.

"You weren't exaggerating," I said, amazed at how fast the dynamic duo figured out how to hack into the cameras.

"The footage shows the SUV stopped *here*." Dillard shared his screen, which showed a map of Emer Aude. "Give me a second … I'm hacking into the cameras in the area around where they stopped."

A few seconds later, Dillard continued. "Bingo! The cameras show footage of them getting out of the car and boarding an airplane." Dillard's shared screen showed a closeup of the plane. "Track those numbers on the side of the plane, Baca."

In a manner of seconds, Baca announced, "Got 'em! Their plane is currently in flight!"

"Any idea where it's headed?" asked Robert.

"One sec," she said, rapidly tapping away at the keys on her computer. "By the course it is currently on, I would guess it is headed for Capital City."

"Alright. We'll head in my jet to Capital City. Keep tracking that plane and let us know if it changes course, or tell us the second it lands," Robert said.

"You have a jet?" I asked him. As soon as I said it out loud, I realized what a silly question it was. Lord Robert was one of the wealthiest men I'd ever met. "But of course you do."

16

PAX'S BIG SECRET

❧ Nick ❧

Twenty-Seven Hours After Disappearance

Nick finished up his last college class and headed to his night shift at PAX Headquarters. On the way, he thought about his phone conversation he'd had that morning with his mom.

She seems so different. Not the mom I left behind when I started college last autumn. But then again, look at how much I've changed in only eight months. I met Peter Williams, joined The Resistance, then met Lord Ranfurly and the incredible CAPE team. My mom would never believe all the things I've seen and done since I've been here. If only I could tell her.

Ever since PAX had stolen his dad's life, Nick was bent on stopping them. He knew about the resistance groups forming and wished he could get involved. Then one of his professors from school invited him to a secret meeting. That was the night he first met Peter Williams.

Nick was amazed to learn that Peter had been a Supreme Court Justice before PAX took over.

Once he had asked Nick, "If you met the person who was responsible for your dad's death, what would you do?"

"I don't know. I guess I'd want to make him pay for what they did."

"How? Would you kill him?"

"I don't know. Maybe. I would definitely want to *hit* him. *Really* hard."

"Understandable. However, *feelings* lead us to do all sorts of things that we may regret later. That's why it's dangerous to let feelings be your *guide*."

"Yeah. I know."

"And then, there is God to consider. Do you believe in the Old Religion, Nick?"

"I mean, I'm not super religious, but..." Nick started to say. He gathered his thoughts before he continued. "PAX rewards human traffickers and drugs and crime are at an all-time high. But before, when the Scriptures of the Old Religion were held up as the law, we were way better off."

"I agree. Have you spent any time studying the Scriptures, Nick?"

"Not really. I get the gist of what they say, though."

Peter chuckled. "Is that right? I've spent a lifetime studying the Scriptures, and yet I've only just skimmed the surface. Take murder, for instance. What do you think of the Holy Commandment, 'Do not commit murder'?"

"I mean, isn't it obvious?"

"Is it? When I asked you if you would kill the person who took your father's life, you didn't have a definite answer. Which means, there is a possibility you would commit murder."

"Well, that's different."

"Why?"

"Because his killer should have to pay for their crime."

"Interesting. Did you know there are places in Scripture where killing is allowed?"

"No. ... That seems like a contradiction."

"Is it? If you look at the original language, it's clear that the Scripture allows a person to take a life under certain circumstances: when defending other lives, in defense of their land, and to punish evil doers. Under all other circumstances, to take a life is to break a Holy Commandment."

"Really? That makes sense to me."

"It does to me as well. But we couldn't possibly know this about Scripture without studying it, digging deeper. ... Now, would you be willing to kill someone in order to save a life, Nick?"

"I mean, I hate the thought of killing someone. I've never done it. And I don't want to have to make that choice. But I hope I would in order to save an innocent life."

Every talk with Peter was a challenging conversation.

When Peter told Nick he was the leader of a resistance group and extended an invitation to join, Nick was shocked, yet thrilled at the same time. His secret dream was coming true. But Peter warned him, "The time for being unsure is over. As a member of The Resistance, you need to be unwavering."

Now that Nick had landed an internship working under a PAX assistant to one of The Ten, he was glad to have Peter's wisdom as a guide.

Since Nick had started part time at PAX Headquarters, he'd tried to learn more about The Ten. Like the fact that nobody, not even the assistants, were allowed in a room with them. Nobody even knew what they looked like.

In his short time there, he'd managed to steal one of the newest chip designs and handed it over to CAPE Tech. Once they reverse engineered them, they found a way to halt progress on the PAX chips.

Nick smiled to himself when he overheard a conversation at the PAX headquarters:

"Somehow our chips keep failing. It's almost as if someone is tampering with them."

"Who could it be?"

"Maybe someone on the inside."

"So does that mean we wait even longer to get our microchips inserted?"

"Sounds like it. They can't afford to keep losing employees and having to hire new ones."

It was an achievement Nick was proud of. And thanks to Dillard and Baca, Nick didn't have to worry about getting a PAX chip.

But it was on Nick to prove himself a worthy and exceptional intern if he wanted to stay on through the summer. So, he always arrived at his shifts early, left late, and went above and beyond in everything they asked him to do.

His boss, Joe, seemed pleased with him. A recent college graduate, he was an awkward, tall young man, only three years older than Nick. Sometimes he shared things with him that the interns weren't really supposed to be told. That night, he was in a heightened state when he came over to Nick's cubicle.

Nick was doin data entry work, tedious and boring, when Joe interrupted him. "Hey, Nick," he whispered.

Nick looked up from his computer. "Yeah?"

"I want to show you something." He signaled Nick to follow him.

When they were in an elevator, Nick whispered. "I'm going to show you a little secret PAX has been keeping. Or I should say a *big* secret."

"Well, is it okay for me to know about it?"

"It is if I say it is."

"You have clearance to tell *me?*"

"Are you kidding? I have unrestricted clearance, Nick. I'm just under the *top*. And I'm not going to just *tell* you. I'll *show* you. Come on."

Joe used his clearance badge to take Nick down to Sub-Floor Thirteen. They went through three different security doors on that level. "Only people with a special badge get to come in here. Pretty epic, right?"

"Definitely," Nick said.

"Okay. Brace yourself, Nick. This is what they are keeping down here, far below the Capital City in the PAX Headquarters." Joe grinned from ear to ear as he opened the final door and waited for Nick to step in. Joe followed Nick inside and closed the door behind them.

Nick's heart leapt into his chest when he saw what was behind the impenetrable glass wall in front of them.

"How the #%!! did they get that thing in here?"

"Very carefully," Joe whispered in a sinister voice.

"I didn't even know they really existed."

"Oh, well, it is PAX's best kept secret. And they certainly do exist," Joe said.

"Are they really carnivorous?"

"Oh, yes, they are. At least *he* certainly is."

"What do they feed him?"

"You might not have the stomach to learn what he eats. I didn't at first."

"What do you mean?" Nick gaped at the beast through the glass. Its gaze met his. Red eyes with black vertical slits that shouted defiance. It was as if the beast was thinking, *do you really believe I can't break through the glass?*

Nick quickly turned away. "Are we really supposed to be in here?" he asked Joe.

"Feeling a little nervous, big guy? You know, if I didn't like you so much, I'd make you spend the night in here, Nick. In fact, that would be fun to do to some of the *other* interns. The ones I like the least."

Nick could have kissed the sky when they emerged out of the underground. He would make extra sure not to get on Joe's bad side.

The next morning, Nick was back in his cubicle at PAX Headquarters when Joe walked in. "I've got a job for you, Nick."

"Okay." Nick stood, ready for action.

PAX Headquarters covered several blocks in the city, from the center of the business district all the way to the waterfront. They hopped on a tram, which took them several blocks down to the waterfront portion of the building. They then rode an elevator to Sub-Floor Three, which also required Joe's security badge for entry. While they were inside of the elevator, Joe said, "Now, you know I like you. But this next job is one you can't mess up, or I will have to make you sleep in the room downstairs, with Big Red. Understand?"

Nick swallowed down the rising bile that rose up into his throat. "Yeah. Of course."

After they reached Sub-Floor Three, they walked down a very long hallway. On one side of the hall was the largest aquarium Nick had ever seen. "Wow. They have an aquarium down here? What kind of fish do they keep in it?" Just as he asked the question, a great white shark swam by.

"That's not an aquarium," Joe said. Another shark, a hammerhead, swam past. "Those sharks look at us as if we are in an aquarium."

"What do you mean?"

"We're underwater right now. In the bay."

"Woah..." Nick contemplated the water again and understood. "What is down here?" Nick asked.

"The food bank."

"The food bank?"

"I told you that you might not have a stomach to find out what Big Red eats. Well, you're about to meet one of its future meals. But this meal refuses food right now and if it doesn't eat, it'll die. Then it'll become shark food. Big Red only eats his food if it's *alive*. Your job today is to get the nasty thing to eat. I know if any of the interns can deal with it, you can, Nick."

Joe stopped in front of Cell 333. A small window in the door showed there was water outside. "Am I about to try to convince some kind of a fish it needs to eat?" Nick asked.

Joe laughed. "Not a fish, no." He pushed a yellow button, and Nick watched as a large tube extended across the water and connected to a cell twenty feet away. He heard a loud click as the tube sealed and locked. Next, Joe pushed a blue button, and Nick realized he was now looking into an airlock, as the water was being flushed out of it. After a few minutes, a light flashed green above the door. "Okay. It is now pressurized and safe to enter."

"Anything you need to tell me before I go in there?" Nick asked.

"Hmm. Let me think. Oh! Sadly, Big Red doesn't tolerate drugs in his food, so we can't drug it. Tried that once before, and Big Red got pissed.

Ended up killing one of the interns. We won't make that mistake twice. So, you'll just have to deal with it. But don't worry, it's tied up."

"Do I get a weapon, at least? In case it attacks?"

Joe shook his head. "Sorry, big guy. Interns aren't allowed to carry weapons. You know that."

Nick stepped into the airlock tube.

Joe continued. "You only get five minutes before water fills the tube and then it retracts. You'll have thirty minutes inside the cell to get it to calm down and eat this." He handed Nick a candy bar. "Then you'll have five minutes to come back through the tube. Now, always be sure to close the airlock doors behind you, otherwise you'll get flooded. Good luck, Nick." Joe closed the door and left him alone in the airlock tube.

Nick felt uneasy as he stared at the solid steel cell door in front of him. But he couldn't exactly take his time or avoid opening it, unless he wanted to be washed out to sea. It was either face the thing inside the food bank or face the sharks out in the bay.

DILLARD'S DOTS

❧ *Lord Robert* ❧

Thirty-One Hours After Disappearance

The first words out of Winnie's mouth after Baca announced where the plane was headed, "How fast is your jet? Maybe we can catch them."

"We?" Both of Robert's eyebrows shot up.

"What? You're not going to look for Elizabeth without *us*," Winnie put a hand on her hip.

Robert planned on going after that plane. But the last thing he wanted was to put Courtney and Winnie in harm's way. *How do I convince them to stay behind?*

It wasn't that he didn't appreciate their help. In truth, he did. Very much.

But he couldn't bear the thought of something happening to Courtney. He was used to being focused, single-minded, and worrying about her would only serve to distract him from the mission.

It surprised him, the way she handled the news when he told her he was with The Resistance. *She even seems agreeable to it—in fact, she jumped right in on the action.*

Then there was Winnie. Robert knew she was more than competent. Not only had Peter told him numerous times, he'd seen her in action. But she was like a niece to him. *If something were to happen to her, I could never forgive myself.* He shook his head at the pair of them. "I can't risk your lives."

"We're talking about your little girl. She's worth risking everything," Courtney said.

"Unless you're implying that we're incompetent." Winnie crossed her arms.

"Of course that's not what I'm implying, Winnifred!"

"We care about Elizabeth too, and we want to help find her!" Winnie said.

They're ganging up on me! Robert was angry that he couldn't come up with a reasonable argument. "You two are impossible! … Fine! Have it your way. Come along."

Courtney and Winnie exchanged a triumphant glance.

Robert drove the Whipper at high speed all the way back to the river island and down the long road that led to the entrance gate of Ranfurly Manor. But before they reached it, they turned into a different driveway. Robert stopped the car at the entrance of a huge double wide cast iron gate. Over the top were letters, also made of cast iron, that spelled out *Ranfurly Park.*

"Ranfurly Park?" Courtney squinted at him. "You told me about this place when you gave me the tour of the grounds on my first day of work. I thought you said it was wild and abandoned."

"It *is* wild and abandoned. Mostly." Robert tapped a few times on his Digi-watch and the gates opened. Berry bushes were trailing onto the gravel road, making it difficult to see at times. The winding road went uphill for a while until they came out of the thick foliage into a clearing. A long grass runway and airplane hangar came into view.

Robert said, "Ran Park Hangar Two" into his Digi-watch and one of the hangar's giant roll-up doors opened.

Winnie whistled. "So, this is the hangar Kila and McGregor told me about, where you keep your jet. Kila told me she got to see your estate from the sky on a recent rescue mission. … What's in the other garages?"

Wouldn't you like to know, Robert thought, still bitter about having to bring them along. His flying car Vivienne was in another compartment of the hangar, but he was in no mood to reveal *that* secret. "Nothing *you* need to worry about." He changed the subject. "Once we're in the air, we'll call Baca and Dillard to see if they've been able to keep tabs on the plane Elizabeth is in."

"Elizabeth just landed south of Capital City on a PAX runway," Dillard said.

Baca bounced up and down. "I just hacked into the camera feeds at the airport where they landed. It looks like there are three children getting off of the plane. Two men are loading them into a black van with *Lambert's Laundry Service* written on it."

"Do you see any children with red hair?" Robert asked. "Elizabeth has red hair."

"Yes!" Baca pointed at her computer screen. "There! There!"

Dillard's eyes grew wide in horror. "The one who just bit the guy that was dragging her into the van?"

Robert lit up. "That sounds like my Elizabeth. I taught her to fight like a tiger if she was ever in trouble. Track that laundry van!"

Three hours later, it was sunrise in Capital City when Robert's plane landed. Kila Jeffries, Winnie's best friend and a fellow CAPE member, picked them up out in a private field located thirty minutes outside of town. They followed the coordinates to the place where Baca and Dillard said the van had stopped.

"A parking lot," Kila said.

Courtney pointed at the black laundry van. They stopped to peer inside. It was empty.

"Where did they go?" Robert asked, scoping the area.

"We hacked into the cameras in the parking lot and its surroundings!" Baca's high-pitched voice announced over the Digi-watch. "Three hours ago, the two men got out of the van and hauled a large commercial laundry cart out of it."

"Was the laundry cart large enough for three small kids to fit inside?" Robert asked.

"Easily," Dillard said. "They pushed the cart down Second Street, toward the waterfront. After that we lost them."

The four of them combed the area for a clue as to where the men might have gone. "There's not anything down here," Winnie said. "This street comes to a dead end at the waterfront."

"And it doesn't look like there are any more cameras in this area, either," Courtney said.

"There are three boats in the harbor," Robert pointed out. "We should check them."

"Wait!" Dillard stopped Robert before he headed toward the docks. "You don't need to board the boats to check for the kids. I recently designed a new app. Plug in a location, and it will show heat dots where there's human life. Just give me a sec and I'll see if there are any heat dots on the boats."

"What if the person is dead? Do the heat dots still show?" Winnie asked.

"No. They only show up for the living," Dillard said. "Okay, I've got your area loaded into my app."

"Oh! I see four heat dots right where you guys are standing!" Baca bounced.

"Obviously, Baca." Dillard said. "That's Lord Robert, Courtney, Winnie, and Kila you're seeing. ... Also, looks like there's two dots by a dive shop."

"Oh! And there! I see another dot!" Baca jumped up as if it were a game.

"Yes, Baca," Dillard said. "That one you're seeing is at a boat rental shop."

Robert put a hand on the small of Courtney's back and pointed. "There. The boat rental shop. And there's the diving shop. Any more dots?"

Baca was excited. "Yes, out in the water. There are about ten dots directly east of you."

Robert scanned the water and confirmed. "There are a group of divers out on the water in that direction."

"And there are a whole bunch of dots to the south of the divers, out on the water!" Baca said.

Robert squinted in the direction that was south of the divers. "No. There's nothing out there, except open water. No boats. Nothing." He and Courtney exchanged a confused glance. "Are you sure the dots are *south* of the divers?" he asked.

"I'm sure!"

"She's right." Dillard in their Digi-watch screens nodded his head up and down profusely. "There are a whole bunch of dots out there. I just counted at least thirty-one."

"Are you sure the dots are *human*?" Winnie prodded, "Could they be dolphins or seals?"

"You're insulting my intelligence, Winnifred. These dots only indicate humans! Alive humans!" Dillard's voice peaked in agitation.

"And you don't have your map upside down, right?" Kila asked.

If Dillard could have shot lasers out of his eyes through the Digi-watches, Kila and Winnie would have been obliterated.

"Maybe there is a group of divers out there under the water," Courtney said. "It would help if we had a boat. Then we could go check it out for ourselves."

"Great idea, Courtney," Robert grabbed her by the hand. "Let's go find ourselves a boat."

Kila was called in for a different CAPE mission. She left Robert the car keys and said, "Good luck finding your daughter, Lord Ranfurly," before she zoomed off with McGregor on the back of his motorcycle. Winnie, Courtney, and Robert headed off to rent a boat.

The only boat available was a large fishing boat stocked with everything an avid sea fisherman would dream to have on their rig. It even came with a built-in steel surface for cleaning and fileting freshly caught fish. It even had a huge chum bucket filled with plenty of dead fish bait to catch the largest of sea creatures.

"You know how to drive this?" Winnie asked Robert.

"I spent my early years on boats like this," he said. "My father was an avid sportsman. He loved to hunt and fish in the channel."

"I can drive it, too," Courtney said. "Keith and I used to go deep-sea fishing."

Robert drove the boat out on the bay, all the while communicating with Baca and Dillard.

"Okay … a little further out," Dillard was watching the dots on his app and guiding their boat toward them.

"Stop! The heat dots are just in front of you now!" Baca said.

Robert scanned the water. "But we can plainly see there's nothing out here!"

"You are absolutely certain that those heat dots only show *humans*, Dillard?" Winnie asked. "Not seals?" She was referring to a couple of seals playing nearby.

"Winnifred, don't ever ask me to do you any more tech favors!" he said.

Winnie whispered to Courtney, "Dillard loves all his inventions as if they're his children."

Just then, a swarm of sharks showed up near their boat. They were feasting on something, because blood turned the water red below them. "I hope that's not…" Winnie started to say.

Reading her thoughts, Robert said, "It's not human. Look." He pointed to the remains of a seal, which the sharks were still devouring.

"Wait—what's that?" Courtney pointed to something ahead of them that was below the water's surface. It was clear enough to see several feet below.

"A submarine?" Winnie suggested.

Robert trolled the boat closer. "I don't think that's a submarine."

THE FOOD BANK

❧ Nick ❧

Thirty-Eight Hours After Disappearance

Nick finally mustered up the courage to open the cell door. When he saw what he had to face, it was far worse than he could have imagined.

It was a child.

She was small. Maybe five or six years old. Bright green eyes peered up at him. Her face was filthy, her hair braided and matted in dirt. Chained to the wall, her tiny hands and feet had bruises where the metal braced her tender skin. There were no beds or chairs in the room—she sat on the cold, damp floor, shivering. Nick observed a bandage on her leg.

"Hi," Nick said softly. "I'm Nick. What's your name?"

The child bared her teeth at him and growled.

Nick slowly squatted so he was at eye level with the girl. He spoke gently. "I'm not here to hurt you."

She snapped her teeth at him.

"Are you hungry?" he asked her. He could plainly see she was starving by the look of her, but she wouldn't speak or nod. Nick brought a candy bar out of his pocket and started to unwrap it slowly.

"You know, I have a dog. His name is Thor." The child blinked. Did he catch a flicker of interest in her eyes? He went on, hoping. "When Thor was a puppy, he didn't like people much. He used to growl at me when I tried to pet him. Do you know why?"

Nick could tell by the way she perked up that she was interested in knowing why, even though she said nothing.

"Because Thor's previous owner was mean to him."

She looked away.

"I know. It's sad that somebody would be mean to a little puppy. They were also mean to his littermate, Loki."

The girl's eyebrows knitted.

"What's wrong? You don't like that he had a brother?"

She shook her head fiercely.

"You don't like puppies?"

"Yes, I do!"

Nick inwardly beamed. *So, she can talk, after all!* "Do you want me to tell you more about my dogs?"

She nodded.

Nick went on. "They're Shays. Have you ever seen Shays before?"

She lit up.

"Yeah? But my dogs aren't puppies anymore. They're big dogs now. Thor and Loki learned that they could trust me when they were puppies, and we became best friends. They used to follow me to school every day."

"I know dogs that are Shays named Thor and Loki too," she whispered.

Nick goggled at her, amazed. "You do? Where do your Thor and Loki dogs live?"

"In Cascadia."

"Cascadia? But that's where mine live, too! Is that where you're from?"

"Yes."

Nick wondered at the coincidence. *I suppose there could be another person in Cascadia who named their Shays Thor and Loki.* "What is the name of the person who owns *your* Thor and Loki?"

"They belong to my nanny."

No way. My mom is working as a nanny, but this can't be the child she was looking after. Surely she would have told me the child was missing. Unless it happened after *I last talked to her.*

"What's your nanny's name?"

"Mrs. Drake."

Nick sucked in air so fast, he nearly hyperventilated.

"I'm hungry," she said, eyeing the candy bar Nick was still holding.

"Oh... Do you want this?" Nick held it out to her. She tried to lift a hand to reach it, but the chain had no slack. She opened her mouth, a look of pain on her face. Nick fed it to her. *Poor child* thought Nick. *She looks painfully hungry.* He smiled tenderly. "What's your name?"

"Elizabeth."

"Do you have a last name, Elizabeth?"

"Ranfurly." A tear streamed down her face. "I miss my daddy." She sucked in snot, as more tears streamed down.

Nick gently wiped her face with his shirt, and fought to keep his own tears from escaping. Both of them were startled when the cell door automatically opened. His thirty minutes had already passed.

"It was nice to meet you, Elizabeth. I'm sorry I have to leave. But they told me I can come back. Do you want me to come back and feed you more?"

"I'd like that," she whispered.

He stood up and left her alone in the room. *Ranfurly? Strange coincidence,* he thought as he walked through the lockout chamber to the main building. *It isn't likely that the girl is a relation of Lord Robert. And if this is the same kid my mom is babysitting, surely my mom would have mentioned that the girl was missing.*

Nick's heart had been ripped into a million pieces. When he signed up to be an informant on PAX, he never imagined the things they were up to would be this twisted. But if that little girl had any hope of surviving, he had to be an award-winning actor when he faced Joe. He had to pretend he didn't care.

"Well ... how did it go?" Joe asked.

"She ate the candy. I also learned her name and where she came from."

Joe clapped, an ear-to-ear grin plastered across his face. "Way to go, Nick! But this means we'll need you back here tomorrow to feed it again. In fact, we'll probably need you every day this week. That scrawny thing needs to get a lot more plump to be tasty enough for Big Red to want to eat it."

"She has a bandage on her leg. What was that about?" Nick asked, masking the compassion he felt.

"It got bit by a wolf. The medics here treated it with rabies shots. Big Red's food can't be rabid."

When Nick left PAX headquarters that day, the first thing he did when he got back to his dorm was get his CAPE phone, which was hidden under a floorboard in the room. He put in a call to Robert.

❧ Lord Robert ❧

Robert, Courtney, and Winnie headed back to shore. They called Peter and filled him in on what they'd seen out in the bay. Afterward, Robert went out in the boat again while Winnie and Courtney stayed in the car and kept an eye out on shore for a sign of the men.

While Robert was out on the boat, despair tried to whisper its way into his mind. *You can't possibly believe she's still alive. And even if she is, what kind of life will she have after this? She's probably been so abused she won't be recognizable.*

A call came through on his CAPE phone. *Nick Drake.* Robert was so swallowed up in the darkest of thoughts that he almost didn't answer.

"Lord Robert, I just came out of PAX Headquarters. This is probably just a coincidence, but I met a child with your last name."

Robert's heart began to accelerate. "What was this child's first name?"

"Elizabeth."

An electrifying jolt surged through Robert, so powerful he stood. "You met Elizabeth? She's alive? How long ago did you see her?"

"Wait ... you *do* know her? Um ... a little over an hour ago."

"Was she harmed in any way?"

"Apparently she was bit by something, and they treated her with shots. But that cell she's in ... it's not good. They have her chained up to a wall, sitting on the cold, damp floor, no bed. I can't believe how cruel they are to a little kid." Nick paused. "I guess she must be a close relative by the way you're taking the news?"

Thus far, Robert had tried to function by locking up his heart behind an impenetrable steel door. He had to fortify it, lest his emotions cloud his judgment. He ignored the reality that it was *his* child who was in danger. To think about that fact would unravel him.

That's why hearing Nick say "she must be a close relative" was like someone taking a crowbar and prying off the steel door.

As Robert spoke the words out loud, "She's my daughter," the door protecting his heart came off its hinges. Walls, grooves, arteries, and blood vessels were exposed to the elements.

Nick was silent for a minute, giving Robert time to slow his breathing and get his voice back.

"I had no idea. I'm … I'm so sorry."

Robert took several deep breaths.

Nick finally broke the silence when he asked, "But Lord Robert … my mom isn't working for you as a nanny, is she?"

"Actually, yes. She is."

"What? But … how?"

"Some might say 'coincidence'. I call it 'divine intervention'. Your mum applied for the job as a nanny for my children and turned out to be the perfect candidate."

"Woah."

"And she knows I'm with The Resistance. In fact, she's here in Capital City with me now, helping me look for Elizabeth."

Nick laughed. "No way. She knows about CAPE? And is *helping*?" Nick paused. "We can't be talking about the same person."

"Yes, we are." Robert smiled. "You don't give your mum enough credit. She's an exceptional woman, Nick." He brought up a map of the city on his phone navigation. "Now, can you give me the exact location of where they are keeping my daughter?"

"It's like a labyrinth on the inside of PAX Headquarters, with several floors aboveground, and belowground as well," Nick explained. "But where she is being held is on Sub-Floor Three which extends out into the bay. She's in a building underwater. Cell 333."

"Then, it is as we suspected."

"Oh, and also … her cell isn't attached to the main building. It is isolated out in the water. They extend a bridge out when they want to access it.

"About how many feet away is her cell from the main building?"

"Judging on how far I walked across the bridge, I'd say about twenty feet."

"If that's the case, then she should be accessible underwater without us having to go into the main building," Robert said, his heart quickening.

"The area is fenced off," Nick said.

"It's worth diving down and exploring. There might be a way through."

"You'll have to avoid the sharks," Nick warned. "Sharks that have acquired a taste for humans."

"I'm aware of the sharks, yes."

"… Lord Ranfurly, does my mom know about my involvement with CAPE?"

"No. But I think you should tell her. As your mum, she should know."

"I'll think about it. But please … no matter what, promise me *you* won't tell her. She has to hear it from me before she hears it from anyone else."

"Understood."

"Oh, and Lord Ranfurly, there's something else you need to know."

"What?"

"The place where they are keeping your little girl is what they call 'the food bank.'"

"The food bank? What's that supposed to mean?"

"PAX is keeping a carnivorous dragon in their restricted underground zone. And it only eats its food alive. Your daughter is in line to become one of its next meals."

WHERE SHARKS SWARM

❧ Lord Robert ❧

Forty Hours After Disappearance

After hanging up with Nick, Robert sat on the boat, stunned for a moment. Then, as the shocking truth set in, a burning sensation rose inside his abdomen. He ran to the boat's edge and hurled chunks out into the water. A guttural sound, a wailing so loud it unnerved the creatures in the depths of the sea, ripped out of him. He stayed there bawling, his head hanging outside the edge of the boat, until he was emptied of all bile and fluids. The brine amalgamated with his torment.

Shark fins cutting through the water snapped him out of his lament.

She's alive. She's just beneath me, alive! I have to find a way to her!

He drove the boat back to shore, and walked to the car to tell Courtney and Winnie what he'd just learned about Elizabeth, careful to keep Nick's name out of it.

"I just spoke with someone from CAPE. Elizabeth is alive! He said she's in an underwater cell." *The mention of the dragon can wait.*

"Who from CAPE told you that?" Winnie asked.

"Nobody you'd know," he said, giving Winnie a warning look. Courtney didn't see it, but fortunately, Winnie caught his meaning and put a zip on the lip about Nick working with CAPE.

Robert placed a wide brim sun hat on my head that he'd bought at the boat shop and tied it around my chin. Then he handed me large, round sunglasses. "There. Now you look like a movie star." He lifted the floppy brim of the hat and kissed my nose. "These will keep your face concealed. Best to remain anonymous."

I waited in the fishing boat, while Winnie and Robert rented wet suits and fins. They came back with their gear in tow.

Winnie said, "Guys, look! Drone. Right over the facility."

"Yes. I'd be shocked if there weren't drones patrolling this area," Robert said. "We'll need to anchor the boat pretty far away from the facility so as not to draw any suspicion to us." He scanned the bay, and pointed in the direction of a group of divers. "Over there. Where all the diving boats are clustered. That's the perfect place to park."

"Okay."

I sat down in the small cabin at the helm of the ship and steered us out into the bay. Once we neared the group of diving boats, I turned off the motor so we could anchor there, as Robert suggested.

After they suited up in their dive gear, Robert handed me his CAPE Digi-watch. "Keep it so you can stay in contact with us. Winnie and I can use hers. There's a homing device in them so you can find us when we emerge." He turned to Winnie. "Are you sure you're ready for this?"

"Are you kidding? You have no idea how long I've been waiting to get some real action! This is so much better than cleaning your mansion's toilets!" She placed her mask on and jumped out from the swim platform into the water.

"Does this make me a CAPE team member now?" I put a hand on my hip and struck a superhero pose.

He smiled. "Super Helmsman. Or Helmswoman, I should say." He swept me up and gave me a dizzying kiss.

"I prefer 'Captain.'" I smirked. "It sounds more sophisticated."

"As you wish, Captain Drake. ... Hey, that actually has a nice ring to it, doesn't it?" He gave my waist a squeeze, then grabbed his scuba mask and concealed his fine face behind it, just before he leapt out into the bay.

The water was clear enough that I could watch them for a few minutes as they swam downward. Eventually they disappeared, and my heart sank into the depths with them. Nauseating "what if" scenarios played out in my mind. Naturally, every one of them had a horrible ending.

I forced myself to distract my mind elsewhere. Some nearby divers in a very clear area of the water were taking pictures of an octopus with an underwater camera. That kept me preoccupied—for a matter of minutes.

Eventually, worry won out again. I made my way to the bow of the boat to get a view of what was happening on the shoreline. *That's interesting.* A rainbow-colored yacht was heading back to shore after an excursion on the water. For a little while, watching the eye-catching vessel with all its lively passengers kept me entertained. *They seem to be having quite a party.*

It was making its way into the harbor, but going way too fast. For a minute, I thought it might crash into the docks. I was relieved when it finally docked safely and its passengers unloaded, all of them staggering. *They all appear to be high as kites.*

After that excitement died down, the dock remained uneventful. I was about to turn and head back to the stern when a capsule-shaped object popped up out of the water, not far from where the rainbow boat was docked.

"What is *that*?" I wondered out loud.

I used binoculars to get a closer look but still couldn't figure out what it was. I panned over to where Robert and Winnie were. The lens became blurred since the water was much closer than the shore.

I moved the focus wheel to sharpen the images. Something moving on the water's surface came into view.

Oh no. Is that a shark's fin?

"Go away!" I yelled. "Find a seal to devour!" My eyes glued to the binoculars, I saw a second shark fin appear. More and more emerged—hovering just above the area where we'd seen the underwater facility—the same area where Robert and Winnie were supposed to be diving!

I have to do something. I scanned the boat, searching for anything that might spark an idea. *The chum bucket!*

I brought up the anchor and steered the boat far away from where Robert and Winnie were diving. After slicing several dead fish in hopes that the smell would lure the sharks, I threw the bait into the water.

My plan seemed to work! Shark fins were headed my way. As soon as I saw the school of fins circling the area, I navigated the boat away from the sharks and back to where I was originally anchored.

❧Lord Robert❧

The taste of Courtney's lips on his mouth, his body heated after holding her in his arms for what was too short a time. What he would give to have his Elizabeth home safe, to be with Luke again, and to make Courtney *his.*

The fleeting thoughts came like a springboard before the plunge. As soon as he hit the cold water, it was a shot of adrenaline. He kicked his fins and dove down to catch up with Winnie, who was waiting for him. They still had to travel a ways to where the facility was.

When the underwater facility at last came into view, they approached it with caution. A tiger shark appeared out of nowhere, but passed in front of them, uninterested. They got a bit closer to the building, which is where they ran into a chain link fence. *Here is the fence that Nick warned me about*, Robert thought.

Winnie pointed up, and Robert saw that she was warning him they were on camera. They pretended to take interest in the schools of fish around them, but Winnie used her Digi-watch to subtly photograph the placement of the surveillance cameras and as much as she could of the building beyond the fence.

They swam along the fence around the facility, hoping to find a way through, but had no luck. Along the way, Robert spied another building.

It was separated from the building they were closest to. He believed it extended all the way to the shore. *That must be the main part of PAX Headquarters that Nick mentioned,* he thought.

Below him, he caught sight of something. *What's that? Two black lines?* Curious, he swam down to find out what it was. On the way, something ran into him. Hard. Had to be a large something. *Dolphin? Seal?* Robert wouldn't let it vex him. He had limited oxygen and limited time. *Whatever it was, let's hope it doesn't return.*

He came to the bottom of the ocean floor. It wasn't very deep in this area, maybe thirty feet to the bottom. The two black lines he'd seen were actually a track that ran along the floor. He followed it, and saw that it led through the fence to the building they were closest to, the one Robert believed held Elizabeth. Looking at the building more carefully, he could make out where the track stopped at an entrance hatch. There were grommets, which he guessed were used to attach a lockout chamber to flush and pressurize the area before opening the hatch.

He motioned for Winnie to get photos of the area. She snapped a few, but they were almost out of time. Winnie started to make her way up to the surface. Robert lingered behind a few more minutes, desperate to get inside the building.

It was at that moment when it appeared, like a ghost manifesting.

A great white shark was headed directly for him. Robert immediately swam upward, to try to avoid being rammed into by the menacing-looking sea creature. Up, up he swam, only to meet a swarm of tiger sharks at the surface.

Where is Winnie?

He treaded in place, sharks circling around him. Something grabbed onto his foot and yanked him down beneath the water. He kicked to try to break free of it. That's when he saw Winnie, holding her diver's knife out. She stabbed it into a tiger shark and streams of blood flowed out of the creature. Robert's foot was released.

At the same moment, Winnie grabbed him and towed him up to the surface. The fishing boat was waiting for them when they emerged.

Courtney threw a lifebuoy into the water, and they caught it. She tugged them in, the divers assisting by kicking their feet to gain speed. At last, they reached the boat's stern, and scrambled their way up the transom ladder. First Winnie, then Robert, until they reached their refuge—the blessed platform of the boat.

Winnie saw Robert's half-eaten fin. "That great white had your foot in his mouth!" she cried.

Robert shook his head. "Thank God it wasn't my foot! Just my fin. But if you hadn't stabbed the tiger shark and created a nice diversion back there, he might have been eating me right about now."

The sharks thrashed wildly in the water, fighting over the tiger shark that Winnie had stabbed.

"You saved his life, Winnie!" Courtney threw her arms around both of them.

"I owe you one, Win," Robert said.

They all were thrown off balance as something rammed into the boat.

"Thank me later. I think we just made some new enemies," Winnie said.

Courtney went to the helm, pushed the button to lift the anchor, and started up the engine. She was about half a mile from shore when six drones appeared in the skies above them. Robert and Winnie slipped their scuba masks back on, to avoid facial recognition.

A robotic announcement echoed out. "Fishing in this part of the bay is restricted. Return the boat rental immediately. Your fishing licenses will be revoked."

"Hang on!" Courtney put the boat in high gear and raced aback to shore. The drones followed them all the way to the docks. Courtney's sunglasses were fogged up, so she took them off, hoping the wide brim of the hat would conceal her face from the drone cameras.

Back at the dock, two armed patrolmen pointed their weapons at them. Courtney steered the boat in, and Robert and Winnie tied it off. They remained inside the boat, intentionally dressed in full scuba gear with their masks on, while Courtney climbed out of the boat to speak with the patrolmen. She forgot to put the sunglasses on.

126

"Why were you in the restricted area, ma'am?" One of the men asked Courtney.

She smiled and played her sweet girl-next-door card. "I'm sorry. My friends were diving and encountered a shark. I was so worried about rescuing them that I didn't even realize I was in an area that I shouldn't be."

"You weren't fishing?" The patrolman squinted past Courtney at Robert and Winnie in the boat.

"No. We like to take pictures of the fish!" she said.

"But that's a fishing boat, ma'am." The other patrolman gave Courtney a look, as if she was a dumb blonde—even though she wasn't blonde.

"I know." Courtney pouted. "It's all they had available for us to rent."

"Well, that area where your friends were exploring is stocked with sharks for a reason," the patrolman warned. "Divers usually know better than to swim over there. You should have read the warnings posted in the dive and boat rental shops."

Courtney covered her mouth, and widened her blue eyes. "We didn't know."

"Well, looks like your friends think they are still going for their dive, with all their gear on. But you can tell them they're out of luck. You won't be allowed back out on these waters again. And we'd certainly rather not have to report you to the authorities." The patrolman gave a signal to the drones that were still hovering above. The drones zoomed away.

"Thank you." Courtney coiled a strand of her hair through a finger. The two men smiled at her before they left.

Back in the vehicle, they discussed what they'd learned on their dive.

"You found a way in?" Courtney asked them.

"Yes. Winnie got some photos."

"I already transmitted them by Digi-watch to Dillard and Baca," Winnie said. "They're analyzing the photos now to help us devise a break-in plan."

"Good work." Robert said. "I also found that there was a track leading up to the building. Looks like a way into the underwater facility."

Robert's CAPE phone rang. It was Dillard.

"We played around with the zoom feature on Winnie's photos, and found some interesting things," he said.

"Like what?" Winnie asked him.

"A whole lot of sharks, for one thing," Dillard said.

"Yeah. We're aware," Robert said.

"We also got a pretty good closeup of a hatch on the building. There was a retina scanner right next to it," Baca said.

"Yes, I saw the hatch too. It looks like a track leads up to it," Robert said.

"Hmm. A submarine pod might be what uses the track," Dillard said.

Robert nodded. "Yes. That's what I was thinking too."

"Wait. Did you say a submarine pod?" Courtney asked.

"Why do you ask, Courtney?" Robert tilted his head.

"I saw something pop up out of the water, over by the docks. I was wondering what it was. It was shaped like a capsule."

"Show us where you saw it," Robert said.

They drove the car to a parallel parking place that gave them a clear view of the docks. Courtney pointed to a rainbow-colored boat. "It came up right there. Next to *Flamboyant Flo*."

The dock was empty. No pod or capsule shaped thing in sight.

"Let's hang out here awhile and see if there's any more activity at that dock," Robert said.

"We've been here forever. We need to *do* something!" Winnie complained.

"Wait … look!" Courtney pointed at the dock.

A submarine pod had just popped up out of the water. A minute later, a white van pulled up, and two men got out with another laundry cart. They rolled it into the pod, and the door closed behind them. The vessel submerged below the water's surface.

"What do we do?" Winnie asked Robert. "We were warned not to be seen diving in this area."

He shook his head. "We'll wait for it to make its return. That pod is our best chance of getting into the facility. Not to mention what Dillard warned us about—the retina scanner at the entrance hatch. We need eyes to get inside the underwater cell."

Less than an hour later, the pod emerged at the dock. Robert leaned in and whispered into Courtney's ear, "Stay here, and warn us if anyone is coming."

"Stay here?"

"Winnie and I still had our scuba masks on when you had those patrolmen captivated by your irresistible charm." He smiled and put a finger in her cheek's dimple, which he found adorable. "They don't know what we look like. But you removed your sunglasses, and those men will remember those bewitching blues of yours immediately." He kissed her on the mouth, a slow savory kiss. "… I feel like we're getting close to seeing my daughter, Courtney."

"Me too!" she said.

Robert kissed her again, once more, before he turned to Winnie. "Winnie, get ready to play a part."

BREAK IN

❧ Lord Robert ❧

Forty-Three Hours After Disappearance

Robert and Winnie acted like a couple of tourists walking out to the docks. As the men came off the submarine pod, Winnie approached them with a smile and pointed at it. "What is *that* thing? It looks like fun! Is it for rent?"

"No, it's a private vessel," one of them answered. "Boat rentals are at Pier Thirteen, if that's what you're lookin' for. A few blocks down the road."

"Oh, okay, thanks! Hey, you guys don't happen to know the best place around here to get fish and chips, do you?"

"We're headed there right now," the other guy answered.

While Winnie had them distracted, Robert came around behind them and pressed guns into each of their backs. "Great," he said. "Let's hang out and grab a bite. *After* you take us for a ride on the little pod."

"What's going on?" one of the men said. "Who are you?"

"We're two tourists who want to go on a little ride. To the food bank," Robert said.

"Food bank?" The men asked in unison.

Winnie gave Robert a confused wince, wondering what he meant since he hadn't told her about it. "Cell 333," she told the men.

There wasn't even a fight. With the guns at their backs, the men were compliant and allowed them access to the pod. For the duration of the ride beneath the water's surface along the track to the entrance of the building, the men at gunpoint were sweating profusely.

As they waited for water to exit the airlock tube and for the inside to pressurize, Robert asked, "Is this the only way into the building?"

They shook their heads. "There's another bridge that extends out to it from the main building."

The airlock tube was ready for them to enter. "Kidnappers first," Robert said, ordering them to lead the way.

One of the men wiped the sweat from under his eye and put it up to the retina scanner. The door of the building opened. They were inside.

It felt like the hallway of cells went on forever. Robert's guts churned, knowing that behind each door was a child waiting to face a terrible fate. *God help them. Help us help them.*

His pulse raced as he came to the 300-cell block. *I will soon see Elizabeth! Once she is safe, I'll come back for the rest.*

At last, they reached Cell 333. One of the men put his badge into a reader and the door unlocked with a clicking sound.

"Go in and unchain her," Robert ordered one of the men.

The man pushed open the door and gaped into the tiny, filthy cell. The chains that had kept the child bound were unlocked.

"Where is she?" Robert demanded.

The men were dumbfounded. One of them stammered, "B-b-but she w-was here an hour ago when we ch-checked on her!"

"Where are they keeping the dragon?" Robert demanded, thinking they must have already taken her to feed him.

Winnie regarded Robert like he was off his rocker.

"D-dragon?" the man stammered. Sweat dripped from his forehead.

That's right. They must not know about the dragon. Nick said only the highest clearances knew about it. "Can you get us into the main building?"

They shook their heads. "No. We only have clearance to run the pod and come into this building."

Robert and Winnie exchanged a glance. "Do you value your lives?" he asked the men.

Both men fiercely nodded.

"Then open up these cells and get these children out of here."

The men unlocked some nearby cells and set some of the children free.

After they'd unchained ten children, one of the men said, "The pod has a weight restriction. It won't hold more than ten."

"Are you including the weight of the four of us?"

"Yeah."

"Let's see," Robert said to the largest of the two, "I'd guess that you weigh about two-hundred-fifty pounds, yeah?"

The man gulped.

"These kids weigh around forty-five pounds each, average. If you and I stay here, ten more children can go back with Winnie. Let out five more."

The man staying with Robert dripped in sweat. Ten more kids were freed. Winnie and the other man left.

Robert ordered the man who stayed with him to let out more kids while they waited for Winnie and the other man to return with the pod. A short while later, she was back, and they took the rest of the kids they had freed from cells with them back to shore.

On the way back, Winnie told Robert, "The team sent us vans for the kids, and for these two. They're taking the kids to a safe house."

"Excellent," Robert said. He asked the men, "How many more kids are locked up in there?"

"At least a hundred," one of them answered.

"We'll have to alert the team that they need to get the rest of the kids out," Robert said to Winnie. To the men, he said, "And you two are going to help them."

Winnie glanced sideways at Robert, "So, what did you mean back there when you said, 'food bank' and mentioned something about a dragon?"

21

A TURN FOR THE WORST

❧ Lord Wellington ❧

Six Hours Earlier

Normally, August would have no interest in the food bank. But today, he happened to be speaking with a couple of The Ten's assistants in the Hallway of Bridges. That was the name of the underwater corridor of bridges that extended out to the isolated cells. One of the bridge doors was opened and extended out to a cell. He heard a voice screaming bloody murder coming from it. Cell 333.

"What is going on in there? That kind of disturbance is unacceptable," he snapped at the two assistants. They quickly went to ran to find out what the commotion was about. They came returned a minute later and explained.

"The kid has an animal bite. She's feral."

"Is she foaming at the mouth?"

"No."

"What bit her?" Wellington asked them.

"We heard it was a wolf."

"Feed her to the sharks. Can't take a chance on the child becoming rabid," Wellington told them. "By the gods, we can't have this kind of disorder in here! If it gets back to *The Ten*, you can be sure it'll be you who'll become shark lunch next."

An adult woman's voice screamed from the open door of Cell 333, "Get back here, you little monster!"

A filthy thing wearing a blue gown darted out of the bridge and looked their way. Seeing them, it made a dash down the hall away in the opposite direction. The woman, who was still screaming after the child, came out from the cell bridge and chased after her.

"This is utter madness!" Wellington said, furious. "Alert the floor to go into lockdown."

For thirty minutes, the floor was in chaos with everyone running to and fro on the lookout for the wild child.

"I swear this has never happened before. She must be rabid!" one of the assistants told Wellington.

They sent their search drones to find her, and she was finally detected hiding inside an office supply closet. A few people gathered around to make sure she couldn't escape again, and brought her to Wellington.

"Take her to the drop off, and let the sharks devour her for lunch!" Wellington ordered, without giving the child a glance.

The child screamed and wriggled to get free. That was the first moment Wellington actually looked her way.

The flaming red hair. That look in her raging green eyes.

"Wait!" he said.

The child growled at him.

"Put her back in the cell. Clean her wound and have her immunized against rabies," he ordered.

Two Hours Later

"Well? How did it go? Did the feral child eat?" Wellington asked Joe.

"My intern, Nick, was brilliant in there." Joe was in Wellington's office at PAX Headquarters giving his report. "He even got a name out of it."

"Is that right?" Wellington asked. "And what is it?"

"Elizabeth Ranfurly," Joe said.

"Ranfurly? Do you know where she came from?"

"Burt brought her in from Cascadia," Joe explained.

"Is that right? Interesting." Lord Wellington tapped his long, bony fingers together. "Get Burt on the phone. I'd like to speak with him."

Once Joe had Burt on the line, Lord Wellington said, "I have some questions regarding one of the children you sold to Joe."

"Which one? I sold him three today."

"The girl with red hair, who had the wolf bite. You found her in Cascadia. Where, exactly?"

"She was out in the woods riding a pony. Redhead girls are worth a load of pins, so I nabbed her."

Lord Wellington became impatient. "The entirety of the region is woods. I want the precise location. Do you know the coordinates?"

"No. It was on somebody's property. That's all I know. I have a friend who works there."

"I see. Do you know who owns the property?"

"No. ... But I can find out."

Wellington's face lit up. He drummed his fingers, thinking. "I'll pay you twice the amount of money if you do a job for me, Burt."

"Twice as much? Seriously?"

"Assuming you don't screw up, yes."

"I'm your man, Your Grace."

"I want the coordinates of the property and intel on the person who owns it. To be clear, I want names. The owner's name, for one. Any love interest of the owner? I want the name. Find out all you can from your friend. Understood?"

"Okay. You just want names? ... Is that it?"

"Oh, no. I have another job for you to do first that will involve some travel."

They hung up and Wellington called one of his guards into his office.

"Bring the prisoner in Cell 333 to me in thirty minutes. I'll be waiting at the emergency exit that leads out into the City Center tunnel."

"Yes, Your Grace." The guard bowed and left the room.

Wellington called his limo driver. "Bring the car to the Central Market location."

Thirty minutes later, disguised as a hunched old man with a bald head, Wellington headed down to one of the PAX Headquarters secret exits into the city. The guard was waiting there with the child, who was blindfolded.

Wellington pressed a panel, and it opened to a passage. Following behind him was Elizabeth, accompanied by the guard. They went through the passage which led into the kitchen pantry of a restaurant in Central Market. Outside the restaurant, a black limo was waiting.

The guard pushed the blind-folded Elizabeth inside the limo doors, and she tumbled onto her knees. Lord Wellington climbed in behind her.

He gently helped her up into the seat of the car and removed her blindfold.

Elizabeth had to adjust to the light after being kept in a dark cell for hours. She cowered into the corner of the limo.

"It's alright, my sweet," Wellington said, disguising his voice. "I'm not going to hurt you. I've rescued you from that terrible place. You're safe now, my dear."

Wellington couldn't help but be captivated by the child, and yet he hated who her eyes reminded him of.

But the red hair, the mouth, the expression on her face all resembled someone else. Someone he once loved.

The limo drove away from the dark alley, and Wellington spoke to her softly. "Shh. There, there. I'm not going to hurt you. I'm a friend of your mother's. You have her beautiful hair, you know."

Elizabeth gasped. "You knew my mother?"

"Oh yes. We were very, very close."

The child's hands were fidgeting, nervous. She wouldn't look up at him.

"I can tell you lots of wonderful stories about her, if you like," he said.

Without looking up, Elizabeth said, "Yes, please."

"Well, for one thing, she was quite clever. Also, she was brave. The bravest woman I ever knew. ... I can tell you are also very brave."

Elizabeth snuck a peak at him.

What she saw was his disguise. A kind old man, who apparently knew her mother. She could listen to stories about her mother all day and night. He had rescued her out of that terrible place and had taken her restraints off of her. She started to relax a little.

It was exactly what Wellington wanted her to do. "Would you like to eat something now?"

The girl was famished. She nodded.

"What would you like?"

"Cheesy fingers."

"Oh, yes. Those are yummy. I'll stop at a drive through and order some, then."

Wellington stopped and Elizabeth requested a few more things on the menu. She barely ate any of it, her stomach had shrunk so much. But with a full belly, she looked a little better.

"Alright, little one. You should try to sleep. You must be very tired after all you've been through." He played with a strand of her red hair. "You do look so much like your mother, sweet thing." She eventually fell asleep against him.

☙Lord Robert☙

By the time all the children were delivered to the safehouse two hours outside of Capital City, and they'd locked up the men who operated the submarine pod, it was after eleven at night in The Capital region. Robert sent a text to Nick before he went to bed.

Robert: "We broke into Elizabeth's cell, but she wasn't there."

Nick: "What? But that doesn't make sense. I'm supposed to go back tomorrow to convince her to eat more."

Robert: "Then what happened?" *God, if we're too late, I'll...* Robert wanted to slam his fist into something.

Nick: "I'll see what I can find out."

The s afe h ouse w as a l arge f armhouse w ith a w raparound p orch. Th e basement had thirty bunk beds and two bathrooms. Closets stocked with blankets and clothing, and full pantries of food served CAPE well for occasions such as this.

They bathed and fed all of the children and provided them with warm pajamas.

"I bet the kids would feel better if they had stuffed a nimals t o f all asleep with," Courtney said as they tucked them in.

"Yes. that's a great idea," Robert said, kissing her on the cheek. "You always have great ideas. I'll tell the team to arrange for it."

Once the children were all tucked in their beds, Winnie climbed up on a top bunk and Courtney took the bed beneath her. As soon as they hit the pillow, they fell quickly to sleep.

Robert lay on a twin bed next to their bunk and stared at the ceiling. *God, protect Elizabeth, wherever she is. And keep Luke safe too.*

A text came through from Nick while he was praying.

Nick: "She was taken out by the head of PAX Intelligence. Nobody knows where they went, or why he took her."

A profanity slipped out of Robert, loud enough to wake Courtney. She instantly came to his side and put a hand through his hair. He stopped himself from shouting out anything more, not wanting to wake anyone else.

"Robert, what's wrong? Why did you shout out like that?" She sat down on his bed. "Did you get a message about Elizabeth?"

Robert quickly deleted the message from Nick. He'd given Courtney's son his word that he would keep his secret. On top of everything else, he had that to feel guilty about as well. "Will you go with me outside, Courtney? We can't talk here."

He led her by the hand up the stairs and out onto a vast hay field. The sound of frogs singing a happy song and crickets chirping in harmony filled the night. They moved briskly, the little critters hopping out of the way as the couple stepped past them. Eventually, they reached an apple orchard. But Robert kept moving, determined to get further from the house. Their path wound through mature apple trees, lit only by streaks of moonlight beaming down through the branches. The orchard ended in another hay field.

Finally, out of sight and earshot from the house, Robert stopped. He let go of Courtney's hand and paced back and forth, wild eyed. "Why? Why is this happening to her? She doesn't deserve this! She's just a child! Why?"

"I don't know," Courtney whispered. "I don't know."

He stared at her with a blank expression, as if he didn't recognize her. But then, it was as if all of his strength was sapped out, and his legs buckled beneath him. He began to collapse. She tried with all her might to catch his fall, but his weight was too heavy. Down they both went, swallowed up in tall grass.

They lay there together, the sound of Robert's sobs tainting the stillness of the beautiful night, drenching her cotton shirt.

A part of him regretted revealing so much weakness. But the comfort of her softness was a balm to his soul. She was the weaker of the two physically, and yet, somehow she had become his refuge, his strength.

He was so tired. Running on no sleep and hardly any food … believing he had a chance of finding Elizabeth, only to learn she'd been stolen away again. *Perhaps this is God's way of punishing me for all my crimes.* "Why? Why am I able to save other children and not my own daughter?"

"I don't know why. But I know you are doing everything in your power to find her, and I also know that if there's anyone who can find her, it is *you*, Robert," Courtney whispered.

Under the blanket of stars that enveloped them out in the field, their tears flowed freely, unashamed. The crickets and frogs no longer sang and chirped. It was as if they were being quiet out of a show of respect for the grieving of the human heart.

It was three o'clock in the morning when Robert's cell phone woke him. "It isn't my CAPE phone this time. It's the regular one," he told Courtney. He answered it. "Hello?"

Ms. Stern's staccato voice barked on the other end. "Lord Ranfurly! Vee received a call on the landline here!"

"Yes?" he asked, noting the urgency in her tone.

"It vas a man! He claims to have your daughter!"

Robert was jolted out of his grogginess. "What else? What did he say? What does he want?!"

"He left a number vare you can reach him."

Robert was surprised. "A number?"

"Yes. A *telephone* number." Ms. Stern repeated the number that she'd written down.

"Thank you." Robert hung up. Courtney was anxiously waiting for him to explain the call. "It might be a lead," he told her, dialing the number Ms. Stern had just given him.

Robert cringed at the sound of the sinister voice that answered.

"Well, well, well. If it ain't Lord %#&!*@ Ranfurly! I had a %#&!*@ feeling I'd hear from you this morning. It's ten here. What time you got?"

Snake. "Let me speak to her. I want to hear my daughter's voice!"

"I'm afraid she's out of my %#&!*@ reach right now," Snake said.

"You told Ms. Stern you had her."

"I did. But now I don't. At least, not here with me right %#&!*@ now."

"Why are you doing this? What do you want?"

"It isn't personal. Just a %#&!*@ transaction. Now, are you ready? These are your instructions if you want your %#&!*@ daughter back."

"I'm listening."

"Go to the town of Lug in Highland. There's a brand-new PAX Exclusive Club Elite that was just erected. Bring Courtney Drake with you."

Robert's chest clenched. *How does he know about Courtney?*

He held up a hand to Courtney indicating he wanted her to wait for him. Then he walked over to the apple orchard and carried on the phone conversation. He didn't want to risk her overhearing the conversation.

"Any request you make is pointless if you can't show me that my daughter is alive," Robert whispered. "Untouched. Unharmed."

"Follow the %#&!*@ instructions of you want to see your kid again. You have fourteen hours. No show equals no kid." Snake hung up the phone.

Robert felt a rush to the head. He wanted to yell at the top of his lungs, to spew out every profanity that existed, to curse Snake, to damn him to the hottest fires of the abyss. He punched a nearby tree instead.

Deep breaths. In. Out.

It was as if smog swarmed into the space where he was standing, preventing him from thinking soberly. After a few minutes, once he regained his composure, he went back to where Courtney was anxiously combing her fingers through her hair.

"Well? Was it a lead?" She shifted her attention to his hand. The moonlight was bright enough for her to see the dark stain covering the back of his hand. "Oh, Robert! Is that blood on your hand?"

"It's fine. The tree looks much worse," he told her.

"So, the call wasn't a lead?" she asked.

"I don't know yet. I hope. I have to go to Highland to know the truth."

"Highland?" she said. "As in The Green Islands?"

"Yes."

"We need to wake Winnie, then," Courtney said.

"Why? Let her sleep. You should go back and get some sleep yourself. You must both be exhausted."

"Robert, we can't waste any time. We should go to Highland if there's a chance she's there."

"We? No. Not this time. This time it has to be just me, Courtney."

"Robert, Winnie and I aren't letting you do this alone, remember?"

"No, Courtney. You don't understand." Robert had to convince her she couldn't come with him. He said the first thing that came into his mind. "I know the person who took Elizabeth. He threatened to kill her if I didn't go alone, and he's the type to do it." Robert avoided eye contact. He had no choice but to lie. He couldn't allow Courtney anywhere near Snake.

"But there has to be a way we can go as your backup without him knowing," Courtney said.

"McGregor is flying me over. He'll be my backup."

Courtney seemed to be holding her breath.

"Hey," Robert lifted her chin. "Stop worrying. I've worked alone most of my life and I'm still here, aren't I?"

Her face was shrouded in fear, and he felt terrible for being part of the reason she was worried.

"They're giving me fourteen hours. Which means I have to be in The Greens by midnight their time. But I want to see my little boy before I go."

When they got back to the safe house, Winnie was awake and on the front porch.

"I was wondering what happened to you two. Uncle Peter called and is already working on a plan to rescue the other children in the food bank."

"It won't be easy. They will be expecting us. But we have to try," Robert said. "Well, now that you're both awake, be ready in fifteen minutes to fly with me back to Cascadia."

THESE DREAMS

❧ Sean ❧

Sixty Hours After Disappearance

"You really won't want to remember, trust me." He couldn't see the face, but it was a man's voice who said it.

Where am I? A hospital bed? *No. He didn't think so. The man, his surroundings, everything was a fuzzy blur.*

The scene morphed into a more clear and vivid picture. He was outside. Mill Pond. The skies were clear and blue, the view of Mt. Ziwa was breathtaking. He was standing in front of a gazebo that was decorated in white tulle.

A string quartet began playing a well-known love song.

Then ... she appeared. The wind was stolen out of his lungs at the sight of her. His own vision became blurred by tears that filled his eyes. He cursed. He'd promised himself he wouldn't be a blubbering idiot.

She walked slowly toward him, her face glowing and radiant, her long auburn hair glistening in the sunlight. Those intelligent blue eyes behind the veil never straying from his face.

She was the perfect vision of elegance and natural beauty wearing that dress. More beautiful than any woman on the planet. And she was his.

Sean woke in a sweat. He tried to joggle out of it, but the picture of her in the wedding dress was fresh and vivid, etched into his mind.

He'd never dreamt *that* before.

She was the missing piece to the year he had no recollection of.

Before he knew she existed, that she was real, not just a dream, he'd believed she was a figment of his imagination. Then, on the day he drove to pick up the person who would be interviewing for the nanny position, he had a sense of déjà vu. The backroads. The town of Mill Pond. The small house on ten acres. It was all strangely familiar to him, even though he'd never been there.

He had knocked on her door, feeling strangeness. Then he heard her voice, before she opened the door. He knew the voice. It was her voice.

When she opened the door and he saw the dark auburn hair, the pale skin, the bright blue eyes, he *knew* her.

It was the reason he had so desperately wanted Courtney to take the job at Ranfurly Manor. He had to see her more. She was the key to his past.

He reached over to his nightstand and checked his favorite analog watch that miraculously still worked. *Three o'clock in the morning.* He forced himself to fall back to sleep.

At seven o'clock, he woke and went to check on Courtney's animals and the horses, as was his usual routine. Even though it was no longer his official job, he couldn't help himself; he sincerely loved the animals. But he chose that time intentionally, knowing it was when Courtney routinely fed her own animals. However, on that particular morning, she didn't turn up.

Thor and Loki were happy to greet him, though. And his favorite of her three cats, Fiona. He spent a few minutes petting them, waiting for Courtney to turn up. When she didn't, he went into the house through the kitchen garden. Mrs. Roth was collecting herbs.

"Morning, Mrs. Roth," Sean smiled at the kind staff member who he'd known since he was a boy. She was the mother of his ex-girlfriend, Marie, who'd recently been murdered. Sean was still in denial that Marie was really gone forever. She was his first love, and later remained one of his best friends, long after the romantic feelings ended between them.

"How are you and Mr. Roth holding up?" he asked her tenderly.

Mrs. Roth shrugged. "As best we can, I suppose. I still can't believe it."

"I know," Sean felt the sting of losing her more now that they were talking about it.

"And now, that dear little child! Poor Lord Robert. It isn't right when a child dies before a parent."

"No, it's not. Do you think she's dead?" Sean asked.

"I don't know. But to think of her still alive and being trafficked is almost worse than her being dead, isn't it?" She sighed. "That reminds me, I'd better look in on Luke."

"Why? Isn't Courtney supposed to do that?"

"She went with Lord Robert to look for Elizabeth, and they put me in charge of Luke. As far as I know they haven't returned yet."

"When did they leave?"

"The night before last."

"Do you know where they went?"

Mrs. Roth shrugged. "They didn't tell me where. I just know they drove off to catch a flight somewhere, and they asked me to watch after little Luke. Fortunately, he's a good boy. But he's terribly anxious about his sister." Mrs. Roth scurried off, and Sean headed outside.

Jasmine passed him on her way into the kitchen. "Well, speak of the devil."

"Speak of the devil? You can't possibly be referring to innocent me?" Sean asked.

"Innocent?" Jasmine scoffed. "That's not what I'm hearing from a certain blonde maid who is telling everyone on staff that you're cheating on her." She touched his arm and let her hand linger there. "Heartbreaker."

"What are you talking about? I'm not cheating on anybody. Ya have to be in a committed relationship to cheat."

"According to Gretchen, you are in one."

"Hogwash."

Jasmine just laughed at him mockingly. She held up her dust feathers and wriggled her hips playfully, showing off her sexy figure in her maid miniskirt as she headed into the kitchen to begin her shift.

I'm not the one breaking hearts, Sean thought. A vacant feeling swept over him as he watched her disappear into the house.

So much had changed since he first left Ranfurly Manor, back when he was a teenager. It was never his plan to return to the place where he was raised. Too much pain, too many terrible memories. He winced as he had a brief flash of his father beating the crap out of him.

But it wasn't all bad here, he thought. *Marie. Mr. and Mrs. Roth. They were good to me.*

Yet, he put them all behind him when he joined the military, and eventually fought in the Tsur War. So many of his memories were dark, painful. So, few moments of happiness. That's why it hurt so much when Jasmine rejected him. He thought they shared happy times together. *To me those were happy times. Apparently, she didn't feel the same.*

After the war … then what? An entire year was lost. It drove Sean mad, as he tried to force the memories to come back. But forcing only seemed to stress him out more.

The dreams of Courtney were always of happy moments. But he didn't understand why he had those dreams. *Perhaps they're visions of a future I'm meant to have?*

The only thing he could recall was getting recruited to work for PAX.

"You are in better physical condition than most of our agents, Mr. Knight," Alejandro Hernandez had said. "But why do you want to become a PAX Intelligence agent?"

"PAX brought us world peace, and I owe them my loyalty. They saved many lives by ending that war, including mine."

Sean passed all the tests and was sworn in as an agent.

But then all of that was turned over on its head when Jasmine and Alejandro revealed the horrendous truth. He couldn't continue down the path as a PAX agent once that was revealed to him.

It was the right choice to fight with DART, he reminded himself.

But doing the right thing didn't bring back his memory of what happened to him during that missing year of his life. And it didn't stop the dreams. In fact, they were increasing in frequency, and Sean was becoming more desperate than ever to understand why.

HURRY UP AND SAY GOODBYE

✆ *Courtney* ✆

Sixty Hours After Disappearance

It was three o'clock in the morning when we returned to Ranfurly Manor. The first thing we wanted to do when we got back was check on Luke, who was asleep and looking like a sweet angel tucked into his toddler bed. His strawberry mop was toppled over his face, and Robert had to brush the curls aside to kiss his boy on the forehead.

The child's eyes popped open. "Daddy! Did you find Elizabeth?"

"Not yet. But keep those prayers up."

A heart-breaking expression crossed the child's face. "Okay."

"We're going to find her, Luke," Winnie told him with a confidence in her voice that made even me feel better.

Winnie and I left Robert alone with his little boy and I headed to my bedroom. I closed my door and rested against it for a moment. The overwhelming urge to cry flooded over me, but my tears were stubborn and refused to come out.

I examined the balcony doors; the ones Sean had come through a couple of times. Honestly ... whose idea was it to hang those floor length, ceiling high drapes that could so easily conceal a person behind them? I certainly wasn't a fan.

I fearlessly marched across the room to check behind the ominous curtains. The glass doors were closed, and I made sure they were locked. No intruders. And no Sean Knight.

Sean. My heart warmed at the thought of him—the way he'd sat with Thor after the wolf attack. I felt a pang of guilt that I hadn't thanked him. Of course, I had a valid excuse, I'd been busy searching for Elizabeth. I made a note to self that the next time I saw Sean, I would be sure to tell him how grateful I was.

He'd been there for me when I was recovering after Simon and Rayeena attacked me in the woods. He'd checked in on me every single day when I was laid up. True, he was a ladies' man, I had no doubt about that. But he had a good heart.

Ah! I yawned. *That bed has never looked more inviting than it does now.* I peeled off my clothes, relieved to finally get sleep, when a knock at my bedroom door made my heart jump. I was stark naked, so I grabbed the closest thing I could find to cover up in – a short, black silk robe with black lace sleeves that I'd left lying on my bed.

"Who is it?" I called out.

"It's me. Robert. May I come in?"

"Uh … um." I slipped the robe on. "Yes."

He cracked the door and peeked his head in. "Oh. So sorry. Did I interrupt something?" His eyes were devouring me in the robe.

Heat flooded into my cheeks. "I was just getting ready for bed."

"I didn't mean to disturb you. You need to get some rest. I just wanted to say goodbye before I headed off."

"Oh," I said, walking over to him, making a sad face. He stood in my doorway and opened his arms to me. I sank into his embrace.

As he held me, he whispered, "I'd also like to see that secret passageway that Sean showed you, that leads into my bedroom closet."

I stepped back and smiled. "Oh! And here I thought you just came to see me!"

Of course I couldn't blame him for his curiosity, having recently learned there was a secret corridor that led into his closet from my room. Crossing to the fireplace, I looked back at him over my shoulder and gave him a wink.

I lifted the portrait that hung on the wall above it. The wall opened.

"Aha!" he said.

"I know. Just like you see in the movies. Makes me wonder how many more secret passages this house might have."

"Yes, I wonder," he said as he peered into the dark passage. He stepped out of the way and gestured for me to go in front of him. "Ladies first."

As I stepped past him, I said, "Hmm. Isn't that gentleman-like of you. Allowing the lady to go into dark creepy corridor first." I hesitated before I went in, and looked back at him. Once again, he had the look of a hungry wolf about to devour me. With any other man, I would have been revolted, but Lord Robert Ranfurly was not any other man.

"Well … what are you waiting for, Mrs. Drake? Go on." He whispered seductively.

"You better not have Alfred the spider with you." I stepped forward into the passage, hugging myself. He closed in behind me. His warm breath on my neck sent fuzzy bubbles of elation through me. His large frame blocked out most of the light that shone in from my room, but there was just enough that I could see where Robert's closet wall was ahead of us. I started toward it.

Unexpectedly, we were standing in pitch blackness. He'd closed the door behind him. Standing there in utter darkness, I became disoriented. "Lord Robert! I can't see anything in here."

I felt his fingers on my back, moving like a spider. I screamed.

He laughed. "It's all right, I'm right here." His strong, firm hands slid around my waist, and turned me around so I was facing him. He closed the gap between our bodies and pressed me into him. "I'll protect you."

My body hummed as he traced over my curves with his fingers. I longed to kiss him, and reached up to feel his face. Standing in that corridor, with not even a hint of light, the kinetic connection between us illuminated the dark space.

I ran my fingers through his shoulder-length hair. "Robert," I breathed, waiting for his lips to reach mine.

"Mmm, Courtney." Robert breathed. "I'd love nothing more than to get lost inside you and forget the rest of the world. God knows I do," he whispered. His lips at last reached mine. The kiss brought on more longing, an unquenchable desire rose in me.

But he broke away.

"But every second that goes by, I wonder what is happening to my Elizabeth…" he said.

"I know," I whispered. "I understand. You have to go. … I just wish you'd let me go with you." I gripped him around the waist, wishing I never had to let him go.

A sudden stream of light into the corridor broke us out of our reverie. Had someone figured out the way into the passage from behind my fireplace? The wall to my bedroom had reopened, it seemed by itself.

But then I realized it was actually just Robert who had reopened it.

"What? Did you get scared of the dark?" I teased.

"Mmm. Not with you here making it so enjoyable." He spun me back around, so my back was once more facing him. With the fireplace wall reopened, I could once again see the way to Robert's closet wall ahead of me. "Back to business. Show me where it leads," Robert's whisper tickled my ear.

I swallowed down my ache for him and led the way forward. We pushed through the wall, and were inside his closet. "Here we are. In your very impressive closet."

"Well, well! I wonder which of my cousins designed this."

"Maybe the most recent one. Sean's dad told him that your cousin, Theodore Ranfurly, used to have mistresses come into his bedroom through here all the time. He was quite a ladies' man."

"Is that right? I never had the good fortune to meet him."

"No? And yet he left you everything. That's interesting," I said.

"You could have snuck into my room and seen me anytime you wished," he whispered. "Why didn't you?"

"Why, Lord Ranfurly, I'm not that kind of girl."

150

"No. Yet you came through there with Sean. He could have been an axe murderer and left you for dead in there." Robert peered into his bedroom. "Coast is clear." He guided me by the hand over to his bed. "It's a bit unsettling to imagine you and Sean alone in there together."

"Sean was a complete gentleman. But I can't say the same for you, Your Grace." I wrapped my hands around his neck. "Shame on you for pretending to be a spider!"

He growled. "Hmm. Sean…"

"What? You're not jealous, are you? He's just a friend."

"A *friend*," he scoffed and broke away from me. "He's a PAX agent, Courtney. We can't trust him."

"Perhaps he was, but … maybe he's not now. If you recall, Simon and Rayeena were convinced Sean went rogue."

"I'm not putting stock in anything either of them have to say, and we can't be certain where Sean Knight's loyalties lie. I don't trust him. Nor should you."

An uncomfortable silence passed between us where I walked back into his closet and observed the rows and rows of shoes.

"Do you actually wear all of these?" I asked him, to lighten things up.

"No."

"Oh. Kind of a waste of space in here, isn't it?"

"Yes." He came to me and gently tilted my chin; his lips close enough to kiss. "Seeing you in that lacy lingerie is making it difficult to say goodbye."

My sultry gaze met his. "Then don't. Take me along in your suitcase. I don't take much space."

Without any warning, he grabbed my wrists and backed me into a fur coat that was hanging in his closet. He growled and bit my neck. I clawed into his back.

"I'd love to stay here with you … let one thing lead to another," he said in a low rasp. "Once I have my Elizabeth back…"

"I know … you have to go," I whispered.

We exchanged one last kiss before I left his room.

I was already fast asleep when a light knock on the door disturbed my peace.

"Uncle Robert wants to see us downstairs in his study before he leaves," Winnie's voice said through the door.

Not another goodbye. The last one was torture enough. I threw on a long, flowy blue robe that was far more appropriate than the one I'd worn earlier, and stepped into my fluffy white slippers.

Robert was waiting for us in his study.

"I don't know why you can't at least take *me*," Winnie complained. She was dressed in her black CAPE gear, clearly expecting to go. "I'm your *partner*, remember?"

"McGregor will be with me on this mission. I need you *here* to be a guardian for Luke." I blinked a few times. *Did I just hear him correctly? I thought I was Luke's guardian.* Robert continued to say to Winnie, "I'll feel much better about leaving him knowing you're here."

"Alright," Winnie said. "Even though you've got a whole force of CAPE security guards around here protecting the place."

"Winnie, we still don't know how Snake managed to get on and off my property. While you're here, work on finding that out, as well."

"Right," Winnie succumbed. "Okay. I'm on it."

"Also, I need you to test every security camera that I had installed to make sure they all work properly. The front gate code was changed while we were in The Capital."

"Okay, Chief. You and McGregor bring Elizabeth home, and I'll do my part here." Winnie saluted him like a soldier before she left us alone in the study.

"You've accomplished a lot." I played with a strand of his beautiful hair, which was loose and falling over his shoulders. "Do you ever sleep?"

"Sleep is overrated."

"I notice you trust Winnie with a lot. Enough to put her in charge of Luke."

"Winnie's like family to me. I esteem her Uncle Peter greatly, and he raised his niece to be a trustworthy and highly capable young woman."

"Yeah. I've never met anyone quite like her. I like her. ... I never really had any female friends. Other than my best friend, Meg, who died when I was seventeen."

Robert kissed my forehead. "Yes, Meg. You mentioned her to me once before. I'm sorry for your loss."

"Winnie's refreshing to be around, I can see why you trust her. ... But what about *me*? Do you trust me as much as you trust her?"

"Why would you ask such a silly question?"

"Well, you're leaving me behind, and firing me from my job as Luke's nanny. So, what am I supposed to think?"

"I'm not *firing* you!" He folded me into his arms. "Goodness, no. Courtney ... don't you see? You've become far *more* than my children's nanny. Which is why I need you to go back to Mill Pond while I'm away."

"What?" I broke away from him. "Go back to Mill Pond? Why? Why can't I stay here?"

He said nothing in response.

"You don't even have a reason?"

"I do. But I need you to trust me."

"Oh. You're using *that* one. That's what I used to tell my kids when I couldn't come up with a good reason for something."

"No, that isn't what I'm doing here."

I sighed loudly.

"Don't look at me that way. I'm doing my best. Trying to get my daughter back. Trying to keep sane. But if I have to worry about you or Luke as well ... I can't! I can't handle ONE. MORE. THING. Do you understand?!"

"I mean, yes, of course I understand." I gently put a hand on his shoulder and rubbed his arm to soothe him. "But ... Robert, I don't even have security in Mill Pond, and after the break in, why do you think I'd be any safer there than I am here? At least CAPE guards are here. Winnie is *here*."

"You do have security in Mill Pond, Courtney. I've arranged it so that you are completely protected there. After the break-in I took the liberty of having a fence and gate installed. You will be safer than you've ever been."

"You had a fence and a gate installed at *my* house?"

"Of course I did. I can't believe you never fenced off the place."

"It was too expensive. But ... I feel so awkward about this. You really shouldn't have—"

"Courtney, please. I couldn't live with myself if I didn't. You'll be returning to a completely secure home. On top of that, the CAPE Tech team installed surveillance cameras throughout your forest. Should there be a breech, the CAPE phones will be alerted. Peter plans to get you your own CAPE phone, now that you're part of the team, but in the meantime, here's the gate code to your house. The code to mine is there, as well." He handed me a sealed envelope.

My emotions were all mixed up. I felt gratitude for all he had done, while at the same time resentment as I realized he wasn't giving me any options.

"As you wish, Lord Robert," I whispered.

"Just Robert," he whispered. "Courtney, if you can't trust me, then what do we have?"

As his gaze met mine, the stormy sea inside me calmed.

"I do trust you. I do."

He laced his fingers through mine, and squeezed my hand.

"Oh ... and Courtney, the guards aren't there to keep you in, but to keep bad guys out."

I made a sour face. "Guards?"

"I told you; I've made sure you'll be protected. They are CAPE guards."

"Will they be inside my house? It isn't very big, if you recall."

"No. They will be posted outside. Two guards per shift. They don't need you to feed them or entertain them, just carry on as usual."

"Okay." I resigned with a loud sigh. "Thank you," I whispered. He dabbed my nose with a finger. "Am I really part of the CAPE team now?"

"If you want to be. You've proven yourself to Peter." He smiled. "And he isn't easily impressed, by the way."

A smile crossed my lips. *Am I dreaming this? Working as a member of The Resistance. Keith would never believe it!*

Robert bent down and kissed me. … A long, slow, torturous kiss.

I pushed him away gently. "Go," I whispered. "Before I find a way to stow away on your plane."

A SNAKE AWAITS

❧ Lord Robert ❧

Sixty-Four Hours After Disappearance

McGregor met up with Robert two hours outside Capital City, and together they flew another two hours to Highland.

They landed the plane on the private grass runway of Robert's Highland property, The Retreat. After crossing the Western Ocean, and accounting for the time change, it was ten o'clock in the evening in The Greens and the summer sun had recently set.

Robert didn't alert the caretakers that he was there. It had been many years since he'd seen them. *They might be surprised to know I'm alive. Still, I'm taking the car. I should alert them.* He left them a note.

> *John and Millie,*
>
> *I hope this note finds you both well. I'm in the area for an urgent meeting. Took the car. Sorry I was unable to see you.*
>
> *-Lord Robert*

He and McGregor headed to the small sea village known as Lug, which was an hour and a half away by car. On the way, Robert had a request of McGregor. "Open that bag that I brought with me, McGregor. It's there, by your feet."

McGregor opened it and peered inside. "What is this thing in here? A dog?"

"No. It isn't a dog, McGregor. It's a hairpiece. And you're going to wear it."

McGregor, a manly man who was used to women falling at his feet, gave Robert a stone-cold stare before he busted up laughing. "Yeah, right."

"I'm serious. Snake says he expects Courtney to be with me. So, you need to look like her."

McGregor goggled at Robert. "You've lost it, bro, if you think there's any chance that *I'm* going to pass for Courtney."

"You will if you're sitting in the car and a good distance away. Just put on the wig, McGregor … and the dress."

McGregor's jaw dropped. "I'm not wearing a frickin' dress. I'll be in the car. He won't see what I'm wearing!"

"He'll see the top half of you, so you need to look as convincing as possible. Wear the dress, McGregor. Oh … and all that stuffing in there … that is for the dress's built-in brassiere. You won't pass for Courtney without it." Robert smiled to himself as he let his mind wander to thoughts of Courtney's delicious curves.

McGregor gave Robert a look that could kill, but he obeyed orders.

They reached Lug and Robert parallel-parked across the street from a brand-new building in the quaint town of Lug. The modern building, painted red and black, appeared vulgar in comparison to the ancient small stone houses and shops, many of which had thatched roofs. Outside the building, written on a neon sign: *Club Elite. A PAX Exclusive Experience.*

He passed through a scanning machine that searched him for weapons. Once he cleared through the scanner, he surveyed the place. The entrance hall was painted black, with photos of nude models lining the walls.

He approached a tall desk, where he was greeted by an employee dressed in a tuxedo. "Name please?"

"Lord Robert Ranfurly. I'm to meet a man here at midnight."

The employee lifted his chin. He motioned for Robert to go through a red door. "Wait in there."

On the other side of the red door was a room also painted red, and large enough to be considered a ball room. A chandelier made of crystal wineglasses dangled from the center of the high ceiling, its flickering flames creating a magical illusion throughout the room.

Two gorgeous women wearing exotic, sensuous mesh gowns and sheer veils covering their noses and mouths walked past him. One was a platinum-haired bombshell, the other a raven-haired beauty with striking green eyes.

The platinum-haired woman smiled at him through her see-through veil. Most would see her and admire her beauty, but what captured Robert's attention was not the woman, but the shimmery jewel hanging from her ear lobe.

Serpents made of emeralds with rubies.

The other woman, the one with the raven-hair, wore identical earrings.

The women left through the red door. *Dear God. Are these Snake's next victims?*

Robert decided to follow them and see where they were headed. He watched them leave out the front of the building. They stood outside on the sidewalk and chatted with each other. A few minutes later, a fancy car showed up, and they climbed inside.

You have to do something!

To act was always his first instinct. And knowing full well those earrings were a warrant for their deaths, Robert felt compelled. *But what can I do? I have to save Elizabeth!* He wouldn't abandon his daughter to save someone else. He had to let the women go.

He walked back into the Red Room, despairing, praying he was making the right decision.

After some time, a man walked in. Robert recognized the flat nose and beady black eyes immediately. *Snake.*

Robert had suspected all along that it was Snake who had kidnapped Elizabeth, and now his suspicions were confirmed.

The last time Robert had seen him, Snake was leading a trafficking ring out of an abandoned warehouse near the Ranfurly estate. Robert broke up the operation, but Snake had escaped in the forest outside the Ranfurly estate boundaries.

"Where's the %#&!*@ girlfriend?" Snake spat out.

"She's in the car. I wasn't about to bring her into a place like this."

Snake looked at him narrowly. "You're %#&!*@ with me?"

"Look out the window … she's there—in the black car parked across the street. That's as close as I'm letting you get to her, Snake."

"Afraid I might bite her, and she'll enjoy it too %#&!*@ much?"

Robert ignored the question. "So, how did you manage it? Getting onto my property? We found more of the deadly earrings along with two cans of aerosol in your backpack. What's in the cans, Snake?"

"Wouldn't you %#&!*@ love to know?"

Robert's imagination ran wild as he envisioned the ways he would punish Snake for his crimes. But first, he had to get Elizabeth back, safe and sound. "You said you would show me proof that my daughter is alive. Untouched, and unharmed."

"But to do that, I need your %#&!*@ girlfriend. That was the %#&!*@ deal!"

"As I said, she's across the street."

"I'll need to get a closer look to be sure it's really her."

Robert smiled. "Be my guest."

Robert followed Snake out of the building and across the street. Snake approached the front passenger window of the car. McGregor had his head turned so all one could see inside the car was a busty woman with reddish brown hair.

Snake tapped on the window. "Open the %#&!*@ window, pretty thing!"

The window of the car rolled down, revealing the barrel of McGregor's gun. McGregor batted his eyes.

At the same instant, Robert drew a tiny gun out of the wing tip shoe he wore. Dillard's invention. The shoe had a thick rubber sole that concealed the gun from metal detectors.

"Checkmate," he whispered behind Snake.

"You bloody %#&!*@" Snake hissed.

Just then, a car drove up in front of the club across the street. It was the same car Robert had seen earlier—that had picked up the two women wearing serpent earrings. The women stepped out, and the car sped off.

The women, still wearing the veils and earrings, were about to head back inside when they spotted Robert. Curiosity on their faces, they smiled his way. He ignored them.

The platinum blonde waved and giggled. "Hello there, Prince Charming!"

Robert glanced back and feigned a smile. The other woman, the one with the raven hair, smirked. She made a motion to her blonde friend to stay put, while she crossed the street to approach him.

"Everything alright?" She was now standing behind him.

Robert kept the gun between him and Snake, aimed at Snake's back, so she was unable to see it. He turned his head to the side to respond. "Splendid. Enjoying your evening?"

"Oh yes, it's a beautiful night."

"You and your friend there weren't gone for very long," he said.

"Were you actually keeping track of how long we were gone? ... I saw you in the club earlier. I'm surprised you didn't leave with a woman. That's why most men go to the club. To either leave with one, or to stay with one in the rooms there."

"Do you live in one of the rooms?"

"Me? Oh no! I only go in there for rehearsals." She took a step toward him, so that he could get a better view of her face. "Why were you in there anyway? Did they not offer a selection that pleased you?"

"I had my reasons for being in there."

"Hmm. Well, perhaps we can discuss the reasons over a drink?" A coy smile crossed her lips through the see-through veil. That's when Robert realized something about her features sent a stabbing reminder through him of his late wife.

"Unfortunately, I have some business to take care of right now. Raincheck?"

She was now standing in a place where she could see Snake. He was standing with his back to her, blocking her view of the car window. It appeared to her as if he was conversing with the person in the car.

"Burt? You're out here too? You aren't giving this dashingly handsome man any trouble, are you?" she asked.

Burt answered her without turning around. "Just handling business for Wellington, love. What the %#& else would I be doing?"

Robert perked up at hearing the name. *Wellington? Hmm. Could it be the same Wellington I once knew?*

The woman seemed to assess the situation. "Oh, I see. Well, I'll leave you two to carry on, then."

She walked back across the street. Robert heard the doors of the club open and close as the women went inside. Once again, it was just McGregor, Robert, and Snake.

Robert demanded, "Show me my daughter, Snake!"

"Okay, okay. Calm the %#&! down. If you'll just let me grab my phone out of my pocket, I can show you."

Robert and McGregor clicked the safety off their guns at the same time, as a warning not to try anything.

Snake quickly pulled out his phone and waved it in the air. "See? Just my phone."

"Okay. Where is she?!" Robert was out of patience.

Snake tapped a number in and lifted the phone up high. "Here she is. Untouched. Unharmed. Alive. As promised."

Realtime footage showed on the screen. There was Elizabeth, holding on to a game controller. "She's experiencing an all-time high playing that video game. It's like she's never seen one before." Snake sneered. He pressed a button and the screen went black. "I told you, the ticket to getting your kid is to bring me Courtney Drake. Come back with her and if you're lucky, your kid will still be alive. But if you keep delaying things, I can't make no %#&!*@ promises!"

Five drones appeared; their guns aimed at McGregor and Robert. "Drop your weapons or be fired upon," the drones' robotic voices said in unison—an ominous sound that made Robert's insides churn.

Snake turned around, a victorious grin on his menacing face. "So nice to have the %#&!*@ law on my side. And now that I'm working for the Head of PAX Intelligence, I'm not someone you want to %#&!*@ mess with. Now you get a choice. You can kill me, but then those %#&!*@ drones will kill you. Elizabeth will live a life as a trafficked slave. Nobody wins.

"Or you can drop your weapons, and get one more %#&!*@ chance to meet Wellington's demands."

Robert and McGregor lowered their weapons. Snake slipped out from between them and stood under the protection of the drones. His beady eyes glistened in satisfaction as he watched Robert get in the car and drive away.

Once they were down the road, away from the scene, Robert pounded the steering wheel in frustration.

McGregor tore off the wig and scratched at his head. "This thing itches like crazy." McGregor examined it on the inside. "How do actors do it—wear these things for hours on end without scratching their skulls to a bloody pulp?"

Robert was too preoccupied with what their next move would be to pay attention to McGregor's rantings. He turned onto the highway that headed back to The Retreat. "I'll call Peter to see what ideas he might have."

They were climbing on the highway, headed into the forest, a good thirty minutes from Lug when Robert spied headlights in his rearview. "We're being followed."

He knew the area well and took a detour off the main highway. It was an unpaved logging road that was not maintained.

"Uh … this car of yours isn't exactly four-wheel drive, Lord Ranfurly," McGregor said.

"It'll have to manage!" Robert checked the rear-view mirror again. "Looks like I lost them. I know these old logging roads – grew up exploring them. There's only one other road that meets up with this one, but nobody uses it except the family who owns the surrounding property. They won't be out here at night."

Just after the words came out of his mouth, the SUV that had been following them appeared in front of them and stopped, blocking the road ahead.

"You were saying…" McGregor said.

Robert had two choices. *Option one: speed up and ram into the SUV hard enough to knock it out of the way, but risk the car he was in becoming undriveable. Option two: drive in reverse.*

Option two it is.

Robert shifted the car into reverse and floored it. They were jerked forward when the car rammed into something.

"That was an elk you just hit!" McGregor shouted.

Looks like we'll be going with option one. "Hang on!" Robert yelled. He pushed the accelerator to the floor. They were headed straight at the SUV.

When the SUV's driver door opened and he saw the person who stepped out in front of his headlights, he slammed on the break.

THE RAVEN-HAIRED BEAUTY

❧ Lord Robert ❧

Seventy-Two Hours After Disappearance

Their car stopped inches away from the person that stood between them and the SUV.

"Who is *she*?" McGregor's view of her had been blocked by Snake, so this was the first time he saw her.

The raven-haired beauty wearing the veil and see-through mesh dress didn't cower. Either she trusted far too much that his car would stop in time, or she was a fool. Or perhaps she thought she was invincible.

A moment later, the blonde stepped out of the passenger seat, smiling brightly. She waved at them.

Robert and McGregor slowly stepped out of the car.

At first, the women only had eyes for Lord Robert. But when they saw McGregor, their gazes drank him in, a look of amusement on their faces. A smug smile crossed his lips, as McGregor assumed it was because of his good looks. (It was true he usually had a way with the ladies.) Little did he realize the real reason for their amusement; he was still wearing the dress with the stuffed brassiere.

Robert raised a brow and addressed the one with the dark hair. "When I said raincheck, I was thinking maybe another day."

Her sultry gaze was back on him. "Oh. Well, you did *promise*."

"Did I?"

"You're not the type who *breaks* a promise, I hope," her gaze held him captive.

What is her game? Is she in league with Snake?

Swaying like a samba, she went around the SUV to the boot of the car, and started to open the hatch. Robert reached for his weapon, ready for whatever might be next.

She conjured up ... a wine bottle. "How about we enjoy that raincheck *now*? Right here." She patted the inside of the back of the SUV and hoisted herself, so she was facing out the back, her long, bare legs dangling in spiked high heels.

McGregor raised an eyebrow. "My kind of woman."

Seemingly out of nowhere, a wine corkscrew appeared in her fingers. "Would you mind coming over here and doing the honors?"

Robert wasn't sure if this was some sort of trap, but he played along. He opened the bottle with ease. All the while, thoughts raced through his brain. *How can I get these women to leave? I have to find Elizabeth! I don't have time for this!*

However, the fact that they were wearing the serpent earrings, and still alive, did intrigue him. He'd only seen the earrings with the rubies on the *dead*. Under any other circumstances, he would be using this opportunity to get information out of the women.

With too many conflicting thoughts racing through his mind, he handed the raven-haired beauty the open bottle, but refused to sit down. She drank a swig, her posture straight and regal, then offered the bottle back to Robert.

"You brought along a corkscrew, but where are the wine glasses?" he asked.

She lifted her eyebrows, as if challenging him to drink out of the bottle. "You aren't too squeamish to share germs, are you?"

He held up a hand. "Why yes, you've sussed me out. I'm far too squeamish."

"You're sure you don't want a sip?" she asked. "You could probably use this more than the rest of us." She held out the bottle to the blonde, who took a swig before she passed it to McGregor. His swig was more like a few gulps.

The dark-haired woman flashed a bright smile. "Now, about why we chased after you just now..."

"Mmm. I was curious about that." Robert studied her through slits. "How did you ever manage to get in front of my car?"

"I went down the other logging road," she replied, simply. "It goes through my grandfather's property. I know these woods like I know my own name."

Robert let out a sigh. "Just our luck. ... And why did you follow us?"

"I heard you demanding Burt to show you where he's keeping your *daughter*."

"You heard that? But ... I could have sworn I saw you go back into the club."

With a sly smile, she said. "But you couldn't have really seen me go back in, because I never did. When I was speaking with you, I had this hunch that something was *off*. Then I saw you were with Burt, and that confirmed my suspicions were right. Burt's a criminal, and Wellington always calls him to do unpleasant things. I never know the details. But seeing you, *of all people*, with Burt ... well, of course I was curious to know why you were there. And then I overheard the part about him taking your *daughter*! That's far worse than anything I could have imagined! I didn't even know you *had* a daughter, Lord Ranfurly."

He was startled to hear her say his name. "Wait. ... You know who I am?"

Her laugh sounded like a bubbling stream. "You don't remember me? Well, I suppose I'm not surprised."

"We've met before? That's impossible. I'm certain I would not forget meeting *you*."

"Please. Don't mock me. It's no wonder you've forgotten all about little old me, considering your dubious reputation."

"My reputation? Please, do enlighten me." Robert crossed his arms. *Who is this intriguing woman? And why don't I remember her?*

"Oh, I'm sure you'll just deny it." She met his gaze, her expression cool, absent of wrinkle or blemish.

"Oh, who cares what they say about him! He's the most gorgeous man alive!" The blonde said in a thick Highlandish accent. She laughed and put an arm through his.

McGregor made a face, as if he was wounded. "Hey! I'm standing right here!"

The blonde giggled and snuggled into Lord Ranfurly's burly arm.

"If you're concerned about my bad reputation, then why are you here?" Robert asked, oblivious to the woman hanging on his arm. His question was directed at the dark-haired woman.

Her full, red lips slightly parted. "Because my aunt, Agatha Lundgren, was your nanny and speaks of you and your brother as if you're her own children. But she has no idea that you have a daughter. I believe you've kept that a *secret* from everyone, Lord Ranfurly."

Robert was stunned. "Mrs. Lundgren is your aunt?"

She sparkled with amusement. "Yes. You don't remember me at all. When we were younger, you and I used to play together. And then those silly summers we spent together when we were teenagers."

"Impossible. I never spent my summers with anyone."

"Oh, and I believe the last time I saw you, I was around nineteen. We danced the entire time. It was the last ball you ever threw at Ranfurly Castle."

"Ball? I never in my life threw any balls at Ranfurly Castle. And I rarely dance."

"Oh, you *rarely* dance! Now you're just being comical, Your Grace." Her long lashes fluttered. "Well, we were much younger then. Eleven years ago. You had just turned twenty-five and your brother Robert was twenty-six. Of course, he didn't want to dance with anyone. He was always *hiding* himself away. But you … oh, you were always the life of the party, Lord Leo!"

Robert sighed. "Ah! Now I see where the confusion lies."

She cocked her head. "What do you mean?"

He shook his head. "I'm not Leo." He put a hand on his chest, gesturing to himself. "I'm Robert. And please, forgive me for not remembering your name?"

She suddenly had the look of a deer in headlights.

"Kat. Her name is Kat. And it looks like the cat caught her tongue!" The bubbly blonde giggled at her friend, who was abruptly struck speechless. She grasped the opportunity to fill the void with her own voice. "And I'm Raquel! But people call me Kelly," she beamed.

Kat broke out of her momentary silence, and was once again at no loss for words. "*I* don't call her that," she said flatly. "She looks like a Raquel to me." She held out a hand. "And your family would know me as Katherine. But in the entertainment world, I'm known as Kat Stewart."

"Pleasure to meet you, Katherine … *again,* apparently. As we've likely already met." He cradled her hand in his for a moment. Their eyes locked. Robert swallowed audibly.

McGregor cleared his throat. "And I'm McGregor," he said, feeling a hair jealous of Robert, considering he'd been wanting to impress Kat and win her over since he'd first seen on her. The poor fellow was still forgetting he had a dress on.

"Well, it's been a time, meeting both of you. But I'm afraid McGregor and I really need to get cracking. … As you're aware, I need to find my daughter." Anxiety brimmed inside Robert as he started back to his car.

McGregor and Raquel followed him. Kat closed the back hatch of the SUV before she joined them.

"Those earrings make quite a statement. What's the story?" McGregor asked the women.

Raquel did a twirl. "These earrings are our ticket to paradise!" She sang the words out in a lovely voice.

Robert stopped. "What do you mean?"

168

Kat spoke in a calm, collected manner. "She's actually being *literal*. We were hired to perform at an event next month. In The Tropics. Hence, paradise."

Robert lifted his eyebrows. "What kind of event?"

"A stage show that will be streamed worldwide. We'll be singing and dancing for PAX elites," Raquel bubbled. "We were chosen out of millions of other women."

"Not millions, you ninny. More like hundreds," Kat corrected.

"And the King will be there!" the blonde bubbled in her thick Highland accent.

"The King of the Green Isles, you mean?" Robert asked.

"Is there any other?!" the blonde asked.

Kat murmured, "He isn't the only king in the world. You silly girl! Rumor is that the King of The Northlands will be there, as well."

"Oh!" Raquel's blues shone in surprise. "I've never heard of The Northlands. I've never been outside of Lug before."

"Which island in The Tropics are you going to?" Robert asked.

"One that's only for PAX elites!" Raquel bubbled.

"All the islands are now only for the elites, Raquel. PAX stole all the best real estate for themselves," Kat impatiently waved off Raquel like she was an annoying fly. A moment later, her expression softened as she turned to Lord Robert. "We have no inkling which island."

Robert's phone rang. "Peter? Yes, let's plan to meet in three hours. We'll be flying back in stealth mode."

Robert felt Kat's eyes burning into him. "Flying?" she asked him. "In *stealth* mode? That sounds exciting."

"Yes. *We* have an airplane," McGregor told her, emphasizing the word *we*. "A very *special* plane."

"You're going to brag about it, and not invite *us*?" Kat seemed offended. "So un-gentleman-like."

"Of course you're welcome to come with us, ladies," McGregor flirted. "I'll even show you my *cockpit*."

Robert eyed McGregor. *Dear God, he's certainly not thinking with his brain at the moment.*

Raquel giggled. Kat raised an eyebrow. "Why, thank you, McGregor. We'll gladly accept, won't we, Raquel?"

Robert exhaled loudly. It was difficult to not let his frustration show. "…I'll just need to let my friend Peter know you'll be coming." He nodded in the direction of the SUV that blocked the road. "Katherine, do you mind moving that beast of a car out of the way?"

"Oh, yes. Of course."

"Your carriage awaits, ladies!" McGregor opened the back door of their little car and bowed.

Robert cleared his throat and got into the driver's seat. The last thing he wanted was to bring them along. He still wasn't sure about them. Although, Kat was Mrs. Lundgren's niece, which made her as good as family. And he was sure those earrings were as good as a death warrant. *I can't very well let Mrs. Lundgren's niece become the next victim in the earring case.*

But he hated that he'd already been robbed of so much precious time.

Once Kat and Raquel were in the backseat of the car and McGregor was situated in the passenger front, Robert sped out of the area and hurried back to where the plane was parked. On the way, he asked the women, "So how much does PAX pay you for your … er … work?"

Kat answered. "We don't get a salary. Being a PAX entertainer is a prestigious position, and we're paid by getting wined and dined, and given elaborate room and board."

"A life you enjoy, by the looks of it," Robert asked.

She flashed a smile. "Who wouldn't?"

Luxury comes with a price, thought Robert. Kat and Raquel were unaware of the fate of those who wore the earrings. *Perhaps we can kill more birds with one stone. Save Elizabeth and these women.*

VIRGINS UNVEILED

❧ *Lord Robert* ❧

Seventy-Three Hours After Disappearance

"I promised I'd show you around. Do you want to feel what it's like to sit in my pilot seat, Kat?" McGregor shamelessly flirted with Kat, while Raquel shamelessly flirted with Robert, to which he paid no attention.

As they got ready for takeoff, Robert sat by a window. Kat slipped into the seat next to his before Raquel could beat her to it. Raquel pouted. She sat in a seat facing him.

Robert looked out the window, distracted by his anxious thoughts.

"So here I mistook you for your brother, Lord Robert," Kat said. "You two always *could* pass for twins."

He turned to look at the woman sitting next to him. *Katherine.* Her cheeks had deepened to a rosy pink. Her lips were plump and slightly opened. *A low hanging, juicy piece of fruit,* Robert thought.

"There were rumors that you were dead." She seemed to drink in every inch of him.

He peeled his eyes away from her. "Rumors? Did you listen to them? It was *your* aunt who first gave me the advice to never listen to rumors. Didn't she never teach you that?" he challenged.

Once the plane had reached maximum altitude, Robert offered the ladies something to drink. He was careful to avoid meeting the gaze of the seductress, Katherine.

"So, is Burt one of your clients?" he asked. Finally, he knew Snake's real name.

Kat answered. "What do you mean by *clients*? No. Burt is a foul, ill-mannered beast who does jobs for Wellington. I try to stay away from him as much as possible."

"Aye. The *sleekit*," added Raquel.

"You keep mentioning this Wellington person. You wouldn't happen to be speaking of Lord August Wellington?"

"Yes," Kat replied.

"Really? Then you *know* him?" Robert's curiosity got the best of him. Without thinking, he looked into her eyes.

Raquel giggled. "Yes, we know him. He's the one with the huge…"

"Ego," finished Kat, her gaze once again holding Robert captive.

Raquel snorted and laughed loudly.

"Ah! Yes. Sounds as if it's the one and the same Wellington," Robert said, breaking his eyes away from her bewitchery.

"He's the one who hired us," the cool, enigmatic Kat said.

"And he'll be taking us to The Tropics for the big event!" Raquel said.

"Ah. Is that right?" *So, Wellington weaseled his way into working for PAX, did he? Why am I not surprised?* "Do you enjoy working for him?"

Raquel answered, "We like that he's filthy rich."

Robert recollected the way Wellington gave the *impression* that he was rich. He had even bought his own title.

Kat moaned. "Of course, we have to endure listening to him go on and on about himself." Her eyes flickered. "Unlike you. You seem more interested in asking us about other *men*." Her lip curled into a teasing smile.

Raquel leapt out of her seat and stood between Robert's legs, putting her arms around his neck. She toyed with a long strand of his hair. "Would you like me to entertain ya? I could show ya one of the dances we've been rehearsin'. The choreographer tells me I'm the best dancer he's ever worked with." Raquel wiggled her hips. "No offense, Kat."

"Oh, none taken," Kat said. "It's no secret that our male choreographer prefers blondes. And you, Lord Robert? Do you prefer blondes?"

Robert had no doubt the blonde was an exquisite dancer by the way she moved. But if he were to choose to watch anyone dance, it wouldn't be Raquel.

He recollected Courtney's first day of employment at Ranfurly Manor when he gave her a tour of the house and showed her the ballroom. Luke was sitting on his shoulders and Elizabeth cried, "Dance with me, Daddy!" He twirled his little girl around the room while Luke held on for the ride. Nothing delighted him more than seeing his Elizabeth beam with joy when he danced with her. *My sweet Lizzie.* It tore him up, remembering.

"Let me dance for you," Raquel's voice broke into his thoughts.

"Actually, at the moment I'd rather just sit and converse," he said, looking out the window. He quickly brushed away a tear.

"As would I," Kat agreed, never taking her eyes off of his face.

Raquel put her hands on her hips and pouted. "Yer killjoys, the pair of ye. I live for dancin'!" By her loud and sloppy speech, it was evident she'd already drank a bit too much.

Kat stole a glance at Raquel. "One more glass, and she's going to pass out."

"Kat, by your accent, you're clearly not from Highland," Robert said, still looking out the window.

"My accent is a hybrid of Bellais and Uplandish, mostly. But I spent a few years in The Northlands as well. My father was in the military, so we traveled everywhere. ... Speaking of travel, where are we headed now?"

"Chantelle. Or Zone B, as we now call it. The Capital City."

"Oh! Glorious! That's one place I've never been."

Robert glanced her way. It was a mistake. Once he caught sight of her, he couldn't seem to draw his eyes away. "Does your father still serve in the military?" he asked.

Her face was a still picture. "My father was executed on The Day of Cleansing," she said, absent of expression.

"I see." Robert studied her. *Is it that she doesn't* care *that her father was executed, or that she doesn't want to let on that she* does *care?*

"Those earrings, I've seen them before."

"You have?"

"Yes. But sometimes they have sapphire stones. Do you happen to know why?"

"I'm not really sure *why*, exactly. I mean, we're all marked as PAX property. All the women I work with. I think the sapphires show a slightly lower rank. Many women at the club wear the serpent earrings with sapphires. All I know is that those of us who were given the rubies are *the select*," Kat said. "We were chosen out of hundreds of others to wear them."

"Ah. What was the criteria to be chosen?"

"We must have the right 'look' and body type, be able to sing and to dance."

"Ah," Lord Robert said.

She smiled. "And we have to be virgins."

"Excuse me?" This came as a total shock to him. "Then you … and Raquel … you were virgins when they chose you?"

"Were? We still *are* virgins, Lord Ranfurly."

"Oh. But I assumed you both were experienced with men, being that your job is to entertain them."

Kat's cheeks flushed. "Oh! Wait … is that what you meant earlier by asking us if Burt was a client? No, no! We aren't *those* kinds of entertainers."

Robert thought back on all of the women he'd found dead who were wearing the earrings. He had proof by the autopsies that none of them had been virgins. *Hmm.* "These are PAX orders, then? You must remain virgins?"

"Yes. I-I'm offended, Lord Robert. You actually thought we were *prostitutes*? My mother taught me it wasn't wise to ever assume, Your Grace. Didn't my aunt teach you that?"

Robert cleared his throat. "Touché. Well, I..." Feeling foolish, he changed the subject. "So, how did you get the job with PAX?" With the new information, Robert saw Kat in a different light.

Raquel was the one who answered his question. "I auditioned! I was so nervous, there were so many beautiful dancers. I could hardly believe it when I was chosen!" She was far louder and wilder than she'd been earlier. "Come on, Kitty Kat! Have more wine and shake, shake, shake it!" Raquel stripped off her veil and tried pouring wine into Kat's glass, as well as her own. She only made half of the liquid into the glasses, the rest spilled all over the floor. She downed her own glass and started spinning in circles, giggling uncontrollably. Eventually, she collapsed into her seat.

Kat was gobbling Robert up with her eyes like he was a decadent morsel. *How is it possible that a woman as enticing as her has never been with a man?*

A question popped into his mind, and he had to ask it. "Why do you wear the veils?"

"Part of the job. *The Veiled Virgins*–that's the name of the production we're going to perform in. All the dances we are learning tell a story of a wedding."

"A wedding?"

"Mmhmm. Some ancient ritual of the gods or something. I don't know. None of us have seen the script yet. So far we've just learned a couple of the dances."

"Gods? What religion is it?"

"I have no idea."

"Ah. Did Raquel just break the rules, then, when she removed her veil? Or are you allowed to remove them?"

"We can't remove them in public, but in private we can do whatever we like." She unhooked her veil and let it drop to the floor.

"I see."

Kat changed the subject. "So where have you been all these years? Even my aunt thought you were dead. She was very upset about it."

"I never meant to worry your aunt. She means the world to me."

"The media said you murdered your wife. But when I asked my aunt, she said, 'Lord Robby would never do anything evil. Never!' To this day, she sings nothing but your praises."

"The media says a lot of things. But they probably won't mention that the murderers of my wife have been discovered and put behind bars."

"Oh! Well, that's wonderful news! You're proven innocent, at last!"

"I was proven innocent years ago. This simply confirms it."

"Right … Even so, Wellington doesn't like you. I've heard him talk about you. He questions your loyalty to PAX! Which makes me question whether you might be more like my father."

"I don't give a toss about what Wellington thinks." He spoke quietly. "I just want my daughter back in my arms."

Kat put a hand on his bicep. "I'll do all I can to help you find her."

"Thank you. … Kat?" he whispered.

"Yes?"

"Are you aware that many women who wear the ruby earrings end up dead?"

Her face clouded over. "What?"

"By the look on your face, I see you didn't know. Listen, I don't want to see you and Raquel suffer the same fate as the other women who wore those earrings."

Kat, who had forgotten Raquel, became aware that her friend had passed out.

Her chest rose, and she began to breathe quickly. "May I speak freely?"

"Of course."

"If you were any other man, I'd doubt you were telling me the truth." She leaned into him, so her thigh was against his. He could see her silky skin through the mesh. "But you're *not* any other man."

Robert felt increasingly uncomfortable, sitting at such close proximity to her. He found an excuse to break away. "May I offer you something to eat Kat?" He got up and crossed to the wet bar. As he brought out some prepared meals, he continued to ask the questions that were on his mind. "Tell me, Kat, what made *you* want to work for PAX?"

Kat sank into her seat. "I was living in Upland, singing and dancing at a club. That's when I met Wellington. He invited me on a date." She played with an air vent above her head. "He isn't at all my normal type, but when he told me he was the Head of PAX Intelligence, I agreed."

"What? *He's* the Head of Intelligence?" Robert froze. *So, it was Wellington! He has my Elizabeth!* It was far worse than Robert imagined.

"Yes." Kat was puzzled by his reaction. "You didn't know that? So, obviously, one can't say no to the Head of Intelligence. I had no choice. He questioned me during the date, discovered I was still a virgin." Her cheeks turned a shade of pink as she laughed. "I suppose it surprised him, considering I'm almost thirty years old and was performing in a rather risqué production."

"You look like you're too young to be drinking legally."

"I know. I take after my mother, who was a model. Lord Wellington had already heard me sing and watched me dance at the club, so all I had to do was model in a bikini for him. Thank God he was looking for a virgin, so I didn't have to worry about him trying something inappropriate."

Robert tried to push the visual of her in a bikini out of his mind, but the thought was already planting itself.

"It was so degrading, having to stand there alone in the room, while he appraised me to decide if I was perfect enough."

"That's the entertainment industry for you. My wife, Desiree, lived it."

"Yes. Desiree Diamond was amazing in *The Mermaid*. She was one of my idols, you know."

"Really?" Robert wondered if that was why Kat's mannerisms reminded him of Desiree's. Perhaps because she'd watched her in films and imitated her. "Well, I'm sorry you had to be alone in a room with Wellington. In a bikini, no less."

She waved it off. "I've gotten used to it since then. We have to wear ridiculous leotards while rehearsing. Might as well be in bikinis. Kind of numb to it now. My father would hate it ... he was old-fashioned and proper. Lieutenant General for the King of The Greens!" She beamed with pride. "Before PAX executed him."

"He must be turning over in his grave, knowing his beloved daughter is being used to entertain PAX now."

If he was hoping to get a reaction, he was successful.

A tear trickled down her cheek. "I didn't ask for this. It isn't like I have a choice, Lord Robert. How else am I supposed to pay for food? It's either work for PAX or starve. Not everyone was born into privilege as you were! No disrespect intended."

Robert went to her and handed her a tissue. "None taken." He grabbed Raquel's empty wine glass and walked back to the wet bar.

After she gained composure, Kat stood and joined him. "Wellington brings you up an awful lot. I overhear him speaking to people about you, and my ears always perk up. If you're not a PAX loyalist, how are you managing to survive? I hear they've started to confiscate lands in The Northlands. It's only a matter of time before they do that here in The Greens." Her expression changed, her softness became alive and animated. She moved in so she was close enough to kiss, and whispered, "You're not with The Resistance, are you?"

Her hair was soft against his cheek, giving off a smooth and luscious fragrance of vanilla and chocolate. "If I was, do you think I would admit it?"

She became animated once again. "I wish I could join The Resistance. I just don't know how to get free of PAX's clutches."

The instinct to protect came over him. His hands went around her waist. "You might not want to tell people that, Kat. In fact, how can you be sure I'm safe to tell that to?"

She pressed into him and rested her head on his chest. "I trust you, Lord Robert. You know, I had a secret crush on you when we were young. Oh, yes, your brother was always the outgoing, flirtatious one. He was my first crush. But you always intrigued me. And yet you never even noticed me."

Feeling uncomfortable, he broke away and coughed. "I didn't pay any attention to women until I met Desiree. I had a lot of responsibility to carry after my father died."

"My aunt told me that when your father died you carried the burden of it on your shoulders, while your brother ran away from responsibility. She was always so worried about you."

Clearing his head, he moved away from her. It felt like an appropriate moment to bring up the earrings again. "Perhaps you can help me, Kat. The earrings you're wearing are of some interest to me. You say Wellington gave them to you?"

"Yes. Last week."

"Do you know all of the others who were chosen, besides the two of you?"

"Yes, we all attend rehearsals together."

"How many are there?"

"Eight others. Raquel and I make ten."

"Kat, I fear your life is in danger. I'd never forgive myself if something happened to the niece of Mrs. Lundgren. Will you take them off for me?"

Holding his gaze, she slowly removed the earrings. She might have been a virgin, but every move she made dripped with seduction. She slowly placed the earrings into his palm.

"Kat, I can make you and Raquel disappear from Wellington's radar and take you to a place where you will be safe from PAX. Where you will be provided for. Would you like that?"

Her eyes glistened. "You could really do that for us?"

He nodded. "You'd best make sure you and your friend there get buckled in. We're about to fly in stealth mode. Chances are, you'll pass out from the g-forces."

He headed into the cockpit, distancing himself from her. It was obvious she wanted him. If he weren't with Courtney, no doubt he'd pursue things with Kat. But his heart was spoken for.

He spent the rest of the flight in silence next to McGregor, worried about his little girl in the hands of his enemy, Wellington.

IN SEARCH OF PERFECTION

⮞ Lord Robert ⮜

Seventy-Five Hours After Disappearance

It was eight o'clock in the evening Capital Region Time when they arrived on a runway in a field two hundred miles outside of Capital City. Peter Williams was there to greet them.

Before introductions were made, Peter said, "Those are interesting earrings," referring to the ones Raquel still wore. Robert had Kat's pair in his pocket.

"Peter, this is Katherine, and that's Raquel," Robert said. "I've already explained to Katherine about the earrings. When Raquel sobers up, she can be filled in."

"I see," Peter said. "Are these the only two with you who will be going to the safe house?"

"Yes."

"Alright. We've got it ready."

"Thank you," Katherine said to Peter.

Robert's mind was preoccupied–playing out how he was going to rescue Elizabeth. *Bringing Courtney to Snake isn't an option. But then again, what if there isn't another way? … No. I will not risk her life!*

"Alright, ladies," Peter said to Kat and Raquel. He pointed to the sedan that drove up. "That's your ride. My wife, Nina, is waiting at the house for you to arrive. She'll make sure you have everything you need."

"You are too kind," said Kat.

"But before you go, I'll need those earrings," Peter said to Raquel.

Everyone turned their attention to her.

"Nooo!" She made a pouty face. "I'm one of the chosen!"

"Raquel, you need to give him the earrings," Kat told her. "I'll explain why later."

Raquel huffed. She reluctantly removed the earrings, grumbling incoherent words as she handed them over to Peter. She staggered as Kat pulled her by the arm to the car.

Once the women were gone, Peter said, "I hope we can trust them, Robert."

"Kat is the niece of my childhood nanny. I don't think she's anyone to worry about."

"She could be the niece of The Dragon Rider Himself, and she'd still have to earn my trust."

"I'm fully aware."

"Now I see why you couldn't speak freely when you were on the plane. Were you able to get any information out of Snake?" Peter asked him.

"No. He found out I didn't bring Courtney, and now we're back to square one. He's demanding I bring her in exchange for Elizabeth."

"There has to be another option."

"Do you have any ideas? Because I seem to have run out."

"Does Snake know what Courtney looks like?" Peter asked.

"I don't know."

"Because if he doesn't, we could send one of the CAPE team members with you. Someone with field experience."

"And if he knows what she looks like?"

Peter frowned. "CAPE Tech might have an idea."

Robert and Peter met with CAPE Tech to discuss a strategy.

Dillard was the first one to chime in his idea.

"Easy solution. There's this thing called a mask," Dillard said.

Baca beamed and clapped, bobbing her head up and down. "Oh yes! What fun! Dillard and I can make a lookalike Courtney! We learned how to do that back when we were, like, ten!"

"You just need to pick a field agent with the same body type, skin, and eye color as hers," Dillard said. "We'll take care of hair and face."

"Okay..." Robert wondered how they were supposed to find someone as perfectly designed as Courtney in so short a time. "And do you two have someone in mind?"

"Hmm. Let's take a peek," Baca said. Faces of CAPE female agents appeared on her screen.

"How about her?" Dillard pointed to a woman who was three inches too short.

Robert raised an eyebrow at Dillard. "Are you feeling well? No."

"That one? She has nice blue eyes," said Dillard.

"She's six foot one. Courtney's five foot seven," Robert said, impatiently.

"That one has hair just like Courtney's." Baca pointed to another photo. "Lush and long, and chestnut."

"Courtney's hair isn't *chestnut*. It is a deeper brown, with just a hint of red. And gold highlights that glisten in the sun."

"Last I checked, chestnut *was* brown with a hint of red," Baca muttered to herself.

Robert went on. "Besides, can't you see? *That* woman is far too thin. Most of the field agents you've shown me *are* far too thin. They're all built like gymnasts. No curves. You'll never find someone with her shape. It's absolute perfection."

Baca made an audible noise as she exhaled; the same sound a kid might make when playing with toy cars and pretending they are crashing into each other. Dillard and Baca scrolled and scrolled through photos of more female agents, to no avail. Robert found something wrong with everyone they pointed out.

Baca was looking deflated and a bit timid about pointing anyone else out when she said, "Her?" She zoomed in on the one she found. This one had an hourglass shape like Courtney's.

"She doesn't have the right hair," Robert said.

"Hair and face can be transformed. Her height and figure are what matter," Dillard said. "And this one is the closest match we've found."

"She has blue eyes, too," Peter pointed out. "And we're running out of time, Robert."

"If this one doesn't work, you might as well go get Courtney and take her with you. We're out of options," Dillard said.

Robert sighed. "... She does have blue eyes," he admitted. "Who is she?"

"That's Sharon Campbell. She was with Zone B Intelligence before the PAX takeover."

Robert studied the photo. Short blonde hair and large blue eyes. Nice figure too, that made him ache all the more to hold Courtney again.

"Okay," he finally relented. "Let's see you two work your magic."

Baca perked up. "I know how to pick 'em!"

"But what about the voice?" Robert asked.

"Oh ... we've got *that* covered." Dillard waved off the idea as if it was nothing.

28

AGITATED KNIGHT

Eighty-Seven Hours After Disappearance

Another night of dreams about Courtney. Sean woke up feeling frustrated and restless. He walked into his mini kitchen. The studio apartment in the staff quarters at Ranfurly Manor was one big square, with a separate bathroom. A note had been slipped under his entry door. He picked it up and read:

Hey partner. Going for a jog. Want to join me? -J

Jasmine. She'd come so close to dying on their last mission. The thought of losing her … he didn't want to entertain it. He couldn't imagine a world without Jasmine in it.

Was she serious when she said that about getting married? He laughed at himself. *Don't be an idiot. Of course she wasn't serious.*

A few months back, when Sean had proposed marriage, she flat out laughed in his face. He wouldn't make the same mistake twice.

On his way to meet Jasmine for a run he stopped by the barn to check on Courtney's animals again. *I wonder when Courtney will be back.*

Inside the barn, he was surprised to see Gretchen petting Xavier, his horse. It had been a while since he'd seen her. For some reason she had a sour look on her face. *This is the first time I see the resemblance to her mum, Ms. Stern,* Sean thought.

"Hello, Gretch. Something wrong?"

"Hmph!" She stuck her nose up in the air and stomped past him.

Sean caught her by the hand. "Woah, woah! What's this about?"

"Like you really care!" She looked as if she'd been crying.

"I do care. Tell me what's wrong."

"You! *You* are what's wrong! I was so worried about you when you went missing! But ever since you came back, I have no idea what's going on with us. It's like you've been avoiding me…" She started sobbing.

In fact, he had been. The truth was, he hadn't given Gretchen a thought since he met Courtney.

"Oh, Gretchen." Sean drew her in and comforted her. He regretted it instantly. She started kissing him passionately and drug him into an empty horse stall, the one they used to romp around in. Her hands were at his buttons, trying to rip the clothes off of him.

"Woah! Slow down!" Sean could hardly believe the words were coming out of him. "We … we can't do this. Not here!"

"Why not?" She was like a rabid animal. "We've done it before!"

"Okay … no." He moved her hands down. "No, Gretchen. I have a busy day, and I can't do this right now."

She growled like a cat, a playful smile on her face.

"Gretchen, I'm serious. I don't want to play tiger with you today."

"Promise you'll come to see me tonight!" she demanded.

"Actually, I have plans…"

She started tearing his shirt off.

"Gretchen!" It was Ms. Stern's voice calling out from the direction of the manor. "Gretchen!"

Saved by the terrifying Mummy, Sean thought.

Gretchen covered her mouth with a hand and giggled.

"I think you better go now. Mummy's calling," Sean whispered.

"Don't be surprised if you find a tiger in your apartment tonight," she purred into his ear.

Gretchen hurried out the back door of the barn to avoid her mother. Sean felt a sense of relief flood over him.

Where are the dogs, I wonder? When he saw Davey bailing hay outside the barn, he asked, "Have you seen Thor and Loki around?"

"Courtney and her animals went home," Davey told him.

"Wait," Sean was more confused than ever. "Courtney came back? When?"

Davey shrugged. "I think she got back early yesterday morning. She went home sometime yesterday afternoon. I helped her load the animals into her truck before she left."

Sean rummaged through the cabinets where all of Courtney's pet supplies were kept. Almost all of it was gone, except for a few dog bones that were left behind. "Why did she go home?"

"No idea," Davey went back to bailing. "All I know is Lord Ranfurly left for The Greens to search for Elizabeth, and Courtney went home sometime after that."

Sean borrowed Ranfurly's car, the one he liked to drive best—the Royal Rodney.

While driving, he got a call from Jasmine on his DART phone.

"Jasmine? Where are you that you're able to call me on the DART phone? Ranfurly Manor didn't all of a sudden get cell service, did it?"

"Like that will ever happen. I was waiting for you to meet me to go jogging. Then I saw you leaving in the Royal Rodney. So, I rode one of the bikes down to the little town of North Ireland so I could call you."

"Well, well. You're stalking me now. I'm flattered."

"Oh, please! I'm not stalking. But for your own protection, you should at least let me know where you're going before you leave. The last time you took that car, you were chased off into the Wildwoods." There was a pause, as if Jasmine expected him to fess up where he was headed. When he didn't, she went on. "You could have at least had the decency to bring me with you. I hate being stuck out here all the time. Do you know how long it has been since I had a shopping day?"

"Sorry, Jazz."

"So, where are you off to in such a hurry?"

"Just taking a little drive, that's all."

"Taking a little drive to a place called Mill Pond, by any chance? You're going to see *her*, aren't you?"

"Her who?"

"The #$@!%& nanny, Sean!"

"Jasmine, I'm surprised at you. I didn't think you were the jealous type."

"I'm not jealous, Sean. I'm worried that you're going to run into trouble again, and I won't know where you are to be able to drag you out of it like I did last time."

Sean's heart thawed a little as he thought about the way they once were. But as he recalled how she rejected his marriage proposal, it took all but two seconds to re-harden.

"Yes, I'm headed to see Courtney."

Silence on the other end.

"Jasmine? Are you still there?"

"I'm here. I figured as much. Well, if you get in a bind, you know who to call."

"Thank you. I'll keep that in mind." Silence again on the other end of the line. Sean felt a twinge of guilt. "Jasmine…" he started to say.

"Gotta go," she said, and hung up.

Sean sighed. *She only wants me when she can't have me.*

He drove into Mill Pond, and it happened again. A scene flashed through his mind.

He was hanging out by the pond, trying to catch fish with a couple of other teenage boys. One of the boys asked him, "You're playing football this year, right, Keith?"

"Course," he answered. "You?"

Sean rattled his head, as if he could jog out the memory.

Why did that scene just flash into his head? He'd never been to Mill Pond before he'd met Courtney. He never played football, either.

He rolled the car up to Courtney's gate. "Why is there a gate here?" It irked him, seeing the massive cast iron structure that must have cost a fortune.

He saw the dock on the pond, and another scene flashed in his mind.

Courtney was standing on the dock speaking to him. "The kids are at summer camp. We can run around naked all week," she said, laughing. She started to peel her clothes off, and he couldn't keep his hands off of her. "I love you, Keith," she whispered.

"Why am I having these memories where everyone is calling me Keith?" Sean pressed his fingers into his temple. Sweating profusely, he hesitated to push the button on the gate post to alert Courtney that he was waiting. In the end, he decided it would be best to leave.

He got back into the car, and put it in reverse. But then he saw Courtney's truck coming down the road. She waved, and he was forced to stay.

WHILE THE LORD IS AWAY, THE KNIGHT MAKES A PLAY

❧ Courtney ❧

Eighty-Seven Hours After Disappearance

I'd asked Robert to check in with me as soon as he reached The Greens, to keep me updated. I still hadn't heard from him.

Maybe Winnie knows something. I dialed the landline at Ranfurly Manor.

"Hello?" Ms. Stern answered the phone.

"Hi, Ms. Stern. This is Courtney. May I speak with Winnie?"

"Vinnie is vorking and cannot speak vith you at the moment."

"Can you please tell her to call me when she gets off work?"

"I am not Vinnie's secretary, Mrs. Drake." Click.

"Okee…" I let out a long sigh.

I decided my best option was to keep busy so I wouldn't have to tear my hair out waiting by the phone. The first thing I needed to do was go to the local market and stock up on groceries.

On my way back from the store, the Royal Rodney was sitting in front of my new gate that Lord Robert had installed.

I drove up next to it and got out of the truck. "Sean? What are you doing here?" I asked.

"Hi."

"Hi. Have you heard any news about Elizabeth?" I asked, hopeful.

"No. Haven't heard from anyone. ... In fact, I was surprised to find out you weren't looking after Luke. Why'd you leave?" Sean asked. "Aren't you still working as his nanny?"

I felt frustrated, because the truth was I didn't understand it myself. "Yes, but ... Lord Robert wanted me here."

"That makes no sense," Sean scoffed.

"I'm sure he had his reasons."

"He didn't tell you his reasons?"

"Well, his mind was a little preoccupied with his little girl being taken from him!" I snapped. "But I can't expect you to understand. You don't have kids."

"Oh. Nice! Thanks so much for reminding me that I'm half a human because I don't have kids," Sean growled.

"What? That wasn't what I was implying at all."

"Whatever. Well ... how is Thor? That's why I'm here. To check on him."

"He's healing well. The cone is off, so he's much happier."

"Yeah. Bet he was glad to be rid of the cone o' shame."

"Exactly."

An awkward silence passed.

I started to say, "Well, I..."

At the same time, he started to say, "Well I just..."

"Oh... I'm sorry. What were you going to say?" I asked him.

"I just saw that you left a few things behind. I brought them with me."

"Oh! Thank you. It's a long drive, though. You didn't have to."

"I'm aware of how long it takes. I've driven it a few times, if you recall. And I don't consider it a burden. Besides, it's an excuse to get away from the manor. Can I say hello to your animals, now?"

190

I felt a little uneasy. How would Lord Robert feel about Sean visiting me? *And if it is as Robert suspects, and Sean really is a PAX agent ... I don't know what I'll do. I hope Robert is wrong about that.*

"Fancy gate. You finally fenced off the place, I see."

"Yes. Well, no. I didn't. This is all Robert's doing."

"Oh? Robert, is it?" Sean scowled. "Dropped the formalities, have we?"

"Yeah. We've gotten a little closer."

"Could have fooled me, the way he flew off without you, then kicked you off the nanny job."

"It wasn't anything like that, Sean!" I said, annoyed. "Come on, I'll open the gate, and you can follow me down."

Once we got to the house, Thor and Loki greeted us on the porch before Sean helped me carry groceries inside.

"Hey there, boys! I bet you two are glad to be back home!" Sean scratched behind their ears.

I laughed. "Keith used to say that exact same thing to them when they came home from a search and rescue job."

"Yeah?"

A security guard came around the side of my house. Sean pulled out his gun and aimed at the guard. The guard mirrored him.

"Woah! Sean! Stop! That's a security guard!" I shouted.

Sean slowly lowered his weapon. The guard waited until it was back in Sean's pocket before he put his gun back in its holster.

"Ranfurly's doing, I take it?" Sean said.

I nodded.

"Are there any more surprises I should be aware of?" He scrutinized the surroundings.

"There's another guard around here somewhere."

191

We brought in all the groceries, the dogs at Sean's heels the entire time. Sean presented a bone. "Look what Mummy forgot back at Ranfurly Manor?"

Thor and Loki sat, alert.

"So that's why they were at your heels. They smelled that you had a treat. I hope you didn't drive all this way because I forgot one of their bones." I smirked.

"No! Of course not. You forgot *a few* of their bones. Here's another one." He was like a magician, manifesting a second bone.

Shaking my head, I told Sean to make himself comfortable while I put the groceries away.

When I finished, I sat next to him. That's when I noticed the grey shadows under his eyes. "You look tired, Sean."

At first, it seemed like he was far away in his thoughts. He finally said, "Oh? Yeah. I haven't slept well lately."

The dogs barked to be let outside, so I opened the sliding glass door, and they ran out, bones in their mouths. "Neither have I. Not with Elizabeth missing." I pointed to the teal armchair he sat on that was taped up. "I apologize for the furniture. Rayeena did a number on it when she broke in."

Sean

Seeing her taped up furniture, looking like it had been in a war zone, caused Sean's mind to glitch.

Everything that day felt surreal.

He didn't understand all the mixed emotions inside him. It made him feel more out of control than ever. *I should probably leave.*

Courtney didn't know about the dreams he'd been having; she had no idea what it was he really wanted.

Do I even know what I really want? he asked himself. But a voice inside him was whispering, "Why should I leave? She belongs with me."

❧ Courtney ❧

My house cozy, with an open floor plan that had a kitchen/dining/living room combination. I could be in the kitchen and have a conversation with people in the living room, so I made us some coffee.

"Do you need my help with anything?" Sean asked, starting to stand.

"Nope." I put up a hand. "Stay where you are. I've got it."

"I wonder where the dogs went?" he said, gazing outside.

"Probably chasing after deer in the woods. Benefit of living on ten acres far from civilization." I walked over and set his coffee down next to him. "Here ya go."

"Thanks," he said, staring at the coffee with a funny look on his face. I sat down and took a sip of mine.

"I must admit, I make a great cup of coffee. I've been using the Vinosian press, and it tastes so much better, don't you think?"

"Hmm. I should admit something as well, Courtney."

"What?"

"I don't really care for coffee," he said.

"But … last time you were here, I made you coffee. You were just pretending to like it?"

With that same funny look on his face, Sean blinked slowly.

"You could have just told me," I said.

He half grinned, but had no verbal response.

"Well, would you like some tea, then?"

"Water would be great," he said.

"Water. … Okay." I got up and poured him a glass of water from my fridge.

"You're kind of a health nut, aren't you?" I made a yuck face.

"Not really. I just eat clean."

"Nobody should have that much self-discipline. It's disgusting."

He shrugged, then sipped his water. I sat back down and tried to enjoy my coffee, even though I was now feeling guilty for putting something "dirty" in my gut.

"So…" I said, at a loss for words.

"So."

I took another sip, and shifted in my chair.

"Mind if I take a look around?" He asked the question the exact same way a policeman does. Then cupped his hand to his ear, then made his fingers on the other hand crawl, like a spider.

"What are you doing? Are you telling me you heard a spider?" I asked him.

After he did a sweep through of my place, he came back to sit. "Clear," he said.

"No spiders? Good. We can drop the charades, then. Phew." I swiped a finger across my brow.

"You had a break-in here not too long ago. I was checking for bugs. You know … listening devices."

"Oh. *That's* what the crawly spider hand meant." It had never occurred to me that there could be listening devices planted in my home. "Thanks for checking. I guess they teach you all that stuff at PAX spy school."

"Actually, I learned it when I was in the military."

"Oh. But they probably taught you even more cool stuff at the spy school, right?"

Sean wasn't giving away anything. He deflected. "So, you dropped the formalities with Ranfurly. Does this mean you two are a thing … or …?"

I hated the question and wished I could think avoid it. But I wasn't a master at deflecting, as Sean was. "A *thing*?"

"Yeah. Like, are you dating each other? … Exclusively?"

I laughed uncomfortably. *How am I supposed to answer that?* Robert and I hadn't established what we were. "We're … we've gotten close … er. Closer."

He narrowed his eyes. "Closer. How close are we talking about? Inches away, or bodies melding together close?"

I choked on my coffee. "Oh, please, Sean!"

194

"It just seems odd to me. If you're so *close*, why didn't he take you with him? Or at least, why didn't he want you to stay at Ranfurly Manor?"

I felt my cheeks grow hot. "He had his reasons, Sean." I changed the subject.

"You know, you asked about the dogs. We should have seen them by now."

"Hmm." Sean got up and went to the sliding glass doors. "I'll call them."

"Thanks."

He went out back and called for the dogs but instantly curled his top lip up into a snarl. "It smells foul out here. Where is your septic tank?"

I showed him.

"When's the last time it was emptied?" he asked.

I shrugged. "Keith used to handle it. I have no idea."

"For a house this size, it needs to be emptied every three to four years, Courtney. It's probably overdue to be serviced."

"Oh. I didn't realize that. I guess I better find someone."

"You've got someone. *I* know how to do it. But the equipment I'll need is at the manor. I'll come back tomorrow and take care of it for you."

"Oh? Wow. Are you sure?"

"I wouldn't have offered if I wasn't," he said.

"Okay, then. Thanks!"

The dogs came running out of the forest, both still carrying their bones. "Ah, there they are! I'll just say goodbye to the dogs before I head off," Sean said. "Thanks for the chat. And the water."

"Oh. Alright. You're welcome." *Thanks for the chat? He came all the way out to pet the dogs, and question my relationship with Robert? Sean is so strange sometimes.*

WINNIE'S WINDFALL

❧ Winnie ❧

Ninety Hours After Disappearance

Since Lord Robert had left, Ms. Stern was a slavedriver of a boss. Winnie wasn't the sort to put up with it, but she didn't want to blow her cover, either. So … she had to suck it up and play along like she was one of the regular hired help.

When she was working, Winnie watched the minute hand pass and counted the seconds until she clocked out. Every chance she had, she eavesdropped on staff conversations. *If one of them helped the intruder get on and off the property, I'll find out who.*

She wrote out a list of all the facts she had thus far:

1. The intruder was the one Uncle Robert called Snake.

2. Lord Robert's first encounter with Snake was when he found one of the dead victims in an alley in Emer Aude. The victim was wearing the serpent earrings with the rubies. Snake had been at the scene of the crime when he stabbed Robert and got away.

3. His second encounter was when he found Snake coming out of a club in Emer Aude. Snake escaped a second time.

4. His third encounter was when he busted up a traffic ring in an abandoned logging warehouse close to Ranfurly Manor. Snake got away a third time that night on foot.

5. Days later Snake turned up on the Ranfurly property and kidnapped Elizabeth and her pony.

6. Courtney found the pony's tracks and a backpack that contained more serpent earrings with rubies, plus two aerosol spray cans. But nobody knew what liquid they contained. Also found inside the backpack was an address of a café written on a piece of paper.

7. Lord Robert had a top-notch security system around the perimeter that should have triggered loud alarms if a human crossed it.

"There has to be another way to get on the property," she said audibly, in the habit of talking out loud to herself.

For days, she searched all over, but was having no luck finding anything. Until, at last, the wind blew in her direction. Literally.

During one of her daily run around the grounds, a gust of wind blew so hard, it knocked a huge evergreen over. The tree landed across Winnie's path. If she wouldn't have glanced up in time, she'd be trapped under it. Fortunately, she did look up and got out of the way, but now it blocked her from going the normal way.

She took a detour through the gated pool terrace. It was quiet. Not even the CAPE guards were in sight. She peered into the giant drained hole that was once the swimming pool. "I'm gonna tell Uncle Robert he needs to fill it. This job could use a perk."

A strange noise caused her to whip her head around. "Where did *that* come from?" she said to herself.

She heard the noise again, this time she could tell it was coming from the direction of the pump house. "What is that?"

She opened the large double glass doors and stepped inside.

"Hello?" Nobody was in sight. She took in the tall ceilings with high windows that let in the sunlight, and it reminded Winnie of a grand ballroom. She spun around and did some awkward looking dance moves. (She wasn't much of a dancer.) *This really would make a great pool cabana,* she thought.

A scraping noise inside the room caused her to freeze. She looked around, mortified that somebody might have been watching her little dance number. She heard the noise again. Scraping. Then a whinny. "Why does it sound like there's a horse in here?"

The night they followed Lady Rose's hoof tracks it had been dark when they checked inside the pump house. Now it was daylight, and the room was obviously empty. "No way is there a horse hiding in here," Winnie said out loud. "Unless Lady Rose died and her ghost is haunting me."

Scrape. Scrape.

"Lady?" Winnie called out to the ghost.

"Neigh!"

"Wait. That sounds like it is coming from the floor!" She knelt down and tried lifting up the floorboards. That's when she found some of them weren't nailed in. She lifted them out, and beneath them was a sub-floor.

"Neigh!"

She lifted up more boards until the entire sub-floor was visible. "There's a trap door here!" She opened it, and found herself looking at the top of a pony's head.

"Neigh!"

"Lady Rose!" Winnie said, shocked. "How did you get down there?"

Lady Rose snorted.

"Hang on, girl. I'll find some help to get you out." *The poor thing. How long has she been trapped in there?* Winnie ran back to the stables and found Davey. "Davey, I need your help in the pump house."

"Why? What were you doing in the pump house?"

Winnie explained.

"*Lady Rose* is in there?" Davey wobbled his head, baffled. "How is that even possible?"

Winnie shrugged. "I have no idea. The creep that kidnapped Elizabeth must have forced her down into the hole. I hope to God her legs aren't broken. But if we don't get her out of there, she looks like she might drop dead any second. Can you help me get her out?"

"Okay. Did she still have a saddle on her?"

"Yeah," Winnie said.

"Good, we can use it. Grab a couple of ropes, and some gloves. I'll try to find the Butters brothers to see if they'll help."

A little while later, they were working with the Butters brothers to lift the pony out of the hole.

Once they successfully hoisted the Lady up and out, Davey checked out her legs. "Good news. They don't appear to be broken." He patted Lady Rose on her snout. "Poor girl. Bet you'd like some food and water, and a nice brush down." The Butters brothers went back out to work in the gardens, and Davey led Lady Rose back to her stable.

Left alone, Winnie jumped down through the trap door to get a look at the space. It was quite a drop down into it. She landed on all fours, scraping up her knees and palms on gravel. "Ow!"

She tapped the flashlight on her cell phone. "This isn't just a little hole in the ground. A semi-truck could fit inside here."

Winnie shone her light on the gravel and walked around, expecting to eventually run into a wall. But she never did. "It must be a tunnel," she said out loud.

She came to switchbacks and was heading down a steep decline. She considered turning back many times. But curiosity won out, and she continued.

The tunnel seemed to go on forever, until she finally, heard the rushing sound of water. Soon after that, the tunnel opened up into a low canyon. Drawn in by the sound of the water, she walked toward it. Vertical walls of granite towered high above her, and a waterfall, maybe two-thousand feet tall, poured over one of the granite walls and crashed into the river.

"Wow, Ranfurly Manor is way up there," she said to herself. "The only way to reach it is to scale those slippery granite cliffs. Unless you know about this tunnel. This is how Snake must have escaped. He must have abandoned Lady after he got out of the tunnel and reached a vehicle. Fortunately, the pony found her way back home."

DOTH MINE EYES DECEIVE ME?

❧ *Lord Robert* ❧

Ninety Hours After Disappearance

Robert had to wait far too long for Dillard and Baca to "work their magic."

Peter finally gave him notice that they were ready to meet him at a private runway. Robert arrived first, and sat inside the airplane while he waited for Peter and Sharon to arrive.

Robert was watching out of the airplane window when a car finally drove up and the driver stepped out. To his amazement, it wasn't Peter or Sharon.

He ran down the airplane steps. "Courtney!" She smiled up at him, and he lifted her off of her feet. "What are you doing here?" he whispered. "You shouldn't have come. I told you to stay in Mill Pond."

"I missed you," she said.

"Hmm." He inhaled her. She smelled different. Not like her usual, irresistible scent. "What is that fragrance? You've never worn it before."

"Do you like it?" she asked. "I wore it especially for you."

"It's … interesting." Robert couldn't possibly tell her that he didn't really care for it. "I've missed you terribly. Forgive me for not calling. I've wanted to, but it's been a whirlwind."

"I understand," she said.

"Have you heard from Winnie about how Luke is doing? I haven't had a minute to check on anyone."

"Luke is fine."

"Good. And Winnie's alright? Any news about finding out how Snake got on the property?"

"Winnie's great. But no news."

"Oh, Courtney, I still can't believe she's gone."

"I know." She put a hand on his arm.

"By the way, how did you find me here?"

"Peter told me where you would be. You aren't mad that I came, are you? I just had to see you."

"Peter told you?" *Why did Peter tell her?* Robert drew her in to hug her.

Something felt … not normal. His fingers usually tingled when they touched her. But today … the chemistry between them wasn't happening. He stepped back and searched her eyes, hoping to find the unspoken connection between them.

That's when he understood. "Good lord…"

She smiled and held out a hand to shake. "I'm Sharon. Pleasure to meet you, Lord Ranfurly."

"Unbelievable. Even the voice is the same…"

"All thanks to CAPE Tech," she said loud into her comms.

Dillard and Baca were listening in on the entire meeting, munching on licorice. They toasted with their licorice vines.

They arrived on the grounds of The Retreat and headed to Lug, arriving just in time for their midnight deadline.

Courtney's lookalike—Sharon—accompanied him into the club. They were told to wait in the Red Room.

Snake came out to greet them, sneering. "So, you decided to follow orders this time. Good boy."

"Where's Elizabeth?" Robert said through gritted teeth.

Snake snickered. "Follow me." He led them through a black door, down a black painted hallway, and into a manmade cave. Waterfalls fell into a pool filled with koi.

Robert stopped short when he saw what looked like a real mermaid swimming in the pool. It wasn't the fact that she seemed real that sent a jolt through him, though. It was the face, the eyes, the long red hair that covered her bare breasts.

Desiree.

The woman could have been his dead wife's identical twin. She was wearing the exact costume Desiree had worn when she starred in the film, *The Mermaid*. One of the songs she sang in the film was playing through a sound system. At first, Robert believed it was a recording of Desiree singing. But then he entered another room and saw who the voice belonged to – a different lookalike Desiree, singing on a stage. She was dressed in the di Bianco dress that Desiree had worn the night he met her at his cousin Raymond's party. The woman crooned away through a retro-style microphone.

How is this possible?

There was a man in the room, watching the singer, his back to them. When the singer finished the song, he clapped. The singer's icy blue eyes flickered and focused on the man. *Desiree's eyes.* The look she gave the man was the look Desiree used to give Robert. That look of love and devotion. She smiled as the man praised her performance. *Desiree's smile.*

But it isn't really Desiree. It can't be.

As if she could read his thoughts, the singer's gaze flashed over and focused directly on Robert. An unsettling feeling came over him. In her eyes, he found no warmth, no look of love. It was as if he was looking into glass.

The man in the room stood and turned around to face Robert and Sharon.

His hair was whiter; his skin had a few more lines. But there was no mistaking who the man was.

"Wellington."

"It has been quite some time since we last met, hasn't it?" Wellington smiled, his teeth shimmering in the dimly lit room, reminding Robert of a vampire.

"I see you're trying to replace the irreplaceable," Robert said. "Found a couple of actresses to play the part?"

"True, there is no replacing Desiree Diamond. It isn't possible. But I do like to have daily reminders of her. She was always my favorite. As I know she was yours." Wellington smiled at the one he believed was Courtney.

Robert vomited in his mouth. "Where is my daughter?"

"All in good time, Robert. All in good time. One must show patience, mustn't one?" Wellington grinned. "I've certainly been a patient man, all these years ... I never believed for a moment that you were dead. No ... I just had to wait. And now, my patience is paying off."

"What is it you want from me?" Robert tried to maintain his calm, but couldn't. He slammed a fist into the table he was standing next to.

"I want so many things, Robert. So many things." He pointed his chin at Sharon/Courtney. "For starters, I want *her*."

"She's not available," Robert said.

"Then your daughter is as good as lost to you forever." Wellington's thin lips curved up at the edges. "Come here, Courtney. Robert and I are going to have a little chat, and you get to listen."

"She'll stay with me," Robert tightened his grip on Sharon/Courtney's hand.

"Do you want to see Elizabeth alive or not?" Wellington asked.

"It's okay. I'll be okay," Sharon/Courtney said. She let go of Robert's hand and crossed the room to stand next to Wellington.

"Now, that's better. Let's all have a seat, shall we?" Wellington sat, forcing Sharon/Courtney onto his lap. "Do you remember when you stole Desiree away from me, Robert? Because I do. All too well."

"I remember you were an abusive monster who never deserved her."

"Me, abusive? Is that what she made you believe? Well…" He laughed.

"Desiree was always a good actress. I suppose she had her own selfish reasons for turning on me like that."

"I saw the way you treated her. We were outside a restaurant, and you hit her after she said something about your gambling problem."

Wellington glowered at Robert. Then his expression lightened. He snorted. "That was nothing. You caught us in the middle of a petty lover's quarrel. Then you decided to interfere in our business. No, Robert. I wasn't ever a monster to Desiree. In fact, I was the one who *rescued* her."

Robert scoffed. "You're deranged."

"Do you know who the real monster was? Her father. And do you know what she was before I met her?"

Robert clenched his jaw, refusing to speak.

"I have a feeling you don't. Desiree was careful to keep her past from leaking out." Wellington spoke softly, directly to Sharon/Courtney. "She was only sixteen when I met her. The girl could convince anyone of anything. She was raised by a drunk. Grew up picking pockets on the streets." He clicked his tongue. "A tragic, terrible childhood."

Sharon/Courtney swallowed. Wellington continued, speaking softly to her, as if she was his lover. "Her real name was Katie Smith, but her father called her Kitty. He sold her to men from the time she was only eight years old, all to line his pockets with gold pins. She learned from a young age how to play any part, how to trick any man."

Robert's fists clenched, his knuckles went white.

"But then she met me, and I offered her an alternative to that life."

He would not give Wellington the satisfaction of knowing the story was ripping into him. But the truth was, Robert never really knew his late wife. He'd fallen hard and fast and was taken in by her charms. She was the damsel in distress, he her rescuer.

Wellington continued. "I connected her with all the right playhouses, and she rose to the top in no time. I even came up with the perfect stage name. *Desiree Diamond.* I knew she would be a smash. Of course I knew. I came from a family of actors myself, back in The Goldens. I also had to play roles to get where I am now. Kitty and I understood each other that way."

He beckoned for the singer to come to him. She obeyed. His free hand caressed her hip. "She was sixteen when she fell in love with me. And I loved her. We married."

Robert shuddered. "No." Even Sharon/Courtney was shocked.

"Yes." Wellington continued. "A few years after we married, I became an agent with Zone A Intelligence. They needed someone to get information, and I knew Kitty was perfect for the job. No, I didn't want to share her with other men, but I knew she was mine at the end of the day. So once again, she slept with men, but this time it was to learn their secrets.

"Still … she was always mine." Wellington's steely gaze bore into Robert. "Until you came along and ruined her." Wellington began to grope Sharon/Courtney inappropriately. She pushed him away. He smiled a sickly grin. "It's your fault Desiree is dead, Robert," Wellington said.

"I didn't kill her," Robert said through clenched teeth.

"Maybe it wasn't by your hand, but you are the one to blame. She was too sharp to be taken off guard before you came along. You weakened her. I didn't know the full picture back then. But *now* I can see *why* she was weakened," Wellington glowered. "She was bloody pregnant!"

"So that's why you stole my daughter from me? This is all your sick way of getting revenge?"

"*Your* daughter? I'm certain she is Desiree's. But I'm not certain she's really *yours*. After all, Desiree was still sleeping with *me* while she was married to you."

Robert had to hold himself back from lunging at the monster.

Wellington continued to dig the knife in. "You must have known it. The times I came to your house in Upland when you were away. … You were so jealous of me. And you had every reason to be. I was her rightful husband."

Robert remembered. He was on his way to kill Wellington, just before Desiree told him she was pregnant. The news is what stopped him. *I should have killed him years ago, when I had the chance.*

Wellington went on. "And the child's eyes are something … Yes, you have green eyes. But then again, so does Simon DuPont. If I recall, Desiree was sleeping with him as well, because I told her to. It seems that a DNA test is the only way we'll ever know who Elizabeth's *real* father is."

Robert was out of the chair and at Wellington's throat. The Desiree lookalike moved like a cheetah, and stabbed a knife into Robert's hand, causing him to release his grip. At the same time, Sharon/Courtney lunged at the Desiree lookalike. But the mermaid Desiree had Sharon pinned to the ground, the tip of her knife at Sharon's throat.

"You really don't want to see your daughter alive, do you?" Wellington ticked his tongue. Pressing a button in his chair, he alerted his men. "Take them to the holding cell." A fiendish grin crossed Wellington's face. "Have you heard of The Heights, Robert?"

Robert glowered.

"I'm sure you must have, since you spent summers in Highland. In three days, you'll be a special guest in my lodgings there. I'm getting your room prepared now. It has a lovely mountain view. But alas, I just got notice that The Ten need me. They *are* very demanding, mustn't keep them waiting.

❧ Peter ❧

The CAPE Tech team was listening closely to everything through the listening devices they'd placed inside Robert's and Sharon's shoes.

"He will be taking them to The Heights," Peter repeated.

"The tallest, most deadly mountains in the world are there," Dillard added.

As they were listening, the line went static.

"Oh no! Guys?" Baca said. "We just lost the signal to the trackers that Robert and Sharon are wearing!" Baca said.

COURTNEY'S
CLAG-FREE DAY

❧ *Courtney* ❧

One-Hundred-One Hours After Disappearance

Another day and I still hadn't heard from Robert, Winnie, or Peter. I was sick with worry. But for better or for worse, I had Sean to distract me again.

"This thing will let off some toxic fumes when I open the cover. You might want to stay inside the house."

I obeyed and headed back inside, leaving Sean to deal with the septic tank.

It was six in the morning when he showed up at my house to work on it. Way too early, but I couldn't exactly complain. The foul odor was becoming more unbearable with each passing hour. Even the guards were walking around with twitching faces, looking as if they were about to gag.

Mid-morning, Sean came up and tapped on the sliding glass door. I slid it open a crack, fearful that I might let fumes inside. "You survived!"

"All fixed. Should be good for a while." He sighed. "Well, I need a shower now. Better be on my way."

207

"Oh! Well ... thank you for helping me today ... I'll definitely pay you for doing that. But I need to go get some pins at the bank. I don't have anything on me."

"No, you don't have to *pay* me. I'm not doing this for *pins*." He dismissed the idea with the wave of a hand. "I'll go around to get to my car. You don't want me traipsing through your house with the smell of your clag on me."

"My clag?" I wondered if I heard him correctly.

"Yeah. Don't you know what clag is? ... Jobbies?" He gave me a sideways smirk.

I squinted up at him. "Can you speak in *my* language now please?"

"I suppose I could just call the dump in your septic $#!%, but I like my Highlandish better."

I laughed. "Oh! That's what you call it in Highland? Jobbies? And what was the other word you said?"

"Clag."

"Clag. Okay, fair enough." I said. "Well then ... thank you for eliminating my jobbies, Sean."

He nodded as he turned and headed back around my house to his Royal Rodney. Before he rounded the corner, he stopped. "Call if you need anything else."

I lifted a shoulder and smiled. "Thanks."

He gave me a nod before he disappeared from view.

   ***

The phone rang. As usual, my heart skipped, hoping it was Lord Robert with news about Elizabeth.

It was just Sean. Again.

"Hi Courtney."

"Oh, hi Sean."

"Sorry to disappoint you."

"What? No! I'm not disappointed. ... I was just hoping to hear news about Elizabeth by now. *You* haven't heard anything, have you?"

"No. Haven't heard. But, um … I'm out at your gate. Want to let me in?"

"You're at my gate? Really?"

"I have a little surprise for you," he said.

"A little surprise? It isn't a puppy, is it?"

"You'll have to let me in if you want to find out what it is."

What kind of a surprise could he have brought me? I pressed the remote and let him through.

A few minutes later, he showed up at my door looking freshly showered and wearing a very nice black button up shirt and black pants. In his hands were two large, insulated bags.

"What do you have there?" I asked.

"Dinner. From a world-renowned Vinosian restaurant in Emer Aude."

"You did *not* drive all the way out there after you left today—just to get that."

"No. After I left today, I drove all the way back to Ranfurly Manor. Then I showered off the contamination of your septic full of jobbies, and put on these nice, freshly washed clothes to make me feel like the swoon-worthy guy that I truly am. It was then that I drove all the way to Emer Aude to pick up this meal. And now, here I am." He smiled brightly and lifted the bags up.

"You're definitely a little cray cray!" I rattled my head.

"I've been accused of worse. … But wait 'til you've had a taste. Then decide for yourself if you wouldn't have gone all that way for it."

I smiled. "Well, come in!" I beckoned him to come inside. "You caught me just in time. I was just about to sit down and eat."

"Oh? I hope you didn't slave in the kitchen cooking up something."

"Not exactly." I smiled, knowing how little effort I put into my dinner.

We went to the kitchen/dining/living room. Sean spied the bowl of cereal sitting on my dining table and gave me a disgusted look. "You know that isn't real food, don't you? Processed flour. Corn syrup. It should be outlawed, Courtney! It's terrible for you!"

"Yeah, well, if I knew the nutrition police were going to show up tonight, I would have hid the evidence."

"Oh, Courtney, I can't wait to see you try this." He raised his eyebrows up and down. "Then you'll understand what real food is."

"You expect me to trust your judgment when all you ever put in your body is that disgusting shake thingy." I curled up a lip in disgust.

"Oh, that's just a daily routine for me. On special occasions, I eat like a king." He puffed out his chest.

"But this isn't a special occasion."

"It most certainly is. It's the day your jobbies were eliminated, which makes it a very special day."

"Oh. Is that right?"

"Courtney's Clag-Free Day."

"Lovely. I always wanted a holiday named after me."

"And now you have one. So…" He went into my kitchen and searched through cabinets and drawers until he found plates and forks. He brought them to the table. "Here you are. And one more thing…" He found wine glasses and set them down by the plates. Then he bustled around looking for something. "… Ah, here we go!" He snagged an apron that was hanging up near the stove, and put it on.

"Wow. Chef Sean. You put on quite a show!" I clapped for him. "But it must have gotten cold by now. I have paper plates that you can use to reheat the food in the microwave. Besides, there will be fewer dishes to clean if we use paper plates."

He shot a disdainful look my way. "Microwave? Lardie, woman! What is wrong with you. If I did have to reheat the food, I certainly wouldn't nuke it inside that little box. No, no, no. The restaurant provides these insulated bags which keep things hot, cold, or frozen for up to six hours. No need to reheat or chill."

"Fancy that!" I felt the bags. One was warm, the other cold to the touch.

"That's because people travel from far, far away to get this takeout. I'm not the first, and I won't be the last." After opening a couple of kitchen drawers, he found the oven mitts and proceeded to pull a foil tray out of the hot bag. "Bop bah bada!" he sang, as he lifted the lid off the foil

210

tray. A tangy aroma wafted through the air, filling my senses, causing my mouth to water.

"Oh … I need something to dish this out," he said. I started to get up to help. "You, lassie, sit back down. Can't have you working on your holiday."

He found the serving spoons and a wine opener. It was impossible not to giggle a little. He was so entertaining.

Sean twirled a fork of the colorful pasta and plated it. My stomach growled, as the pungent scent of garlic blended with herbaceous notes of basil and oregano made its way to my nose.

He revealed something else out of the hot bag. "I ordered this especially with you in mind, Courtney."

"Ooh! What is it? Smells fantastic!" He set the box down in front of me, and opened it. "For you."

A beautiful display of fresh, warm garlic bread with basil leaves baked into the top of each piece was before me. I reached out to try a piece, and he swatted my hand.

"Wait. We have to do this meal the right way, Courtney."

"But … it's bread. People eat bread before the meal, as an appetizer," I said, desperate to try it.

He gave me a warning look.

"Okay," I pouted.

Next he presented a tray from out of the cold food bag. Inside was a salad with black olives, tomatoes, feta cheese, and salami chunks. "There should be a dressing with it. Let's see. Oh, here it is, in this cool little pocket built into the cold bag. Very good."

He proceeded to toss a side of vinaigrette dressing into the salad, then dished a healthy pile of it on smaller plates and set them on the table. "Oh! I left the wine in the car. Be right back." He went out the front door and returned a few minutes later with a bottle of red wine. He opened it and held the cork to my nose.

"Mmm. Hints of blackberry?" I guessed.

"Marionberry, actually. This will be a nice pairing, I think." He poured us each half a glass. "Ah! Here we are!" He sat across from me at my little dining table.

"Wow. I must say, quite impressive, Sean."

"I know. I am. Oh, wait ... We aren't quite ready yet. We need the right music." He found a playlist of Vinosian music on his phone. An operatic baritone's voice bellowed out through the phone speaker. "Now, we're ready."

I started to reach for a piece of that bread I'd been dying to taste. He swatted my hand. Again.

"But first, we must thank the gods of Vinosa."

"Thank the gods of Vinosa?"

"I always thank them when I'm about to eat at this restaurant."

I laughed. "I think I better just thank the one God, and leave the rest out of it. Since Elizabeth went missing, I've been doing a lot more talking to Him lately. I don't want to get him jealous by praying to the others."

"That works too." We both bowed our heads and prayed in silence. Then I bit into a piece of lettuce.

"Mmm. This salad ... is so fresh! And the dressing ... mmm. Amazing."

Sean pointed at my pasta with his fork. "No, no. You're supposed to eat the salad last. Try the pasta now," he ordered, his mouth full of food. He watched me intently as I slowly forked in a bite.

Growing up with a Vinosian grandmother who was an amazing cook, I wasn't easily impressed when it came to Vinosian restaurants in Cascadia. But this ... the pasta was so fresh, and the sauce ... oh my, my, my. Absolutely addictive. I devoured everything on my plate, and wished I could find room for more. But I was so full!

"I told you." Sean gave me a warning look. "Now, you'd better never question my taste again, lassie."

"Believe me, I've learned my lesson!" I laughed.

"Okay ... stay put. I'll do the dishes." Sean stood and bussed our plates.

"I don't know if I'll be able to get up, I'm so stuffed."

After he finished in the kitchen, I was wishing to burn off the feeling of heaviness from the hefty meal. "Since you've been on the road way too much today, and since you bought my dinner, and cleaned out by jobbies, why don't you let me treat you to something fun, now."

Sean raised his eyebrows. "What kind of fun do you have in mind?"

"Let's go out! I'll pay!"

"Yaldi! Are you asking me on a date?"

I didn't want him getting the wrong idea. "No, Sean. This isn't a date. I'm with Lord Robert."

"Really? You're *with* him. The only ones I see here are you and me. Admit it … you're asking me on a date, Courtney. It isn't anything to be ashamed of. I don't blame ya. I've got these chiseled abs, and this very handsome face. I'd ask myself out too, if I were you."

I rolled my eyes. "I'm asking you out *as a friend*. And because I owe you big time for doing that *jobby* today."

"Ooh … a friend. Right. So … what do you have in mind?"

"There's a new bowling alley in Mill Pond. I've never been there yet. Wanna go?"

He chuckled. "Well, that wasn't what I had in mind, but okay. I like bowling."

I found out the humbling way that the Highland-born man was an experienced bowler.

"Another strike, Sean? Seriously? You should have warned me that you were a champion bowler."

"If you're going to be with me, you might as well get used to losing. I'm a natural at pretty much every sport." Sean flexed his biceps as he lifted the bowling ball and flashed that grin of his.

"And you're so very humble about it, too."

We finished the second game, and he scored two-hundred-ninety to my one-hundred-fifty. "You couldn't even pretend to be bad for my sake?" I asked him.

"So, what now? Is there a good place to get ice cream around here?" Sean asked.

"You want ice cream? After that hefty dinner? Do health nuts like you even eat ice cream?" I raised an eyebrow.

"On occasion. And tonight is definitely the right occasion."

"Actually, there's a cute little ice cream parlor and candy store on Main Street, and luckily they stay open late. Can you believe it's almost ten o'clock? It's still light out too!"

Sean's eyes widened. "Oh my! That's so late!" He was clearly mocking me. "Come on! The sun is only just setting! The night is young!" He put his hand on the small of my back and led me over to a brown leather couch, where we changed out of the bowling shoes we'd rented. "This was a great idea you had."

"Thanks. I do have great ideas," I said.

He chuckled. "On the tame side, but..."

"Tame? Bowling is too tame for you, Sean?"

"Well, it isn't exactly *wild*. The next time we go out, I'll show you what less tame can be like." He flashed a wicked grin.

His insinuation didn't fly over my head. "Woah..." I scrunched up my face as if I'd tasted sour milk.

He glanced at me sideways. "You might like it, Courtney. Just wait 'til you try it."

"Shame on you, bad boy." I smirked.

Maybe hanging out like this was a mistake. I hope I'm not leading him on. But on the other hand, he went out of his way to help me, then the dinner. That was nice. The truth was, I liked being with Sean because he was a great distraction from reality—Elizabeth missing, not hearing from Robert. When I was alone, I did nothing but literally pull my hair out, worrying about them.

We headed to the Mill Pond Creamery where we enjoyed splitting a hot fudge sundae. Once we'd finished, Sean asked, "So, what now?"

"Now? I'm about to turn into a pumpkin if you don't take me home," I said.

"Ah. And here I am, all amped up after winning two games and eating sugar."

"Well, glad I could help inflate your ego even more by losing to you."

"How would you like to come back to Ranfurly Manor and keep me company for the long drive? I can bring you home tomorrow."

"And endure the mighty Ms. Stern? No thank you." No way did I want to go back there. Besides, if I showed up with Sean, the staff might get the wrong idea about us. The last thing I wanted was a false rumor going around about us, that might get back to Robert.

Sean let out a long sigh. "Very well, then. I'll drop you off and drive all the way back *by myself*." He yawned. "Hopefully I can stay awake."

"I can make you some coffee. Oh wait, you don't drink coffee…"

We arrived at my house. Sean got out of my truck and unlocked the Royal Rodney. "Hey … have you heard back from the chemist regarding that aerosol can yet?" I asked him before he left.

"Not yet. I'll let you know when I do."

SACRED SECRETS

⤙ Peter ⤚

One-Hundred-Forty Hours After Disappearance

"Still no signal from the trackers on Robert or Sharon?" Peter asked Dillard.

"No. Nothing," Dillard said.

"All we have to go on is that they will be headed to The Heights tomorrow," Peter said. "I'll send McGregor and Kila there to search for them."

⤙ Courtney ⤚

The weather was hotter than usual in Western Cascadia, which wasn't helping my mood. I still hadn't heard anything from Robert. It was difficult not to think the worst.

Laurel was too busy writing essays to have long phone chats, and I hadn't heard from Nick, either. That concerned me, because he was usually good at texting daily to check in.

That day, I wanted to get outside and breathe in the fresh air of my forest. It was cooler beneath the giant evergreens. Sean rolled up in the Royal Rodney just as I started to walk down a trail.

"You know, it isn't safe to go traipsing around the woods alone, little girl," he said, acting like he was a Big Bad Wolf.

"I'm not alone. I have the animals to protect me." On cue, Thor and Loki came down the trail to greet Sean.

"May I join you on your little hike?" Sean asked.

We walked through the forest, listening to the sounds of different birds. As we approached the mound that led to the mine where I'd first spotted the dragon in my forest, Sean stopped abruptly.

"Is something wrong?" I asked, my mind instantly flitting back to the dragon sighting, which he knew nothing about.

"I've been here before. In a dream," he said. There was a strange, perplexed look on his face.

"Here? In my forest? What was the dream about?" I asked.

He pressed his fingers into his temple and closed his eyes. "There was a mine on the other side of that mound." He pointed to where I saw the dragon emerge. "And an older boy ... a brother. He died inside it."

I gaped at him. *He couldn't have dreamt that. It was impossible. He must have known about the cave-in, must have read about Keith's brother, maybe in an old archive.* I narrowed my brow. "If you find that funny, then you're twisted, Sean."

Sean stepped back. "What? There isn't *really* a mine on the other side of that mound, is there?"

"Stop trying to mess with me."

"Mess with you? Is that what you think I'm doing?" He looked as annoyed with me as I was with him. "I'm not. I really did have a dream about this place."

I crossed my arms, and I'm pretty sure my nostrils were flaring. "You must have learned about Keith's brother dying in the mine."

"Keith had a brother who died in a mine?" Sean slowly turned his head in the direction of the mine, as if it was a giant portal to another dimension and something terrible was coming out of it.

"Why would you dream about Keith's brother if you didn't know about it?"

A wild look came over him. "I have no idea."

A silence as thick as stone filled the space between us. As usual, when I feel uncomfortable, I resorted to blurting. "Well, I saw a dragon come out of that mine a couple of times."

Sean had a glossed-over look. "Hmm?"

"A dragon. I think it might actually live inside the mine."

A half smile crossed his face. "Now *you're* messing with *me*."

I didn't smile. "I'm not. It's true."

"Wow. I hope it wasn't one of those carnivorous red ones." Now he was just being a smart ass.

I put a hand on a hip. "You think I'm joking. Well, I'm not. And for your information, it's orange."

"Right," Sean said, staring at the cedar that had been struck by lightning—the same tree Keith once carved our initials in when we were teenagers. He ran over to it. "What happened to this tree?" he asked. Then he mumbled, "It was always my favorite."

Once again, he baffled me. I followed as he walked around the huge trunk to the spot where the initials were carved. He traced his fingers over the carving.

"How could this be your favorite tree?" I demanded. "You've never been in my forest before! At least that's what you told me. Clearly, you lied!"

"No. I wasn't lying!" He was now shouting, red faced and angry. "I haven't been here before! I don't know how I knew these initials were here!" He tugged at his hair like a madman. "... I used to climb this tree as a boy! I mean—*I* didn't. But in my dreams, I did!"

"*Keith* used to climb the tree as a boy." I said quietly, watching him. "Nobody knew about those initials except Keith and me. Nobody. Not even my own kids." I traced a finger over the carving. It had been years since I'd visited that spot. *If Sean has never been in my forest, how could he know this?*

"Sean, who are you?"

"Courtney..." He paused. "I don't know how to explain this. ... You're going to think I'm crazy."

"Too late. I already think that."

218

We sat on a log. "Okay, look," he began, "… the truth is, ever since the first day I drove to this property, the place was familiar to me. Then I met you. But I'd already seen you many times before. In dreams."

I half believed him, and half thought what he was telling me must be impossible.

"Do you remember the day I came here and played your piano?" he asked.

"The day you told me I was already hired at Ranfurly Manor?" I asked. "Then you went missing?"

"Yes. That day."

I crossed my arms. "It's hard to forget that day. You lied to me about being hired."

"I lied about you being hired because I was scrambling for some way to keep you in my life."

"You said you were drawn to me … said I had magnetic powers."

He smiled. "That was true. But the part I didn't tell you is that I felt I already knew you." He paused, as if he was going to stop talking altogether.

"Go on."

"Look, I know it sounds crazy, but it's the truth, Courtney. I have no idea why, no idea what it means, but I was dreaming about you a year before I met you. I even dreamt that I made love to you by a cove somewhere. *Somewhere here* … on this property, I think. We called the place The Swing. The dream was so real, Courtney, it is still etched in my mind. It was our first time making love and…"

I stood up and covered my ears, shouting. "Stop! Stop! What are saying? That you're *him*?"

He stood up and roared. "No, I'm not saying I'm Keith! I'm *not* him! I should know if I was!"

"But that is *my* memory! With *Keith*! How could you know about it? Nobody knew! It was a secret. Nobody knew!"

"Oh really? Then why do *I* know? In fact, I can probably find the place myself, I know it so well."

"That's impossible." I challenged him with a glare. He returned the glare, then stormed off in the direction of The Swing. "Fine! Be my guest. Lead the way!" I called after him.

He marched on toward the place where my most sacred secret had been kept from the rest of the world. I started to shake uncontrollably, shivers causing goosebumps to form on my skin. He led us through long abandoned, unmarked trails.

"There used to be a trail here," he said.

He was right. There once was, but I'd let it grow over with weeds. It had been years since I'd gone to The Swing. The last time was long before Keith died. But Sean found another way to go, and continued in the right direction. We climbed through some thick areas, thorns pricking my arms and legs, until we were back on the trail that led to the cove. Then he stopped and stood, looking at me.

"Nick wasn't planned!" Sean said in his fury. "He was conceived right here, the very first time we were together!"

He caught the look on my face and his countenance softened. He seemed to have realized what he'd said, and regretted it.

I broke down, fell on my hands and knees to the dirt. *What is going on? Who is this man? How does he know?*

Sean helped me up and folded me into his arms. "I'm sorry ... I'm sorry. I didn't mean it to come out like that." He nuzzled my neck. "Courtney-coo."

Courtney-coo? ... That was Keith's pet name for me.

"Stop! Stop telling me you aren't him! You have to be! You are! You are Keith!" I beat my fists into his chest with all my strength, overcome with emotions. Hate, fear, regret, longing.

He stood firm, and allowed me to hit him until I was so exhausted, I collapsed into him and sobbed.

He held me there for a long time, and my body ached for what it once had in that exact place, where I'd first given myself to Keith. The feelings I had were so strong, they felt true. I thought for certain my husband was actually alive, in the form of Sean Knight. I kissed him. "Keith."

Sean backed away. "No. I promise you ... I'm not Keith."

"Then … how do you know the things only he should know?"

Sean brushed my cheek with the back of his hand. "I'm sorry. I wish to God I knew. And I never meant to hurt you by telling you this. Never. It's just that, well … it's been driving me crazy. I don't understand any of it. It's … it's as if your husband's ghost is invading my dreams."

LITTLE DISCOVERIES

One-Hundred-Sixty Hours After Disappearance

Heart racing, dripping in sweat, he cried out so loud he woke himself.
Why do I keep having the same dream?

In this repeating dream, Courtney was running from a faceless person, and he was shouting at her to stop. He had no idea what it meant, but he always felt unsettled when he woke up from it.

After he'd left Courtney's house the day before, he regretted ever telling her the truth. He knew he had just confused her by saying anything, and what good did it do, anyway? She didn't have any answers for him.

He downed his green drink, threw on jeans and a white tank, and went out to the barn to take care of his horse, Xavier.

As he was leaving the staff quarters, he bumped into Jasmine rounding a corner quickly.

"Woah!" Jasmine said as they collided. "Oh, Sean! Thank God, it's just you."

Sean grabbed her elbows and steadied her. "Why? What's wrong?"

"Remember when I told you I found a secret passageway inside the house?" she asked.

"Yes. You were going to show me where that was."

"I know. But you've been gone every day. I haven't had a chance."

"Well, did something happen that has to do with the passage?"

"Yes. Just now! I found more cans of aerosol and more earrings inside it! But someone was coming, so I ran back here before I was caught. At least, I hope I wasn't seen."

"Show me the secret passage, Jazz."

"Okay. But we have to be careful that whoever is using it doesn't find us in there."

Jasmine led Sean back into a separate wing of the manor, where the guest rooms and movie theater were. It was connected to the main part of the huge house by a long passageway. They passed an attractive male guard on their way. Jasmine smiled flirtatiously.

When she went through glass doors to an outside courtyard, a confused look came over Sean. "I thought you said it was *inside* the manor?"

"It is. I consider this inside the manor. Don't you?"

"No. This is a courtyard *outside* the manor, Jasmine."

"But it has a roof."

"Yes. We call it a covered patio. But there are no walls and we're lookin' out at the barn and horses. We're outside, Jazz."

"You say *potato*, I say *patata*, who cares?" Jasmine pointed to a white grand piano in the center of the courtyard terrace. "Play!" She commanded.

Sean mockingly bowed. "As you wish, Your Majesty." He sat at the piano and began to play. Jasmine smiled in approval when she heard the way his fingers glided over the keys, covering a beautiful rendition of one of her favorite songs.

She went over to a fountain that had a statue of a raven in the center. She glanced over her shoulder at Sean and said, "I could listen to you play all day," as she turned the statue to the right. Large paving stones in the patio slid open, revealing a staircase going down. Sean stopped playing and got up. Jasmine motioned for him to keep playing the piano. She pointed to the inside of the manor, where there was a guard passing by on patrol.

Sean understood and went back to playing. This time he sang along.

Jasmine's jaw dropped. She walked over to him and sat next to him on the piano bench. Sean finished the song, and Jasmine clapped. "Wow.

You're actually really good!" she said loudly. Then she whispered, "Go in and check the place out. I'll stay here so they think we're still tinkering on the piano." She conjured up a flashlight out of her apron and handed it to Sean.

"Okay," Sean said. "How did you figure out that statue turned?"

"One time, when I was in here cleaning, the fountain stopped working, even though it was plugged in, so I tried to fix it. That's when I accidentally turned the raven."

"Lucky accident, " Sean said. "I heard Ranfurly added more security cameras to the place," Sean said, looking around, "but I don't see one out here. Let's hope that's more luck for us." He went over to the open passage and headed down the steps to have a look, while Jasmine plucked out a song with one finger.

The hidden area wasn't actually a passageway, as Jasmine had said. It was more like a room.

He saw the earrings and aerosol cans on the floor. *Should I take them with me? It would be impossible to hide the cans.* He left the cans and pocketed one pair of the earrings with rubies. *I'll get DART to inspect these.* He hurried back up the stairs. Jasmine was still toying around on the piano.

"Good work finding that, Jazz."

"Dusting has its perks, I guess," she said. "So come over here and sing me another song."

Sean smiled and sat down on the piano bench next to her. He started in on a slow, sad ballad. When he started singing, Jasmine put her head on his shoulder. "I had no idea you could sing like that!"

"It's a secret weapon. I only pull it out when absolutely necessary." He almost put an arm around her and kissed her. It was so natural to do that. But then he stopped himself. "I have to go. Courtney's property is out of control. I'm going to help her out."

"What? Her *property* is out of control? That's the lamest thing I've ever heard. While the boss is away trying to rescue his kid, you're trying to steal his girl? Shame on you, Sean!"

"She doesn't belong with him. She'll figure it out soon enough. You behave yourself with those guards, Jasmine. Looks like you've already got all of them on a string."

"I can't help that I'm irresistible." She wiggled her hips at Sean, then headed back into the house. Sean headed outside to the garage.

A tickling, wet sensation on his toes woke him. He was confused at first, not sure where he was. Then he remembered. He was home. In the hammock by the pond.

No. Not home. He juddered, shaking himself out of the dream state he was still partly in. *I'm at Courtney's house.* The wet feeling had been Thor, licking his toes. Sean scratched the dog behind the ears, then stretched his arms and checked the time on his favorite, ancient, analog watch that somehow still worked. "One o'clock in the afternoon? Must be the heat that made me take such a long nap."

The day *was* unusually hot. Sean had been toiling away in the vegetable garden at Courtney's and had taken off his tank. *I must have left my shirt in the garden.* He'd planned to just sneak in a short break when he found the hammock. Apparently he'd dozed off.

Two hours later, sun scorched, Sean tumbled out of the hammock, his bare chest sunburned.

He headed inside the house to the kitchen to get some water, where he found Courtney putting away dishes.

"Well, look who finally woke from the dead." Courtney smiled at him, and stole a glance at his bare chest. He gloried in the way her face flushed. *She is pretending not to be flustered, but I can tell; she finds me irresistible.*

"I know. The sun had its way with me."

"Oh! You're burned. Cut off a piece of aloe vera plant, it'll help."

Sean did as ordered and put the leaf on his sunburn. "Ouch! It has spikes!"

"You're not supposed to put the outside part on your skin! Here," Courtney slit the succulent leaf open, so the slimy flesh was exposed. "Now just put the slimy part on the skin. That slime works miracles."

He made a disgusted face. But after the sting of the burn was relieved, he smiled. "Wow. Good stuff."

"I know." Courtney pointed to the table, where a sandwich was waiting for him. "I made you a roast beef dip. With my homemade recipe for *au jus*."

"Sounds delicious. Although I had my carb quota for the month the other night when we had dinner on your *holiday*. I don't usually eat bread. It ruins the figure."

"That's just the part that makes it a sandwich. Mr. I-am-in-love-with-my-perfect-body."

Sean grinned. "Oh, so you think my body is perfect, do you? I'm touched." He put a hand on his chest.

She laughed. "*You* definitely think your body is perfect, that much is obvious."

"What I usually have for lunch is a delicious drink, packed with nutrients and vegetables."

"I don't have any of that awful green drink you like, sorry. And if you don't eat bread, you'll have to feed your roll to my dogs."

"That isn't good for them."

"Gaw! You're so annoying, Sean!"

He picked up the sandwich and bit into it. With food still stuffed in his mouth, he said, "Happy with me now?"

"Hmph. You do realize that when you say bread ruins a person's figure, you are insinuating that you think my figure has been ruined? Because I eat bread."

"No! No, of course, I'm not insinuating that!"

"Whatever. Good thing I'm not insecure or I'd starve myself of the best things in life. Bread. Coffee. Ice cream. Pasta. But I'm perfectly happy with my curves."

"As am I." Sean's gaze moved downward. "Very happy with them, in fact. Women are much more enjoyable when they are soft and curvy." He eyeballed the sandwich in front of him. "I, on the other hand, do not want my body to get soft and curvy. But for you, today, I shall eat the bread." He had another bite.

"You're exasperating." Courtney said. She went to pour him a glass of water from the fridge.

"Thanks." Sean drank down the entire glass. Courtney wiped down the counter, while Sean admired her tight-fitting shirt and yoga pants. "That bread actually looks good on you." He flashed her a charming smile. He was delighted when he saw the pink rise in her cheeks.

Sean's phone interrupted them. "It's the chemist. I need to take it," he told Courtney.

After a brief conversation, he hung up and said to Courtney, "You'll never believe what was inside the aerosol can."

CUBE OF GLASS

⧫ *Lord Robert* ⧫

One-Hundred-Sixty Hours After Disappearance

After the meeting with Wellington, Robert and Sharon were separated. He had no idea where Sharon was taken, but he was locked in a cell in the basement of the club.

Almost three days later, guards came into his cell and cuffed him. He was flown in a rocket-copter to the mountainous region of The Highlands, known as The Heights.

Robert guessed they were close to six thousand meters in altitude, since they were up in the midst of the tallest glaciers in The Heights. With no time to acclimate and very little water in his system, his head throbbed. The rocket-copter set down on a large landing pad, the only flat surface in view. Next to it, built into the side of the mountain, about two thousand meters below the peak, was a building in the shape of a pyramid.

Robert was taken inside the building, up four flights of stairs, then down a long hallway lined with closed doors.

"Welcome to your new home," said one of his captors, a man with a face of stone, void of emotion. They entered through one of the doors to his "new home"– a small, square room with an exceptionally high ceiling. A window covered most of one wall. Video screens hung near the ceiling of the windowed wall. Four screens, one on the right, one on the left, one top center and one just below it.

The view out of the window was familiar to Robert. Four mountains, close together, all around six thousand meters tall. If you were looking down at them from above, their peaks were in a diamond shape, and the straight-line distance from peak to peak was around five miles.

The range was world-renowned for having the most challenging mountains to climb. *Na Ceithir.* (The Four). Very few climbers had achieved reaching the summits. Many had lost their lives trying.

Robert had always enjoyed the beauty of The Heights. To see even one of The Four was a rare sight, as they were usually concealed by clouds. To be among the few who had seen all four at once was to be extremely fortunate.

When Robert was in his twenties, he'd spent time hiking the lower summits around The Four, peaks around three-thousand meters. It was an escape for him from his hectic life in the city.

He grew to appreciate the mountains even more when he decided to follow the Old Religion. He came to view them as God's power on display.

But that day, he didn't see the beauty of the soaring peaks. He dreaded the sight of them. Evil had stolen his serenity and distorted his view. All he treasured as glorious and sacred, he now questioned. He raged at, doubted, even challenged the Creator. *If You are All-Powerful, then why won't You do something?!*

Wellington's men strapped Robert into a chair that faced the window. Speculums were inserted into his eyelids, so he was forced to keep them open.

Outside, a vessel, larger than several airplanes combined, in the shape of a hexagon, flew over the peak directly across from him. As it drew nearer, his window and chair vibrated.

The vessel stopped in the center of the three other peaks and hovered. A sparkly thing, glistening like a diamond, hung from its base.

His focus shifted to movement just outside his window. Tiny drones were flying about. *More than likely outfitted with cameras*, he thought.

The video monitor on Robert's right turned on. It showed a heavy equipment machine called a super snowcat (made for high altitude terrain with a high-torque drill enhanced by advanced robotics). It was drilling into the icy rocks on the side of a mountain to install a titanium cable through the rock.

Next, the monitor on Robert's far left turned on. It showed another snowcat doing the same, drilling into the ice and rock, securing the cable in place. The top center video monitor showed a third snowcat, also securing a cable. *Three super snowcats, on the three mountainsides that I'm looking at outside my window*, Robert realized.

The bottom center video screen flashed on, showing the thing that had given off a sparkly effect. *A cube of glass?* Robert wondered what the purpose of it could be. His naked eye couldn't make out the real size of it, but on screen, he guessed it to be about one thousand cubic feet.

Next, the video screens showed a suspension net made out of titanium cable. It appeared to be floating midair, in the center of the three other mountains, but it was actually being held in place by the cables that the snowcats had secured to the rocks.

The flying vessel lowered the glass cube slowly, until it was situated inside the net.

Once the cube sat securely, two men were lowered down by ropes from the vessel. They disconnected the vessel's cables from the glass cube. Then they were raised back up, and the vessel flew off and disappeared in the distance. With the absence of the vessel's vibration and low hum, an eerie silence loomed.

The video screens flashed, showing new scenes–wide angles of the massive surrounding peaks; himself, sitting inside the pyramid room, bound to his chair, his lids forced open; the cube in the distance, suspended in midair thousands of meters above ground.

The next scene showed a closer angle of the cube. Close enough now that Robert could see two people were *inside*. He felt sick at the sight of it.

At first, the camera angle was too far to make out who the people were. But as it panned in, their faces were recognizable.

A menacing voice came through a speaker and sliced through the silence. "Hello, Robert. I apologize for making you wait three days to come to my mountain lodge. How do you like the view so far?"

Wellington.

Robert wanted to blink desperately. His eyes burned.

"It leaves you speechless, doesn't it? If you look at your video monitors now, you'll see the snowcats have circular diamond saws coming out of their arms, ready to cut the cables, at my command."

Wellington paused, as if he expected Robert to say something. When he didn't hear anything from Robert, he continued. "Can you tell who the people are inside the cube?"

The camera showed a close up of Elizabeth holding onto Sharon/Courtney.

"Ah. Poor thing. She looks terrified, doesn't she? At least she has Courtney there to comfort her," Wellington said.

Robert let out a moan in frustration. "You're diabolic, August!"

"You're the one who stole my wife. And as for Elizabeth, well, who is to say that you didn't steal her as well?"

"She is *my* daughter!"

There was silence for a few minutes. Then Wellington's voice blasted through the speaker again. "But you aren't sure, are you?"

Robert tried to move, but the metal restraints and blades in his eyes made it impossible. He fought the urge to vomit.

Wellington sighed. "Well, I hate to sign off, but sadly The Ten have me doing other things that aren't nearly as fun. I'll have to catch all of this on replay. And don't blink, Robert. *You* won't want to miss anything."

❧ Peter ❧

Nearly three days had passed since Robert and Sharon had been without trackers when Baca announced, "I just got a signal from Robert's tracker!"

"What about Sharon's?" Peter asked.

"Nothing yet," she replied.

Peter put a call in to McGregor and Kila, who were on standby. They were ready to fly a high-altitude heliplane that had the ability to fly over the peaks of The Heights. Another brilliant invention of CAPE Tech.

"Baca just got a signal coming from Robert's tracker," Peter told them. "We have a precise location."

McGregor heard Dillard's voice in the background of the call. "I just scanned the area around Lord Robert and found several camera drones! We're trying to hack them so we can get footage of the surrounding area."

"Great!" Peter said.

Minutes later, Baca said, "… We did it! We're in!"

"Explain what you're seeing on the camera drone feed, Baca, so McGregor and Kila can hear," Peter said.

"Oh no! This is bad. Really bad!" Baca said. "Elizabeth and Sharon are locked inside a glass cube suspended in midair, in the middle of the mountains."

"A glass cube?" McGregor asked.

"Yes," Peter said.

"Is it small enough for my plane to tote?" McGregor asked.

"No. Way too big for *any* of our planes to tote," Dillard replied.

"I could drop down on a cable and get them out," Kila suggested.

"I don't think that's a good idea," Peter said. "We're seeing Snowcat robots with high-speed circular diamond saws, ready to cut the cables that are holding the net that the cube sits in. If you go out there to pull any rescue stunts, it could be the end for Elizabeth and Sharon."

"If only I could be invisible. Then the snowcats wouldn't see me," Kila said.

"Invisible … hmm." Baca pushed her hot-pink-rimmed glasses up off of her nose. "Dillard, what about … you know. *Them*." Her eyes widened like an owl's.

"No." Dillard was adamant. "They've never been tested in this kind of situation."

"But they're designed to be able to pick up and fly huge buildings! They could handle the weight of the cube," Baca argued.

McGregor interrupted. "What are you guys bickering about?"

"Yeah, Baca, what are you getting at?" Peter asked. "Something large enough to fly huge buildings is going to be pretty obvious out there."

"Not if it can become invisible!" Baca's voice moved up an octave in her excitement.

"Baca, no!" Dillard protested. "Even if they could carry it off, the cube is made of glass! And they've never been on a mission. They're like toddlers! You don't let toddlers play with glass!" Dillard threw up his hands.

"What exactly are *they?*" Peter asked.

"Oh. Um … Dillard and I have been keeping them a little secret from you. We wanted them to be a surprise," Baca smiled.

"…They still need to be tested!" Dillard crossed his arms.

"What *are* they?" Peter repeated the question.

"They're a project we've been working on for a couple of years. Robots that have capabilities beyond *anything* PAX has come up with," Dillard added.

"How many of them are there?" Kila asked through her comms.

"Just two right now," Dillard said.

"But if they prove to be a success, we were going to ask for funding to create more of them!" Baca jumped up.

"You're supposed to get clearance to create things like that." Peter's deep, firm voice put the fear of God into a person.

"Oopsie." Baca covered a hand over her mouth.

"Thanks a lot, Baca," Dillard said through clenched teeth.

"Well, let's have a look at them," Peter said.

Baca bounced up and down and clapped her hands. "Oh, I've been dying to see them go on their first mission."

Dillard didn't look happy at all as he got out of his chair and slowly led Peter over to a wall of computer monitors. After typing a few keys into his CAPE phone, the entire wall moved toward them. He stepped around it and disappeared.

Peter followed. "Hmm." Another incredibly large room was behind the wall. It was filled with all sorts of innovations. "You two have been hiding all sorts of things in here."

McGregor and Kila listened in to the conversation, amused. "You sneaky little techies," McGregor said.

"Everything in here is still in testing mode," Dillard said defensively.

Baca ran over to the corner of the room and opened a pink door. "Allow me to introduce Lady Zulabaca!"

Peter was stunned when he saw a giant woman standing in front of them. With blond pigtails, wearing pink rimmed glasses and a pink sweater, and the face of Baca. Only she was missing a nose. And a hand.

"Like I said, I don't know if they're ready yet. I still need to fix her hand and get the entire face completed," Dillard said. He shot a glare at Baca.

"She was able to lift that entire crate of gold with one hand!" Baca pointed across the room at the gold. "She can definitely handle a glass cell with a couple of lightweight humans."

"How did you two get all of that gold?" Peter asked. Dillard and Baca looked like a couple of raccoons caught red handed.

"Very sneaky techies, indeed," Kila laughed through her comms.

"Well, it was a PAX vault, so philosophically, we weren't *really* stealing." Baca said sweetly, the picture of innocence.

"Alright. So, she has one good hand. What about the other robot?" Peter asked.

Dillard opened an orange door that was next to Baca's robot.

"I've got to see these robots!" McGregor said into his comms. "Switch over to video and show us!"

Dillard pressed a button on his phone and stepped back to hold up the camera, to give McGregor a full-size angle of the robot.

"Oh my. It's you, Dillard! On steroids, after several visits to a gym!" McGregor grinned. Kila snorted.

Dillard ignored them both. "Once again, he isn't ready. I haven't tested him enough for a mission like this." He crossed his arms and let out a huff.

"Well, then this will be an excellent way to see if they are ready for action. And it looks like you've got enough gold there to fund several more robots in case these two don't work out," Peter said matter-of-factly.

A look of horror came over Dillard. "Do you even hear yourself? You're speaking as if they're dispensable! Do you realize—"

Kila cut in. "Dillard, we're talking about saving three people's lives. Your robots may be the best chance Elizabeth, Sharon, and Lord Robert have."

"What about the high altitudes of The Heights? Can they fly that high?" McGregor asked.

"These robots can fly into outer space!" Baca squealed.

"Technically speaking, they *should* be able to, Baca. We haven't tested that theory yet, though!" Dillard reminded her.

"Baca thinks they're ready, and I trust her instincts," Peter added.

Baca beamed. "I'm absolutely certain my girl here can carry a glass cube one-handed, and *your* guy will be there too, Dillard! Together, they are invincible!"

She bobbed up and down.

Dillard lowered his eyes at her.

"It's decided then. The robots will fly behind the plane," Peter said.

36

CAPE TEAM
ON MISSION

⚬ McGregor ⚬

One-Hundred-Sixty-Five Hours After Disappearance

As McGregor and Kila flew to The Heights, they remained in communication with Dillard, Baca, and Peter. Flying behind the plane were the two robots, invisible to the eye.

Because McGregor couldn't see the robots, he repeatedly asked Dillard, "Are you sure they are still flying behind us?"

"Yes. They're still behind you," Dillard had to say several times. Finally, after being asked the question too many times, Dillard said, "Here. I'll share my navigation screen with you." Dillard's screen appeared inside the plane monitor. "The pink dot is Baca's robot, and the orange dot is mine. Now, quit asking me where they are."

"Why didn't you share your screen to begin with?" McGregor asked him, annoyed.

The plane and the robots flew over The Heights undetected in stealth mode. As they approached the mountains, Baca said, "Our robots are going to search for the cube."

"Okay. Kila and I are headed towards Robert's tracker," McGregor said. He flew between two craggy peaks, and came so close to one of them, he caused an avalanche.

"McGregor, watch where you're going!" Kila said.

"I am! That mountain just appeared out of nowhere!"

Dillard, on screen and aware of their every move, put in his two cents. "You know, if you put the plane on autopilot, it will do a better job avoiding disastrous situations like that, McGregor. The last thing we need is for you to destroy my plane!"

McGregor muttered something under his breath.

Thanks to Robert's tracker that was still blinking, McGregor found the pyramid building where Robert was being held captive.

"I'm sending out the Pola-Droids now," McGregor said over the comms. Pola-Droids were miniature spy droids with cameras that could fly undetected into areas and get video footage.

"Okay. Following," Peter said.

"The Pola-Droids are in and we're looking at all the footage they're capturing. Are you seeing the footage we're transmitting, Baca? There are cameras outside the pyramid."

"Yes! I'm seeing it. Give me just one second…" Baca said. "Okay! I've hacked into the cameras around the pyramid and just blacked out their screens! McGregor and Kila, you'll be clear to enter!"

"Perfect, Baca," McGregor said. "More Pola-Droids are on their way to infiltrate the inside of the building."

"Good. Once we figure out the main frame for the surveillance system, we'll be able to hack into it and disable all the cameras and communication channels."

A large landing pad could be seen below, where two other copters were parked.

"Good thing CAPE Tech gave this plane a propeller so it can hover and land like a chopper," Kila said. "There isn't a runway up here, and that helipad looks like the only place we'll be able to land. Everywhere else is way too steep."

"There's a guard in the tower. He's looking around, confused. He hears us but can't see where we're coming from," McGregor said.

"Okay, I'm sending the mini bots now before he has a chance to radio the other guards," Kila pressed a button that opened up a panel in the belly of the plane. Mini bots that were designed to resemble honeybees zoomed down to the guard tower. They stung the guard, which sent a drug into his system that would put him into a twenty-four-hour coma.

McGregor set the plane down on the helipad. They unbuckled and stocked up with weapons.

"Okay. Ready for some action, Kila?"

"I'm always ready for action!" She grinned.

He leaned over and gave her a kiss on the lips.

"Woah. What was that for?" Her deer-like brown eyes widened in surprise.

"I know we aren't together anymore. But this could be the last chance I have to kiss you."

"Oh, please, Casanova. Quit being dramatic!"

Kila put a PAX medic shirt over her bullet proof CAPE snow suit. The suits were designed specifically for missions like this one, in high altitudes at freezing temperatures. Fleece-lined to keep them warm, with a white dragon skin shell that was bullet proof and waterproof. Boots were all-terrain, interchangeable depending on the surface. When the sole hit ice, crampons came out automatically, then retracted when no ice was detected.

Assuming they would get him out of the pyramid alive, they brought an extra suit and pair of boots for Robert.

They lowered the airplane stairs and Kila descended first. McGregor remained unseen inside the mirrored plane.

The spikes of the crampons came out of Kila's boots as she approached the pyramid. A guard walked out and spotted her. He aimed his gun.

Kila raised her hands in the air. "Don't shoot. I'm here with medical supplies."

"How did you get out here?" The man cocked his head, confused. "Where's the rocket chopper you usually come in?"

"It's right there." She pointed to the helipad. "Don't you see it?" Not seeing it, the guard had a baffled expression. At that same moment, one of the mini bot bees flew at the guard's neck and stung him. The tranquilizer set in immediately. The guard fell forward onto the ice.

Two guards came from around the back of the building just as McGregor joined Kila.

"Sorry. No time for a chat," McGregor said to the guards. His gun sounded like nothing more than a light pop thanks to silencers. They didn't contain bullets, but released the twenty-four-hour tranquilizers into the guards, who passed out on contact.

He and Kila ran toward the entrance of the pyramid.

McGregor opened one of the entrance doors and threw a gas grenade inside. They waited thirty seconds, then peered into the lobby. "Clear!"

Now inside the pyramid, their boots retracted the spikes, leaving padded rubber soles that muted their footsteps. They found their way to the door that led to the emergency stairs.

Kila pointed up and held out four fingers. McGregor understood. *Lord Robert is four floors up.* They entered the stairwell silently and ascended.

A guard walked in through the door on the second-floor landing just as they reached it. They exchanged fire, but McGregor's tranquillizer hit the mark and the guard fell.

On the fourth floor, they opened the stairwell door to enter the hallway. A guard was on patrol. Kila shot him before he saw her coming. The tranquilizer went in, but the guard was so huge that the dose wasn't potent enough to affect him. He fired back at them.

They retreated into the stairwell, and fired back and forth.

They heard the guard radio in. "We got a breach! Hello? Anyone there? ... Hello?"

McGregor smiled at Kila. "Baca must have hacked into the main frame and shut down their comms and cameras."

McGregor threw a gas grenade down the hall, then fired several shots. They waited thirty seconds.

McGregor checked the hall. Seeing the guard face down, he said, "Clear. But wait here." He held up a hand to Kila. He ran down the hall and checked to make sure the guard was out cold before he stepped over him and yelled, "Lord Robert, are you in there?"

"McGregor?" Lord Robert's voice called back from the other side of the door. "Is that you? Yes! I'm in here!"

"Stay clear of the door!" McGregor yelled.

"I'm not anywhere near it!" Robert yelled back.

McGregor placed explosives on Lord Robert's door. He ran back into the stairwell with Kila and counted on his fingers. *One. Two. Three.*

The door blew off. They stepped over the guard's large body in order to enter Robert's room.

"Lord Robert!" Kila ran to him. He was strapped into the chair, his eyes forced open by the blades of the speculums.

She removed the blades. "That had to have been painful," she said once they were out.

"It's difficult to blink, my eyes are so dry … what I'd give for some drops right about now. Can you find the controls that release the chair restraints?"

"There are a lot of buttons here," McGregor said, wondering which button to press. He tried a few, but they only seemed to work the video screens. At one point, the window blinds came down.

"McGregor!" Kila yelled at him.

"Hey, these things should have labels on them! Oh, wait. Maybe it's this one with the picture of a chair next to it."

Kila shook her head.

The restraints were released. Robert stumbled forward out of the chair. "I don't have a weapon," he said.

"You can still see good enough to aim, I hope." Kila handed him one of her guns.

"I can tell the bad guys from the good guys," Robert said.

McGregor handed him the boots and CAPE snow suit. "Hurry and change … we've got to get back to the plane!" he told Robert.

Robert slipped the suit on over his clothes and exchanged his shoes for the boots.

240

As they were climbing down the stairwell, two guards entered from the floor above and shot down at them. They ducked under the stairs for cover, intermittently returning fire. They continued like this the whole way down, covering for each other, until they were back on the first floor.

The lobby entrance of the building was still clear. Shots flew at them from the guards coming out of the stairwell behind them.

They made it outside and ran toward their invisible plane. Six guards surprised them on the way. With nowhere to take cover, the three of them fired without ceasing until they managed to hit and tranquilize all six men.

As they scrambled up the stairs to the plane, McGregor saw that Kila was bleeding. "Kila's hit!" he yelled.

"No, she's not. The blood is coming from my hand," Robert said. "It was stabbed earlier and the wound just reopened."

They strapped in, and McGregor started the propellers up.

Four more guards came out of the building, but the heliplane was already soaring up into the skies, out of firing range.

"There weren't too many guards due to the location," Robert said. "No doubt, they didn't think they'd need as many in a remote place like this. Not many people would have the means to access it."

"But we've got CAPE Tech on our side!" Kila said through the comms, so Baca and Dillard could hear.

"Yes you do!" Baca squealed.

Kila got the first aid kit out and helped Robert clean and bandage his hand. "That should heal in no time with this dragon tape," she said. "And here are some drops for your eyes."

"Thank you, Kila," Robert said, at last getting some relief.

Baca's voice came over the comms. "Great timing, guys! The robots just found the cube!"

HASTY DECISIONS

✑ Lord Robert ✑

"Robots?" Lord Robert roared. He hadn't been informed of the plan.

In Robert's mind, robots were not a *solution* to a problem. In fact, in his limited experience, they were usually a thing that *created* a problem.

"Robert, there's no time to explain. You have to trust us," Peter said into the comms.

McGregor flew to the coordinates that Dillard sent him, and there it was–the glass cube suspended in midair.

The high altitude heliplane hovered above the suspended cube. Robert shouted at Kila. "Lower me down to Elizabeth!"

Peter's commanding voice came through the comms. "Robert! Hold position! The robots are invisible, and they're going to fly the cube out of there!"

Robert was at his wits end. "Are these robots tested? Proven capable?"

Everyone sucked in air at the same time. Robert read the looks on their faces and roared in fury.

"This is my child's life you're gambling with!" He started to search through the cabinets and storage drawers. "Where are the harnesses in this plane kept?"

"If you jump out, there are snowcat robots out there who will cut the cables!" Dillard yelled into the comms. "And also ... it's possible you could break the cube if you land on it!"

"I'm going to rescue my daughter! Lower me down to the cube! You're wasting time!"

"That wasn't the plan!" Dillard said.

❧ Peter ❧

"Robert is impossible to reason with when he gets like this," Peter muttered to himself. He knew Robert was going to jump out of the plane and nobody would be able to stop him. He had to act quickly.

"Do the robots have fighting capabilities?" he asked.

"Yes!" Baca said.

"No way! No!" Dillard shouted.

"We need to get rid of those snowcats before they cut the cables, Dillard," Peter said in response to Dillard's protest. "Send the robots out to disable them. McGregor and Kila, you two focus on keeping Robert from cabling out of the heliplane until those snowcats are dealt with."

❧ McGregor ❧

McGregor pressed a few buttons to lock the drawers where the harnesses were kept before Robert had a chance to find them. He also put an auto lock on the cable coil, so it wouldn't be going anywhere outside of the plane.

Meanwhile, Robert was searching through a cabinet in a frenzied state, shouting, "I can't find a thing on this bloody plane!" He was in his own head, so much that he had no idea what anyone around him was saying or doing.

Outside, the robots rocketed over to deal with the snowcats. Dillard's went for the one that was furthest away, and Baca's went for the closest. If McGregor could have seen the robots in comparison to the snowcats, he would have known that the super snowcat robots were three times larger than the CAPE robots. The circular diamond saws they wielded extended half the length of Zulabaca's body. The only advantage the CAPE robots had was their invisibility.

"I gave my robot the ability to shoot bullets out of its hands. But these bullets aren't doing anything," Dillard said.

❧ Lord Robert ❧

Robert was in a rage.

"McGregor, you need to unlock the drawer in the cabinet! I have to get down there!"

"Peter, are you hearing this? Robert wants me to let him have the harness," McGregor said through the comms.

"Okay, McGregor. Cable Robert down," Peter said.

Robert fastened himself into the harness and Kila lowered him down. He was jerked back as Kila slowed the cable's speed, so he would be able to land ever-so-gently on top of the net.

Once his feet touched down on the net, he used the side wall of glass to steady himself.

Elizabeth was only a few feet away from him now, through the panes of glass. She had her head down. In his chaotic state of mind, he was tricked for a split second when he saw the lookalike Courtney holding her. *That isn't Courtney, you fool.*

"Daddy's here, Elizabeth. Right here!" he cried out to his daughter.

Elizabeth broke out of Sharon's arms when she saw her father. "Daddy!" She ran to him, sobbing, her hands and face pressed against the glass. "Daddy!"

She can hear me! He thought, seeing the tiny ventilation holes in some of the glass panes. Robert's eyes stung as a chill of wind blew through. *I will not fail her. I cannot!*

"Elizabeth! Hang on! I'm coming!" Robert touched the glass where her hands were. "I love you, Elizabeth!"

"I love you, Daddy!" Elizabeth bawled.

Robert took a step closer toward her. The movement caused the cube to jerk.

"Daddy!" his daughter screamed as she was jolted and landed on her bottom.

"I'm sorry! I'm going to get you out of there. Where's the door to get inside?"

Elizabeth scanned the cube. She shook her head sadly. "I don't know." Tears streamed down her face.

"They drugged us!" Sharon shouted. "We don't remember how they put us inside this thing!"

While Sharon was saying this, a huge bird came out of nowhere and flew directly at Robert. It rammed into him, knocking him off of the net.

He blacked out.

❧ Peter ❧

"What just happened? … Robert?" Peter shouted in the comms. He got no response. "Robert!"

Robert was no longer standing on the net, but dangling on the heliplane cable like a limp dummy. Even worse, his cable was swaying him to and fro like a pendulum, knocking him into the cube.

"Robert! Wake up!" Peter roared.

❧ McGregor ❧

From his vantage point, McGregor could see the snowcat that Dillard's robot was supposed to be fighting. It suddenly started swinging its saw through the air, as if in a fight with an invisible enemy.

"Um, Dillard? What is happening out there? I can't see your robot to know who is winning."

"My robot tried to knock the snowcat out of the way, but the thing doesn't even budge!" Dillard said.

"Oh no, guys. The other snowcat, the one that neither of our robots can deal with right now, is making its way toward the cable!" Baca cried.

"You need to send one of the robots over to stop it!" Peter said.

"I can't!" Baca cried. "I'm dealing with the other snowcat at the moment!"

❧ Baca ❧

Baca was moving her fingers at an insanely rapid speed to maneuver *her* robot.

When she was designing her robot, Baca gave it fighting features. One was the ability to shoot lasers out of her eyes.

The robot's lasers sliced through the snowcat's robotic arm that held the diamond saw. It fell to the depths below. Then Baca's robot sliced and quartered the snowcat.

"One down!" she shouted.

With Tasmanian devil speed, she tapped away at the computer keys to fly Zulabaca to snowcat number two. She had to stop it before it cut through the cable!

By the time she flew her robot over to the other snowcat, it had reached the cable and was raising its diamond saw to begin cutting through. She lasered off its arm, and it fell, shattering on the rocks far below. She sliced that snowcat in half.

❧ McGregor ❧

McGregor watched the snowcat that was fighting Dillard's robot. It appeared to be ramming at something with his saw. "Dillard? What is going on out there?" he asked.

"No! No! No! NO!" Dillard was crying over the comms. "My robot was just completely destroyed! Baca, this is *your* fault!"

"I'm sorry, Dillard. I'm so sorry!" Baca said. "I'm sending Zulabaca to stop the snowcat!"

The snowcat that Dillard's robot had been fighting turned away from Dillard's invisible and destroyed robot and raised the diamond saw to begin cutting the cable.

"Where is Zulabaca?" McGregor yelled. "The snowcat is starting to cut the cable!"

"She's almost there!" Baca cried.

But by the time Zulabaca made it across and cut the snowcat's arm off, it was too late.

The cable dropped.

Elizabeth screamed. Sharon cushioned Elizabeth from impact as they were thrown when one side of the net spilled open. The cube turned like a die rolling on its side. But instead of continuing to roll out of the net, the corner of the cube got caught in the net's holes. By some miracle the cube didn't fall.

FALLING TO AN END

The sound of Elizabeth's scream jolted Robert out of his unconsciousness.

"What happened? How did the cube turn like that?" he shouted through the comms. It was a living nightmare that just kept getting worse.

His eyes were on his daughter, who was crying into the arms of Sharon, while he dangled from the heliplane, there in the sky, unable to do anything.

"Glad to hear you are back with us. You missed some action while you were out cold," Peter said through the comms.

"What is going on?" Robert demanded. "Why did the cube turn?"

"One of the snowcats cut through their cable. The net is only being held up by two cables now."

"But how am I going to get inside the cube now? I can't risk stepping on the net," Robert said. "I don't want the cube to fall out of it."

A nick in the glass in front of Robert caught his eye. He became fixated with it. *Is it growing? Please don't let it grow.*

The nick became a thin line. Then ... a tiny crack began to form.

He shouted into his comms. "Listen, the cube is cracking! Even if the net holds, we can't risk the glass shattering! If I swing over to it, I might cause it to crack more. What can we do?"

"I don't know..." Dillard said over the comms, still crying about his robot's demise.

"You don't know?" Robert roared. "That's the best you can do, Dillard? You don't know?"

"Dillard's robot is destroyed," Peter said. "But the original plan was for our robots to fly the cube out of the net and set it on a safe surface. We can still go with that plan. Zulabaca is strong enough and has the cables on her to attach to the cube and fly it out of the net."

"That's our only option?" Robert asked. "Fine." He still couldn't see a robot, but he could feel its wind and hear the hum of its engine as Zulabaca flew down and fastened her cables to the glass cube's two mooring rings. To Robert, it appeared as if the cube was moving slowly through the sky by itself as the invisible Zulabaca lifted it out of the net.

Robert cried out to his daughter, "Hold on, Elizabeth!" Sharon was holding his little girl and gave Robert a thumbs up.

"Lord Robert, are you ready? We're about to lift you up," Kila said.

"No! Don't pull me up! McGregor, fly slowly behind the robot. When it sets that cube down, I want to be set down next to it so I can get Elizabeth and Sharon out safely!"

They continued through the sky slowly, searching for a flat area to set the cube down. Robert's eyes never left his daughter inside the cube, while McGregor's heliplane kept a safe distance behind the robot.

At first, the plan seemed to be working. Robert caught his little girl's eye and smiled at her reassuringly.

But things took a turn for the worst when the crack in the glass expanded.

Robert heard the sound of the glass breaking, and a ripple of terror shook him. Elizabeth saw her father's reassuring smile instantly change to a visage of fear.

A second later, the sound of shattering glass cut Robert to his very core. The last look on his daughter's face before she dropped was panic-stricken terror.

"Nooo! Elizabeth!"

Robert didn't take time to think about what he was doing. He unhooked his carabiners, unclasped his harness, and dove headfirst after her.

She's falling too fast! Robert thought. He straightened himself into the shape of a bullet to gain speed. *If I can just reach her in time, I can save her.*

It suddenly dawned on him … he had no parachute. In his haste, he'd forgotten to put one on.

Dear God! What have I done?

The anguish of regret clawed at him. *You have failed her. Failed Luke. It is ALL. YOUR. FAULT.*

A memory flashed. It was so vivid, he could taste, hear, see, smell, and touch it.

Elizabeth was an infant, crying in his arms. "Shh, little one." Robert sang her the only song he could recall. "Dragon Rider's coming, don't you cry, don't you cry. Dragon Rider's riding through the sky. Hotter than the sun's fire, blazing through the night, the darkness better run and hide."

"Robert, that's the first time I've ever heard you sing," Desiree said. "You've a wonderful baritone. … But I don't know if that song makes a very nice lullaby."

"Sure, it does. She's quiet now. It worked perfectly."

Desiree smiled, as Luke fed at her breast. "Oh, how I love you. Your love for me has transformed me. And these two—they've ruined me forever—in the best way."

Robert held Elizabeth close, enjoying the sweet smell of her head. She reached up her tiny infant hand to touch his face.

The memory dissipated.

He was jolted back into the present reality, Elizabeth plunging to her death below.

He heard a strange whooshing. *What is making that sound?*

In the distance, it first appeared to be a large bird. As it drew nearer, Robert realized it was coming straight at him. "Not *you* again." Robert said, believing it was likely the same bird that had rammed into him earlier.

As it drew closer, he realized it was a very large bird. Too large. *That can't be a bird, can it? But if not, then what is it?*

And then … blood rushed out of his face; his neck became rigid, his jaw locked.

God, help me.

He was filled with icy dread as its penetrating eyes homed in on him.

It was a dragon. A white dragon.

It was flying directly at him. Its mouth open … razor-sharp teeth exposed … several horns on its back. Its scales glistened in the sun. Its wingspan grew wider and wider with each flap, creating such a force of wind that he was blown back.

But then, Robert saw something else even more terrifying than the dragon. A ball of fire appeared above the dragon. It grew and grew, until it was as bright as the sun. The dragon paled in comparison to the flame. Robert squeezed his eyes shut, but even with his lids closed, the brightness was blinding.

He knew the stories in the Scripture, knew the accounts that described this sight, and his feeble faith made him ashamed that he ever doubted. He wasn't worthy to be in the presence of this Holy Being … God Incarnate. *Dragon Rider. Show me mercy,* he pleaded.

He heard a Voice whisper, "Do not be afraid, Robert."

At the sound of the Voice, fear fled from him. Regret dissipated. Pain became nonexistent. Instantaneous peace permeated him.

"Dragon Rider!" He reached out blindly, trying to touch the One he dare not look upon. "Please, don't leave me."

"I will never leave you, Robert. I've been with you, all this time. Even when you doubted, I was still here."

"Am I dead?"

"Shall those who love me experience death? … But you have come to an end."

As the Being spoke the words, Robert saw his soul, in hundreds of pieces, rise out of his own body. It was as if his spirit had been shattered along with the glass cube.

"Why is this happening?" He reached out to try and touch The Dragon Rider again. "Let me touch You! You can make me whole."

Suddenly, it was as if someone closed the curtains on the brightness.

"Open your eyes, Robert," the Voice said. He obeyed.

Before him, a man with silver hair and a long beard. He had light eyes, a yellowish brown.

"Where's The Dragon Rider?" Robert asked, confused.

"I am He."

"How is it possible that I can look at You?"

"I've changed My form, so that you may look upon Me."

"Is this place we are in … the afterlife?"

"Where*ever* I Am, there is life."

"Then, I am … dead?"

"It is true that you have reached an end … the end of *yourself*. The end is where trust in Me begins. … But it isn't your time to come home with Me. Not yet."

The Dragon Rider put a hand on Robert's head, and Robert saw all the fragments of his soul come back together. His whole spirit reentered his body.

The Holy Being opened His arms, and Robert fell into them.

"Trust in Me, child, and I will keep you from falling," The Dragon Rider whispered. "In your weakness, I am strong."

And then … He was gone.

Pain shot through Robert, reawakening him to the horror of his situation.

Below him, there was Elizabeth. But it appeared as if she was midair, floating on her back, sleeping. He watched in amazement as his daughter began to rise.

How is this possible?

Up she rose, slowly. Until they were eye level. But her eyes were still closed.

She's being lifted up by The Dragon Rider. Take me with You!

He arched his back, and his body flipped over so he now was looking at the sky. He watched Elizabeth rise past him and continue to ascend above him.

A sound like a shooting rocket coming his way shook him. It grew louder, deafening to his ears. He couldn't see what made the sound, but he feared it might collide into him, whatever it was. He coiled into a ball and tucked his head into his knees as he braced for impact.

The sound ceased. All he heard was a low humming.

What is going on?

It felt like arms cradled him. He looked around and realized he was no longer falling, but he wasn't on the ground, either. The ground was about ten feet below.

Did I just hit ground and somehow not feel it? I must be dead. Thank you, God, for sparing me the pain of impact.

The sound of a rocket engine blasted, and he was shot up into the sky, still held by the arms. It was like an amazing dream he'd once had, where he could fly.

Yes. I am most certainly dead.

His ears plugged up from the sudden changes in altitude.

At last, he was lying on the floor of the heliplane, looking into the tearful brown eyes of McGregor.

How is this possible? I'm back inside the plane?

"We thought we had lost you!" McGregor hugged him.

The thing with the arms holding him materialized. Only it wasn't that it materialized, but it no longer had a mirrored surface that camouflaged it.

"Dillard?" Robert said. *Wait... No. That isn't Dillard. It must be the robot.* It resembled Dillard, only it was missing the lower half of its body, two ears, and an eye.

Baca's robot materialized next to him, standing tall. *And that looks like Baca, but she is far too large. Could this be a dream?*

Then he saw *her*. It was enough to defibrillate his heart and set him back in motion. "My Elizabeth!" he cried, reaching for her.

The oversized Baca set the child down, and he swept her up in his arms.

Unable to stop himself from weeping, he cried, "I'm here, Elizabeth! Daddy's here."

Hearing his voice, her closed lids fluttered, then a moment later, he was looking into his daughter's eyes.

"Daddy." Clutching his neck, she sobbed.

"Daddy's right here. I won't ever let you go, baby girl."

McGregor watched with wet eyes, and wrapped his arms around both of them. "I love you guys!"

"Hello?" Kila's voice came through the comms. "Sharon and I are down here! ... A *long* way down here. Any way we can hitch a ride?"

"Kila!" McGregor's face fell. "As soon as the glass cube broke, she dove out of the plane with a parachute. Thank God she was able to reach Sharon in time."

Robert spoke into the comms. "Baca? Can your robots handle one more heroic deed today?"

"On it!" Baca said.

The robots dove out of the heliplane, and minutes later they returned with Kila and Sharon. All were safe and sound.

"What happened with your robot, Dillard? I thought you said it was destroyed?" Peter asked.

"I thought it was! But when Robert was falling, it suddenly shot back up into the sky. At least, its torso shot up. It's legs didn't make it."

"Well, that was exhilarating," Kila said. "Aside from a couple of terrifying moments where we all thought the mission had epically failed, your robots weren't too bad on their first mission, Dillard and Baca."

McGregor set course for CAPE Headquarters in Capital City.

For the duration of the flight, Robert quietly held his little girl. She fell fast asleep in the security of her father's arms. Overwhelmed with relief and gratitude, Robert was contemplative, without words.

When they arrived in Capital City, they were met by Peter and his wife Nina. And of course, Dillard and Baca were there too.

"Welcome home!" Peter said, his arms outstretched. They all enjoyed a bear hug.

"This is a miraculous day! Praise The Dragon Rider!" Nina said.

Robert waited a minute for the excitement to settle down before he said, "Speaking of, I saw Him. He was out there with me."

"You saw who?" Peter asked.

"The Dragon Rider."

Nina asked, "What do you mean? As in a vision?"

"I don't know. It certainly felt like more than just a vision. The dragon was … terrifying. Then the ball of fire, a blinding light as it is often described. But then he became … flesh. A man."

"Did He say anything to you?" Peter asked.

"He told me the painful truth. That my pride nearly cost me my daughter's life. Yet, somehow, at the same time, he took away my shame."

Nina beamed. "Oh! He is good! We need to thank Him now." She reached out her arms, and they all closed in together. "Oh, Holy One, Ancient of Days, thank you. For saving this dear little girl. For showing your mercy and grace to Lord Robert. For revealing Yourself to him, and in doing so, to us." Nina's deep, full voice resonated powerfully. She broke into song:

O praise, o praise the Ancient of Days

Only He can snatch a child from the flames

How He works in mysterious ways

O praise the Ancient of Days

39

HOMECOMING

✍ *Courtney* ✍

One-Hundred-Seventy Hours After Disappearance

"What did the chemist say was in the aerosol cans, Sean?"

"I almost wanted to laugh when she said it," he said. "But she was serious." I waited for him to continue. He was thrilled to keep me hanging. Finally, he said, "Dragon gas."

"Dragon gas?" I gave him a perplexed look. "What's that?"

"Gas that comes from dragons." He looked at me as if I was a dunce. "And before you ask, no, it doesn't come out as flatulence. It's more like a burp."

"I've never heard of that before." I raised my eyebrows and blinked.

"Most people haven't. The chemist told me she just happened to know about it because she did a semester over in Tanai. She worked with a team of scientists who are considered experts on dragons. Apparently, several types of dragon species release gas out of their mouths."

"Wow. But … that doesn't explain why Snake was carrying it around in aerosol cans," I said.

"Maybe he gets off on smelling the belches of dragons."

My phone rang. It was Winnie.

"Hey, I've got great news! Robert has Elizabeth! She's okay! They're on their way home right now and he's hoping you'll be here when they arrive!"

❧ Lord Robert ❧

The nightmare was over. At last, they would all be together again. Luke, Elizabeth, and the woman he couldn't stop thinking about. *Courtney.*

He leaned back against his seat and closed his eyes. A replay of the last time he was with her ran on a loop. *He was holding her by the waist, pressing her into him.* The memory of the taste of her honey lips made his mouth water.

Robert looked out his window as the plane flew over the two-thousand-foot waterfall, just before it entered the dome that concealed his property. As they went through the perimeter of the dome, the Ranfurly Estate and all its surrounding acres became visible. "Here we are, Elizabeth. Home at last."

Elizabeth looked out the window and saw the woods surrounding her giant house below. "I was lost somewhere in those woods, Daddy."

"Yes, you were. And you were very brave. You did all the things I taught you."

"I can see the labyrinth down below! And there's some of our horses!" she said pointing out the window. The plane descended and as they touched ground in Ranfurly Park, Elizabeth's forehead wrinkled. "What's this place?"

"This is where I keep my secret airplane. I say secret because you're not to tell anyone about it."

"Not even Luke?" she pouted.

"I suppose he can know. But nobody else. Pinky promise you won't tell?" Robert held out a pinky.

"I pinky promise," she linked pinkies with her daddy.

Robert drove them in the Whipper to the manor, his little girl cuddling close to him the entire time. It warmed his heart to see the staff out front awaiting their arrival. And … jumping up and down … with an adorable smile on his face…

"There you are! My precious boy!" Robert got out of the car with Elizabeth and held out his arms.

"Daddy! Elizabeth!" Luke ran to his father and sister, and Robert scooped both of his children up at the same time, Luke with one muscular arm and Elizabeth with the other. The twins reached out to each other and held hands. There wasn't a dry eye watching them.

But where is Courtney? Robert scanned faces until he saw her ... tears streaming down her lovely face. Her silky, auburn hair shone in the sunlight.

"Courtney!" He called out to her. She walked toward him with hesitation, as if she didn't want to intrude. "Get over here!" he smiled.

She smiled and ran first to Elizabeth. She hugged the child tightly and kissed her on the cheek. "Welcome home, baby girl."

Elizabeth giggled. "I'm not a baby!"

Winnie wasn't about to miss out. She ran over and joined them. The entire staff eventually closed in around them, hugging and congratulating them.

"Mr. Roth and I have been preparing a feast, with all Elizabeth's favorites!"

Mrs. Roth gleefully announced. "And Mr. Roth made his famous chocolate cake with banana cream filling for dessert!" It was a joyous day of festivities. The household hadn't celebrated like that since the days when Mr. Theodore Ranfurly was alive.

Later that day, Winnie told Elizabeth, "*Somebody* has been missing you."

Elizabeth cocked her head to the side. "Who?"

"Let's see if you can guess. She sleeps standing on four legs, likes to eat apples. And enjoys racing Sir Edgar."

Elizabeth's eyes widened. "Oh! Lady Rose! She's alright?"

Winnie smiled brightly. "She sure is."

Elizabeth looked up at her father, who hadn't left her side. "Can we go see her, Daddy?"

"Of course!"

Winnie grabbed Luke and Elizabeth by the hands, and all three of them skipped out to the barn together.

Robert laced his fingers through Courtney's, and they followed behind at a slower pace. He was hoping to relive the fantasy he'd entertained on the plane. He stopped and enveloped her, his voice a whispery rasp. "I've been wanting to do this for far too long." He made a trail of kisses, starting from her fingertips, all the way up her arm. When he reached her neck, he inhaled her scent. She wore a fragrance that he found deliciously intoxicating. "Ah, you are definitely *my* Courtney."

She smiled. "Last time I checked I was."

Robert's body buzzing with endorphins, they hurried to catch up to Winnie and the children.

On the way, Courtney told him, "Oh! In all the excitement, I almost forgot to tell you Sean's chemist got back to him while you were away. You won't believe what was inside the aerosol cans."

"What?"

"Dragon gas." Courtney glanced over at him, waiting to see his reaction.

Robert's mind instantly thought about the dragon that PAX was keeping below their headquarters. He hadn't told Courtney about it yet.

"Dragon gas. Interesting," he said.

"You don't sound surprised," Courtney said.

"No. I suppose I'm not surprised. … There's something I haven't told you yet. When we rescued those children that were being held in the underwater facility, they were in what PAX calls the 'food bank.' PAX is keeping a red dragon far below ground, and it has a taste for young humans."

Courtney's face paled. "That's pure evil."

"I know." He squeezed her hand. "I'll have to fill the CAPE team in on the dragon gas and see what ideas they have."

I was like a leaky faucet. The tears would not stop flowing. Feelings of overwhelming gratitude and a sense of relief flooded me as I stood in my bathroom, looking in my mirror.

Ever since that very first day in his Parlor, I'd been incredibly attracted to him, and felt a sort of soul connection between us. But I wondered if it was just my imagination. Now, here he was, making it clear that I meant something to him. *How is it possible that a man like Lord Robert Ranfurly, Viscount of Knoxfordshire, could desire a little nobody like me?*

I rinsed my puffy, red face. "Boy, do I cry ugly," I thought, examining myself in the mirror. Robert wanted me to say goodnight before bed, so I powdered up and tried to cover the puffiness before I went to his room.

Robert had his children in his bed with him. Nobody could blame him for not wanting to let them out of his sight. I stayed with the kids for a minute while he ran to get something in his closet.

Luke hopped out of bed and got on his knees. "Thank you, God, for helping Daddy find Elizabeth. Give her good dreams. I love you. Amen."

"Amen," said Elizabeth.

"That was nice, Luke," I said as he crawled back into bed.

"She has drama," Luke said. "Daddy says it can make bad dreams."

"Right. And she's had some trauma, as well, I think," I said.

"That's what Daddy said. Trauma." Elizabeth treated Luke as if he was a child and she was the adult. "Not drama, Luke."

"No. I heard him right," Luke said. "He said drama."

Robert came back into the room. "Okay you two!" Robert laughed. "Time to fall asleep thinking of happy thoughts now."

"Like going to Enchanted World!" Luke said.

Robert smooched his kids once more and said, "I'll come to bed shortly. I'm just going to spend some time with Mrs. Drake first."

He led me by the hand to the balcony that was off of his bedroom.

"It's such a beautiful and warm summer night." I reveled at the moonlit sky. "… Do you think Elizabeth will be alright?"

"After all that she's endured, my daughter still has her same spirit. She suffered a wolf attack, a kidnapping, a horrible underwater cell, that horrendous glass cube prison…"

"All of that would give anyone a lifetime of nightmares," I said.

"It would. But my Elizabeth isn't just anyone."

"No." I thought about how strong she seemed at dinner, the way she held her head high, with a confident light in her green eyes. "She's a warrior!"

"She's a Ranfurly. We're born for the battlefield." He smiled. "And if God allowed this trial, it is only to strengthen her."

"And to strengthen you. Although, I'm pretty sure I've never known anyone as strong as you, Lord Robert."

"*Just* Robert." He dabbed my nose. I smiled. "I believe He did want to strengthen me, yes. To fortify my faith. Through this terrible nightmare, He showed me how weak my faith has been. He showed me that my strength has a limit. But His is limitless."

"Hmm. How did He show you?"

"He appeared to me in the form of The Dragon Rider. I have no doubt that if He wouldn't have intervened, Elizabeth and I would not be alive today."

I hugged him tightly. *Thank You for saving them.* Tears were escaping again.

"Courtney?"

"Yes?"

"I want to give you something." He pulled a silver watch out of his pocket. "It belonged to my mother." He slipped it over my wrist. "Look at that … fit's perfect."

"Oh!" My heart did a little leap. Those darn tears would not stop dripping. "What is this stone?"

"Alexandrite. And *that*," he pointed to the side of the watch, "is an etching of The Dragon Rider. This watch is ancient, but it still works."

"Oh, Robert," I breathed. "This is beautiful."

"You're beautiful."

He cloaked me in and decorated me with kisses. An hour passed like seconds, and I could have stayed there, forever in his arms. But ... even warriors need their rest, and I could see that my poor hero was exhausted. I tucked him in next to his kiddoes and watched him as he sank into sleep.

If only I were a painter, I would have brought out the oils and brushes and immortalized that moment. The strong modern-day knight sleeping soundly next to his strawberry headed, freckly-faced angels. What a perfect picture it would be.

Tracing the etching on the watch Robert had given me, my heart reeled with joy and gratitude. *Thank you, Dragon Rider, for bringing them home. Thank you.*

40

All This Time, We Never Suspected...

⟶Sean⟵

Davey was whistling a famous dark melody as he shoveled old hay out of one of the horse's stalls. He didn't see Sean come into the barn and grab a brush, then disappear into Xavier's stall.

Sean heard Davey whistling, but his own mind was preoccupied with thoughts of Courtney. *Ranfurly. He's no good for her. He's nothin but a hoity-toity Lord that can't see past himself in the mirror! Courtney will never fit in with Upland society—the world of a viscount! He can't change who he is, and she can't change who she is.*

The dreams I keep having must be a sign that she belongs with me. If not, what else could they mean? There has to be a way to show her we belong together.

He was vaguely aware of Winnie coming into the barn. He heard their voices chattering, but it was like background noise to his thoughts.

"Hey, Winnie," Davey was saying.

"Hey."

"What's wrong?"

"I'm tired. Ms. Stern has me slaving overtime."

"Why?"

"Jasmine is sick, so I got all her work on top of my own."

Davey chuckled. "Don't you just love that ole Ms. Stern."

"Oh yeah. God *bless* her, as my Aunt Nina always says about the people she's least fond of."

"I just say it plain. $@#* Ms. Stern!"

Winnie shrugged. "Oh, Aunt Nina would have quite a time scrubbing out *your* filthy mouth. How are things going for you?"

"Same as always. Shoveling dung."

"We're both livin' the dream."

Davey chuckled. "Yeah. Well ... one day I'm gonna buy myself a yacht and sail into the sunset."

"That's what you're fantasizing about when you're up to your neck in horse dung, huh?" Winnie leaned against Epona's stall door.

This next sentence is what made Sean's ears perk up. Xavier's ears also perked up.

"Oh yeah. ... Hey, did you talk to Lord Ranfurly about the tunnel where you found Lady?"

"Yeah. I showed him the entrance we boarded up," Winnie replied. Epona started to munch on her afro. She turned around and put a hand on the horse's long bridge. "Epona! Behave yourself!" she scolded.

"Oh? When did you show him?" Davey asked.

"Last night, during the party." Winnie patted Epona on her long snout.

"What did he say?"

"He thanked me. The last thing he wants is a tunnel to be wide open so people can freely access his property."

"But ... then did he open it up to have a look at it?"

"No ... we went back to the party."

"Hmm. Strange. I was in there this morning and saw the boards were loose again."

"What? How did they get loose? Show me!"

Winnie and Davey left the barn and headed in the direction of the pool pump house. Sean decided it would be a good idea to follow them. He was careful to remain out of sight.

"See? All these boards are loose!" Davey said.

"You're right. But who could have done this, Davey?" Winnie was saying. "Do you have any idea who would have known about a tunnel in here? It has to be someone who has worked here a long time, right?"

Sean crept around quietly so he could peer inside. He wanted to have a look at this tunnel they kept mentioning.

"Ms. Stern is a menacing woman. She's worked here a long time." Davey said. "Maybe *she's* in cahoots with the bad guy. I kind of want to go down into the tunnel and check it out—see if whoever is using it left any clues."

"I've already been inside the tunnel once. It's pitch black. We won't see anything without flashlights."

"There are a few flashlights here—inside the pump house." Davey grabbed them, then walked over to join Winnie who was lowering herself in through the trapdoor.

The next thing that happened stole them all by surprise.

A person dressed in a black ski mask and all black clothing sprang out from behind the door and ran out of the pump house.

The masked figure passed Sean. He bolted after the runner.

The runner grabbed a pitchfork leaning against a fence and knocked it to the ground, causing Sean to trip. "$#!%!" He said as he slammed chin-first into the ground.

Winnie was right behind him. She leapt like a champion hurdler over his fallen body and gained speed on the runner. The runner darted into the trees and started to climb up one of the tall evergreens. Winnie aimed her gun at the runner. "Climb any higher, I'll shoot you out of that tree!"

One of the limbs that the runner was standing on snapped, and the runner fell. Sean and Davey arrived at the base of the tree just in time to break the fall.

Sean had the runner pinned under him.

Davey regarded Winnie, who was still aiming her gun. "You okay, Winnie?"

"Fine." Winnie glared at the masked person who Sean was now sitting on top of. She wasn't about to lower her weapon.

Davey asked Sean, "What were *you* doing by the pump house?"

"I was in the barn when you and Winnie were yip-yapping about some tunnel. You got me curious, so I followed you out there to see what you were jabbering about. That's when I caught this one coming out of the pump house, trying to make a run for it."

"Take the mask off," Winnie said.

❧ Lord Robert ❧

The morning after the staff welcomed Robert and Elizabeth home, he enjoyed waking up with his children snuggled up next to him. He watched them snore away for a little while. *Time with my children is a gift, may I never take it for granted again.*

His thoughts switched back to the concerns he had about Snake. Winnie had found the tunnel that Snake used to get on the property. Robert planned to have a look at it after breakfast.

At breakfast, Courtney entered the dining room wearing a blue dress that brought out her eyes and enhanced every curve. "I could stare at you all day in that dress and never get anything done," he told her. Her cheeks grew pink, and his children giggled.

Mr. Roth had cooked Elizabeth's favorite–pancakes with strawberries and whipped cream– and the four of them enjoyed breakfast together. Robert and Courtney kept the conversation light and happy for the sake of the children.

After breakfast, Robert pulled Courtney aside and quietly asked her, "Will you play with the children upstairs in the playroom for a while? Winnie found a tunnel. It's how Snake breeched the wall. I want to go have a look at it."

"Of course," she said. "But he's still out there. Be careful, Robert."

"Do I seem to you like the type who isn't careful?" he winked.

On his way to meet Winnie, Robert had a strange premonition. *Something doesn't feel right.* He notified his CAPE guards to be on alert. That's when he saw Winnie and Davey along the footpath. *Why is she here? We were supposed to meet at the pump house.* Winnie had her gun out and was pointing it down at something.

"Everything alright here?" Robert asked them.

Winnie grabbed his arm to pull him into the circle. "The boards that Davey and I put in to block the tunnel entrance to the pump house were pulled out, and we have the person who did it."

Robert stepped around Winnie and saw the masked person that Sean had pinned beneath him. *That's a similar mask to the one Snake wore the first time I had an encounter with him in Emer Aude,* he thought. *It must be him.*

"Your game is up, Snake," Robert spewed. "Take the bloody mask off of him," he told Sean.

Sean removed the mask.

Robert blanched.

Winnie was equally shocked.

Davey's jaw dropped.

Sean was rendered speechless.

"Gretchen?" Robert asked, not believing his eyes.

Winnie could have shot daggers out of her eyes at Gretchen, if it were possible. "I usually have good judgment. But I didn't see you coming."

"Surely this is a misunderstanding," Robert said. "What were you doing, hiding in the pump house? Wearing a ski mask?"

"I'm sorry. I just…" Gretchen squeaked.

"Did you let the intruder in, Gretchen?" Winnie was far less kind than Robert in her tone.

"Sean…" Gretchen looked up into his eyes and gave him a pleading look.

Sean repeated the question Winnie had just asked. "Did you let the intruder inside, Gretchen?"

"Please, Sean! Don't tell my mother!" Her big baby blues flooded with tears.

Robert couldn't believe it. "How-how do you know the intruder, Gretchen?" he asked.

She looked up at Sean, who still had her pinned. It was if he were the only person around she acknowledged. "I was seventeen—going through my rebellion phase. I hadn't been with any boys at that point. Other than Davey."

Davey was standing next to Winnie, silent the whole time. At the mention of his name, he shifted legs.

Winnie shook her head in disappointment. "You and Gretchen? Really?"

"Hey, she asked me out!" Davey said defensively.

Winnie shot him a disdainful glare.

"But then I found out Davey cheated on me!" For the first time since they unmasked her, Gretchen broke away from looking at Sean to glare at Davey. "I found pictures and letters from some hideous purple-haired bimbo that he met at cooking school in Vinosa! I had to get over him, so Marie helped me. We snuck out."

Sean nodded. "Yeah, Marie had a wild side."

"She brought me through the tunnel - told me it used to be the way the loggers would drive on and off the property, before the pool was put in. She said the people who once knew about the tunnel were dead and gone. But she found it as a kid when she was hiding in the pump house. … Marie got her friends from Emer Aude to pick us up on the logging road, where the big waterfall crashes into the river. Then we went clubbing in Emer Aude."

"And that's where you met the intruder?" Robert asked.

"Not exactly. I met *him* through this really cute guy named Petra." She shot another glare at Davey. "Petra asked me for my number, but I didn't have a cell phone, of course. I gave him the landline to the manor because there was no other way for him to reach me, since where we live is so primeval!" Her expression was that of someone who has suffered greatly.

So that's why Snake had the landline number, Robert thought. "Petra? Yes, I've met him," he said, omitting that he was one of the traffickers who he'd shot and killed the night he broke up the ring. "Did you know about the old mill with the abandoned warehouse, Gretchen? The one you can only find if you know the old logging roads?"

"Yes. Davey brought me there when I was sixteen."

Sean and Robert both glared at Davey. "You were twenty-two when she was sixteen, Davey!" Robert was furious.

"What? I'm a guy with a healthy libido! And she's ... well, look at her!"

Sean shrugged.

Robert was agitated. When he met Gretchen, she was only fifteen, and seemed so innocent. He still wanted her to be that sweet child. "Why did you tell the intruder about the warehouse, Gretchen?" Robert asked her.

"I didn't show the intruder!" Gretchen said, shaking her head like a poodle that is terrified of getting wet. "I showed the warehouse to Petra! It was our little escape!"

"And Petra must have told Burt," Robert nodded, understanding.

"Burt. Yes, that's the name of the intruder," Gretchen nodded. "Petra told me Burt was his boss."

"Did he tell you what kind of business he was in, Gretchen?" Winnie asked.

"No!" Gretchen's eyes widened. "Well ... okay, y-yes, he told me he worked for the government as a special agent. But ... he said if I told anyone about it, I was as good as dead!" She swallowed audibly.

"I see," Robert said. He realized Gretchen probably thought that working as a government agent made Petra a good guy.

"You're twenty now, and you met Petra when you were seventeen?" Sean asked.

"Yes. Oh Sean, I'm sorry. I was so young and naive back then. That was years before I met you, and..."

"Oh, please, Gretchen! Quit acting so innocent!" Winnie was in a fury. "You're wearing a ski mask, and you pried up the floorboards that Davey and I nailed in, then you ran from us! Why?"

"Because! I had no choice!"

Winnie twisted up her mouth. "You always have a choice!"

"What do you mean, you had no choice?" Sean asked in a gentle voice.

Tears rolled down her cheeks. She sniffed. "It's been a couple of years since I've heard from Petra. He must have given his boss, Burt, the landline number, because ..." Gretchen sniffed again, "... Burt called and asked for *me*."

"When was this?" Robert asked.

"A couple of weeks ago, right after Jake was murdered. He told me he was using the warehouse for government work and that his car broke down. He asked if I could help him. But I don't drive. So, I told him to follow the river east until he reached the old bridge and the big waterfall. That's where the entrance to the tunnel is. It's a challenging hike going uphill, so he was really tired and thirsty when he got to the pump house. I felt bad for him, so I let him in and gave him food and water. I brought him blankets and let him sleep inside the pump house."

"Did anyone else know you let him in?" Robert asked her.

"No! Burt told me I couldn't tell anyone!"

"Gretchen, quit pretending you're so sweet and innocent!" Winnie said.

"But I didn't know, Winnie! How could I have known he was going to take Elizabeth?" Gretchen started bawling uncontrollably.

"Shh, it's alright. You didn't know," Sean said in a soothing voice.

Winnie curled up a lip, disgusted.

Sean continued. "You wouldn't happen to be keeping earrings and aerosol cans inside a secret storage space in the theater terrace, would you?"

Robert and Winnie exchanged a glance, surprised.

She shook her head, "no." Sean held her gaze. Gretchen changed her answer to a nod, "yes."

"Oh, Gretchen." Sean lowered his head in disappointment.

"There's a secret space under the theater terrace, Sean?" Robert asked.

"Aye. I accidentally came across it when I bumped into the raven statue," Sean said.

"Did you hide aerosol spray cans and earrings for Burt, Gretchen?" Robert asked.

"I really thought he was working for the government," she said in a hushed whisper.

"Do you realize what this means? You were aiding and abetting, Gretchen," Winnie said.

She turned her head away from Sean, ashamed. "Burt told me it was top secret work he was doing for PAX," she whimpered. "I was just trying to obey the law. I'm sorry! I really didn't know! I didn't! I swear!"

"You might have believed him *before* he kidnapped Elizabeth," Winnie said. "But today, you reopened the tunnel! And you knew he was a kidnapper!"

Gretchen shook.

Winnie was terrifying when she was angry. "You were planning to let him through again! Even though you knew he kidnapped Elizabeth!"

Gretchen looked like she was hyperventilating.

"Oh Gretchen," Sean wagged his head. "You're not the sharpest tool in the shed, are you?"

"You don't understand! He threatened to kill me if I didn't let him through!" She threw her arms around Sean's neck and pulled him down so she could sob into his collar. "I was so scared, Sean. He said he would kill *everyone*."

❧Winnie❧

After calming Gretchen down and getting all the information from her, Robert privately spoke with Winnie. "Gretchen is young, give her a little grace, Winnie."

"Oh please. Don't blame it on her age. She should know better. Your five-year-olds have more brain cells than she has," Winnie said.

"Perhaps a little time with your Aunt Nina will knock sense into her," Robert suggested.

"Just leave her with me. I'll be happy to knock some sense into her," Winnie said through gritted teeth.

Robert patted her on the back. "I'm certain you would." He sighed. "I'm not looking forward to telling Ms. Stern that it was her daughter who aided and abetted the kidnapper."

"Yeah. I wonder who she'll be madder at ... Gretchen, or you?"

"Me? What right would she have to be mad at me?" Robert asked, confused. "I'm showing Gretchen mercy after she helped the person who kidnapped my child!"

"Ms. Stern may not see it that way. Parental love can be blind," Winnie pointed out.

"Hmm. Let's hope that isn't true for her, then," Robert said. "I'll call your Uncle Peter and see what can be done with Gretchen. She must come to understand the severity of her actions. Until your uncle has a place to keep her, she'll be locked in a room here at the manor, and I'll assign a couple of CAPE guards to make sure she doesn't cause more trouble."

Winnie left Robert and caught up with Sean, who was on his way back to the staff quarters. "Hey, Sean. How did you end up being in the pump house at the right time, anyway?" she asked him.

"I told you ... I overheard you and Davey talking about a tunnel. So, I followed you." Sean shrugged, as if it was no big deal.

"Is that right?" She jabbed him with an elbow. "Eavesdropper!" Her head swayed, as she absorbed the shock of learning it had been Gretchen, all that time, who had betrayed them all. "You were one of Gretchen's many lovers. You must be surprised."

"One of her lovers? Nah. It was never serious. We just had a little romp now and again."

Winnie raised a brow. "Really? Because from the way she talked, you were her future husband."

"Well, apparently the girl's not just stuffing her brain with fluff and feathers ... she's also suffering delusions."

"Hmm." Winnie huffed out of her nostrils.

Sean glanced over at her. "Winnie, enough about me. Let's talk about *you*."

"Me? There's nothing to talk about."

"Really? Because I found it interesting, the way you were talking to Ranfurly back there. As if you're well acquainted. I also found it surprising that you were so invested in finding his daughter. Why did you care *so much*? Unless you knew Ranfurly *before* you got the job here?"

"What? No! I didn't know him before I worked here. I'm from Capital City. How could I know him?"

Sean shrugged. "I don't know ... all the maids act all tongue tied around him, like because he's a lordie lord, he deserves special treatment. But you don't seem to care one iota that he's a pretty viscount."

"Well, I act the same around everyone. He could be a king for all I care."

"Hmm. Good for you."

Winnie tried to think of something else to talk about, to change the subject and get it off of her, while Sean persisted.

"I also noticed you were incredibly steady with that gun back there," he said.

"Thank you." Winnie squeezed her lips together. They walked in step, neither saying anything.

As they approached the staff quarters, Sean touched her arm and said, "I also admired the way you jumped over me and ran like a true athlete. I bet you could almost keep up with me, if we were to race. *Almost*. Of course I'd win."

"Yeah, well *I've* noticed that *you* think pretty highly of yourself, Mr. Knight."

"Hey! I just paid you a compliment, and you return it with an insult. I'm offended." Sean said, smiling. "What I'm getting at here is that you're not *just* a maid, are you?"

Winnie tried to look innocent. "Of course I'm a maid! Do you not see how I've slaved over getting the toilets all sparkly around here?" Sean raised a brow.

"What? Are maids not allowed to be athletic? Are we not allowed to conceal and carry?" she asked. "A girl has to watch her back these days."

He shrugged. "Fair enough."

"If you want to know the truth, I was in the Top Shooters Club in high school. I was Club Champion every year." Winnie blew on her fingers. It wasn't a lie.

The response seemed to satisfy Sean. "Really? Well, you seem very bright. Why did you decide to work here and not do something else?"

"I would guess for the same reason as *you*. The pay is unbeatable!" She fluttered her long lashes, knowing how cute that was to people.

"Ah." Sean didn't know whether the pay was any good, since PAX was the one who put him in his position. If there was pay, Sean never saw it.

"And we don't have to worry about all the new chips. I don't really want one of those inserted under my skin."

"That's a good point. I suppose there are some perks to working out here in the wild frontier," Sean said. "Well, have a nice day. Hopefully it will be less eventful."

"Yeah, see you later. And you owe me a race sometime, Mr. Knight!" Winnie retreated to her room, glad to be free from his interrogation.

41

GILDENRA

❧ Peter Williams ❧

"Lord Robert, good timing. You caught us right in the middle of a CAPE meeting," Peter said over the phone. "I'll project the screen so you can join in." He switched the audio call to video.

A huge Robert on the projected screen was now looking at everyone who had gathered at CAPE Headquarters. "Hello, everyone," he said. "I have an important update regarding the earring case."

"Good. Let's hear it," Peter said.

"First off, we know it is connected to the kidnapping case. The same intruder who breached my security wall and kidnapped my daughter is involved in the earring case. We've learned that he got onto my property through a tunnel. Apparently, it was used as a way logging trucks accessed the property, long before the pool went in. That was over fifty years ago. Sadly, it was one of my staff workers, Gretchen Stern, who let the intruder in."

"Wow. I remember Gretchen from when I came and pretended to be a detective on those recent murder cases. I never imagined that sweet little girl would do something like that." Peter bowed his head, disappointed.

"I don't think she meant any evil by it, but she acted out of fear. She could use an education," Robert said. "As soon as McGregor is able to come pick her up, I'll hand her over to CAPE Headquarters. Perhaps Nina can influence her mind to do better in the future."

"Alright. We'll keep her in a guarded safe house, and I'll have Nina talk with her."

"Good," Robert said. "But that's not all. Snake has been in possession of serpent earrings with rubies. He's also doing something with aerosol cans. One can was tested by a chemist, and it turned out it contained dragon gas."

"Dragon gas?" Peter asked. "What is that?"

Baca raised up a hand. "I know!" Everyone's eyes turned to look at her.

"Yes, Baca?" Peter asked.

"It comes from dragons!" Baca said. "I know a little bit about it."

"Do you know if it's lethal?" Robert asked.

Baca shook her head. "Not by itself. But if it were to come into contact with certain things, it can be deadly."

"What types of things, Baca?" Peter asked.

"Let's see. This one plant, I forget the name. It is tropical. And this particular rare metal."

"What particular metal?" Peter asked.

"I forget." Baca pushed her pink glasses up off her nose.

"Oh … wait! I just saw a documentary about a metal that can be deadly if it comes in contact with dragon gas!" Kila piped in. "It's also only found in mines that tend to be located in tropical climates. There is a lot of it on the isles of Tanai and San Ulios. PAX has been opening mines right and left to find more of it."

"What's the name of the metal?" Robert pressed.

Kila shrugged. "I can't remember. It was a weird name."

Dillard was searching on the internet as they were discussing it. "I found it. Gildenra."

"Gildenra? But I thought that was mythological," Robert said. "All those stories about the magic powers of Gildenra…"

"No, no! I mean, yes, it is true that Gildenra having magical powers *is* just a myth. But the metal itself is not. It's real," Baca said. "It is very rare, found only where there are high populations of dragons, so people make up stories about it. The same way they make up stories about dragons being magical."

"Here's a photo of it," Dillard said. "I'm sharing my screen, Lord Robert, so you can see what it looks like."

Robert studied the image. "Hmm. Resembles sterling." He compared it to the serpent earrings sitting on his desk. "Those earrings appear to be made of sterling as well. But if they're actually made of gildenra…"

Dillard rubbed his hands together eagerly. "We could do an experiment to find out."

"Good idea, Dillard," said Peter. "When McGregor goes to pick up Gretchen at Ranfurly Manor, you send the aerosol can back with him, Robert. Dillard and Baca will run tests on it here."

"We'll need a few rats," Dillard said.

Baca leapt out of her chair and bounced up and down. Her blonde pigtails bounced like bunny ears. "Yes! I'll go to the pet store and get the rats!"

"Okay, Baca, but you can't name them and cry when they die this time," Dillard warned.

42

URGENT CALL

❧ *Courtney* ❧

"Gretchen was the one who let him in?" I was watering plants in the conservatory when Robert broke the news.

Across the huge, sunlit room, Elizabeth played with the pet tarantula, Alfred, while Luke was having a delightful time with his pet boa constrictor, Elsie. A guard stood at the door of the conservatory, as an added measure of security. Robert had ordered a large team of CAPE guards to be posted all over the grounds ever since the kidnapping.

"I can't believe it. I liked her!" I said, thinking of Gretchen. "So do you think Snake can still get in through the tunnel?" I asked.

"We boarded it back up today," Robert said. "He won't be able to come through that way again, unless someone else on the inside helps him."

He wrapped an arm around me, and we watched the children play with their pets. Since he'd returned a day ago, he wouldn't let us out of his sight. Which was fine by me. I felt secure whenever he was close, and it felt so right when it was the four of us together.

Winnie came bursting through the door of the conservatory, past the guard, with an urgent look on her face.

"Uncle Peter wants to have a meeting with you, Lord Robert," she said. "Now."

"What's wrong?" Robert asked.

278

"I don't know, but he said it was urgent. And as you know, he doesn't use that word lightly." Winnie turned around and left.

Robert touched my arm. "Will you be alright in here for a few more minutes?"

"Yeah, go ahead. We're fine." I told him, fully aware of the massive man made of muscles who stood at the door. "And what could possibly happen with that *giant* CAPE guard watching over us?"

"Okay. I'll be back soon." He brushed my cheek with a finger. "Stay here."

There was only one door in and out of the place, so it wasn't like we could go anywhere. "I'm pretty sure even if I tried to escape, your guard would make sure I couldn't," I teased.

Robert smiled. "It's for your protection." He motioned toward his children. "And theirs. I'll be back soon."

❧ Lord Robert ❧

Robert knew that since it was a CAPE meeting, the most private setting with a computer screen was in his secret room concealed behind the cellar wall. He'd never told Winnie about the secret rooms in his manor, and decided that it was time. He led her down into his cellar, and levered the wine bottle that opened the wall.

"What is this place?" Winnie whirled around in amazement.

"I've been keeping it from you. But it is time you knew. There is an entire hidden area in here where I've been handling all business having to do with CAPE."

"Woah. This is epic." Winnie followed him into one of the rooms behind the cellar wall, where several computer monitors were hanging.

Robert put in a video call to Peter. "What's so urgent?"

"Snake was spotted in Emer Aude yesterday," Peter said. "The report came in just a minute ago, or I would have alerted you sooner."

Robert's stomach was churning acid. He turned to Winnie. "He could have come through before we boarded it back up."

"McGregor hasn't arrived to pick up Gretchen yet. I'll go see if she knows anything." She pivoted on her heels and left, a woman on a mission.

❧ Courtney ❧

Being trapped in the Conservatory with the hairy spider … was not my favorite way to pass the afternoon. I shuffled as far away from it as I could get, over to the carnivorous plants, where I picked up a fly and threw it at one of them. It caught it in its pedals and gobbled it up. "Hmm. Never done this before. It's kind of therapeutic."

"Elsie? Where are you hiding?" Luke was calling his boa constrictor.

"What's wrong, Lukey Duke? Did you lose your snake?" I asked him.

"Yes. She likes to play hide and seek with me. And she's really good at it because she can camerfrodge."

"You mean camouflage." I asked him. "I'll help you look for her."

Luke called out for his snake.

It was a massive room, in the shape of an octagon. It had windows for walls, and the temperature was kept perfect for the tropical plants year-round. We followed the path that wound through exotic trees, waterfalls, and plants. It eventually circled back around to the room's entrance.

"Well, we never did find Elsie, did we?" I asked. "She sure is good at hiding." I came into view of the entrance, and wondered where the guard went. Alfred the spider was crawling around on the floor. "Elizabeth?"

I followed the path to see if I could find her. *Where did she go? And where is the guard?*

43

SNEAKY SNAKE

❧ Lord Robert ❧

After he'd alerted his guards, he rushed back to the Conservatory. On the way, he crashed into Sean.

"Why in such a hurry?" Sean asked him. The Highlander read the look on Robert's face. "Has something happened?"

"The man who kidnapped my daughter was spotted in Emer Aude yesterday."

"And? What—you think he's here?"

"He might be. He could have found his way back in through the tunnel, since the boards were taken out in the pump house."

"Right." Sean scanned the area. "Where's Courtney?"

"With my children. In the Conservatory. I'm going there now."

"I need to ask her something. I'll come with you."

Robert gave Sean a distrustful look but said nothing.

They entered through a door which led into an enclosure that kept butterflies from escaping. The security guard was inside the enclosure, lying face down. Blood spilled out from a bullet in the back of the head.

Sean got down and checked for a pulse. "Dead," he said. He and Robert simultaneously drew their weapons, and tiptoed around the guard.

The second door into the main part of the Conservatory was closed. Robert quietly turned the handle and peered into the Conservatory. "Clear," he mouthed to Sean.

Robert held up a hand, motioning for Sean to stay inside the enclosure behind the door, out of sight. He proceeded to enter the Conservatory silently, but left the door slightly open for Sean. Robert's double-action pistol ready, he used the large plants and trees for cover as he tiptoed his way along the path and rounded a corner.

Luke, Elizabeth, and Courtney were sitting on the floor, hands and feet tied, mouths gagged, and Snake was behind them, a gun in each hand, one aimed at Elizabeth and one at Courtney.

"Well, hello there. If it isn't his #%$@!* lordship. I saw you trying to sneak up on us," he hissed. "If I were you, I'd lose the #%$@!* weapon. Unless you want to say bye-bye to one of your little troubles, here."

Robert wondered about Sean, who was still hidden behind the main entrance door to the Conservatory. *Can I trust him? For all I know, Sean might be a PAX agent, possibly working on Snake's side.*

Robert couldn't risk losing Courtney or his children. He dropped his gun and slowly raised his hands in the air.

"That's better," said Snake. "Now, kick the gun to me."

Robert did as he was ordered.

Snake picked up the gun and pocketed it. "Very #%$@!* obliging of you. Now have a seat."

Robert remained standing.

"I said, have a #%$@!* seat!" Snake roared. He shot Robert in the thigh.

Courtney and the children let out muffled yells.

"It's alright. I'll be fine," Robert told them through gritted teeth. He sat back and put pressure on his thigh. "Wellington must pay you well to do this," he said to Snake.

The villain smiled wickedly. "You must have done something pretty #%$@!* bad to make that man despise you so much. And yes, the pay is #%$@!* butter. Your feisty little redhead…" He whistled. "Wellington must really like her for the price he's paying me. I'll be set for life."

"And what about my son?"

Snake smiled wickedly. "Wellington doesn't know the boy exists. I'm hoping he'll pay double when he finds out. If not, I'll get plenty for a boy from one of my other connections."

"You mean Joe?"

Snake's beady eyes gleamed. "How do you know Joe?"

Robert ignored the question. "And what do you want with Courtney?"

"Mmm." Snake homed in on Courtney's figure. Robert cringed. "Wellington wants her too. He plans to show her off in a pair of earrings."

"And will they have rubies, or sapphires?"

Snake laughed. "Let's see…" He put one of his guns into a holster and kept the other aimed at Courtney. With his free hand he pulled an earring out of a large pocket inside his jacket. "How about these ones right here?" He held the earring to her cheek. "Sapphires match her stunning eyes, don't they? But if she misbehaves, then I'll have to punish her by making her wear the *other* earrings."

"If she misbehaves, you'll make her wear the ruby earrings … and punish her … how?"

Snake grinned. "So, you're trying to be a #%$@!* detective, now are ya? Well, let's see if you can figure this out: she's not a virgin, which means the ruby earrings will be *deadly*. Only virgins survive wearing the rubies."

Robert thought over what Snake was saying. Kat told him that her and Raquel were virgins. "Only virgins who wear the ruby earrings get to live," Robert repeated, comprehending. "And if you want to dispose of one of your prostitutes, you put her in the ruby earrings, and spray her with the gas."

The Snake sneered, showing his sharpened fangs. "You know about the gas? Very good. PAX likes to keep that part a secret. Of course, you won't live long enough to tell anyone, so what does it matter?"

Robert ignored him. "So, the sapphire earrings have trackers for the women who work as prostitutes. And when they become difficult to deal with, or undesirable, you put the ruby earrings on them and dispose of them. That's what happened to the dead girls I found in Emer Aude. You sprayed them with the gas because you wanted to dispose of them."

"Maybe they actually teach you something besides how to be #%$@!* fruity boys at those boarding schools in The Greens," Snake snickered. "Yes, pretty boy, only wholesome virgins get to wear the ruby earrings and live. Which is why she," he aimed his gun at Courtney, "can't wear the ruby earrings. She's a defiled little #@^*!"

Robert turned a blazing shade of red. He shot up to his feet and plowed toward Snake.

Snake fired off his gun at Robert.

Robert swerved and the bullet whizzed by him.

The children were screaming through their gags. Courtney wrestled to break free out of her restraints.

Snake pushed the gun into her throat.

Robert urged her to be still.

"Hmm." Snake's eyes turned wild. "I don't like women who forget their place."

With one gun still aimed at Courtney, he dropped the sapphire earring to the ground and conjured an earring with rubies from his pocket. "I think you need a demonstration of how it works." Snake had the look of someone who is possessed.

Robert tensed, unable to mask his fear. This only exhilarated Snake. "Come over here and put this earring on her, pretty boy."

"You sick bastard," Robert said, trying to think of a way to stop the madness. Pain radiated through his thigh, and he felt dizzy with nausea as he walked over to her. He was deliberately slow, hoping to give himself time to think up his next possibly move.

Never taking his eyes from Courtney's, several scenarios raced through his head. Every one of them ending up with someone he loved dying.

Snake handed him the ruby earring. Robert gently pushed the needle of the earring into her lobe, buying time. A tear streamed down her cheek. He brushed it away gently.

"You need the gas to kill her," Robert said.

"Oh, I have enough gas in here to kill her." Out of the same large pocket, Snake brought out a small aerosol can. "Go ahead. Spray it on the earring and watch how it works." Snake handed the can to Robert while pointing the gun at him.

Robert aimed the can at the earring. He hesitated.

"Spray it on the earring! Or watch one of your kids die!" Snake screeched.

Robert pressed the button on the can, and gas shot out. But what Snake didn't see was that Robert had turned the can a quarter when it was first handed to him, so the spray was aimed at Snake.

The spray streamed out into Snake's eyes. He shouted his favorite profanity. "#%$!"

A split second later, a shot rang out from behind Robert. Snake cried out in pain and dropped the gun that he had pointed at Courtney. He'd been hit in the arm.

Sean appeared. "Nice of you to finally join us!" Robert said to him. The Highlander had been watching for the right chance to intervene. With Snake momentarily blinded, he chose that moment to spring out from hiding, and took his shot.

Snake was determined. He grabbed Luke and dragged the boy backward with his other gun aimed at the child's throat until a tropical tree blocked him from moving any further back.

"Put down your #%$@!* weapon!" he shouted at Sean. "Unless you'd like to watch me shoot this little !@#$!"

Sean lowered his gun slowly.

Robert pleaded with the viper. "Snake, please. Let my boy go. Whatever you're getting paid, I'll give you ten times more. Just let him go."

"Ah. Now this is turning out to be more fun than I expected. Look everyone! The #%$@!* viscount is begging me! Hmm. Let me see. I might consider your offer." He cocked his head to one side, as if he was thinking on it. "But ... you'll need to get down on your knees first."

Robert didn't move.

"Get on your #%$@!* knees!" Snake roared.

With an agonizing groan, Robert lowered himself to his knees. The bullet ripped through tendons and lodged further into his thigh.

"That's more like it." Snake sneered. "Now say, 'Burt is king, and I am vermin.'"

Robert glowered.

"Say it! Or watch them all die!"

Robert repeated the phrase, slowly. "Burt is king…"

As he spoke the words, he could have sworn he saw the tree behind Snake's head begin to move. He blinked. Everything was a blur. *I must be lightheaded from losing so much blood.*

He continued to say the phrase, "and I am…" He felt light-headed. The moving tree was distracting him.

Wait … No. It isn't the tree moving. It looks like … what? The branch extended out from the tree and crossed over to Snake's shoulder. Then it started to coil around Snake's neck. Robert blinked several times.

"Finish it! Burt is king and I am_! Finish it!" Snake pressed the gun hard into Luke's temple. The boy started to wail. "Fin…" Snake stopped short as his larynx was squeezed and air left his lungs. He lost his grip on Luke and the gun dropped out of his hand.

"Elsie!" Luke's cry came out muffled through the gag.

It's not a tree! It's Luke's pet boa!

Elsie intensified the squeeze.

Sean raised his gun and aimed it at Snake. "Take your kids and Courtney, Ranfurly. They don't need to see this," he said.

For the first time, Robert agreed with the Highlander. Pushing past the nausea and dizziness, he ran to untie the gags and ropes from Courtney and his kids. He then ushered the three of them out of the Conservatory ahead of him. Before Robert followed them out of the room, he saw Snake twitching in agony on the floor.

A shot rang out. Sean had put the villain out of his misery.

Robert forgot his own pain while he led Courtney and the children outside into the fresh air of the garden. All he wanted was to hold on to the three of them and erase the nightmares from their memories. They reached one of the benches near the large raven fountain, and Robert collapsed into it.

"Robert? You're losing too much blood!" Courtney pressed on Robert's bleeding leg. "We need Mr. Roth!" She called out. "Mr. Roth!"

The children both held on to their daddy's arms. "Daddy?" Elizabeth cried. "Are you okay?"

Ms. Stern swiftly appeared, and saw the blood gushing out of Robert. "Gut Got! I'll find Mr. Roth!" She rushed off in search of the army medic/cook.

"Robert?" Courtney was saying before everything became a blur, and he passed out.

❧ Courtney ❧

"Daddy!" Luke was screaming.

Frantic, Elizabeth joined in. "Daddy! Daddy! Wake up!"

"Ssh. It's alright." I forced myself to remain calm for the sake of the children. I brought my voice down, almost to a whisper, and spoke slowly. "Daddy will be okay. Just hold on to his hands."

With all my strength, I put pressure on Robert's thigh that was bleeding out, hoping it would slow the blood flow. Hoping for some indication that he was alright, I watched his eyelids flutter.

At last, Mr. Roth came rushing out to the garden with a bag of medical supplies. "Keep putting pressure on it, Courtney, until I apply the tourniquet."

Mr. Roth hurried, until I no longer needed to press down on Robert's wound. I became aware of my hands and clothes ... soaked in Robert's blood.

"Don't leave us, Daddy!" Elizabeth and Luke repeated.

I bent over to kiss him. "Don't you dare leave us," I threatened, "or I'll have to..."

"You'll have to what?" Robert asked.

"Oh, thank God!" I smothered his face with kisses. "Oh Robert, you can't die," I whispered. "Ever."

"It will take a lot more than a bullet in my thigh to kill me, Mrs. Drake."

44

INVITATION

❧ *Peter* ❧

After Dillard and Baca ran tests on the cans of aerosol and the serpent earrings, they reported their test findings to Peter.

"I think we figured it out!" Dillard announced.

"Yes?" Peter asked.

"When we tested the earrings on rats, the ones wearing the sapphires were fine after we sprayed dragon gas on them," Dillard explained.

"But then we put the serpent earrings with the rubies on the rats," Baca said. "We sprayed them with the dragon gas, and they all died instantly! Boo!" She stuck out her lower lip and her eyes welled up.

"I see." Peter nodded. "The ruby earrings must be made of the gildenra, and the sapphire earrings are made of regular sterling."

"Precisely," Dillard said.

"But ... we still don't know why the earrings were left on the victims after they died," Peter pointed out. "What would be the purpose in leaving expensive jewels on dead people lying in the streets? That makes no sense."

"Actually, we know the answer to that too," Dillard said. "You see, we ran another test. For Group A, we removed the ruby earrings off of the rats right after they died. For Group B, we left the earrings on for fifteen minutes after the rats died."

"In Group A, we were able to detect traces of poison in the bodies of *those* rats, and the earrings still had traces of the poison as well!" Baca explained.

"However," Dillard continued, "in Group B, there was no trace of any poison in the rat's body *or* in the earrings!"

Baca jumped up and down, unable to contain herself.

"Sit down, Baca! You're agitating my Zen!" Dillard inhaled slowly before he went on. "It seems that after fifteen minutes, the gildenra absorbs all the poison."

"Ah." Peter scratched his chin. "Which is why they left the expensive jewels on the dead girls." He pounded fists with Dillard and Baca. "Well done, you two."

He scratched his chin. "Now we just need to find out *why* the earrings were created in the first place."

❧ Courtney ❧

I was settled into my bed, trying to fall asleep. But with fantasies of Lord Robert racing through my head, I wasn't having much luck.

"Courtney?" Robert was knocking on my door.

"Come in!" I called back.

He slipped in and closed the door behind him. "Am I interrupting anything?"

"Not really."

"I was having trouble falling asleep," he said. "My kids are cover hogs. And Elizabeth is a sleep slapper."

"A sleep slapper? Sounds painful."

"It is. Do I have a bruise on my cheek? She must have slapped me at least three times." He turned his head and pointed to his cheek.

"Poor baby. Would it help you fall asleep if I tell you a bedtime story, Your Grace?" I asked.

"Yes. Tell me a bedtime story," he whispered, crossing to me slowly.

"Once upon a time…"

He interrupted, "There was the most gorgeous woman who ever lived. Her eyes were as blue as the ocean."

I smiled, and continued. "And she met a dashing and daring viscount, who was the most gorgeous man in the universe. He needed a nanny to look after his children so he could fight against the monsters in the land."

He was now standing close enough to touch. He sat on the edge of my bed. "… And then … they began a perfect courtship. Nobody was murdered, kidnapped, and no animals were harmed."

I giggled. "Yes. Exactly. And then…"

Robert interrupted. Again. "…And then the viscount thought, I must take this beautiful woman to see my ancestral home in Knoxfordshire."

I cocked my head, wondering if he was hinting at something.

He went on. "So, he asked her: 'Most gorgeous woman that ever lived, would you like to see my castle?' The viscount hoped and prayed she would say yes."

Is this still just a bedtime story? "And what was her answer?" I asked.

"I don't know. It's your turn."

"Oh! Well … let's see. She said to the viscount, 'Why, Your Grace, I thought you would never ask!'"

"Oh. I like that answer." Robert tickled my ribs. I squealed, which only made him tickle me all the more.

"Stop!" I rolled away from him and grabbed pillows to throw. Then I ran across the room, and he chased me. We finally both crashed on the bed together, laughing.

After the laughter settled, he said, "In all seriousness, I am planning on going back to Knoxfordshire."

"Oh. When?"

"Soon. Once things the children have a chance to feel a sense of normalcy. I'm bringing them with me, of course. My childhood nanny is there, and I just wrote to her and told her about my children. She's anxious to meet them."

"You just told her about them?"

"I've kept them a secret all this time to protect them. A lot of good it did, though. My enemies still found a way in." He cleared his throat.

I put a hand on his arm. "At least now you know the tunnel is boarded up. Gretchen won't be letting anyone in again. And Snake is dead."

"Yes. That's why it is time I return to Knoxfordshire. ... I've been away far too long. The last time I was there was two years before PAX took global power. The Green Isles still ruled as a monarchy then. No doubt it will be different there. I need to upgrade security at the castle, but the place is ancient. It's going to cost a fortune."

"I bet it's beautiful."

"Oh, it is. The castle is smaller than Ranfurly Manor, though, and it is quite outdated. Leaky pipes, old appliances, all that. But it is still one of the larger castles in The Greens. There's a wall around it, and next to it sits the quaint village of Knoxfordshire."

"Does it have a garden?"

"A garden?" Robert laughed. "Oh Courtney, you haven't seen a garden until you go to The Greens. Beautiful gardens are everywhere. Ranfurly Castle has several."

Wow. "It sounds dreamy."

Robert grabbed my hands and brushed his lips against them. "Would you like to come?"

Would I like to come? I threw my arms around his neck. "I thought you'd never ask!"

SNEAK PEEK

The Ranfurly Mysteries Book Three

✦ Lord Robert ✦

She'll never forgive me.

He watched her board the plane, his chest caving in as the doors closed behind her. He didn't take his eyes off the little jet as it made its way down his private runway in Knoxfordshire and eventually disappeared in the distance.

Why did I make the promise to Nick? I should have known better than to keep the truth from Courtney about her son being a member of CAPE.

Robert was trying to be honorable, a man of his word. *But what has it cost me? Nick's life is in danger, and I'm partly to blame. Now the woman I love is gone.* He gazed in the direction of the western sky. Half of his soul was on that plane. *Courtney.*

"Daddy!" Elizabeth and Luke ran across the freshly mowed lawn in front of Ranfurly Castle. They'd just returned from going to town with Mrs. Lundgren.

Robert spread his arms wide, and his little daughter jumped up into them, fully confident her father would catch her. "Where did you get the lolly?" Robert asked her, pretending to try to steal a lick. Elizabeth giggled, and kept the sweet away from him.

"Oh, Ron gave it to her," Mrs. Lundgren said. "You remember him from the market, don't you? He always made the balloon animals. A few years ago, he started dressing up like a clown to do birthday parties, and now he's known as the village clown."

"A clown gave you the lolly?" Robert asked his daughter.

"No, it wasn't a clown. It was the nice man," Elizabeth said.

"What man?"

"The one who helped me," she replied.

Robert tried to think of who Elizabeth could be referring to. *Who helped her?* It was the first time he'd allowed her to go anywhere without him since she'd been kidnapped. He hadn't let her out of his sight. The only reason he allowed his children to go to the village today was because he was trying to patch things up with Courtney, and Mrs. Lundgren offered to take them.

Someone was crossing the vast lawn on the castle grounds, coming toward them.

"Katherine? Is that you?" Mrs. Lundgren called.

Katherine? Robert squinted to get a better look at the person headed their way. As she came closer, he recognized her. The first time he met her, she was wearing a very revealing dress, and today, she wore something equally provoking. A see-through deep green blouse with a black bra that showed through, and a black lace skirt, with a slip that covered only her privates. She wore thigh-high boots that matched her dark green blouse.

Katherine ran up to Mrs. Lundgren and hugged her.

"Well, well! Look at you, my dear!" Mrs. Lundgren stepped back and looked her niece over. "Looking more grown up than ever these days. But my word! What *is* it you're wearing? Not much left to the imagination in that outfit, is there? Your father would most certainly not approve." Mrs. Lundgren clucked her tongue. "Oh, Lord Robert, forgive me. This is my niece, Katherine."

"Yes. We've been acquainted," Robert said.

"Oh! You have?" Mrs. Lundgren's arches went up.

"Hello, Your Grace. Lovely to see you again." Katherine's sultry eyes met his as she held out a hand.

Robert suddenly found himself aware of the effort it took to swallow.

"Well, well! How is it that you two have met?" Mrs. Lundgren asked.

"When I was here as a teen," Katherine answered quickly.

"Oh? But I thought Lord Robert was already away at university by then," Mrs. Lundgren tapped her nose.

"No, Auntie. You must have forgotten that I came here every summer until I was fourteen. Lord Robert was often here. Lord Leo used to throw balls in those days."

"Oh, the balls! That's right. Lord Leo and his parties. But I don't remember Lord Robert ever attending."

"No, he didn't. He was usually in the garden, reading. Or in the library," Katherine said.

Robert recalled the parties. "Yes. How I hated Leo's parties. I was studying for my degree during that time."

Luke squealed, interrupting their conversation.

"The ponies, Lizzie!" Luke cried. He grabbed her hand, and they ran together toward the fenced off pasture, where two golden ponies were waiting for the children to come say hello to them.

Mrs. Lundgren patted Robert on the arm. "I'll go keep an eye on those two. Ah, it is so good to have children here again!" She scurried after the children, leaving Robert alone with her niece.

"What's wrong?" Kat studied him. "You look bothered by something." Her eyes flickered to the watch he was holding. "That's a lovely watch."

It was his mother's watch. He'd given it to Courtney as a gift and she'd handed it back to him before she left him. Kat didn't know any of that, and Robert didn't want to discuss it with her. He pushed the thought out of his mind. "What brings you to Ranfurly Castle, Katherine?"

"I wanted to see my aunt, of course."

"Is that all?"

"Isn't that enough?" she asked, with a half-smile.

"Certainly," Robert said dismissing the topic. His thoughts were back on Elizabeth. "A man just gave my daughter a lolly. She told me she got it from a man who helped her."

"Oh. That's why you look upset. And here I was thinking perhaps you were unhappy to see me."

"No. Why would you get that idea?" Robert asked. "What man could Elizabeth have been referring to, I wonder?"

"I have no idea," Kat said.

"Good lord, you don't think she meant Wellington, do you? He was the one who took her out of that terrible food bank cell," Robert said. "Perhaps she believes he helped her."

Kat took a step toward him. She was so close he could breathe in a whiff of her delicious vanilla and cocoa scent. It was difficult to not notice her exposed flesh. Most women who dressed in a provocative manner were a turn off to him. But the way the outfit accentuated her figure didn't cheapen her. She reminded him of his late wife, Desiree, who could make any outfit she wore look high class.

"After all you've been through, you have every right to be worried," she said, putting a hand on his arm and caressing it lightly with her fingers. "I'm here for you, Your Grace. Together, we'll make sure Wellington doesn't get near your little girl, ever again."

In *The Ranfurly Mysteries Book Three,* Lord Robert returns to his ancestral home with Courtney and his children. But when Courtney learns that her son is working with CAPE on a dangerous rescue, she is furious with Robert for not telling her. She breaks things off with him, leaving him behind at Ranfurly Castle in Knoxfordshire.

Katherine Lundgren happens to drop in for a visit with her aunt at the castle. She seizes the opportunity to snag up the man who she has fantasized about since she was a girl.

But Robert's archenemy, Lord August Wellington, has become the Head of PAX Intelligence, and now knows Robert has a daughter. Will Robert be able to protect his family from his archenemy?

Meanwhile, Sean Knight is more desperate than ever to unlock the memories of what happened to him during the forgotten year. With Courtney back in Mill Pond and no longer with Ranfurly, his hopes rise that he might finally win over the woman of his dreams.

ACKNOWLEDGMENTS

It takes a village to get any job done well. Even as an independent author, I relied on a team of beautiful people to complete this book. A few are mentioned here. Forgive me if I am forgetting someone. *I hope I'm not.*

First off, I owe heaps of gratitude to my developmental and copy editor, Jessica Powers, who has been with me from the start of The Ranfurly Mysteries. *You are an amazing mentor and oh, the many lips that would be bleeding, had you not intervened.*

I also want to thank my proofreader, Kim Beckham, who never ceases to amaze me with her little grey cells, even after a long day of babysitting her toddler grandchild. *Ms. Savina, get ready. Grey verses Gray. Grey will always win.* (Inside jokes.)

Special thanks to my beta readers, Sally Bryan, Koralyn Driskill, and Kim Beckham! *Your feedback is often laugh out loud funny and sometimes humbling.* But it is always spot on and perfect. *Which is why I love you.*

I want to thank my husband and four kids for being my constant support, sounding boards, and for putting up with my crazy creative flow. You're the best!

Special thanks to Nathaniel, for helping me design the maps for The Ranfurly world. I'm blessed to call you my son.

Thanks to those of you who inspired characters in my book. My sister, Sharon, my niece, Kilee who Kila Jeffries is based upon, Angela, McGregor, and Nina.

As always, I can't forget my parents, Maxine and Houston Knox. If you're lucky enough to know them, then you know they are the coolest, hippest nanny and papa on the planet. Which is why I wrote them in as Courtney's parents.

Thanks to Ron and Diana, Nicole, Rowan, Neisha, Wanda, and the rest of the gang over at Centralia Farmer's Market. You guys made selling my books at the local market a whole lot of fun. I appreciate your support!

Thankyou to Sean-David and Jenna McGoran at The Tuned-In Academy, and the team of amazing music teachers I work with. I'm blessed to love my day job!

Thank you to Shanna and the design team at 100 Covers for the new cover concepts!

Last, I want to thank *all* of my wonderful readers and promoters! You make creating this series worth it, and your kind reviews help get this book seen and sold.

Xoxo K.M.

OTHER BOOKS
BY K.M. KRENIK

Inevitable Danger (Prequel to The Ranfurly Mysteries)

Danger Lies Within (The Ranfurly Mysteries Book One)

Kids Dig This (Coloring Book)

Draw Color Write (Activity Book for Kids)

Fire Lilies Prayer and Meditation Journal

Fire Lilies Out of the Ashes (Women's Bible Study and Devotional)

Family Favorites Recipes (Cookbook)

Visit Kmkrenikbooks.com and subscribe to her newsletter.

Did you enjoy

Dangling and Dangerous?

Consider rating and reviewing it wherever you purchased the book.

If you'd like to hear about book giveaways, read my travel blog, and get updates, you can sign up for my newsletter on my website at: *kmkrenik-books.com*

You can also find me on Goodreads and Bookbub!

While you are waiting for Book Three,
have you read *Inevitable Danger* – the prequel
of *The Ranfurly Mysteries* yet?

kmkrenikbooks.com

www.ingramcontent.com/pod-product-compliance
Lightning Source LLC
Chambersburg PA
CBHW010831250626
47157CB00010B/3239